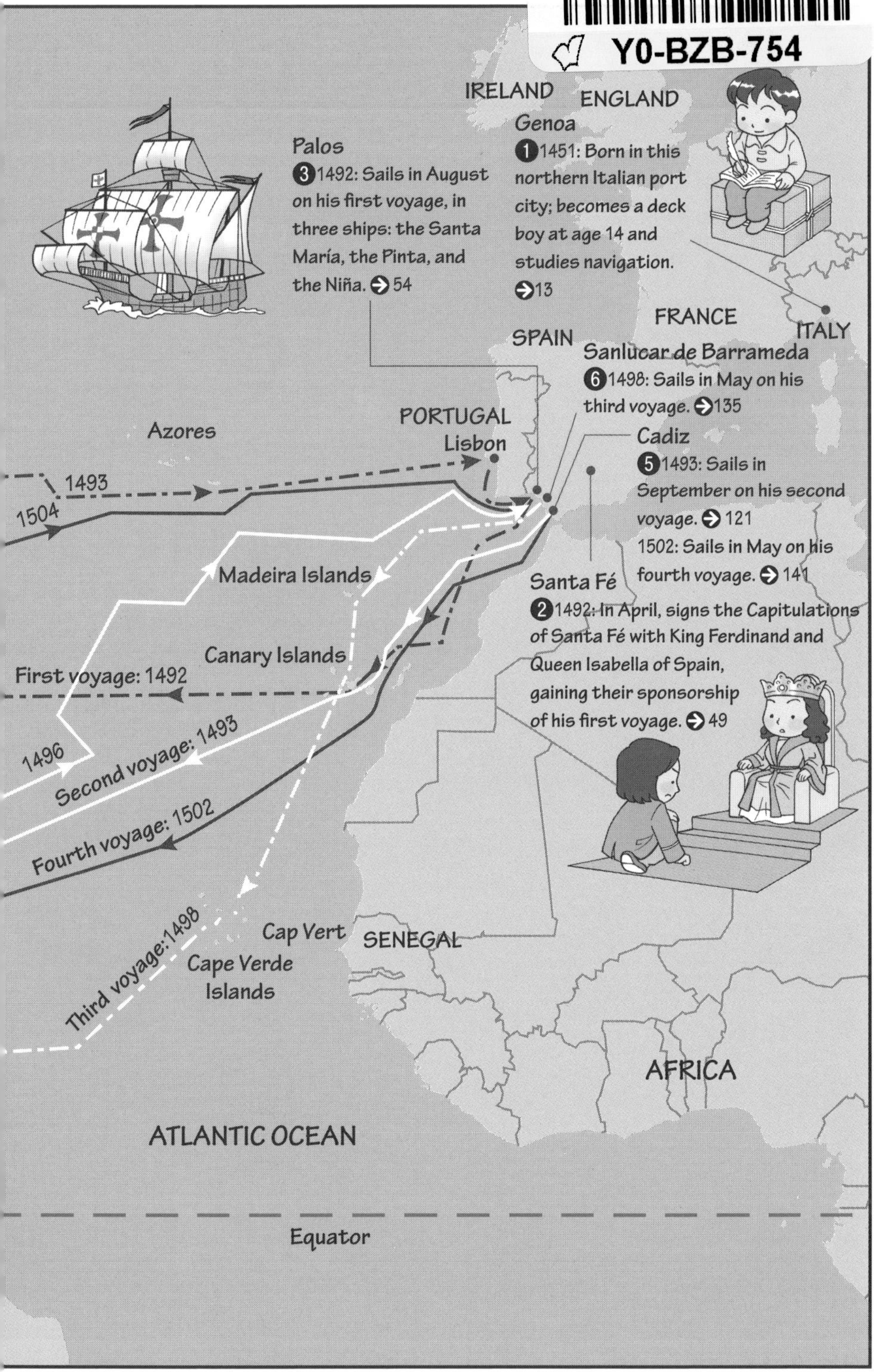

IRELAND
ENGLAND
Genoa
1 1451: Born in this northern Italian port city; becomes a deck boy at age 14 and studies navigation. ➔13
Palos
3 1492: Sails in August on his first voyage, in three ships: the Santa María, the Pinta, and the Niña. ➔54
FRANCE
SPAIN
ITALY
Sanlucar de Barrameda
6 1498: Sails in May on his third voyage. ➔135
PORTUGAL
Lisbon
Azores
Cadiz
5 1493: Sails in September on his second voyage. ➔121
1502: Sails in May on his fourth voyage. ➔141
1493
1504
Madeira Islands
Santa Fé
2 1492: In April, signs the Capitulations of Santa Fé with King Ferdinand and Queen Isabella of Spain, gaining their sponsorship of his first voyage. ➔49
Canary Islands
First voyage: 1492
1496
Second voyage: 1493
Fourth voyage: 1502
Third voyage: 1498
Cap Vert
SENEGAL
Cape Verde Islands
AFRICA
ATLANTIC OCEAN
Equator

Christopher Columbus

✳

The Merchant Adventurer

Christopher Columbus
(Hardcover)

Illustrations copyright © 2012 by Ikuo Miyazoe / Shogakukan Inc.
Story copyright © 2012 by Kensaku Saguchi / Shogakukan Inc.
All rights reserved. No part of this book may be reproduced, scanned,
or distributed in any printed or electronic form without permission.

Published by VIZ Media, LLC, a member of the Shogakukan group
San Francisco, CA, the United States of America
Published simultaneously in Canada
Printed in Japan
First Edition, September 25, 2012

For information about permission to reprint any portion of this volume, write to:
Permissions, Shogakukan, VIZ Media, LLC
P.O. Box 77010, San Francisco, CA 94107

ISBN-13: 978-1-4215-4973-6

Publisher: Hiroyuki Kawaguchi (Shogakukan Inc.)

Translation: Wayne P. Lammers
Copy Editing: Alan Gleason
Coordination: J-Lit Center

Book Design: Koichi Hama
DTP: Showa Bright
Supervision: T. C. Kusuda (Shogakukan Inc.)

Shogakukan Biographical Comics, VIZ Media, LLC
295 Bay Street, San Francisco, CA 94133

Christopher Columbus

The Merchant Adventurer

Ikuo Miyazoe
illustrator

Kensaku Saguchi
writer

Shogakukan

Christopher Columbus
Table of Contents

Main Characters

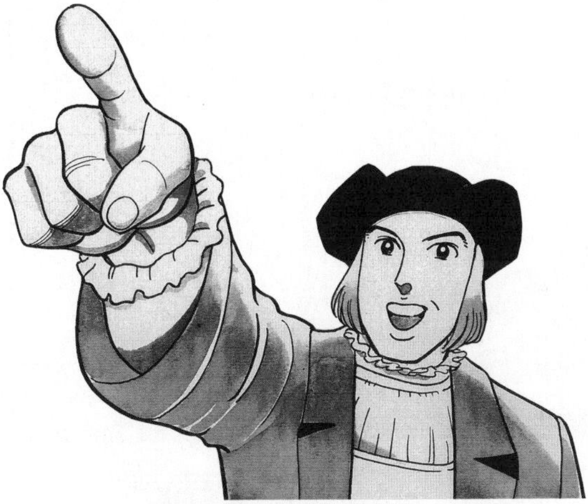

Christopher Columbus
A seafarer born in the Italian city of Genoa; he believed he could sail west to reach Asia

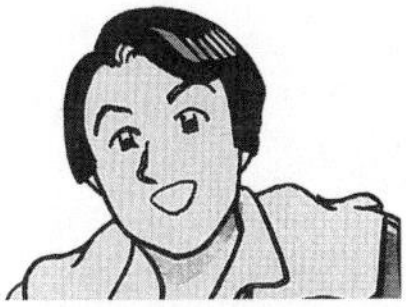

Bartholomew
Columbus's younger brother, a maker of maps

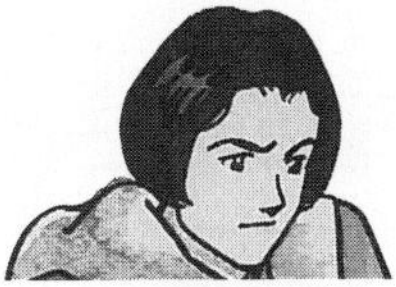

Diego
Columbus's firstborn son, Fernando's older brother

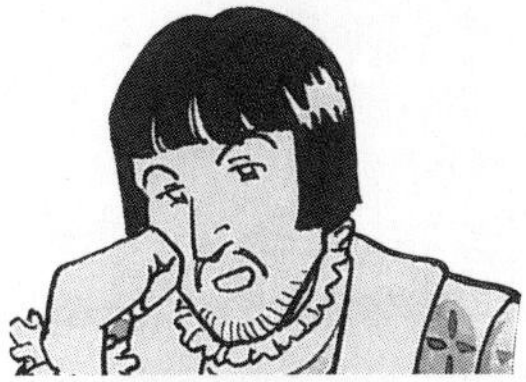

King John II
The ruler of Portugal and a strong backer of African exploration

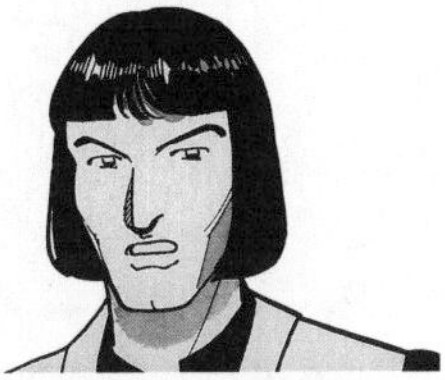

Martín Alonzo Pinzón
Captain of the Pinta on Columbus's first voyage

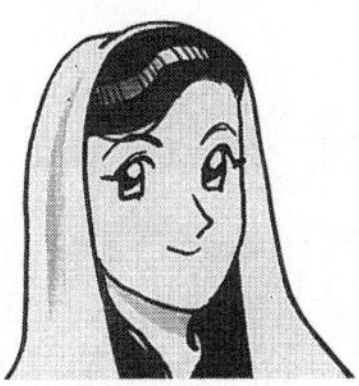

Filipa
Columbus's Portuguese first wife

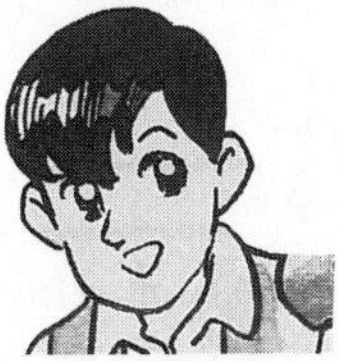

Fernando
Columbus's second son; sailed with his father on his fourth and final voyage

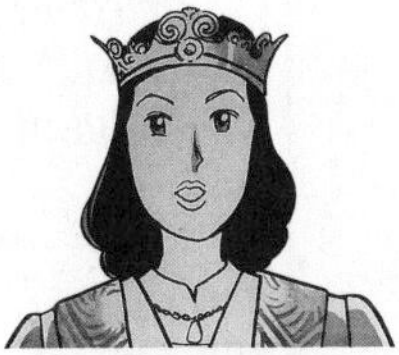

Queen Isabella I
Ruler of Castile (today's Spain)

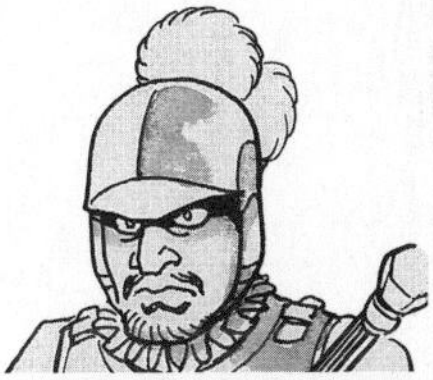

Francisco de Bobadilla
Royal judge who arrested Columbus

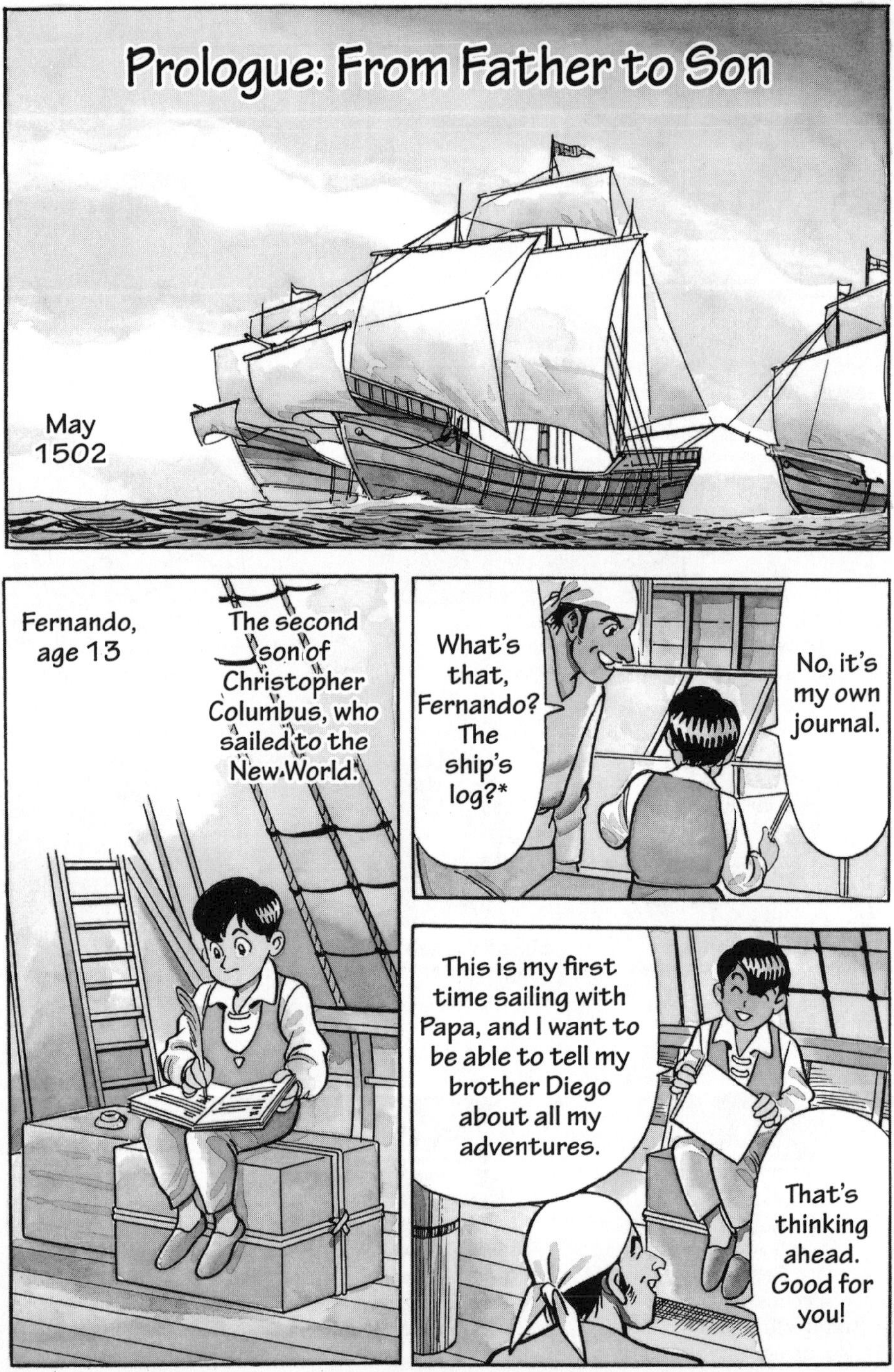
Prologue: From Father to Son
May 1502
Fernando, age 13
The second son of Christopher Columbus, who sailed to the New World.
What's that, Fernando? The ship's log?*
No, it's my own journal.
This is my first time sailing with Papa, and I want to be able to tell my brother Diego about all my adventures.
That's thinking ahead. Good for you!

*Ship's log: a book to keep track of the weather and how far a ship sails each day.

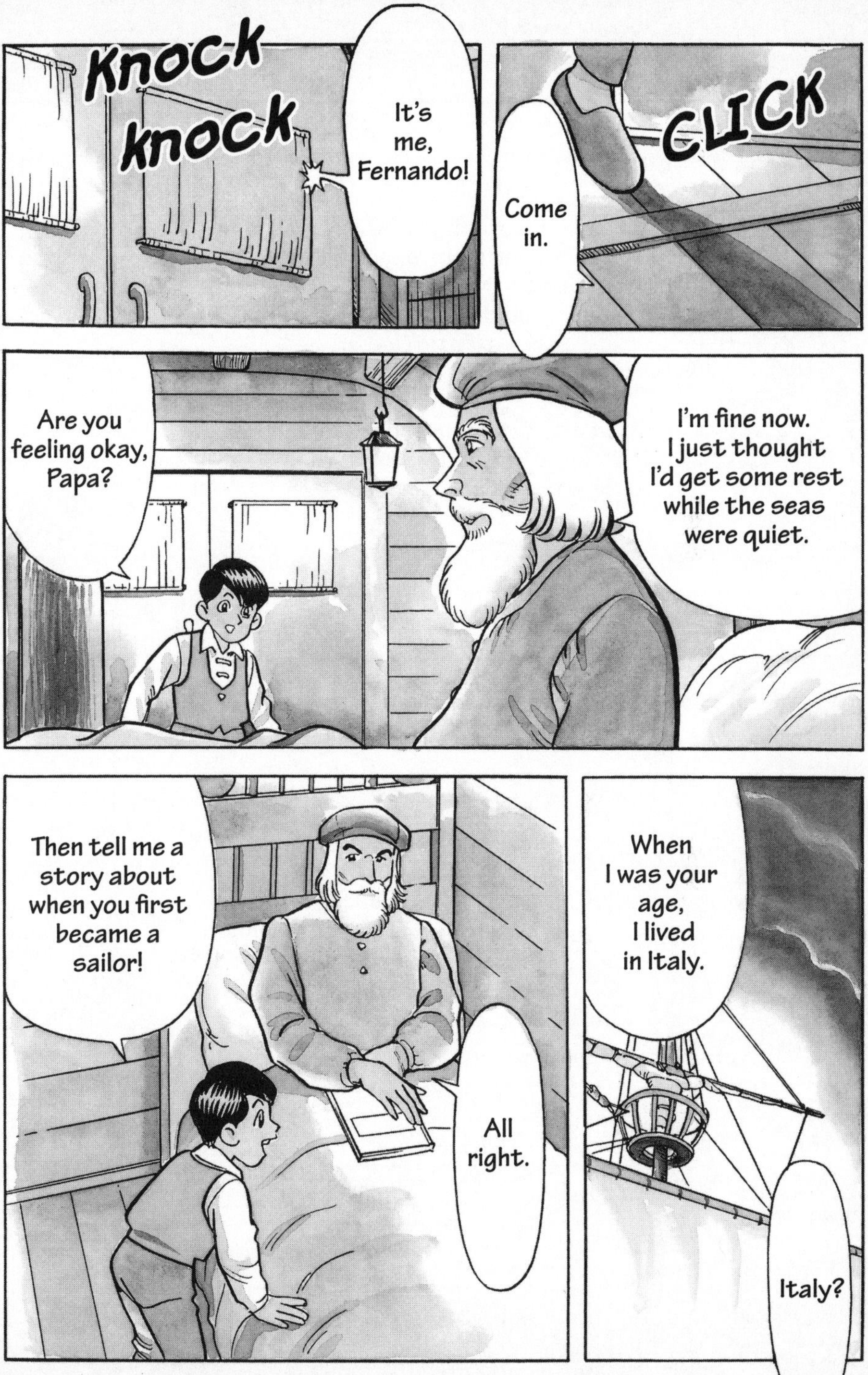
Knock knock
It's me, Fernando!
Come in.
CLICK
Are you feeling okay, Papa?
I'm fine now. I just thought I'd get some rest while the seas were quiet.
Then tell me a story about when you first became a sailor!
All right.
When I was your age, I lived in Italy.
Italy?

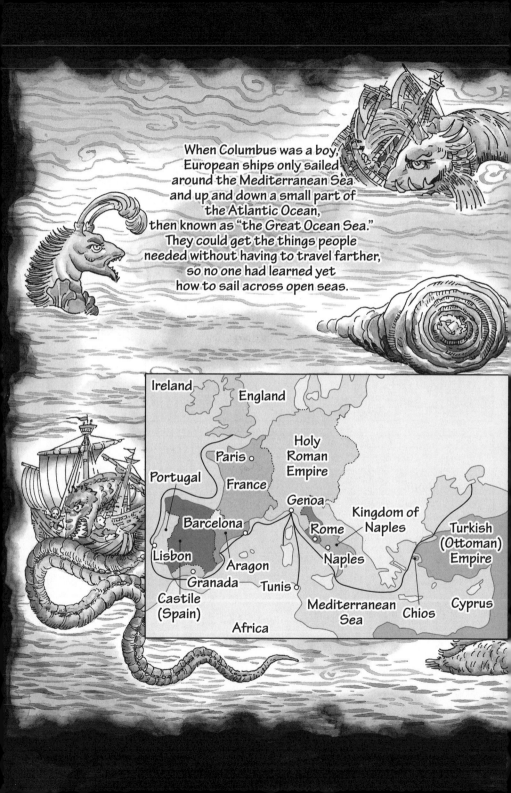

When Columbus was a boy,
European ships only sailed
around the Mediterranean Sea
and up and down a small part of
the Atlantic Ocean,
then known as "the Great Ocean Sea."
They could get the things people
needed without having to travel farther,
so no one had learned yet
how to sail across open seas.

Ireland

England

Holy
Roman
Empire

Paris

Portugal

France

Genoa

Kingdom of
Naples

Rome

Turkish
(Ottoman)
Empire

Barcelona

Lisbon

Aragon

Naples

Granada

Tunis

Castile
(Spain)

Mediterranean
Sea

Chios

Cyprus

Africa

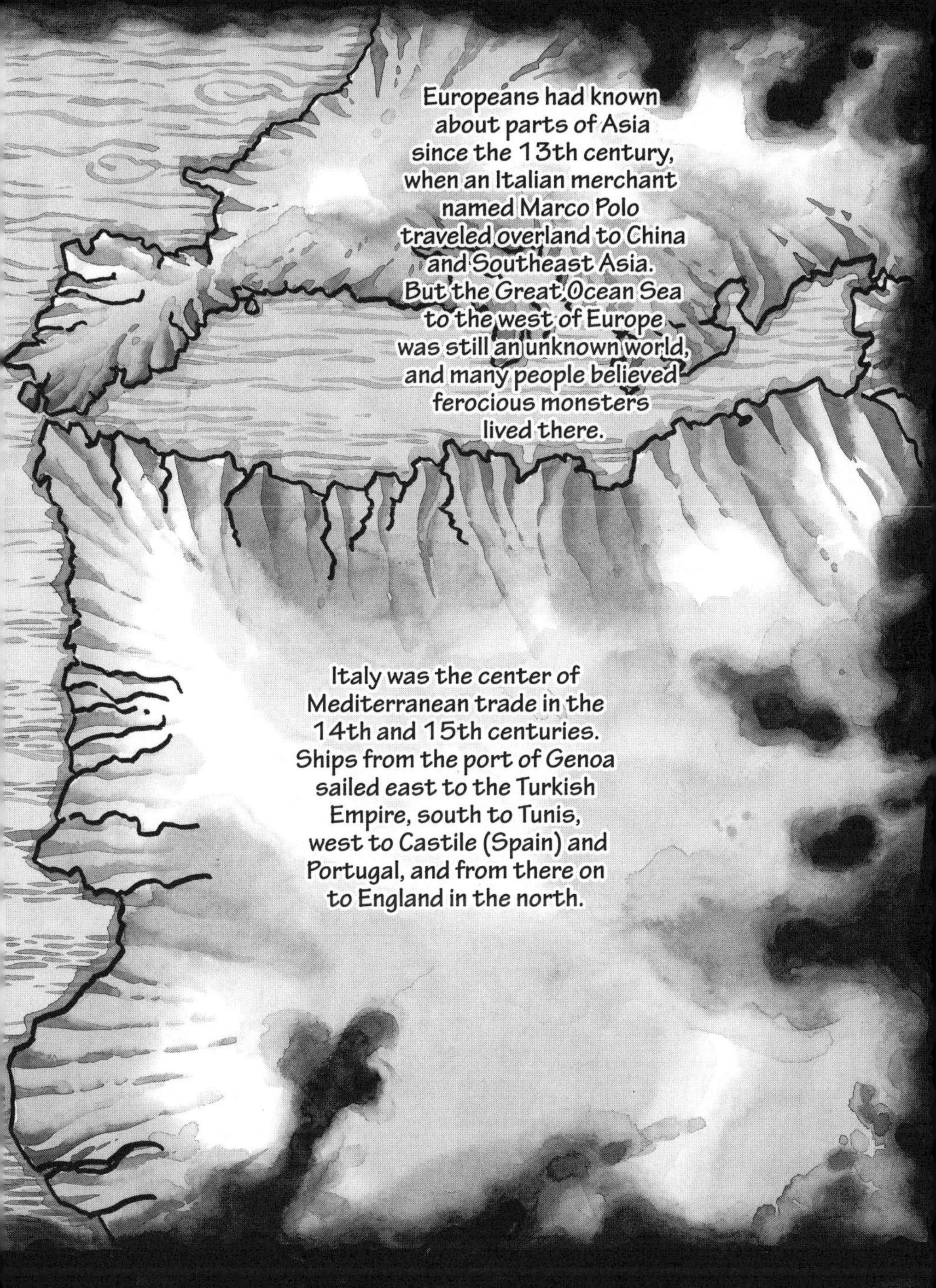
Europeans had known about parts of Asia since the 13th century, when an Italian merchant named Marco Polo traveled overland to China and Southeast Asia. But the Great Ocean Sea to the west of Europe was still an unknown world, and many people believed ferocious monsters lived there.
Italy was the center of Mediterranean trade in the 14th and 15th centuries. Ships from the port of Genoa sailed east to the Turkish Empire, south to Tunis, west to Castile (Spain) and Portugal, and from there on to England in the north.

Chapter 1: The Seafarer from Genoa

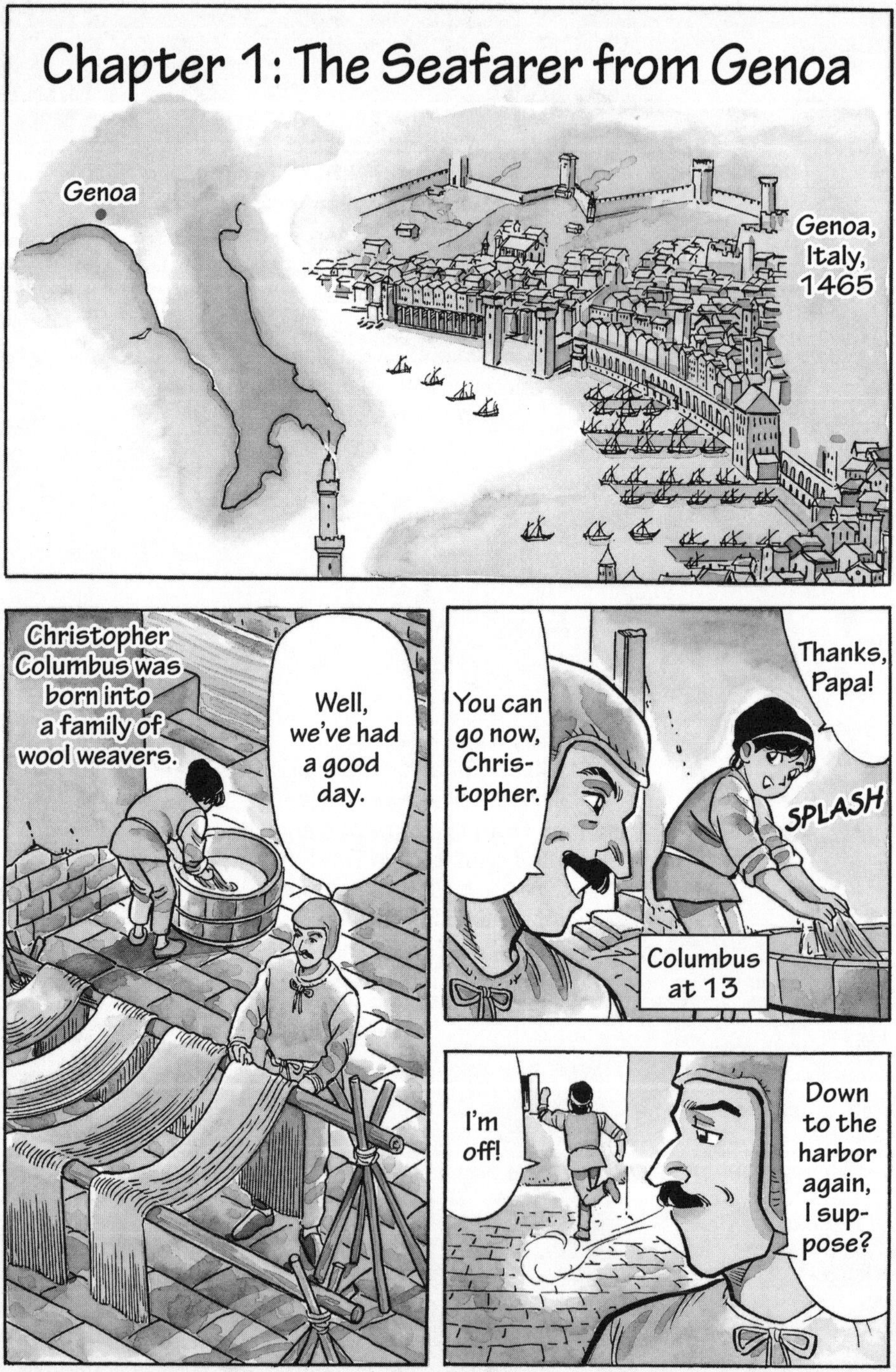
Genoa
Genoa, Italy, 1465
Christopher Columbus was born into a family of wool weavers.
Well, we've had a good day.
You can go now, Christopher.
Thanks, Papa!
SPLASH
Columbus at 13
I'm off!
Down to the harbor again, I suppose?

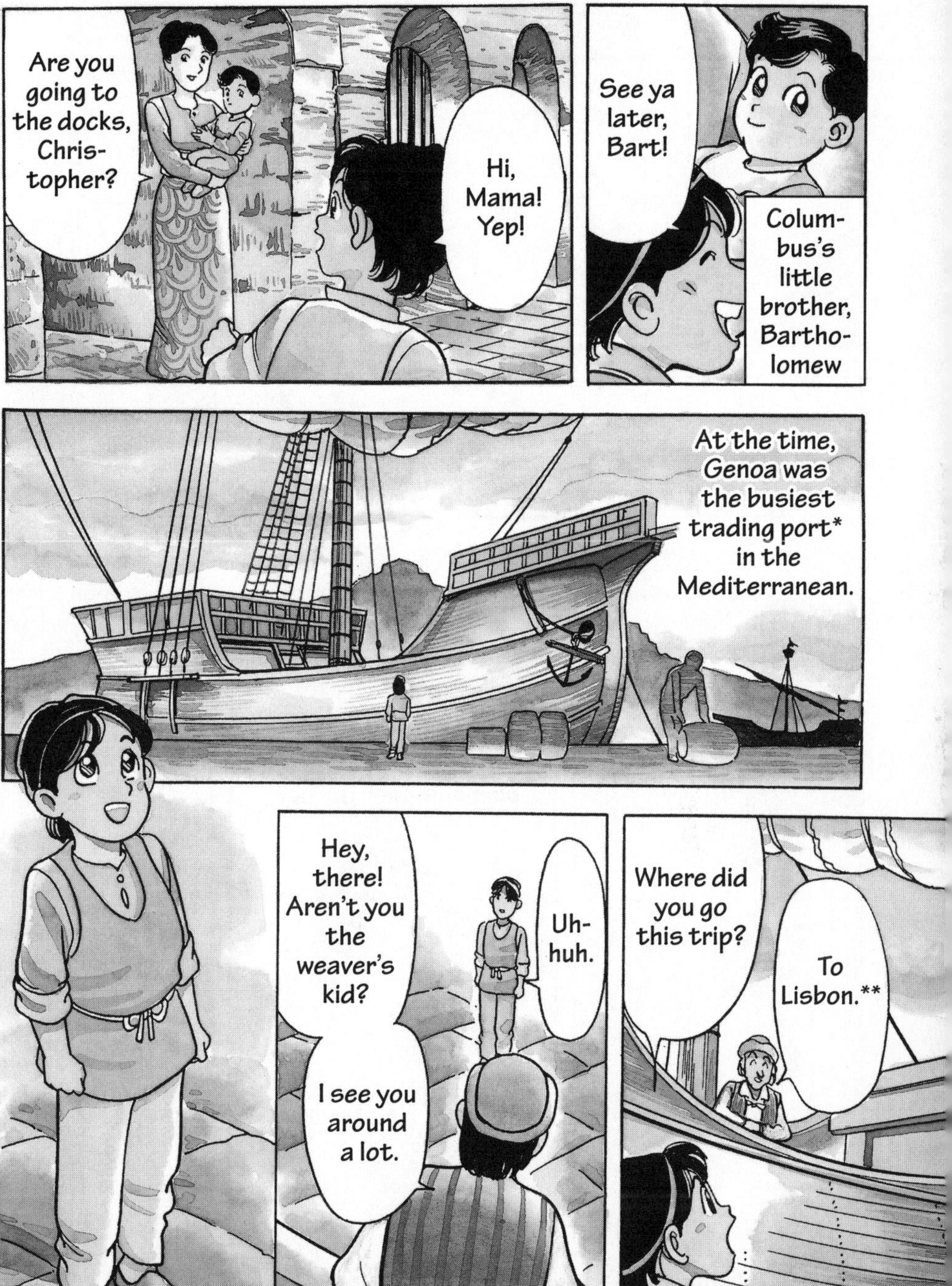
Are you going to the docks, Chris-topher?
Hi, Mama! Yep!
See ya later, Bart!
Colum-bus's little brother, Bartho-lomew
At the time, Genoa was the busiest trading port* in the Mediterranean.
Hey, there! Aren't you the weaver's kid?
Uh-huh.
I see you around a lot.
Where did you go this trip?
To Lisbon.**

*Trading port: a seaport where many merchant ships gather to buy and sell goods from near and far. **Lisbon: See map on page 8.

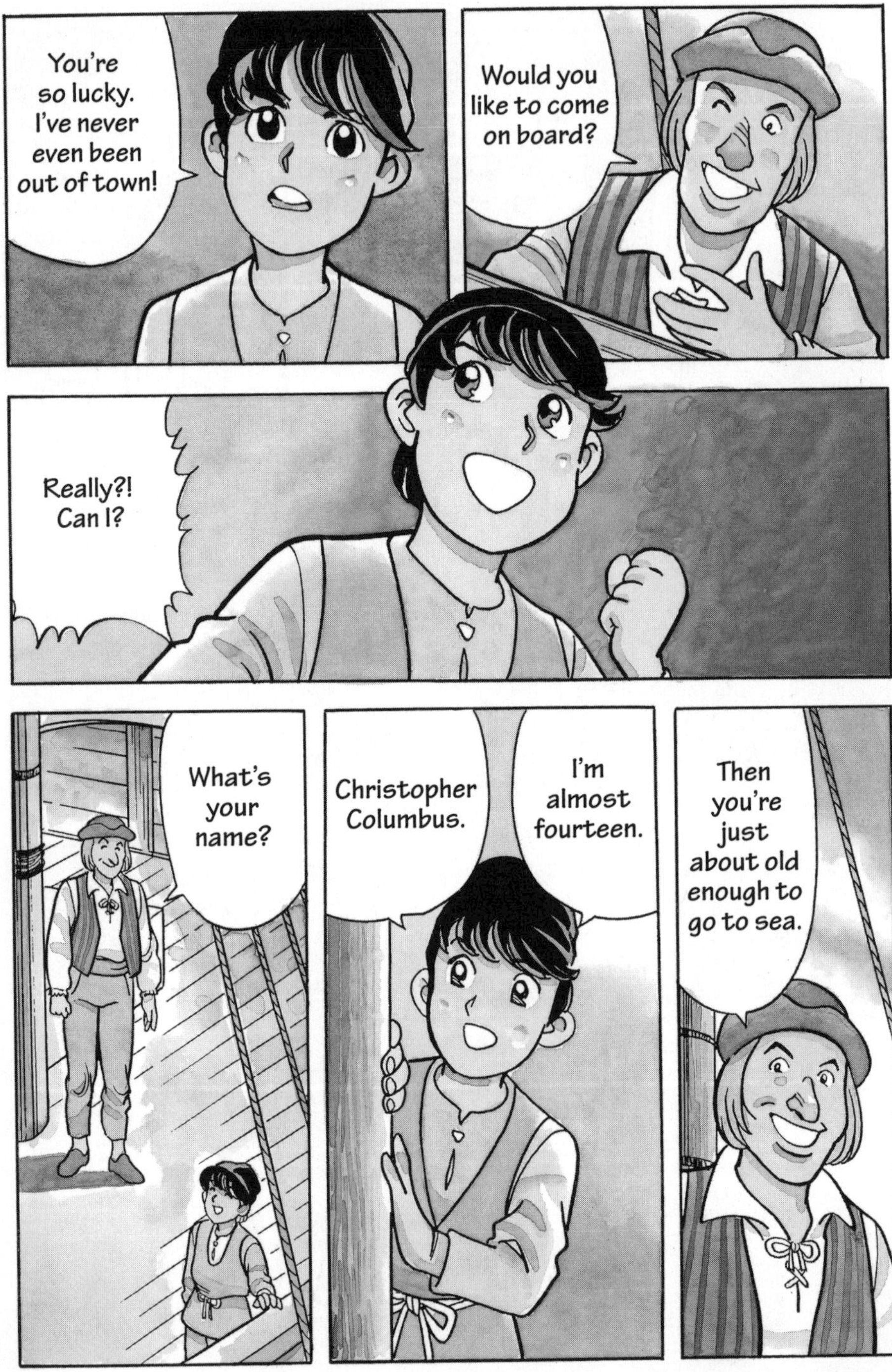
You're so lucky. I've never even been out of town!
Would you like to come on board?
Really?! Can I?
What's your name?
Christopher Columbus.
I'm almost fourteen.
Then you're just about old enough to go to sea.

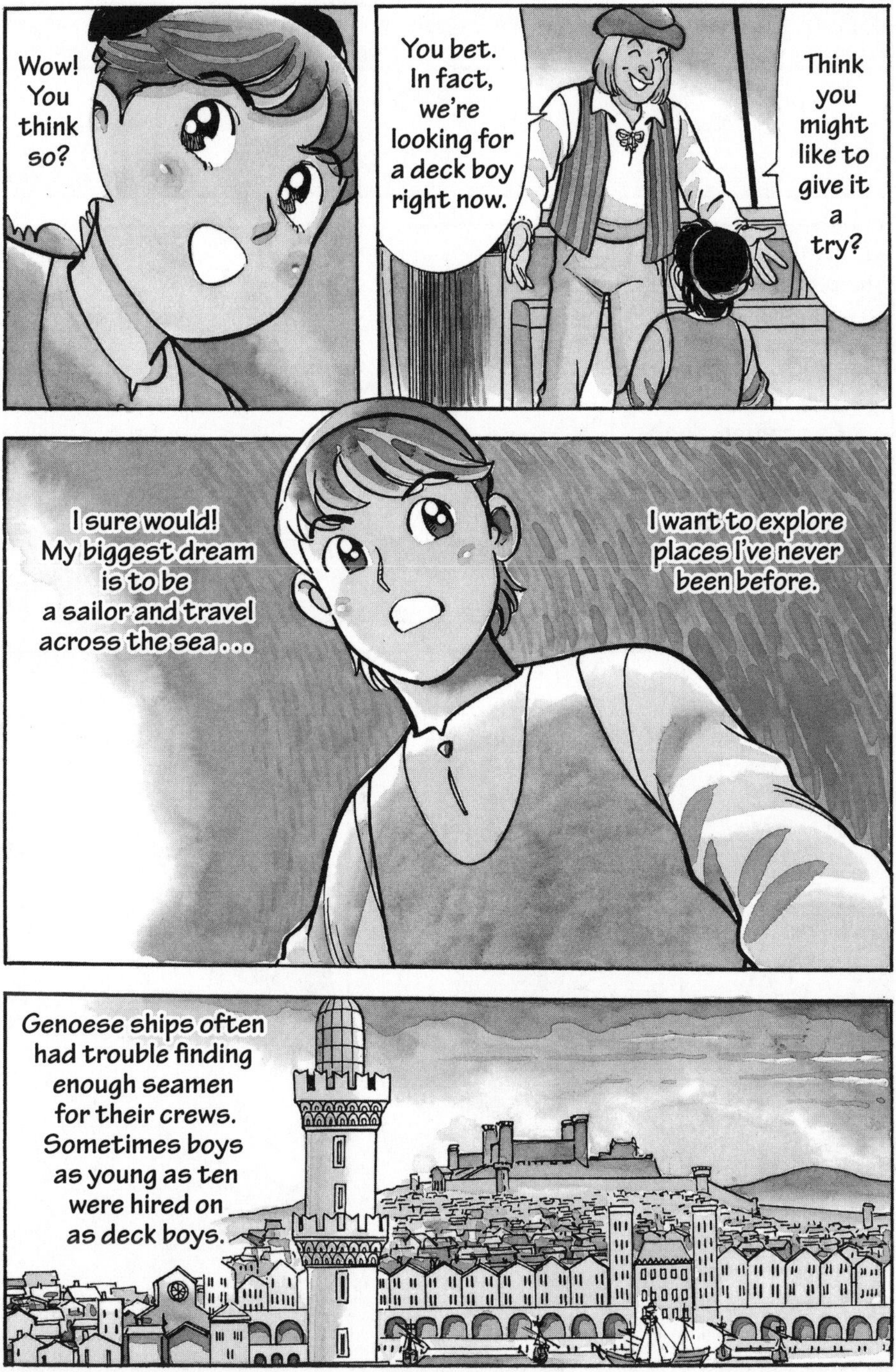
Wow! You think so?
You bet. In fact, we're looking for a deck boy right now.
Think you might like to give it a try?
I sure would! My biggest dream is to be a sailor and travel across the sea . . .
I want to explore places I've never been before.
Genoese ships often had trouble finding enough seamen for their crews. Sometimes boys as young as ten were hired on as deck boys.

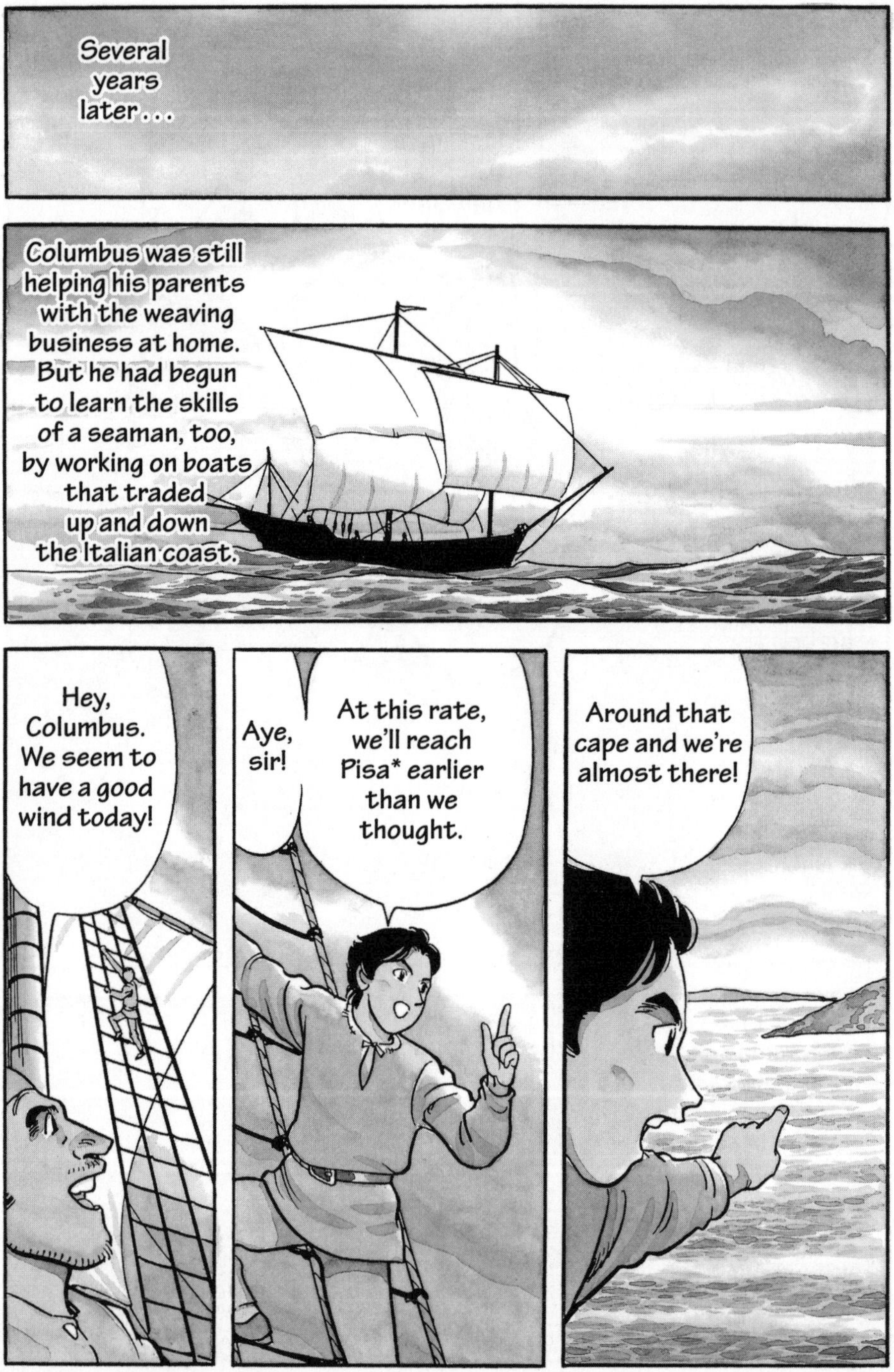
Several years later . . .
Columbus was still helping his parents with the weaving business at home. But he had begun to learn the skills of a seaman, too, by working on boats that traded up and down the Italian coast.
Hey, Columbus. We seem to have a good wind today!
Aye, sir!
At this rate, we'll reach Pisa* earlier than we thought.
Around that cape and we're almost there!

*Pisa: a city about 90 miles from Genoa in northwestern Italy.

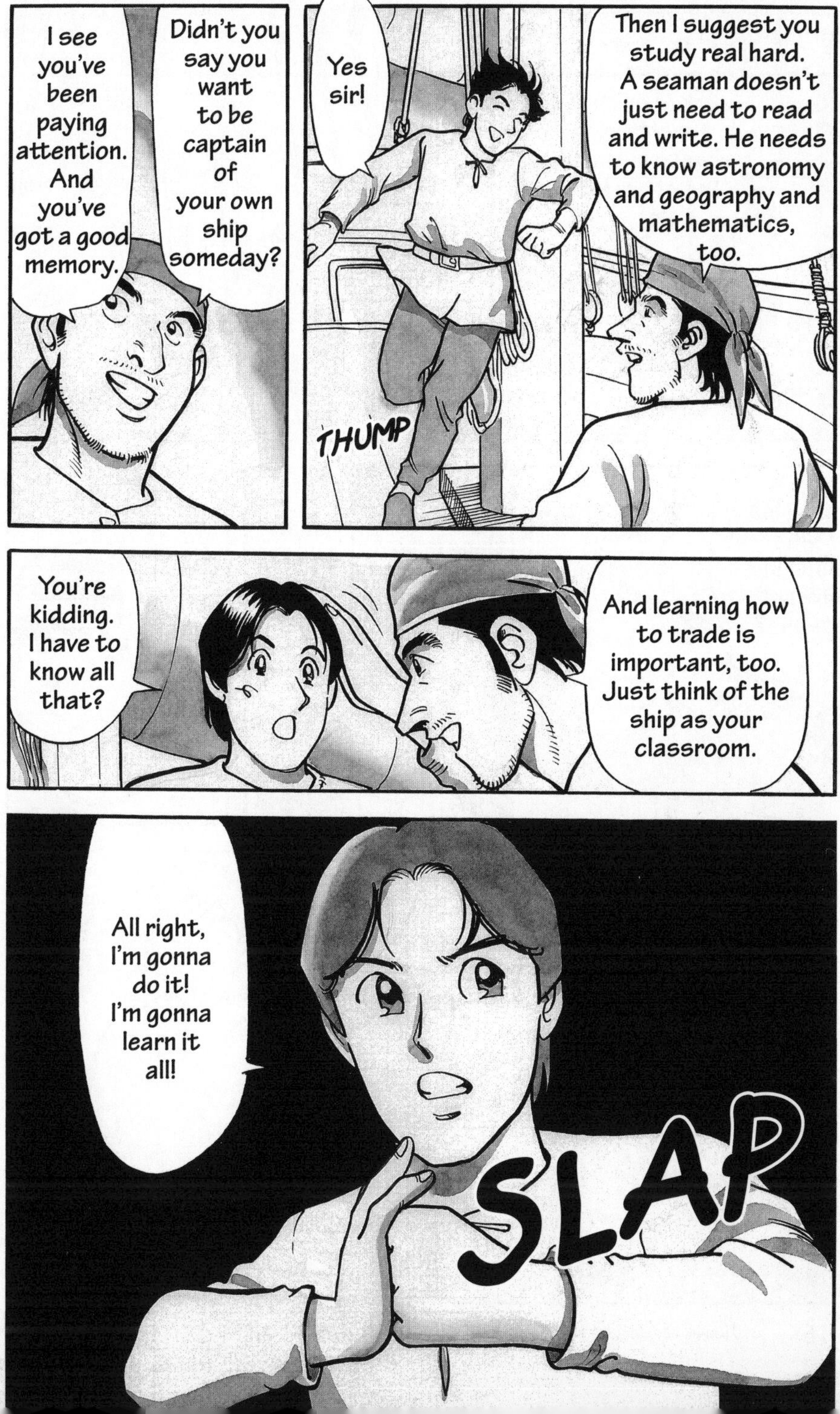
I see you've been paying attention. And you've got a good memory.
Didn't you say you want to be captain of your own ship someday?
Yes sir!
THUMP
Then I suggest you study real hard. A seaman doesn't just need to read and write. He needs to know astronomy and geography and mathematics, too.
You're kidding. I have to know all that?
And learning how to trade is important, too. Just think of the ship as your classroom.
All right, I'm gonna do it! I'm gonna learn it all!
SLAP

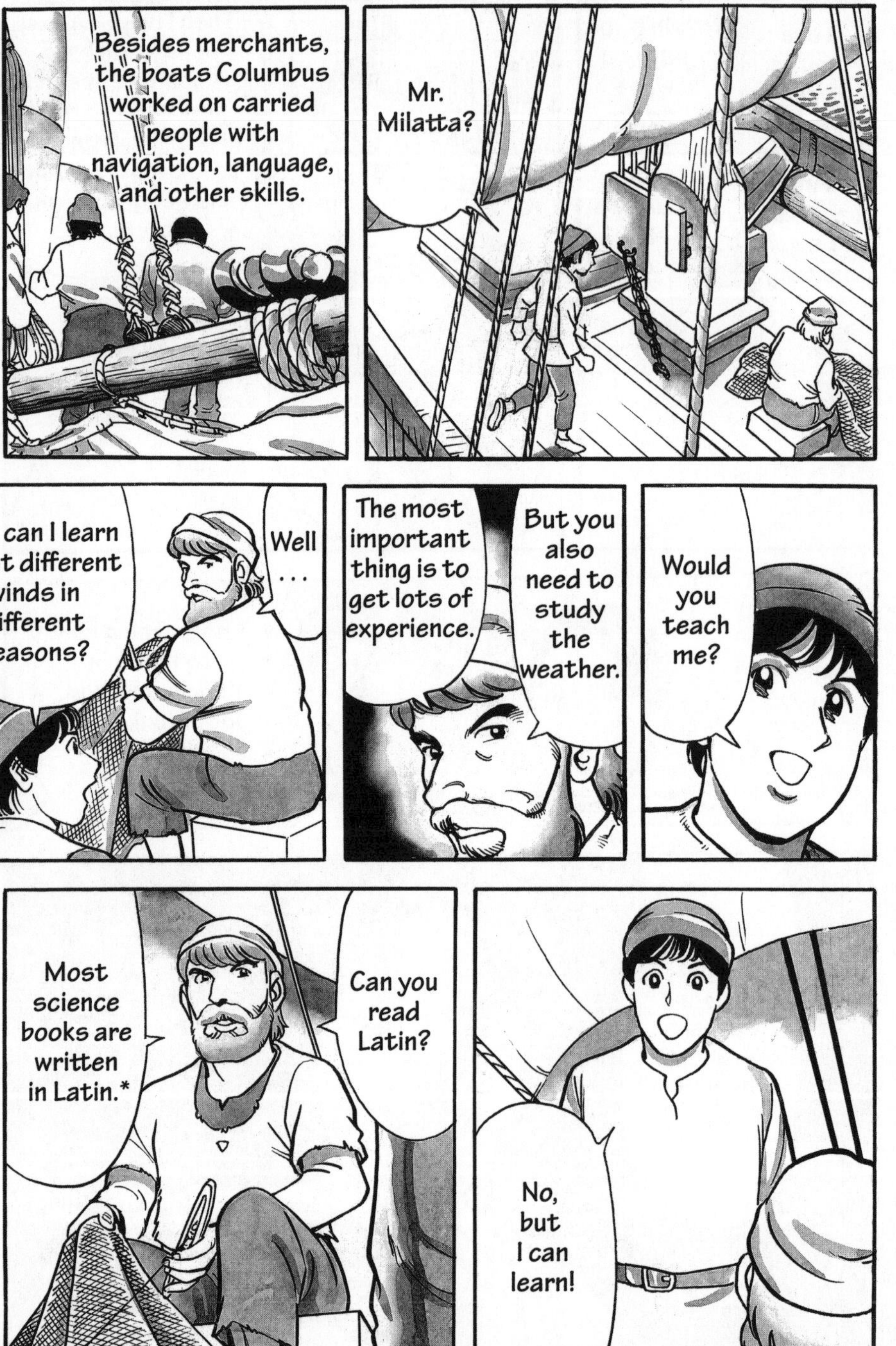
Besides merchants, the boats Columbus worked on carried people with navigation, language, and other skills.
Mr. Milatta?
How can I learn about different winds in different seasons?
Well . . .
The most important thing is to get lots of experience.
But you also need to study the weather.
Would you teach me?
Most science books are written in Latin.*
Can you read Latin?
No, but I can learn!

*Latin: the ancient Roman language that came before Italian, French, and Spanish.

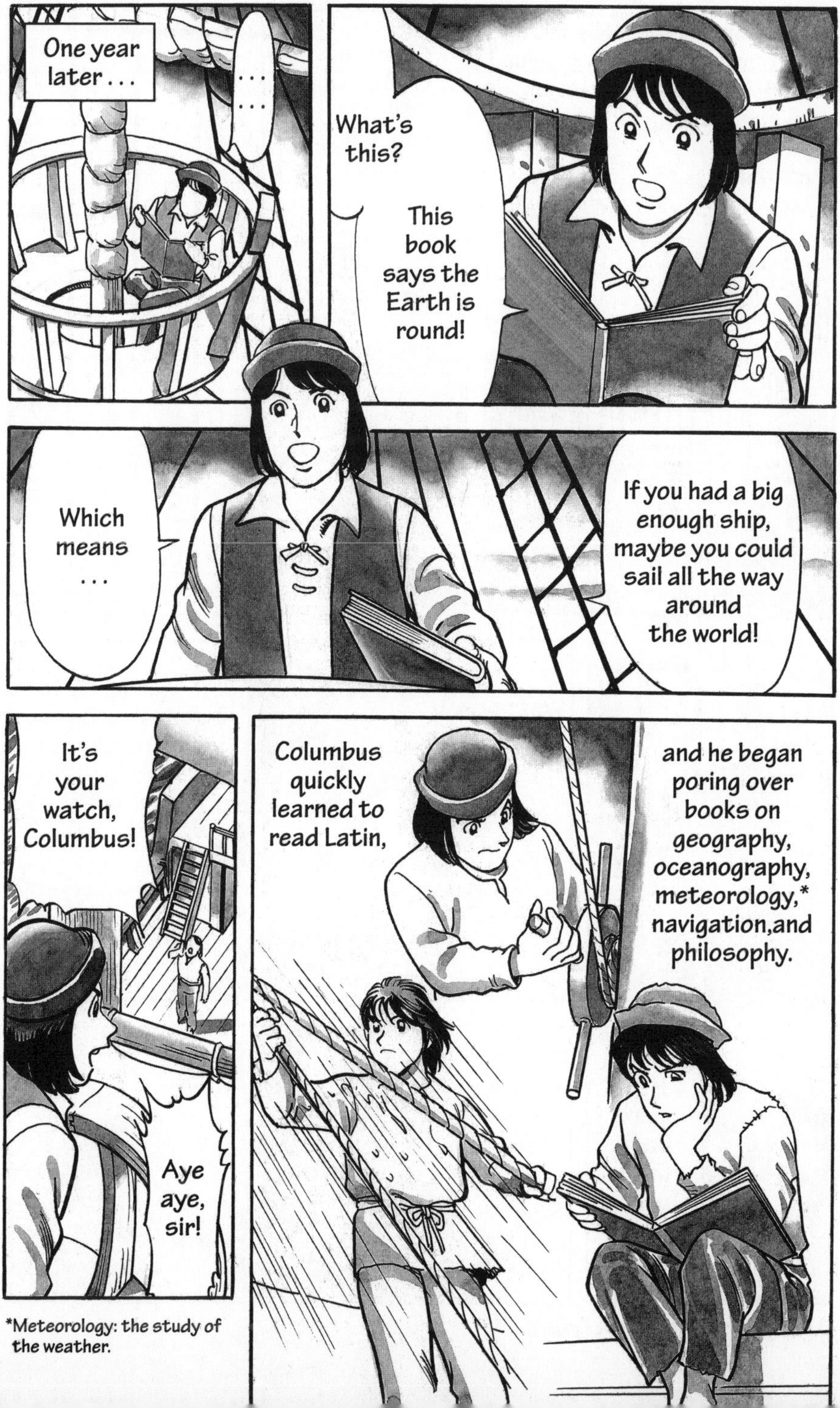
One year later . . .
. . . . . .
What's this?
This book says the Earth is round!
Which means . . .
If you had a big enough ship, maybe you could sail all the way around the world!
It's your watch, Columbus!
Aye aye, sir!
Columbus quickly learned to read Latin,
and he began poring over books on geography, oceanography, meteorology,* navigation,and philosophy.

*Meteorology: the study of the weather.

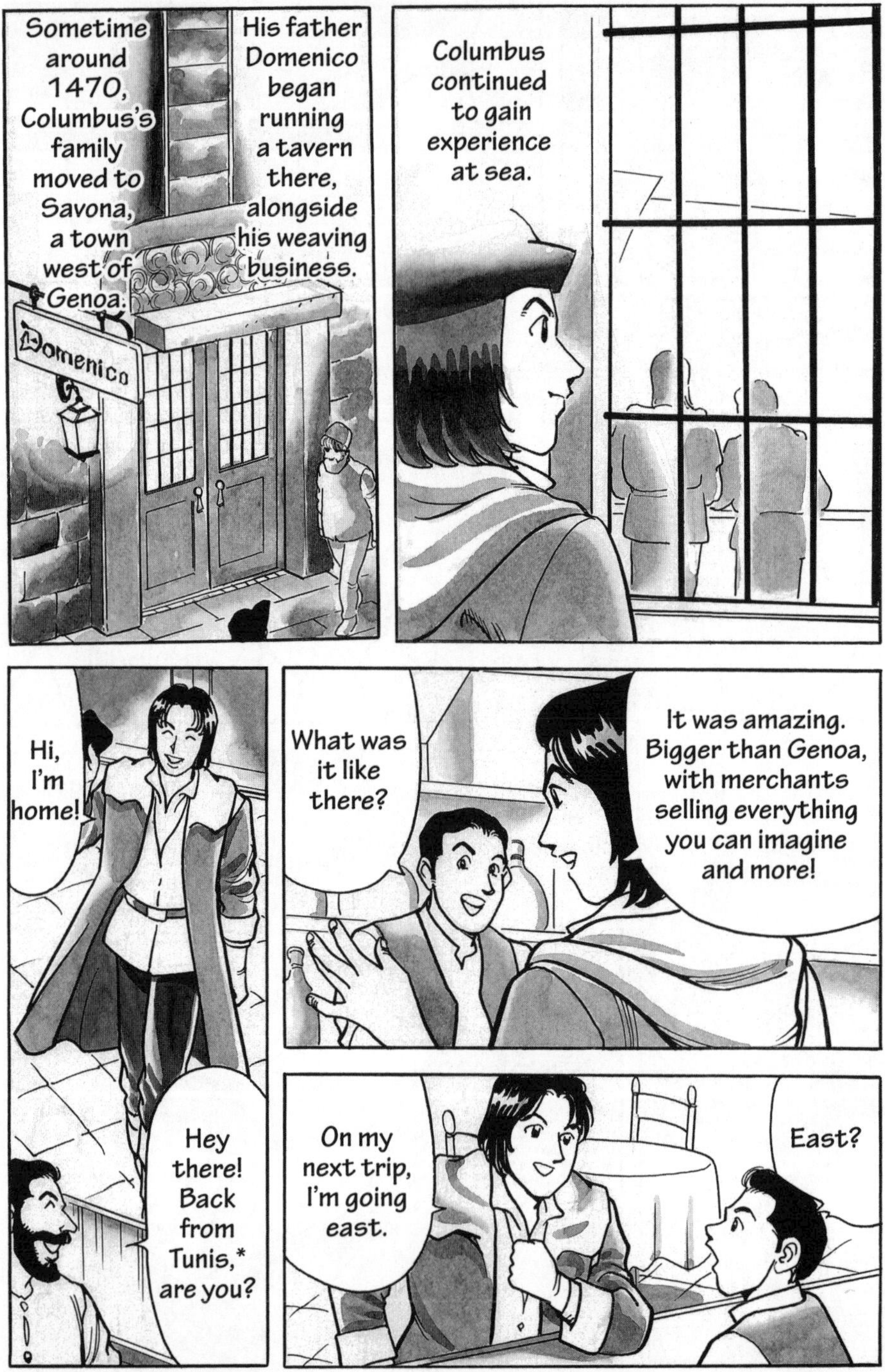
Sometime around 1470, Columbus's family moved to Savona, a town west of Genoa.
His father Domenico began running a tavern there, alongside his weaving business.
Domenico
Columbus continued to gain experience at sea.
Hi, I'm home!
Hey there! Back from Tunis,* are you?
What was it like there?
It was amazing. Bigger than Genoa, with merchants selling everything you can imagine and more!
On my next trip, I'm going east.
East?

*Tunis: See map on page 8.

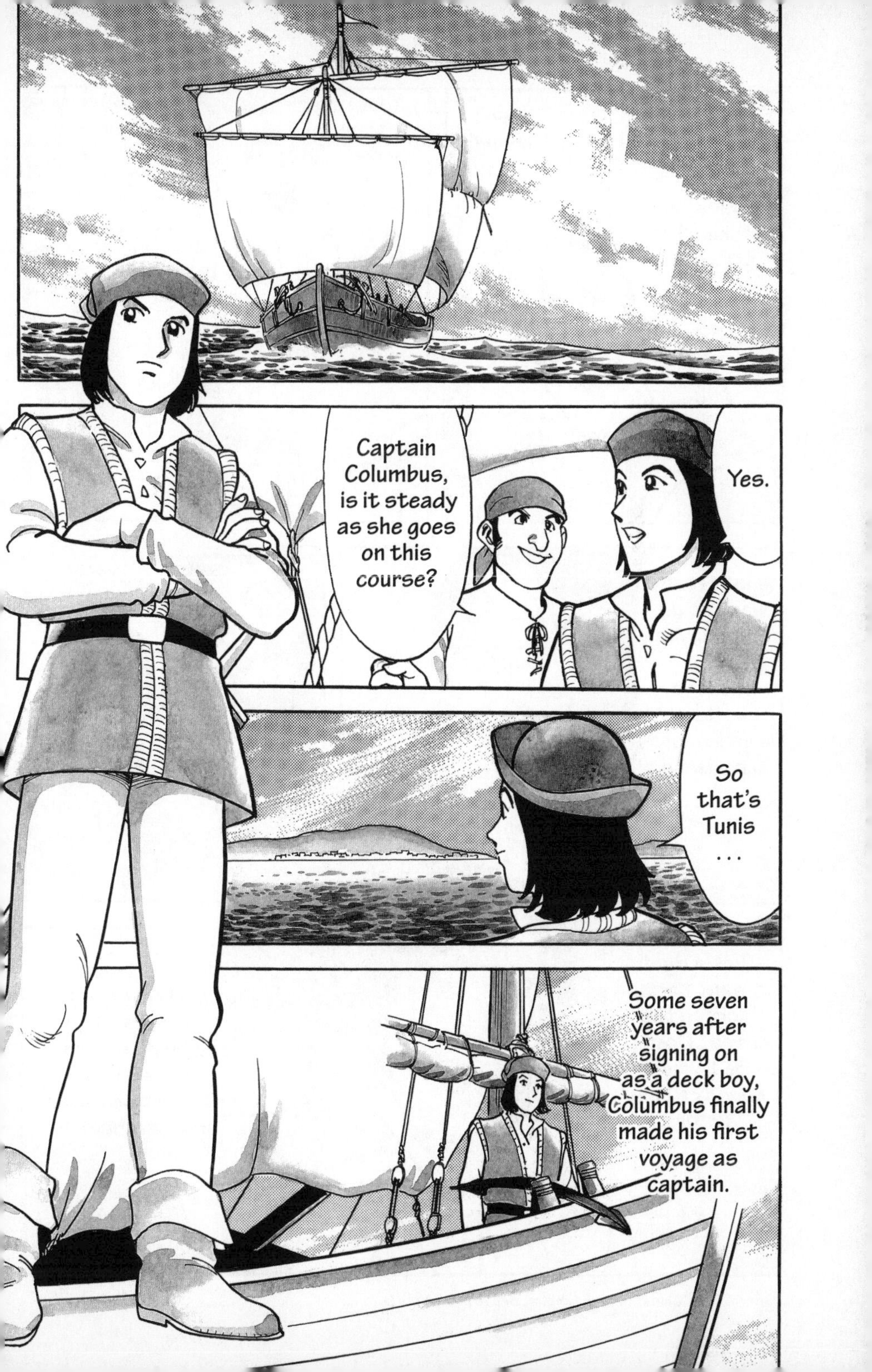
Captain Columbus, is it steady as she goes on this course?
Yes.
So that's Tunis . . .
Some seven years after signing on as a deck boy, Columbus finally made his first voyage as captain.

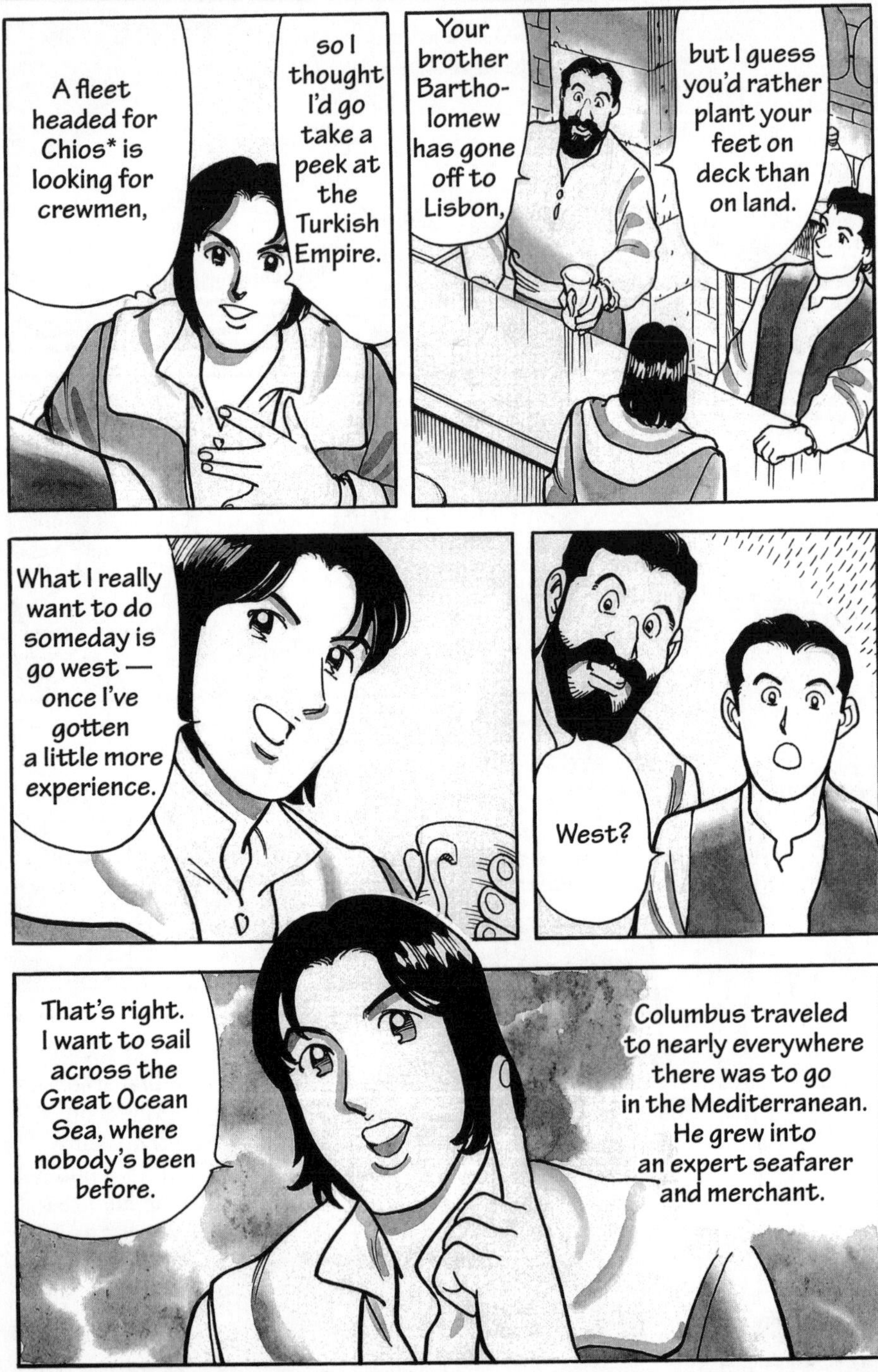
A fleet headed for Chios* is looking for crewmen,
so I thought I'd go take a peek at the Turkish Empire.
Your brother Bartholomew has gone off to Lisbon,
but I guess you'd rather plant your feet on deck than on land.
What I really want to do someday is go west — once I've gotten a little more experience.
West?
That's right. I want to sail across the Great Ocean Sea, where nobody's been before.
Columbus traveled to nearly everywhere there was to go in the Mediterranean. He grew into an expert seafarer and merchant.

*Chios, Turkish Empire: See map on page 8.

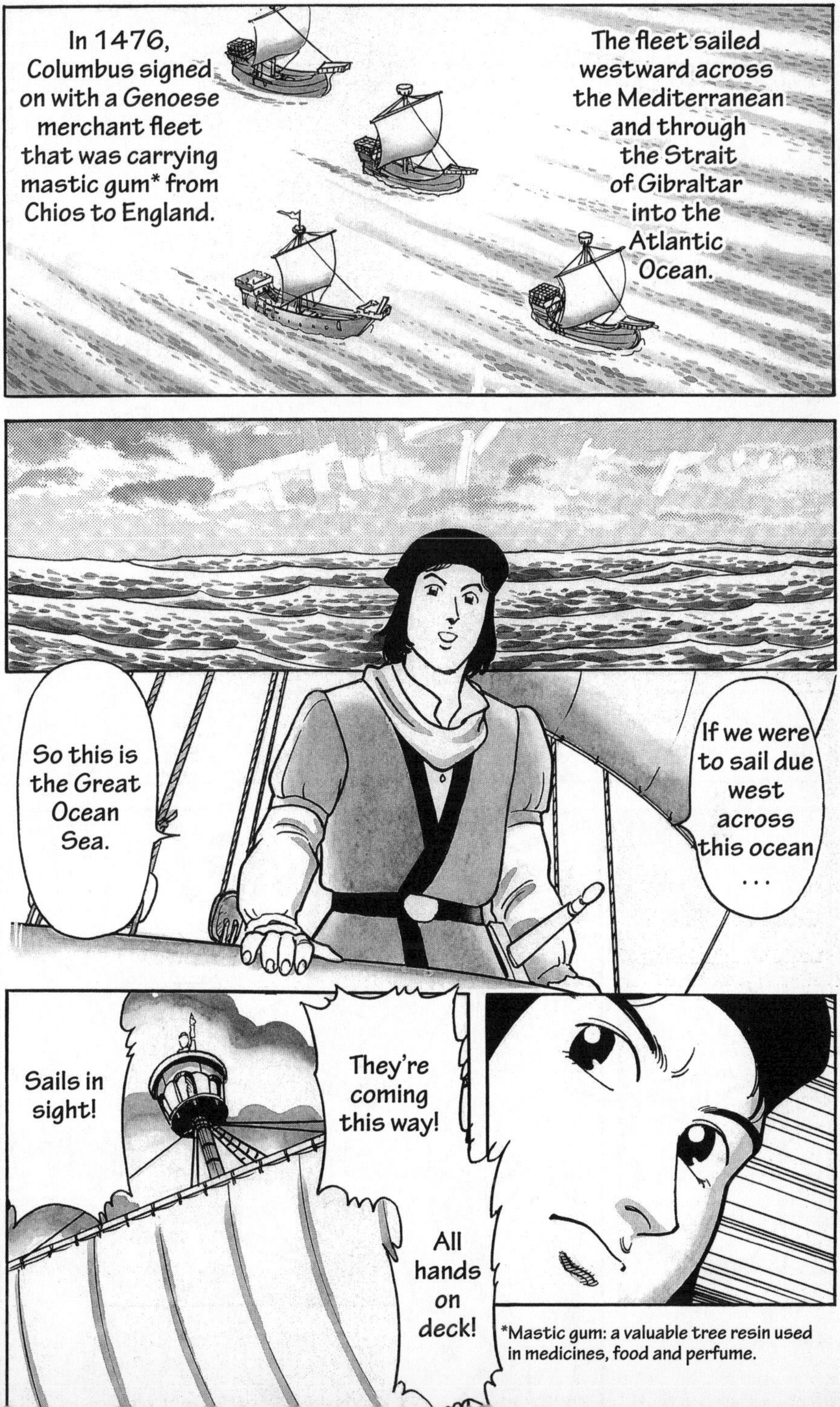
In 1476, Columbus signed on with a Genoese merchant fleet that was carrying mastic gum* from Chios to England.
The fleet sailed westward across the Mediterranean and through the Strait of Gibraltar into the Atlantic Ocean.
So this is the Great Ocean Sea.
If we were to sail due west across this ocean ...
Sails in sight!
They're coming this way!
All hands on deck!

*Mastic gum: a valuable tree resin used in medicines, food and perfume.

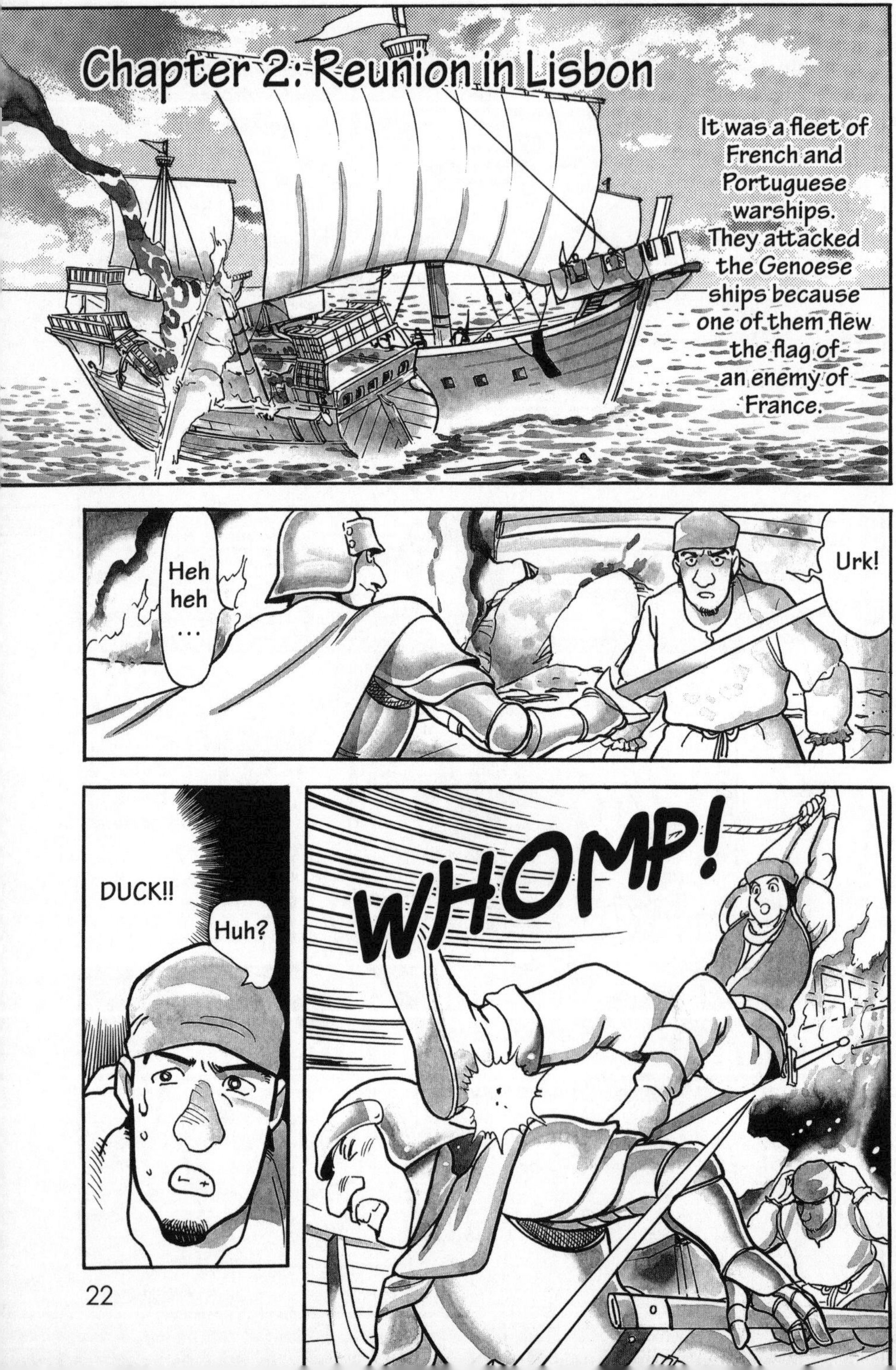
Chapter 2: Reunion in Lisbon
It was a fleet of French and Portuguese warships. They attacked the Genoese ships because one of them flew the flag of an enemy of France.
Heh heh ...
Urk!
DUCK!!
Huh?
WHOMP!

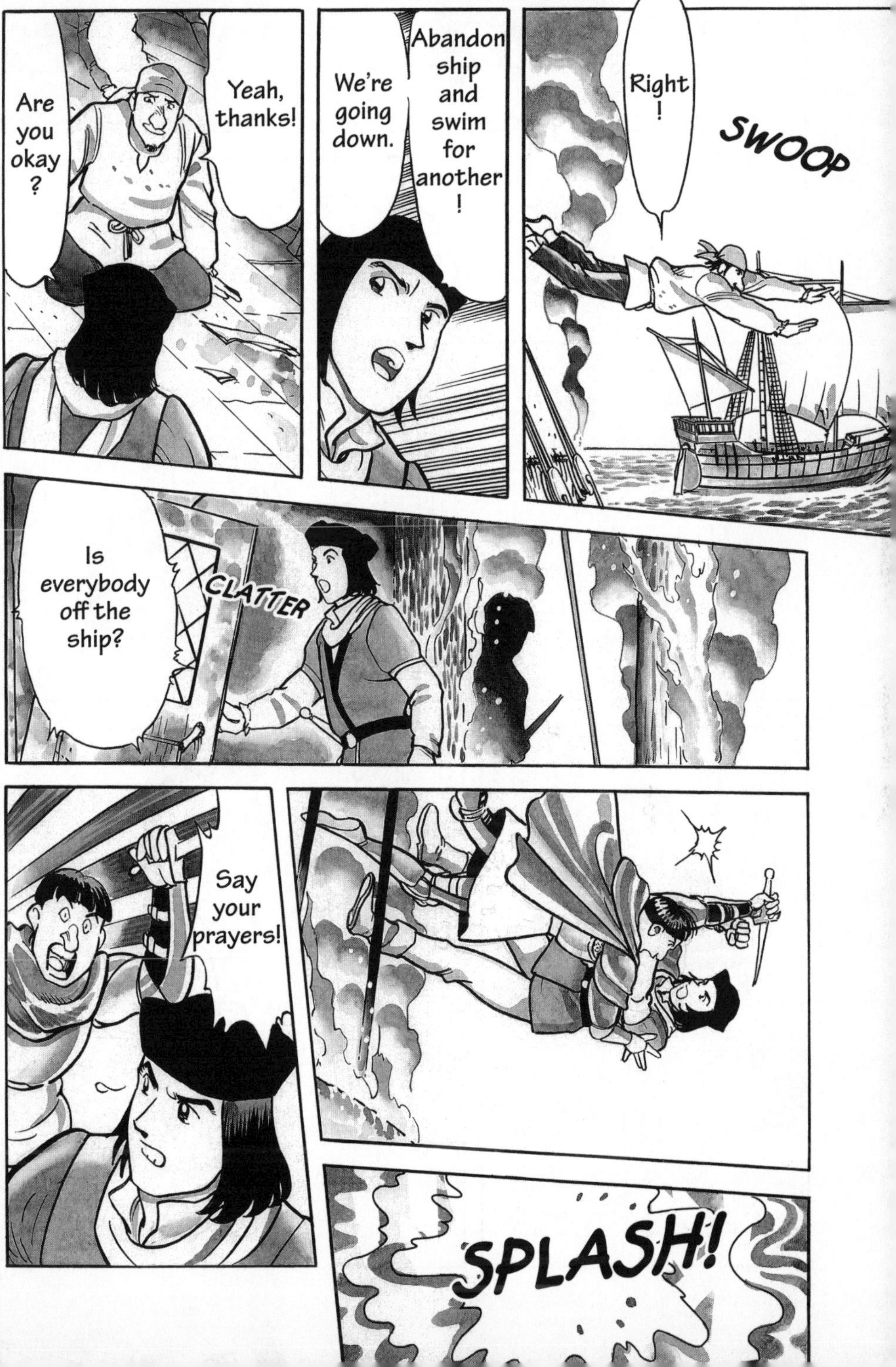
Are you okay?
Yeah, thanks!
We're going down.
Abandon ship and swim for another!
Right!
SWOOP
Is everybody off the ship?
CLATTER
Say your prayers!
SPLASH!

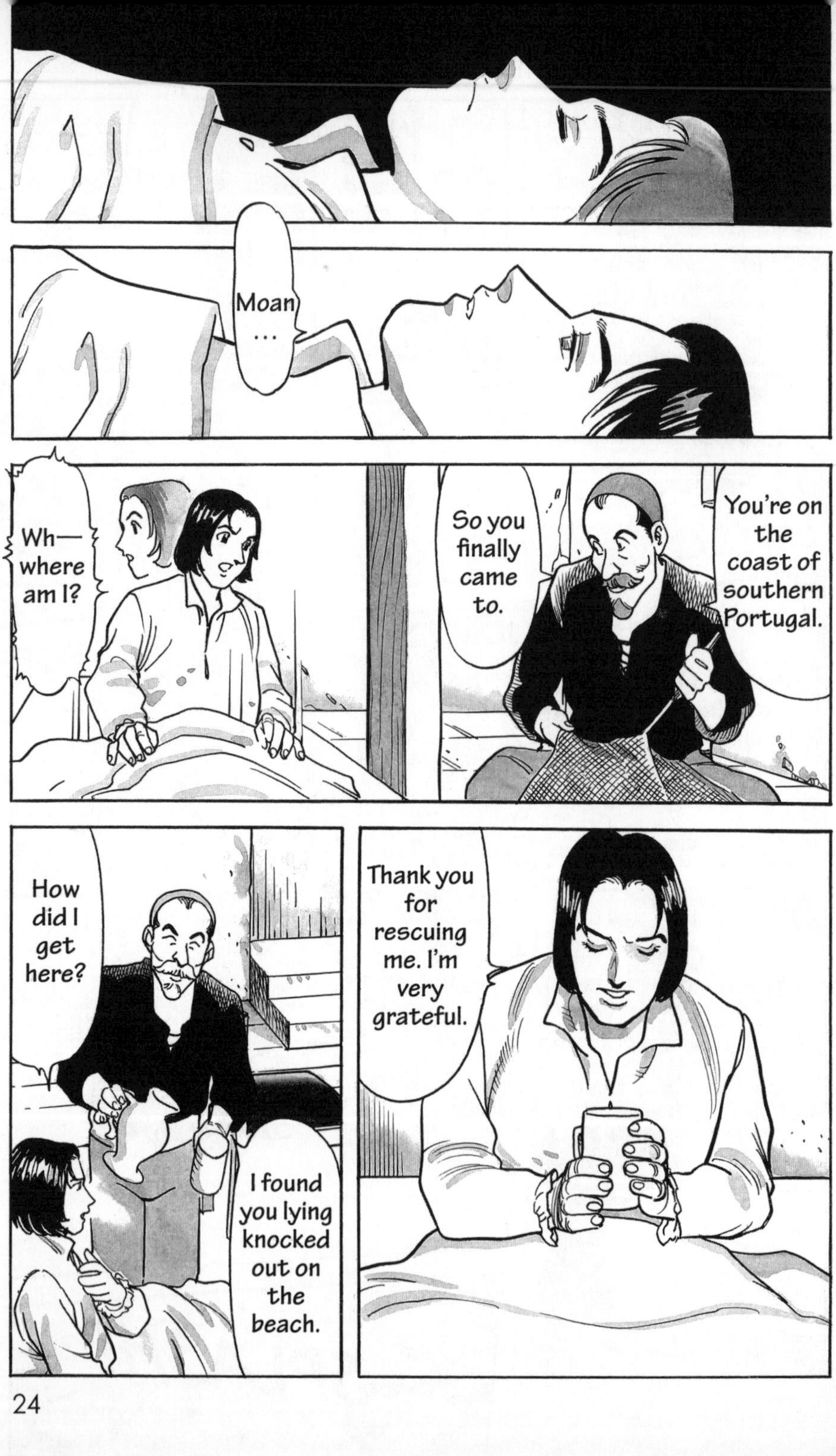
Moan
...
Wh— where am I?
So you finally came to.
You're on the coast of southern Portugal.
How did I get here?
I found you lying knocked out on the beach.
Thank you for rescuing me. I'm very grateful.

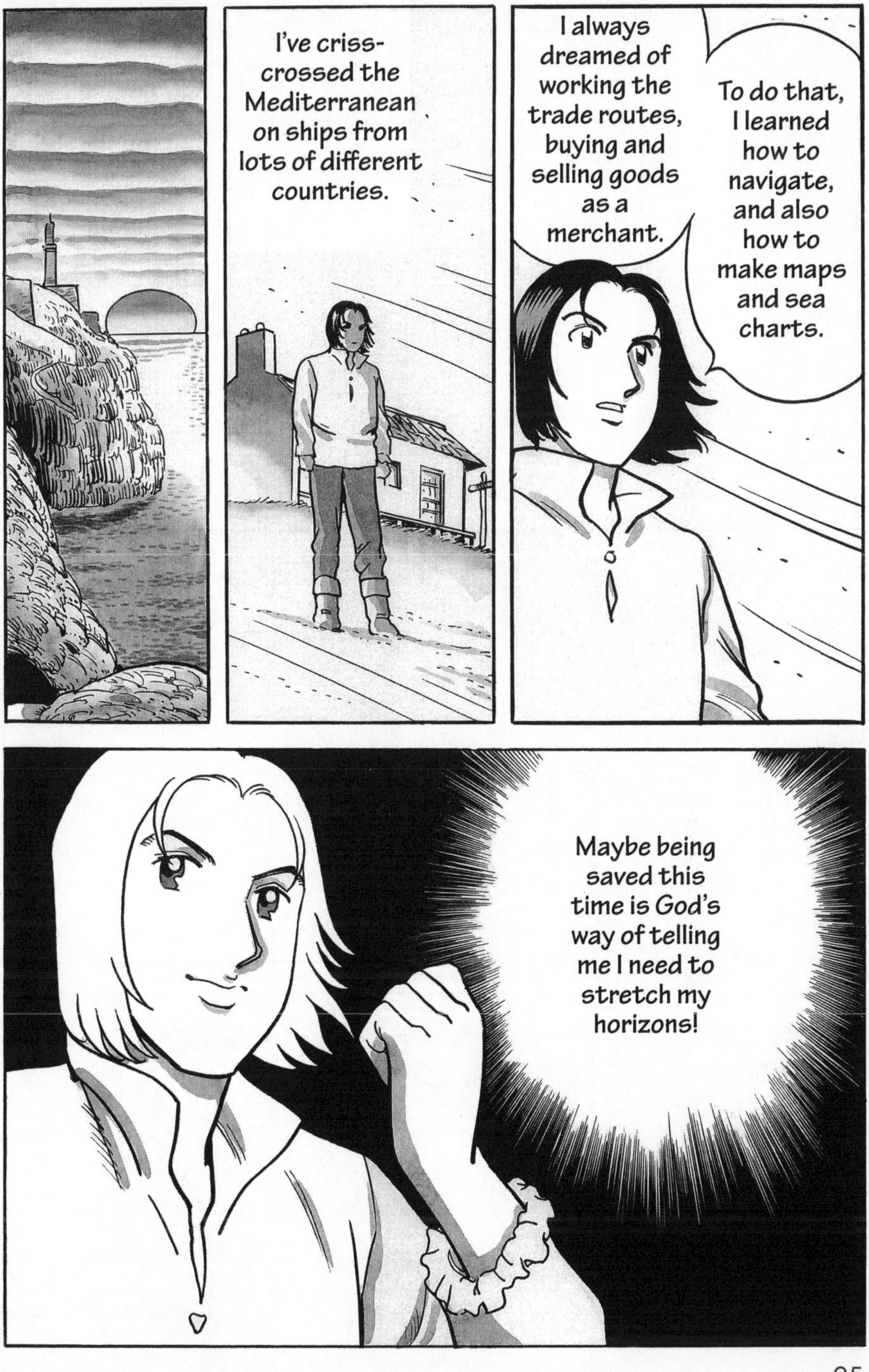
I've criss-crossed the Mediterranean on ships from lots of different countries.
I always dreamed of working the trade routes, buying and selling goods as a merchant.
To do that, I learned how to navigate, and also how to make maps and sea charts.
Maybe being saved this time is God's way of telling me I need to stretch my horizons!

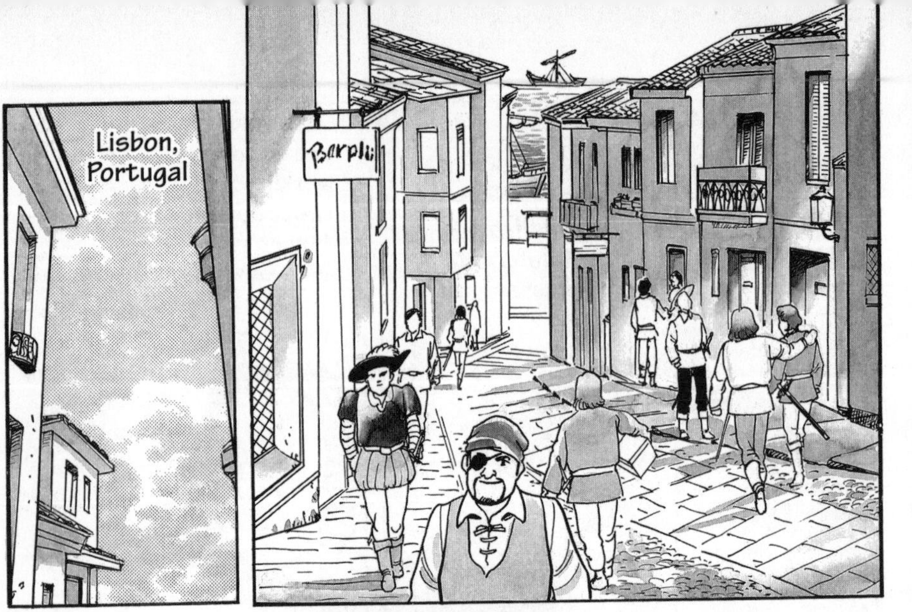
Lisbon, Portugal

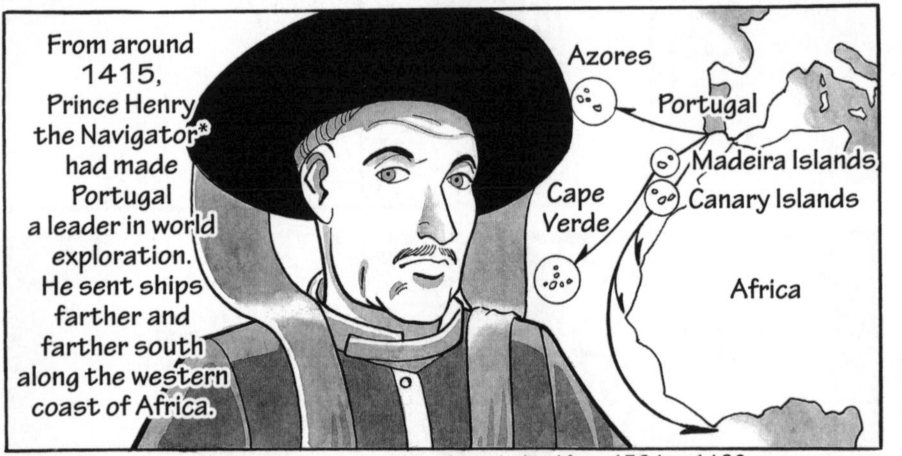
From around 1415, Prince Henry the Navigator* had made Portugal a leader in world exploration. He sent ships farther and farther south along the western coast of Africa.
Azores
Portugal
Madeira Islands
Canary Islands
Cape Verde
Africa

*Henry the Navigator: a Portuguese prince who lived from 1394 to 1460.

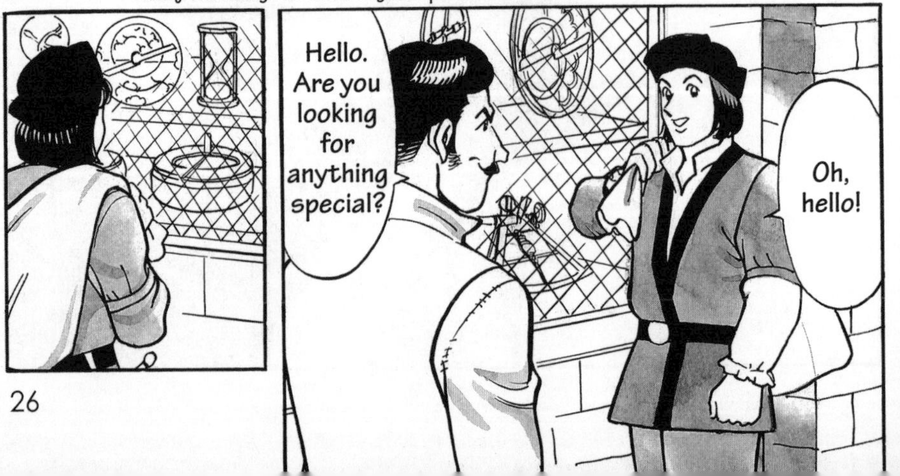
Hello. Are you looking for anything special?
Oh, hello!

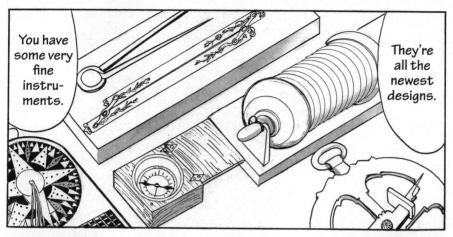

You have some very fine instruments.

They're all the newest designs.

They must be expensive.

Maybe you can come back when you strike it rich!

R— right.

By the way, I heard a man named Bartholomew was working here.

Oh, yes, Bartholomew.

He's on an errand right now.

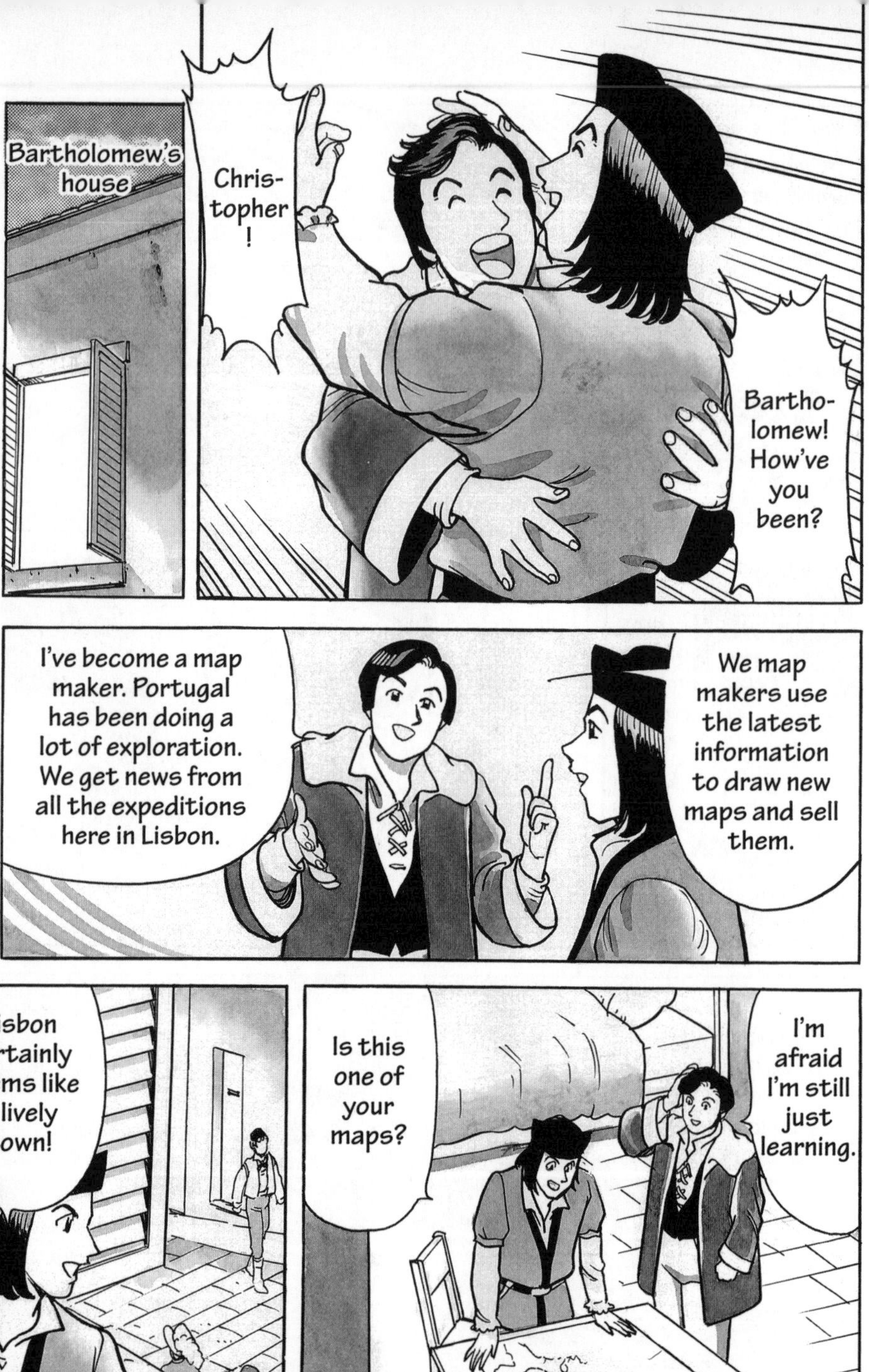
Bartholomew's house
Christopher!
Bartholomew! How've you been?
I've become a map maker. Portugal has been doing a lot of exploration. We get news from all the expeditions here in Lisbon.
We map makers use the latest information to draw new maps and sell them.
Lisbon certainly seems like a lively town!
Is this one of your maps?
I'm afraid I'm still just learning.

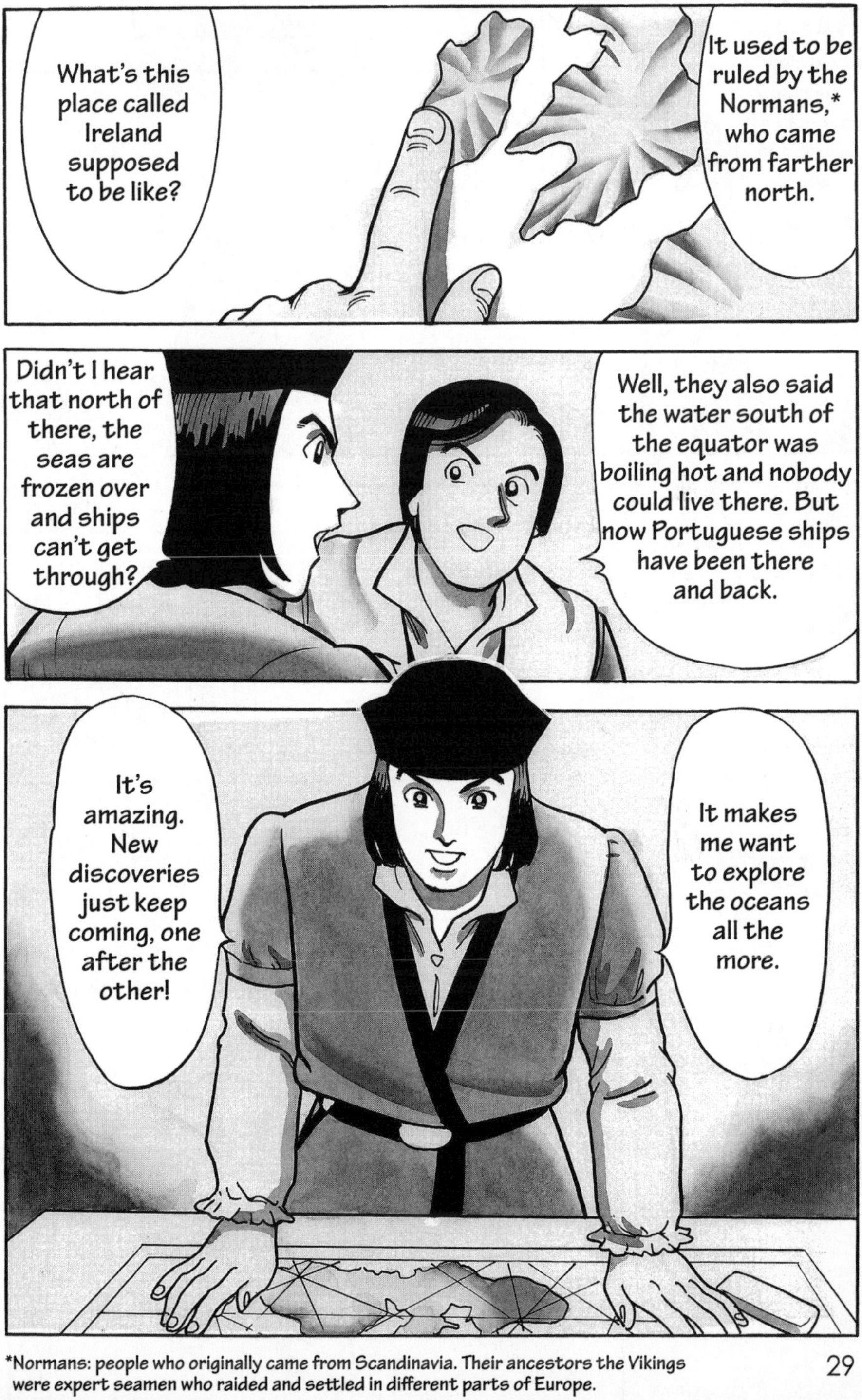
What's this place called Ireland supposed to be like?
It used to be ruled by the Normans,* who came from farther north.
Didn't I hear that north of there, the seas are frozen over and ships can't get through?
Well, they also said the water south of the equator was boiling hot and nobody could live there. But now Portuguese ships have been there and back.
It's amazing. New discoveries just keep coming, one after the other!
It makes me want to explore the oceans all the more.

*Normans: people who originally came from Scandinavia. Their ancestors the Vikings were expert seamen who raided and settled in different parts of Europe.

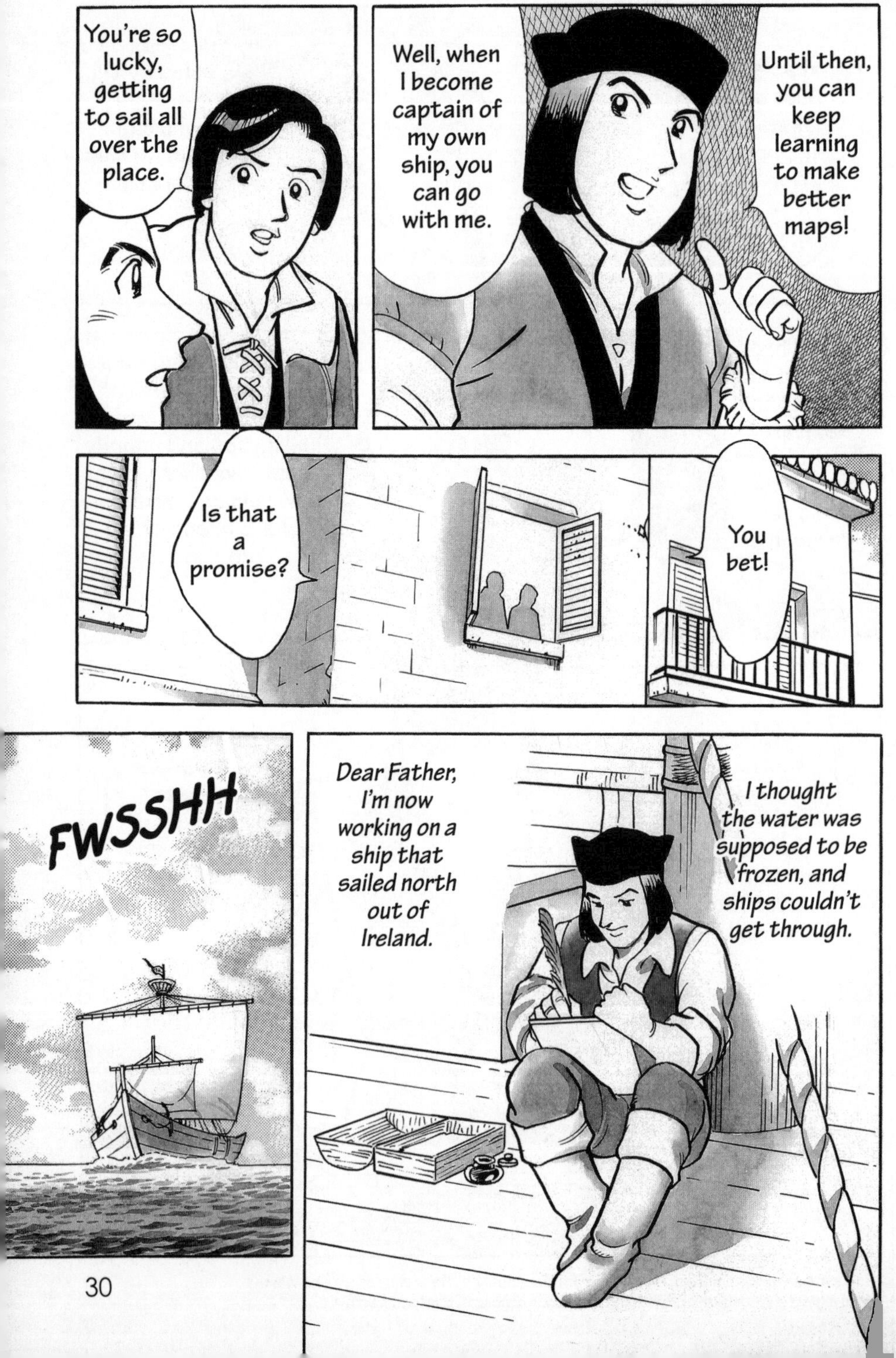
You're so lucky, getting to sail all over the place.
Well, when I become captain of my own ship, you can go with me.
Until then, you can keep learning to make better maps!
Is that a promise?
You bet!
FWSSHH
Dear Father, I'm now working on a ship that sailed north out of Ireland.
I thought the water was supposed to be frozen, and ships couldn't get through.

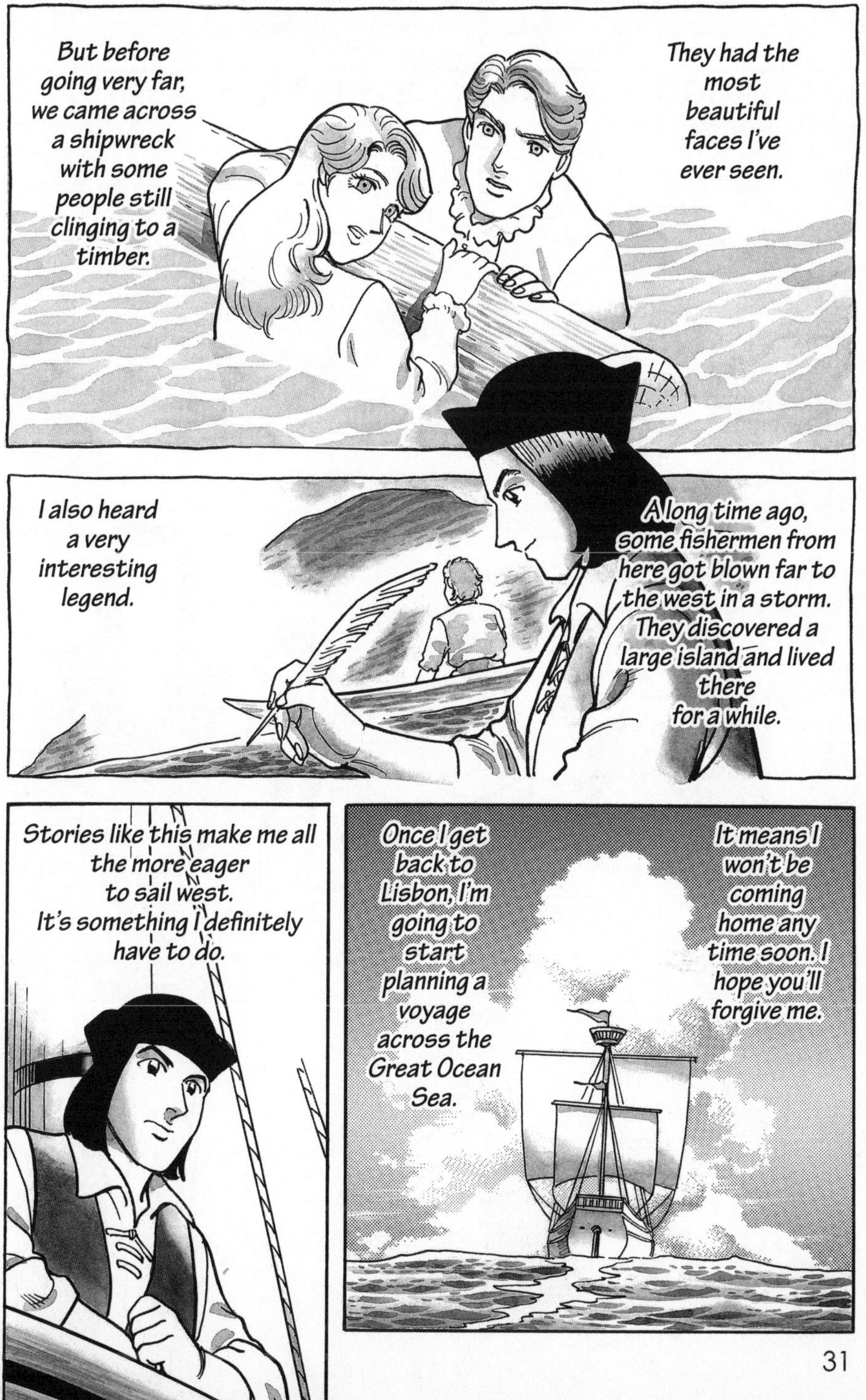
But before going very far, we came across a shipwreck with some people still clinging to a timber.
They had the most beautiful faces I've ever seen.
I also heard a very interesting legend.
A long time ago, some fishermen from here got blown far to the west in a storm. They discovered a large island and lived there for a while.
Stories like this make me all the more eager to sail west. It's something I definitely have to do.
Once I get back to Lisbon, I'm going to start planning a voyage across the Great Ocean Sea.
It means I won't be coming home any time soon. I hope you'll forgive me.

Chapter 3: The Dream Must Wait

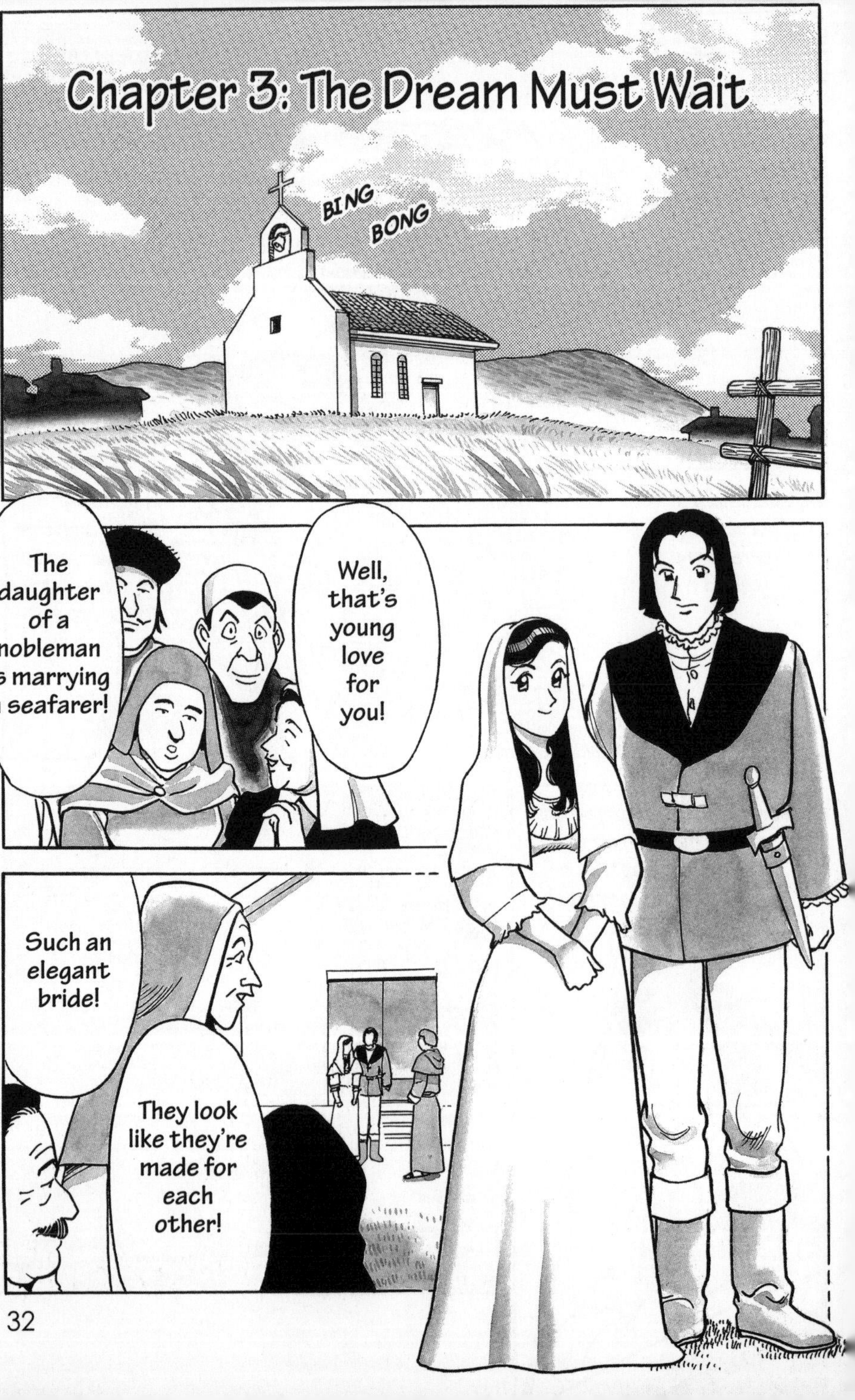
BING
BONG
The daughter of a nobleman is marrying a seafarer!
Well, that's young love for you!
Such an elegant bride!
They look like they're made for each other!

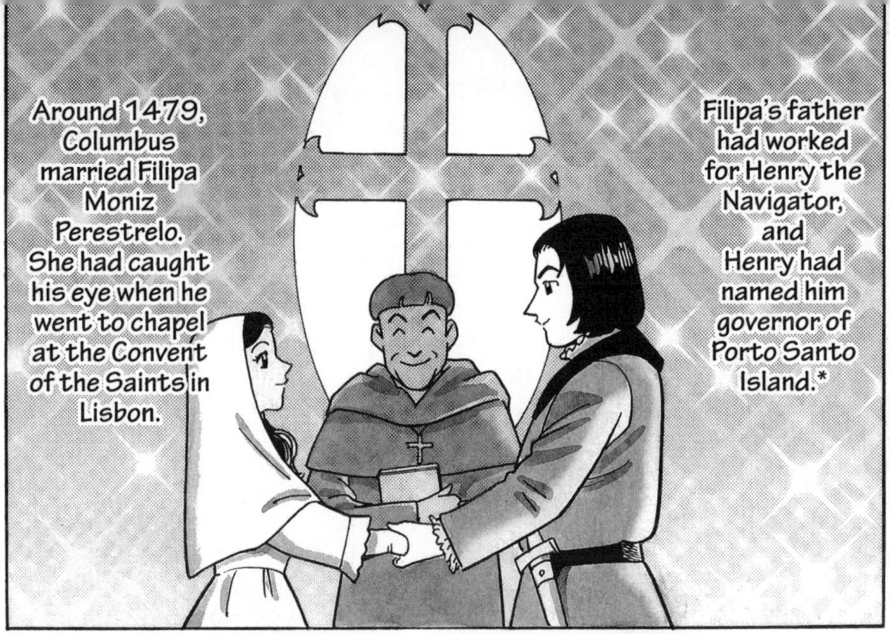
Around 1479, Columbus married Filipa Moniz Perestrelo. She had caught his eye when he went to chapel at the Convent of the Saints in Lisbon.
Filipa's father had worked for Henry the Navigator, and Henry had named him governor of Porto Santo Island.*

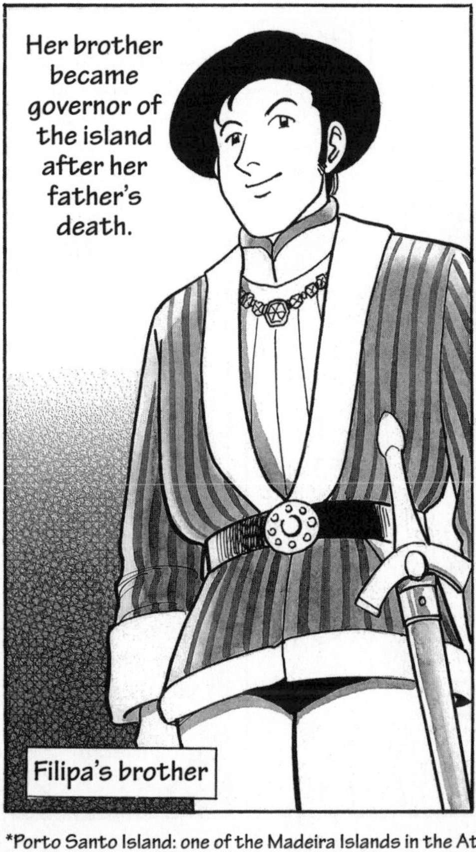
Her brother became governor of the island after her father's death.
Filipa's brother

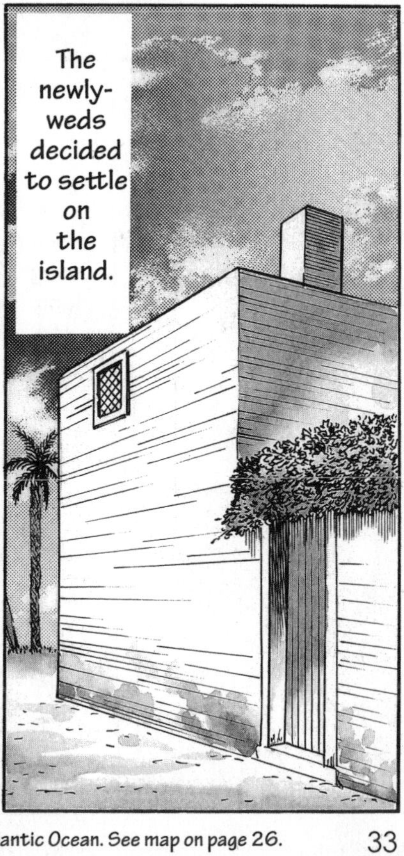
The newly-weds decided to settle on the island.

*Porto Santo Island: one of the Madeira Islands in the Atlantic Ocean. See map on page 26.

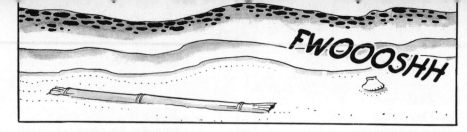
FWOOOSHH

What did you find, dear?

It's a strange piece of drift-wood.

Lots of unusual stuff washes up on this island from the west.

Since moving here, I've read the logs your father kept on his voyages ...

And I hear amazing stories from seamen who stop at the island.

I know it gets your sea-faring blood going.

But please promise not to do anything dangerous.

Stop worrying. It's not healthy for the baby you're carrying if you fret too much!

34

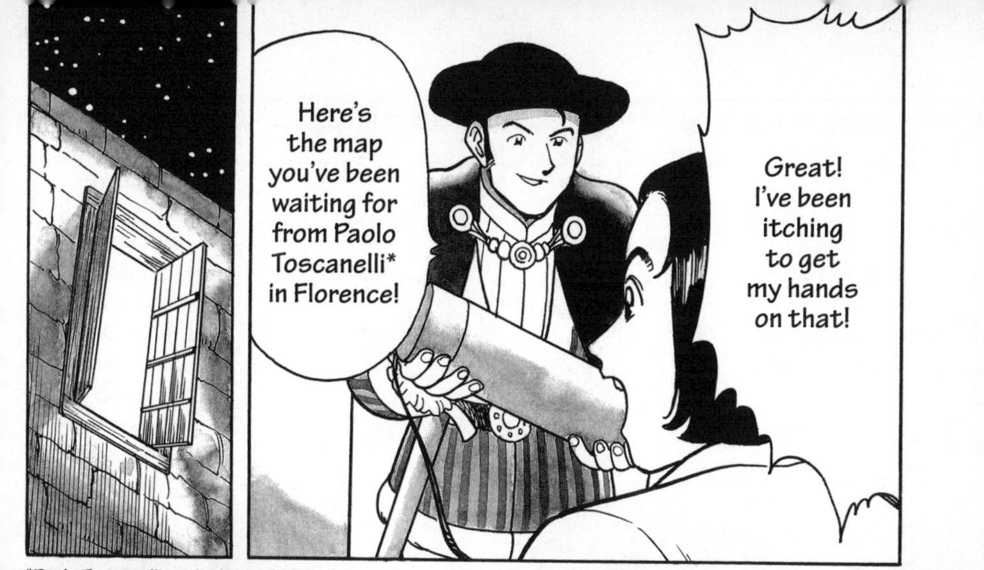
Here's the map you've been waiting for from Paolo Toscanelli* in Florence!
Great! I've been itching to get my hands on that!

*Paolo Toscanelli: an Italian scholar of astronomy, geography, and mathematics, who lived from 1397 to 1482.

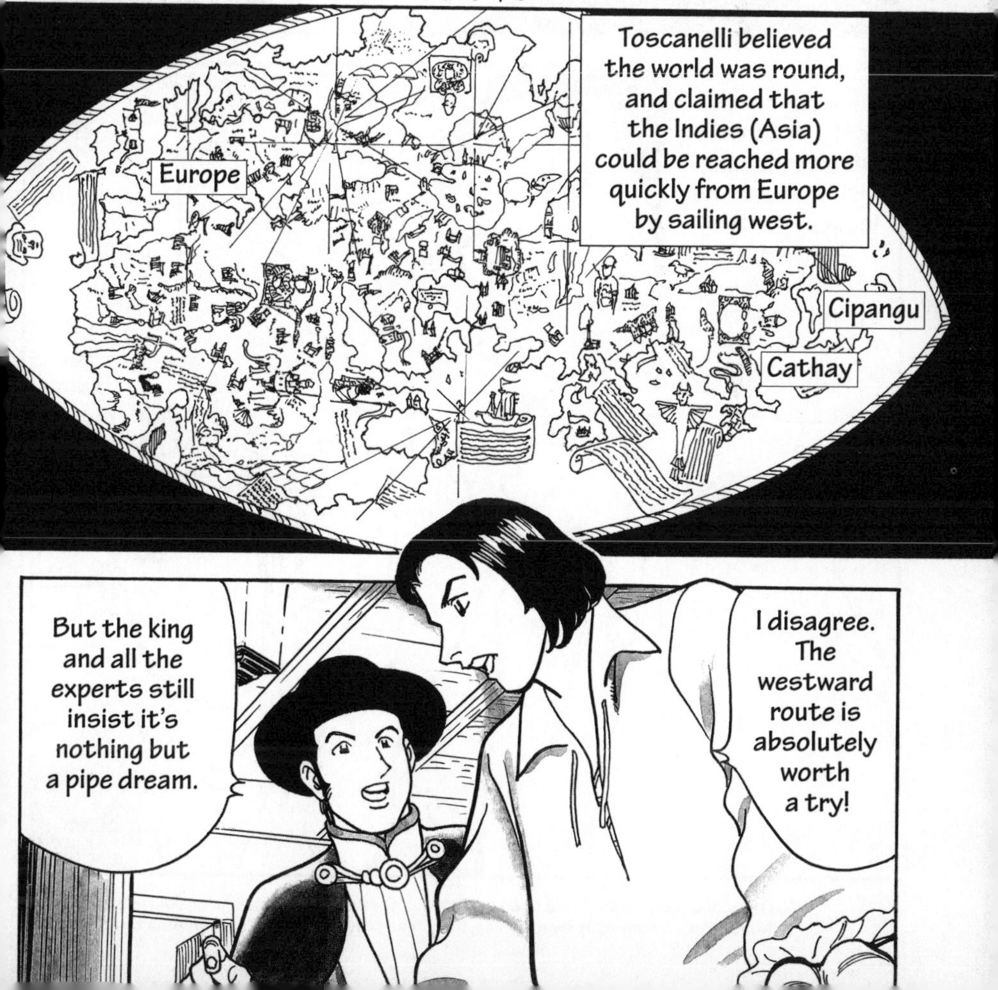
Europe
Toscanelli believed the world was round, and claimed that the Indies (Asia) could be reached more quickly from Europe by sailing west.
Cipangu
Cathay
But the king and all the experts still insist it's nothing but a pipe dream.
I disagree. The westward route is absolutely worth a try!

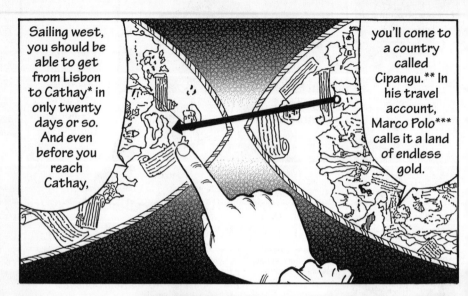

Sailing west, you should be able to get from Lisbon to Cathay* in only twenty days or so. And even before you reach Cathay,

you'll come to a country called Cipangu.** In his travel account, Marco Polo*** calls it a land of endless gold.

He says the ports of Cathay are overflowing with spices. And in Cipangu, they use gold for making everything from houses to dishes.

SNAP

Spices and gold!

It'll be like finding mountains of treasure!

*Cathay: the name Marco Polo used for China. **Cipangu: the name Marco Polo used for Japan. ***Marco Polo: a merchant from Venice, Italy, who traveled by land across Asia to China.

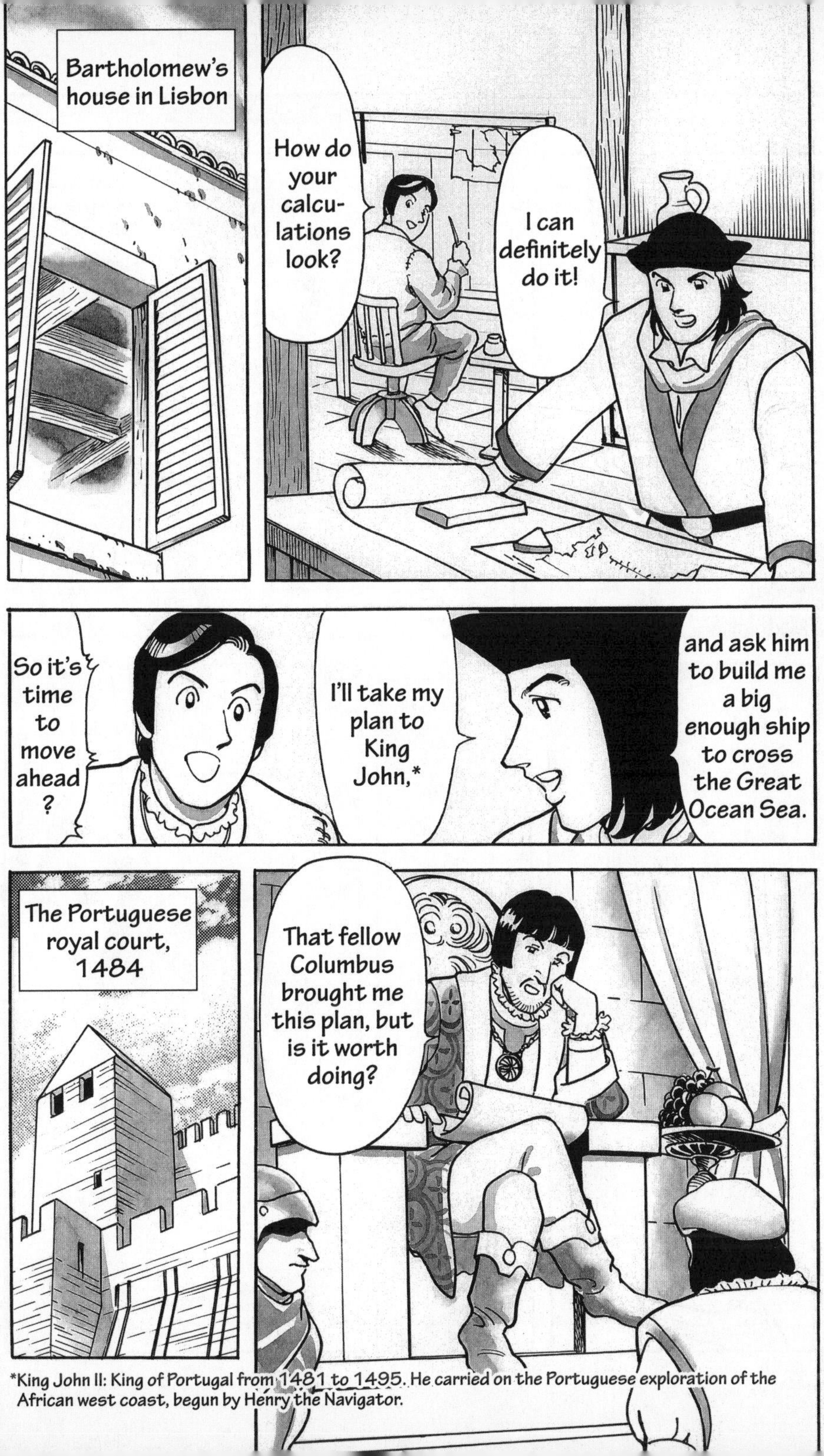

Bartholomew's house in Lisbon
How do your calcu-lations look?
I can definitely do it!
So it's time to move ahead?
I'll take my plan to King John,*
and ask him to build me a big enough ship to cross the Great Ocean Sea.
The Portuguese royal court, 1484
That fellow Columbus brought me this plan, but is it worth doing?

*King John II: King of Portugal from 1481 to 1495. He carried on the Portuguese exploration of the African west coast, begun by Henry the Navigator.

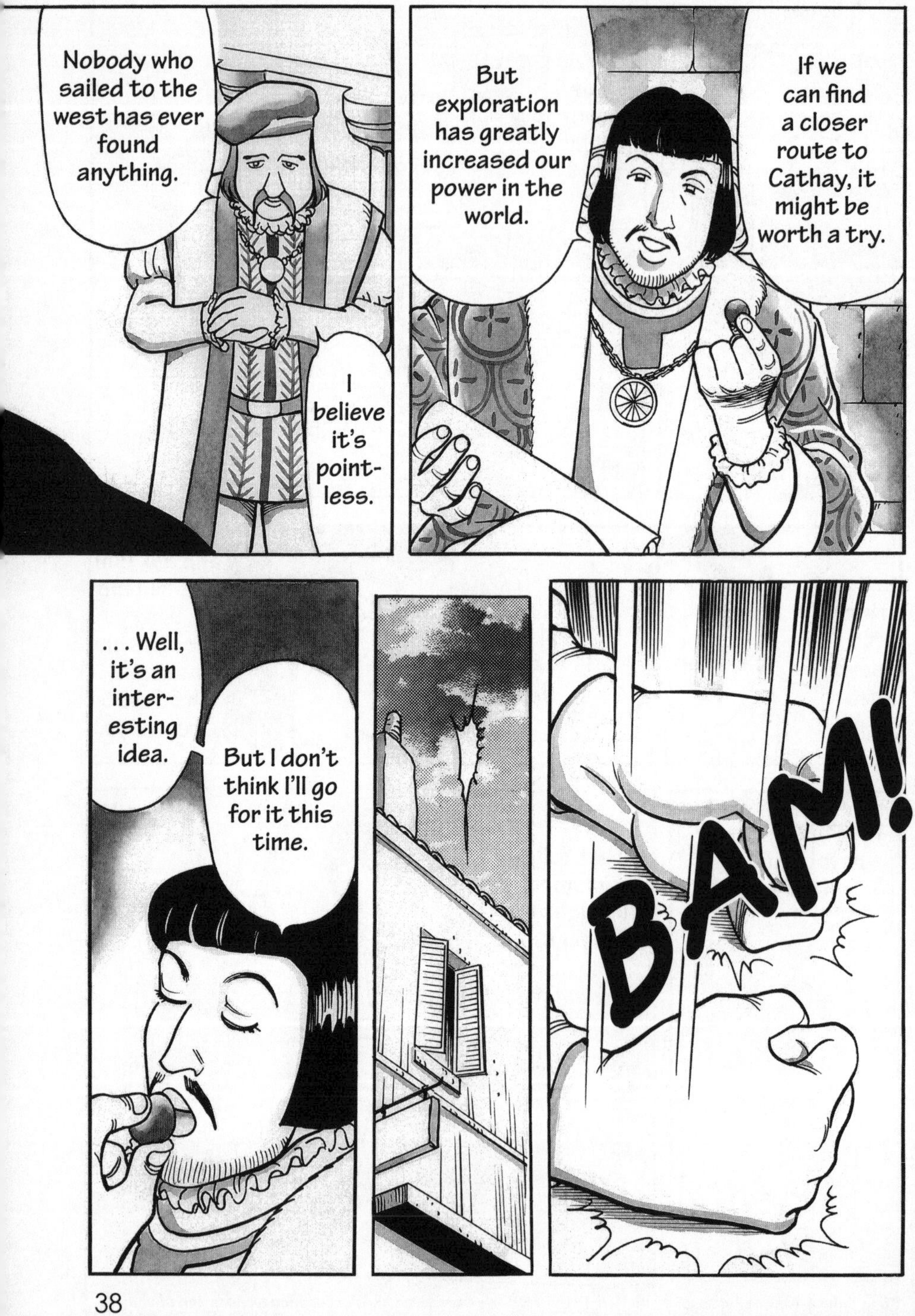
Nobody who sailed to the west has ever found anything.
I believe it's point-less.
But exploration has greatly increased our power in the world.
If we can find a closer route to Cathay, it might be worth a try.
. . . Well, it's an inter-esting idea.
But I don't think I'll go for it this time.
BAM!

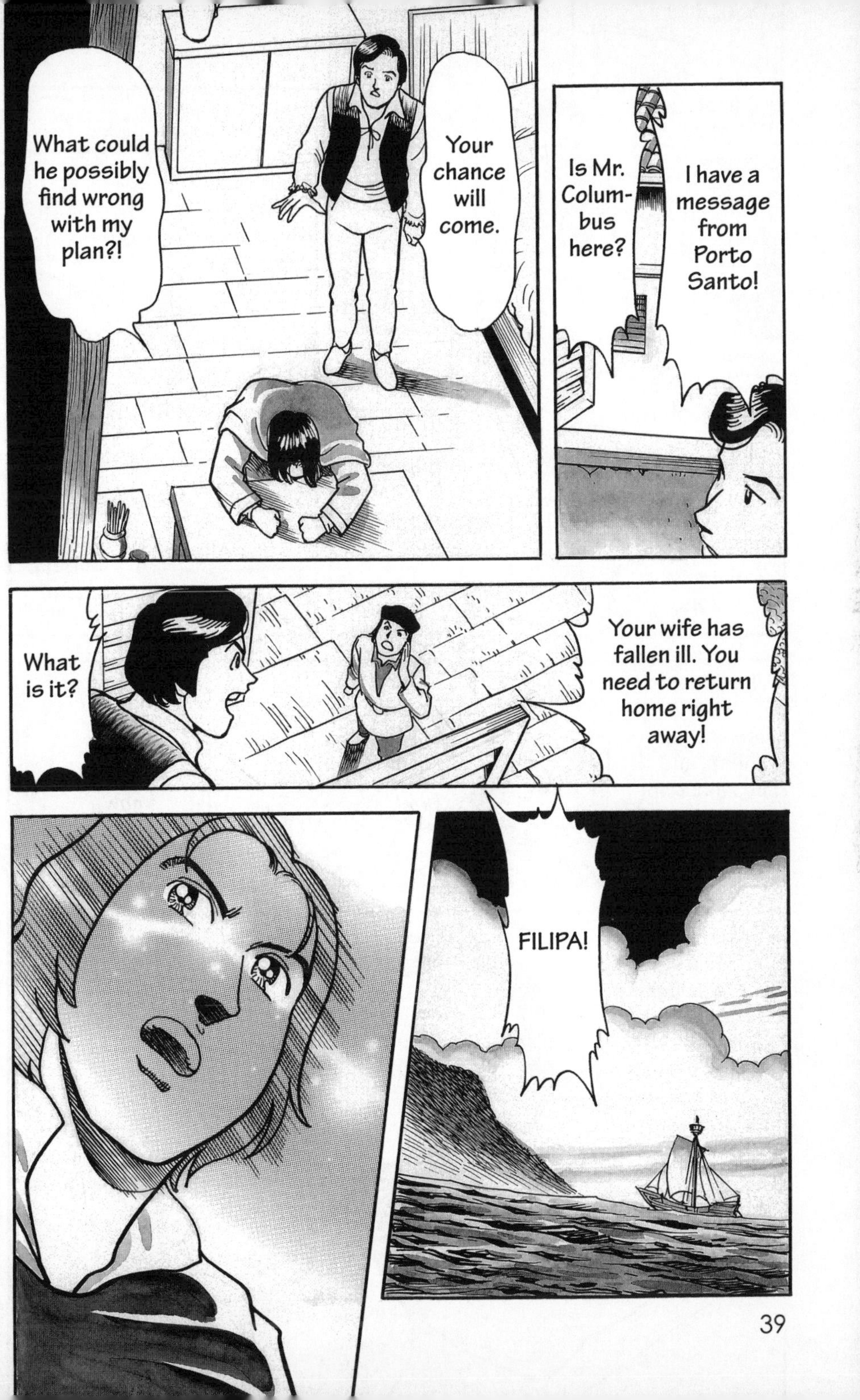
What could he possibly find wrong with my plan?!
Your chance will come.
Is Mr. Colum-bus here?
I have a message from Porto Santo!
What is it?
Your wife has fallen ill. You need to return home right away!
FILIPA!

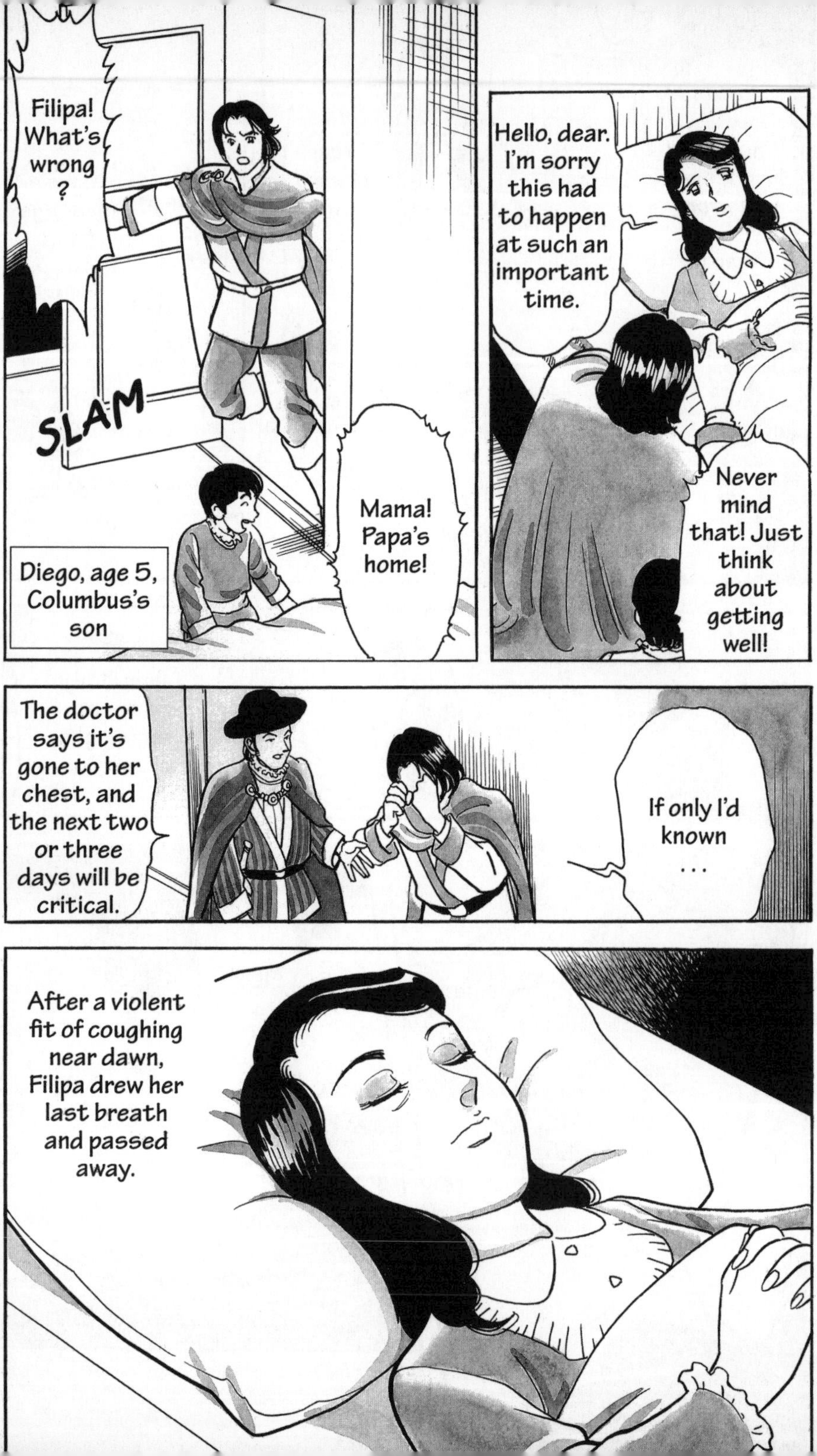
Filipa! What's wrong?
SLAM
Diego, age 5, Columbus's son
Mama! Papa's home!
Hello, dear. I'm sorry this had to happen at such an important time.
Never mind that! Just think about getting well!
The doctor says it's gone to her chest, and the next two or three days will be critical.
If only I'd known . . .
After a violent fit of coughing near dawn, Filipa drew her last breath and passed away.

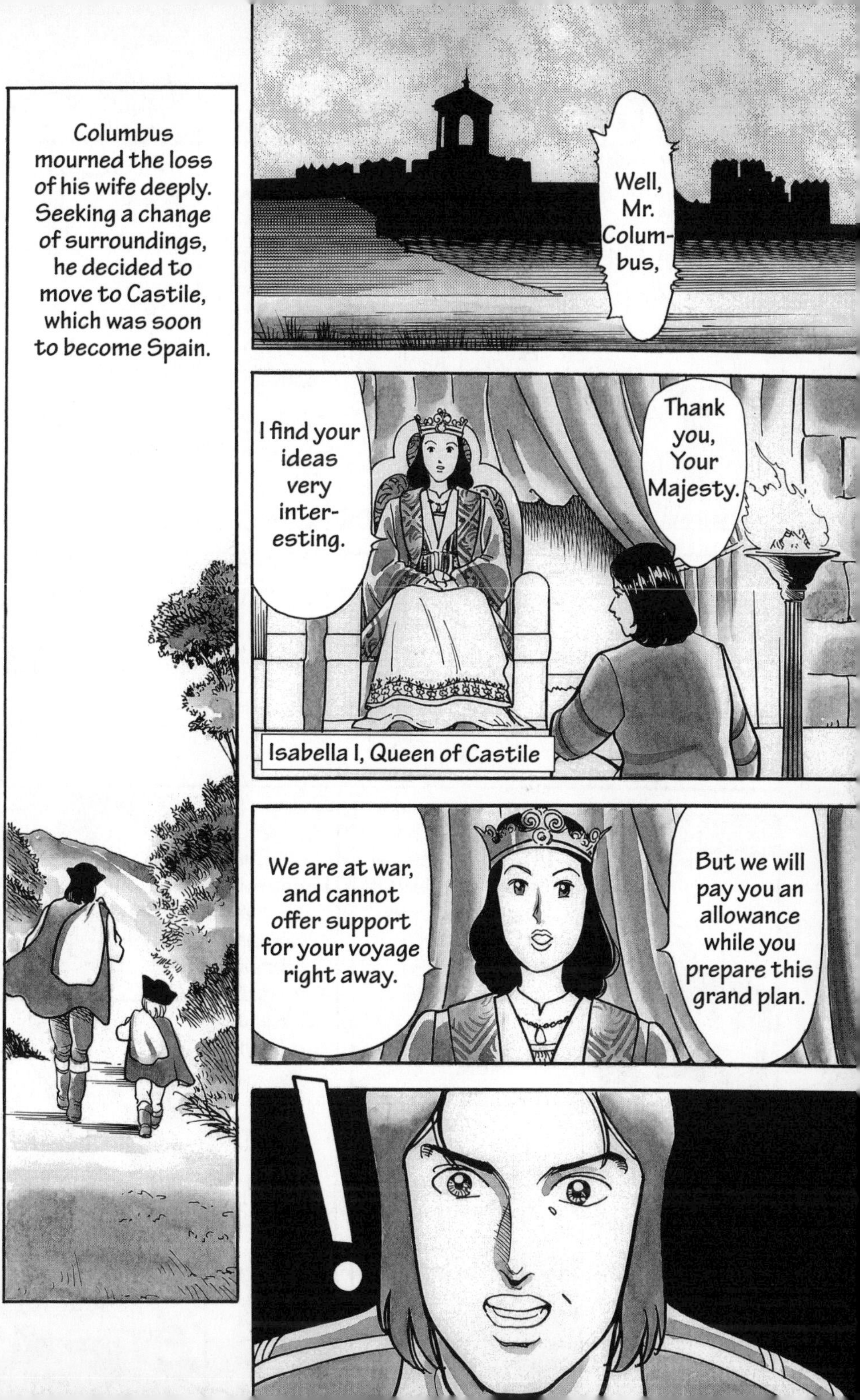

Columbus mourned the loss of his wife deeply. Seeking a change of surroundings, he decided to move to Castile, which was soon to become Spain.
Well, Mr. Columbus,
I find your ideas very interesting.
Thank you, Your Majesty.
Isabella I, Queen of Castile
We are at war, and cannot offer support for your voyage right away.
But we will pay you an allowance while you prepare this grand plan.
!

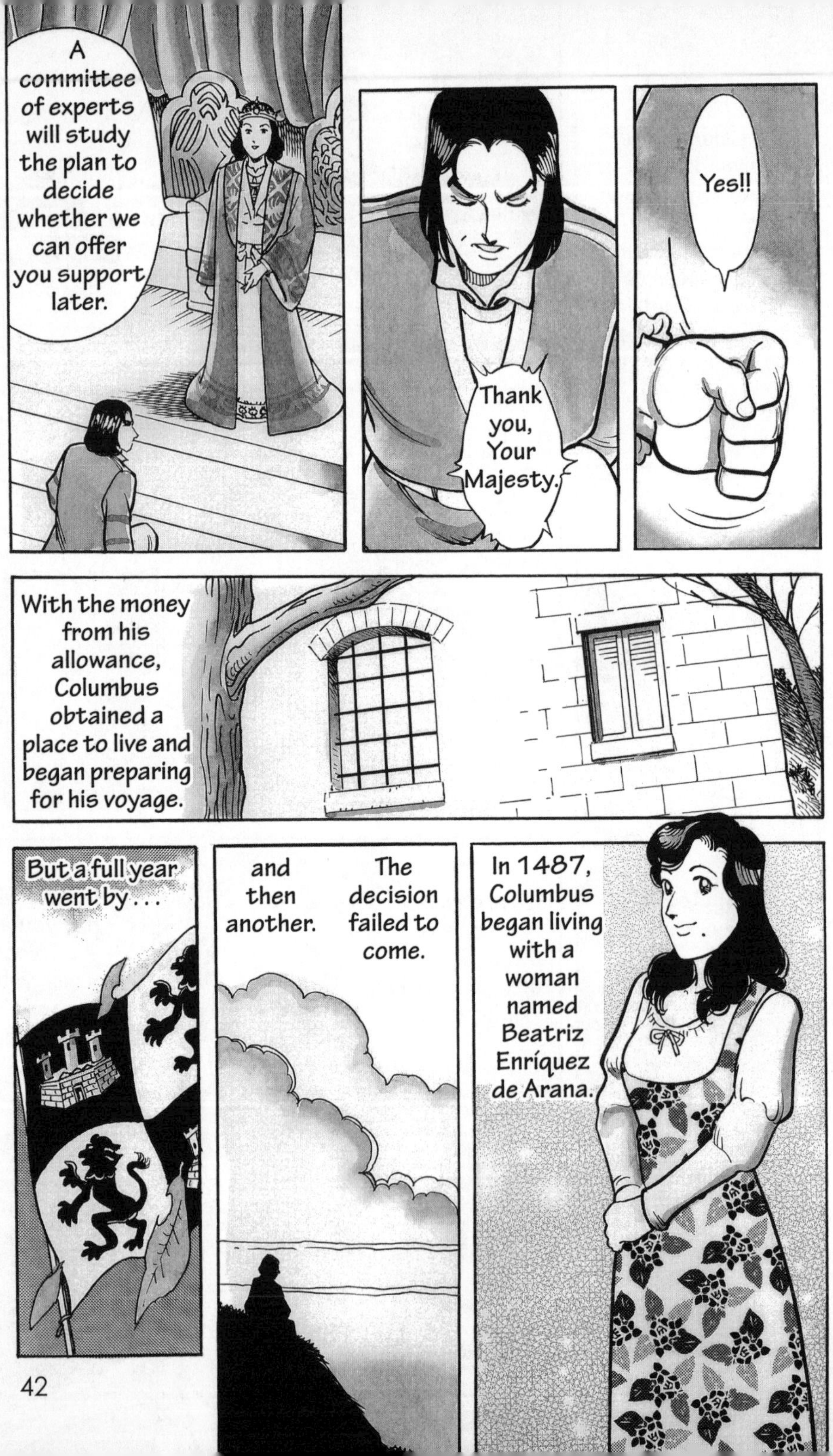
A committee of experts will study the plan to decide whether we can offer you support later.
Thank you, Your Majesty.
Yes!!
With the money from his allowance, Columbus obtained a place to live and began preparing for his voyage.
But a full year went by . . .
and then another.
The decision failed to come.
In 1487, Columbus began living with a woman named Beatriz Enríquez de Arana.

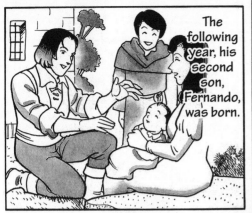

The following year, his second son, Fernando, was born.

In 1488, the Portuguese explorer Bartholomew Diaz sailed around the southern tip of Africa.

This meant Europeans could now reach India by sea.

There's no way Portugal will help me with a westward voyage now.

The months and years continued to go by.

The war that's gone on for nearly ten years is finally winding down.

Counting back to Lisbon, I've been at this for 14 years.

Now may be my last chance.

I can't just keep waiting forever. I'll never get to Cathay this way.

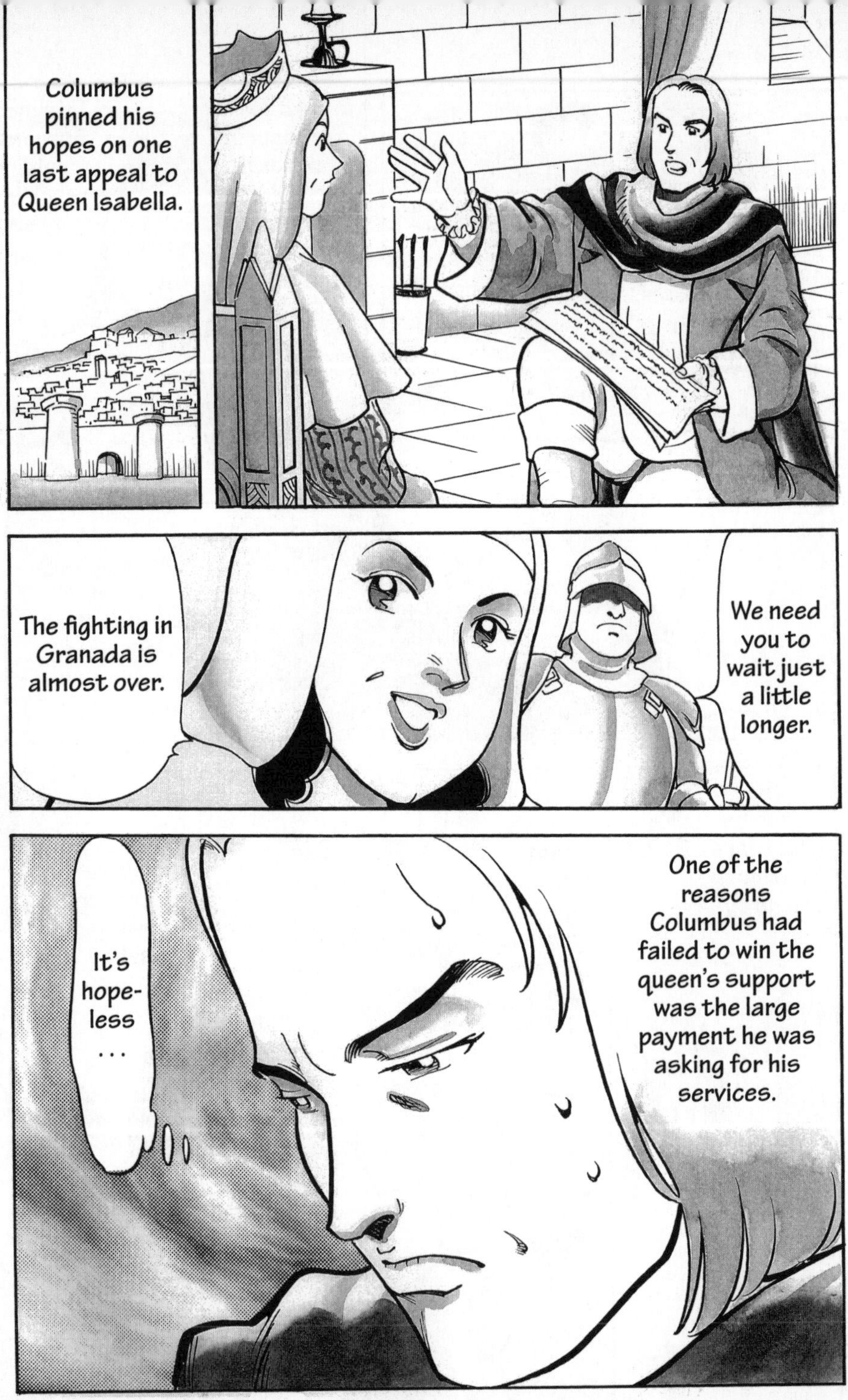
Columbus pinned his hopes on one last appeal to Queen Isabella.
The fighting in Granada is almost over.
We need you to wait just a little longer.
One of the reasons Columbus had failed to win the queen's support was the large payment he was asking for his services.
It's hopeless . . .

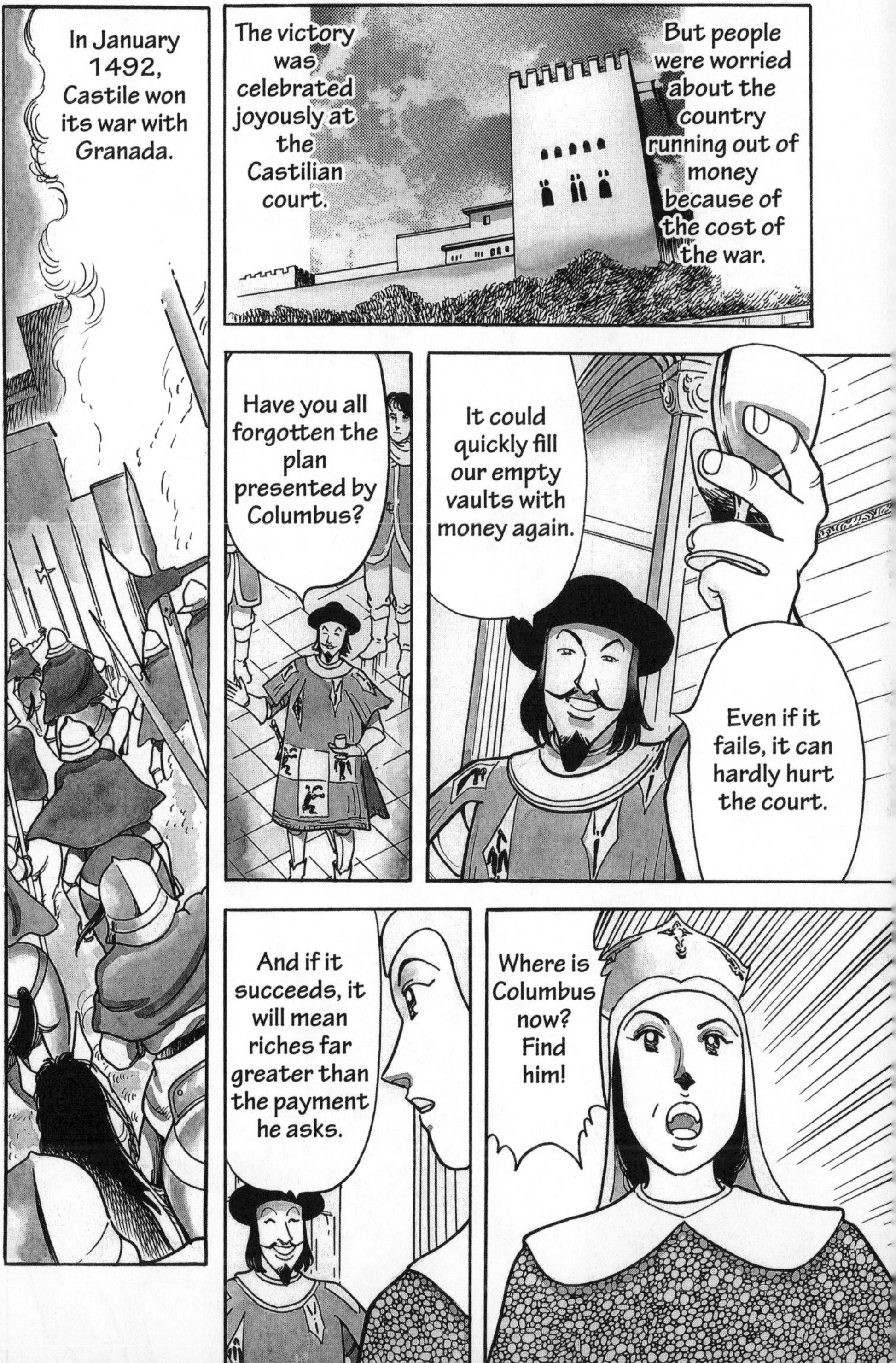
In January 1492, Castile won its war with Granada.
The victory was celebrated joyously at the Castilian court.
But people were worried about the country running out of money because of the cost of the war.
Have you all forgotten the plan presented by Columbus?
It could quickly fill our empty vaults with money again.
Even if it fails, it can hardly hurt the court.
And if it succeeds, it will mean riches far greater than the payment he asks.
Where is Columbus now? Find him!

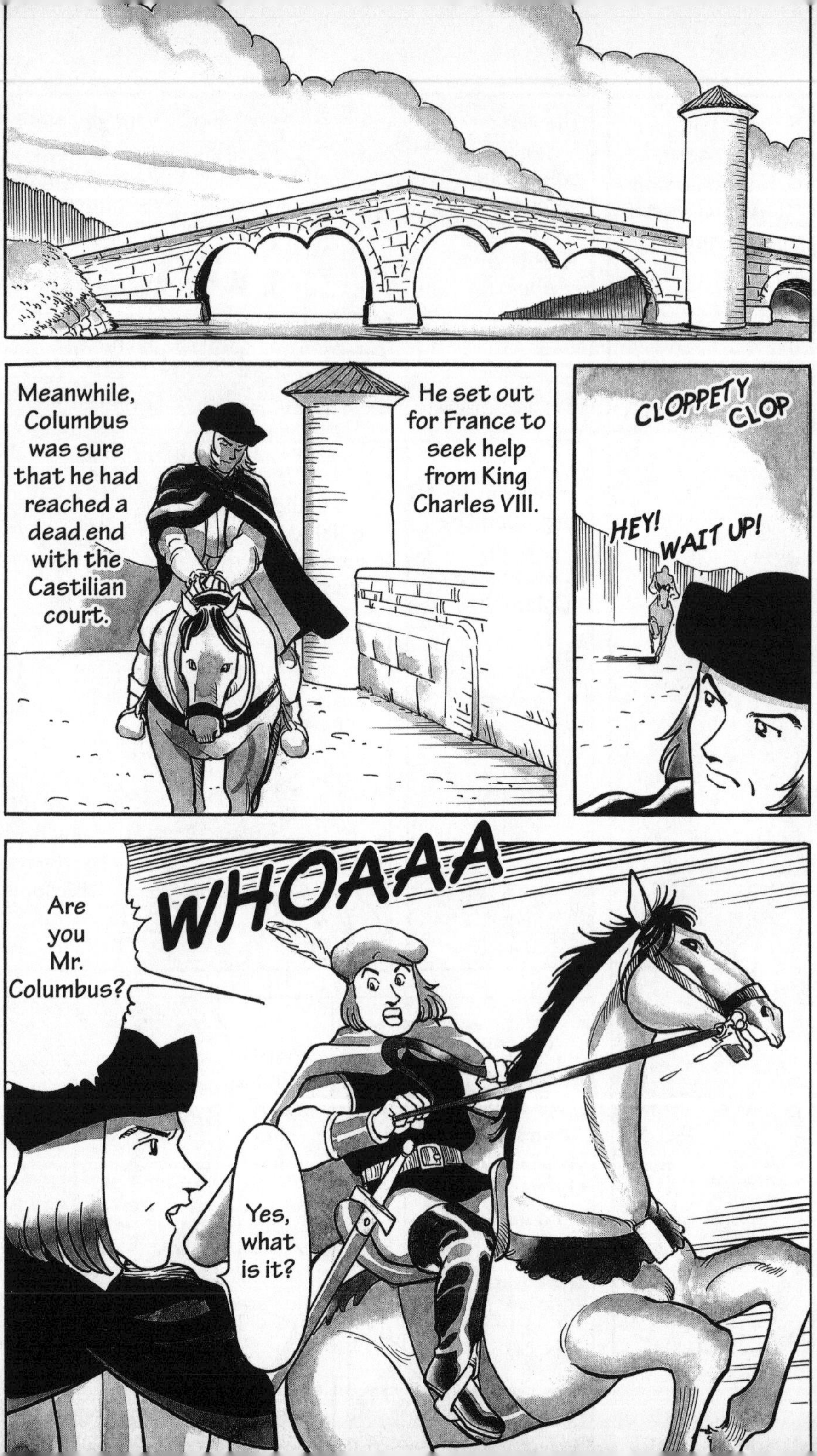
Meanwhile, Columbus was sure that he had reached a dead end with the Castilian court.
He set out for France to seek help from King Charles VIII.
CLOPPETY CLOP
HEY!
WAIT UP!
WHOAAA
Are you Mr. Columbus?
Yes, what is it?

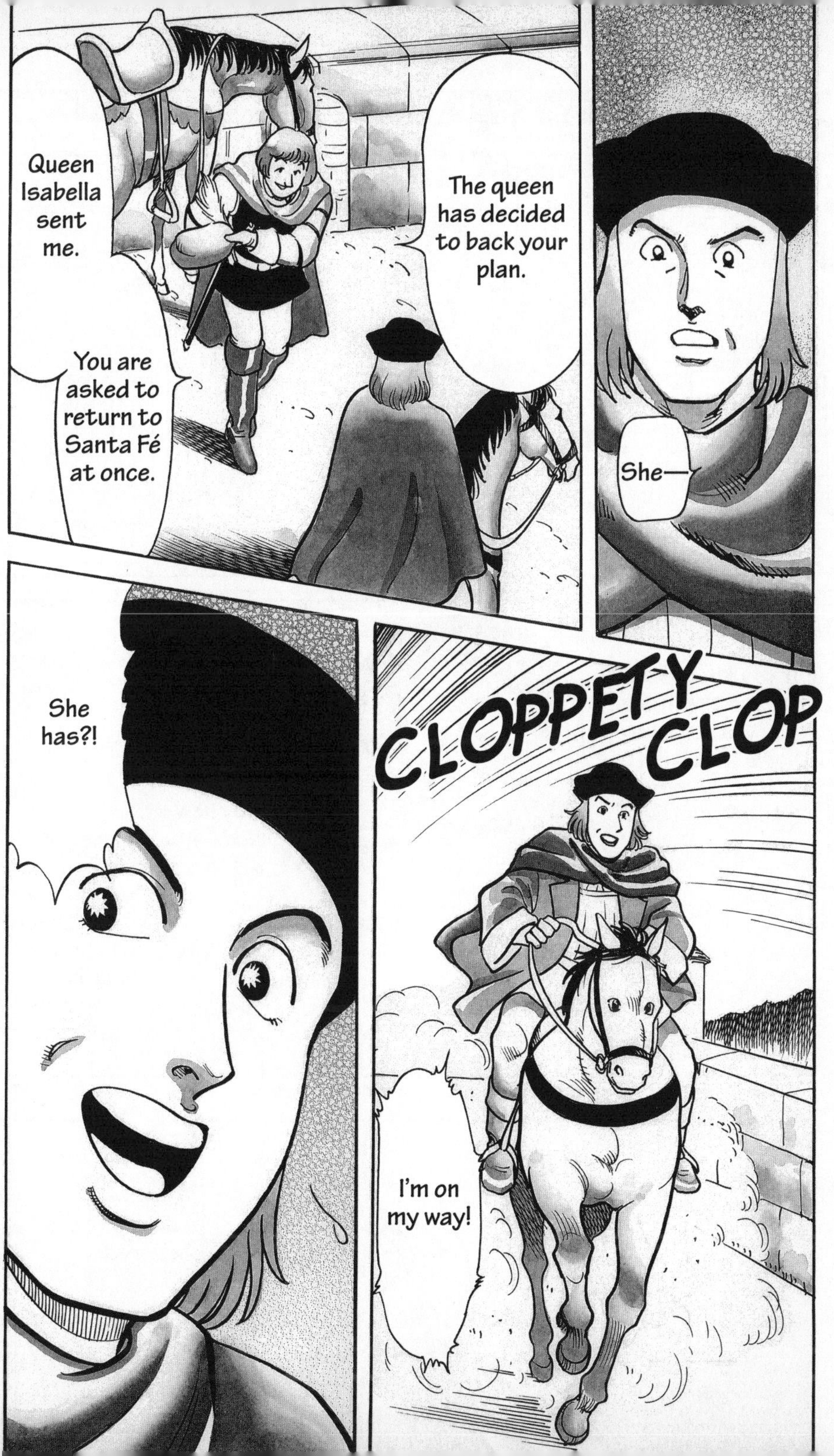
Queen Isabella sent me.
You are asked to return to Santa Fé at once.
The queen has decided to back your plan.
She—
She has?!
CLOPPETY CLOP
I'm on my way!

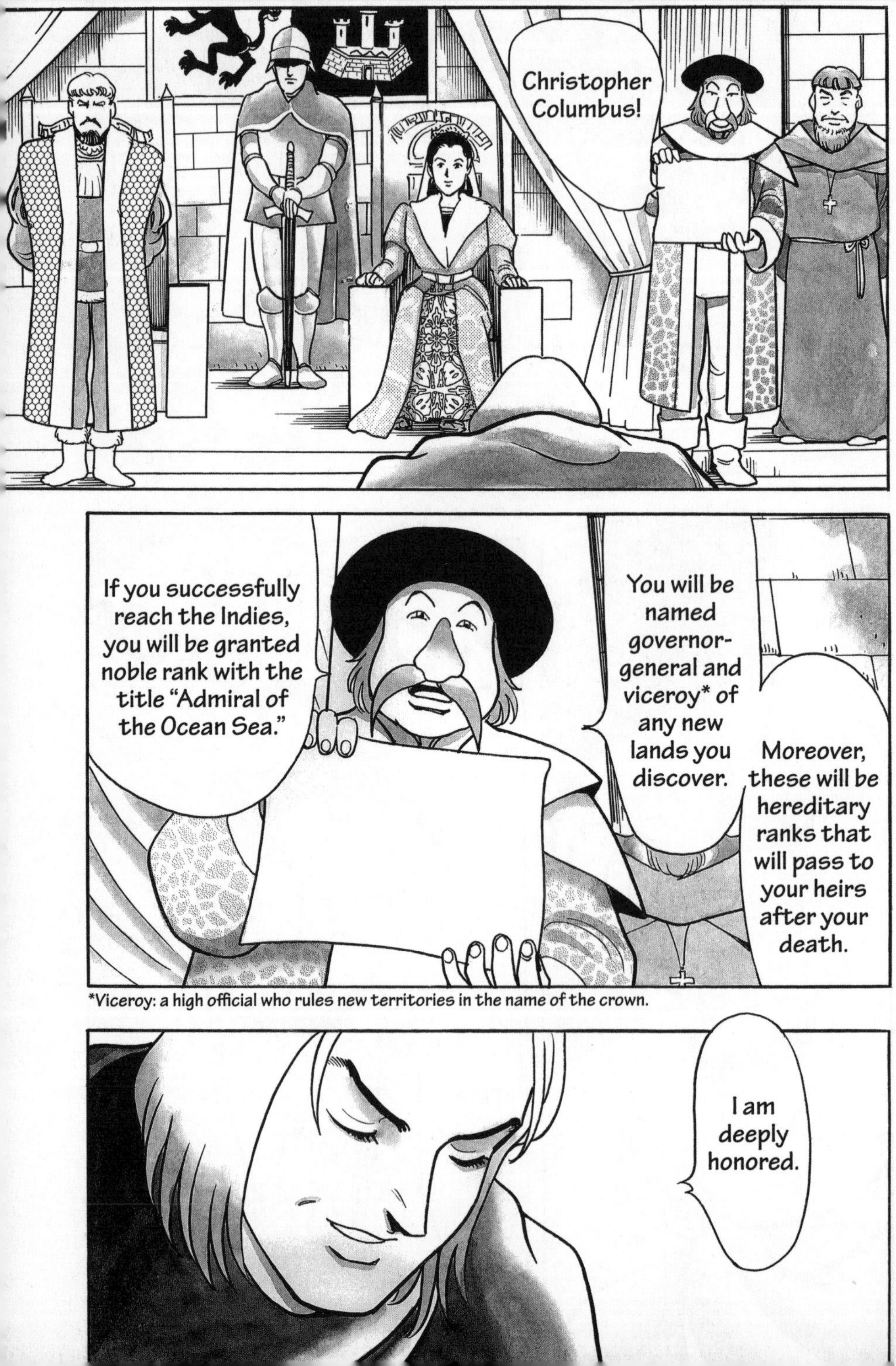
Christopher Columbus!
If you successfully reach the Indies, you will be granted noble rank with the title "Admiral of the Ocean Sea."
You will be named governor-general and viceroy* of any new lands you discover.
Moreover, these will be hereditary ranks that will pass to your heirs after your death.
*Viceroy: a high official who rules new territories in the name of the crown.
I am deeply honored.

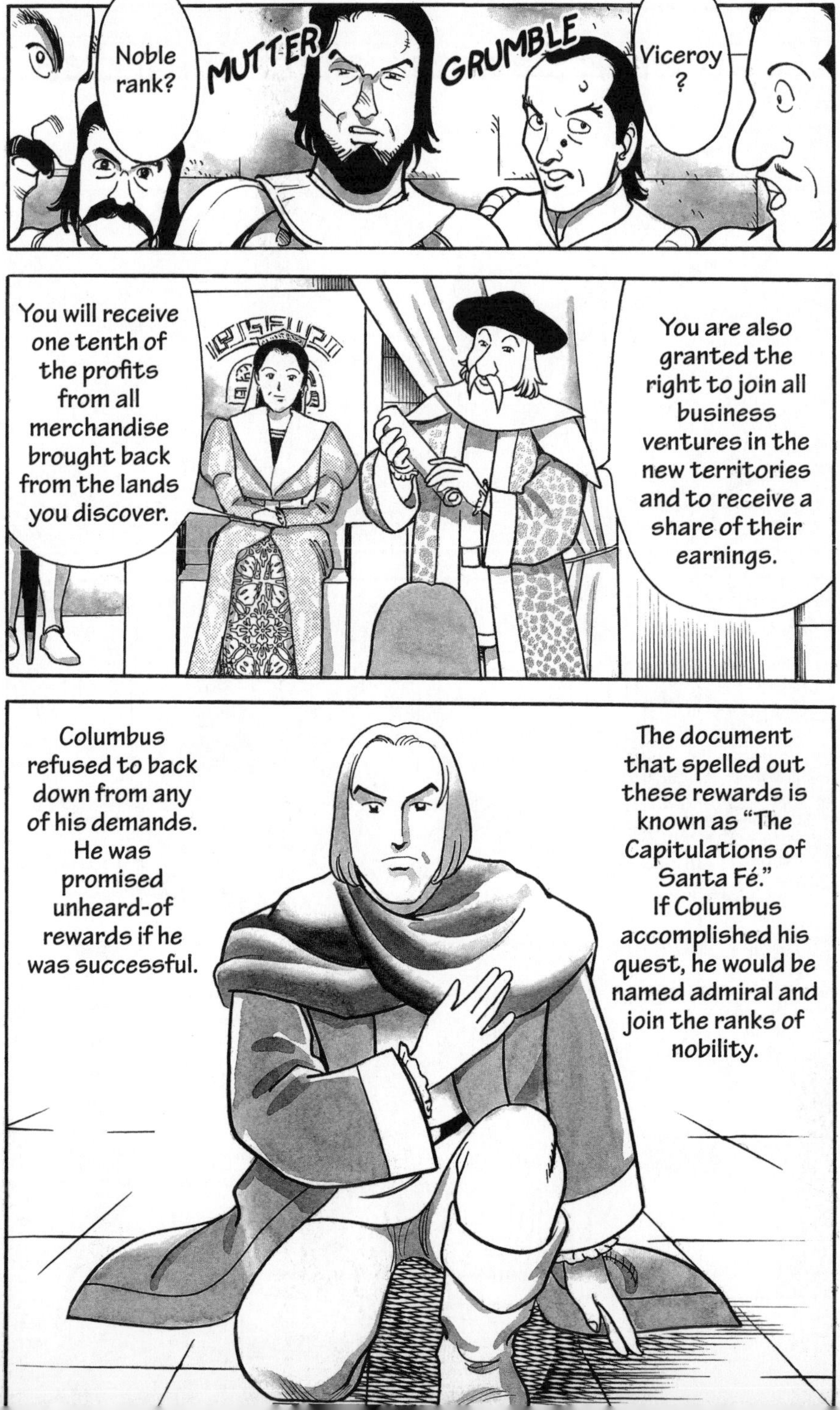
Noble rank?
MUTTER
GRUMBLE
Viceroy?
You will receive one tenth of the profits from all merchandise brought back from the lands you discover.
You are also granted the right to join all business ventures in the new territories and to receive a share of their earnings.
Columbus refused to back down from any of his demands. He was promised unheard-of rewards if he was successful.
The document that spelled out these rewards is known as "The Capitulations of Santa Fé." If Columbus accomplished his quest, he would be named admiral and join the ranks of nobility.

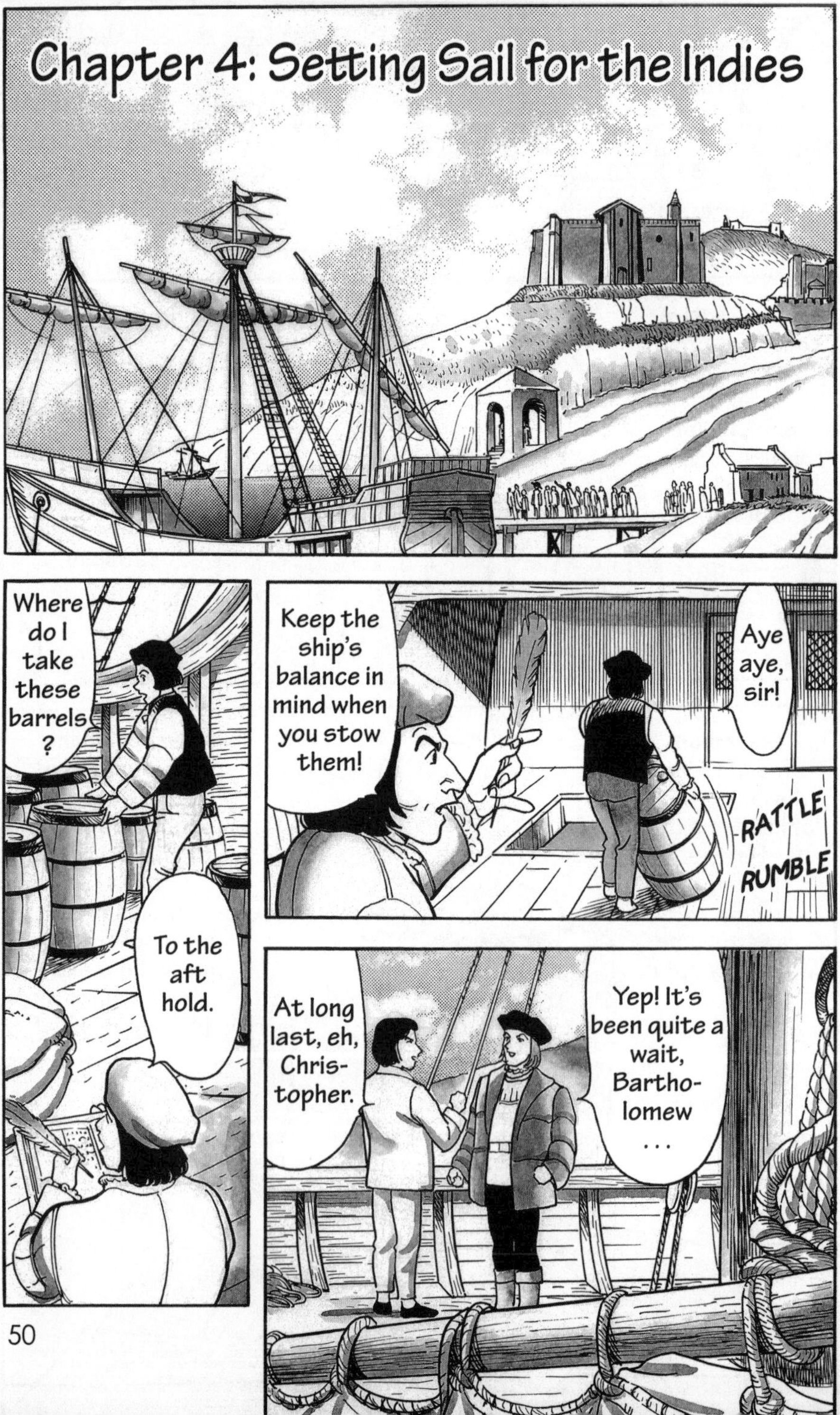
Chapter 4: Setting Sail for the Indies
Where do I take these barrels?
To the aft hold.
Keep the ship's balance in mind when you stow them!
Aye aye, sir!
RATTLE
RUMBLE
At long last, eh, Christopher.
Yep! It's been quite a wait, Bartholomew...

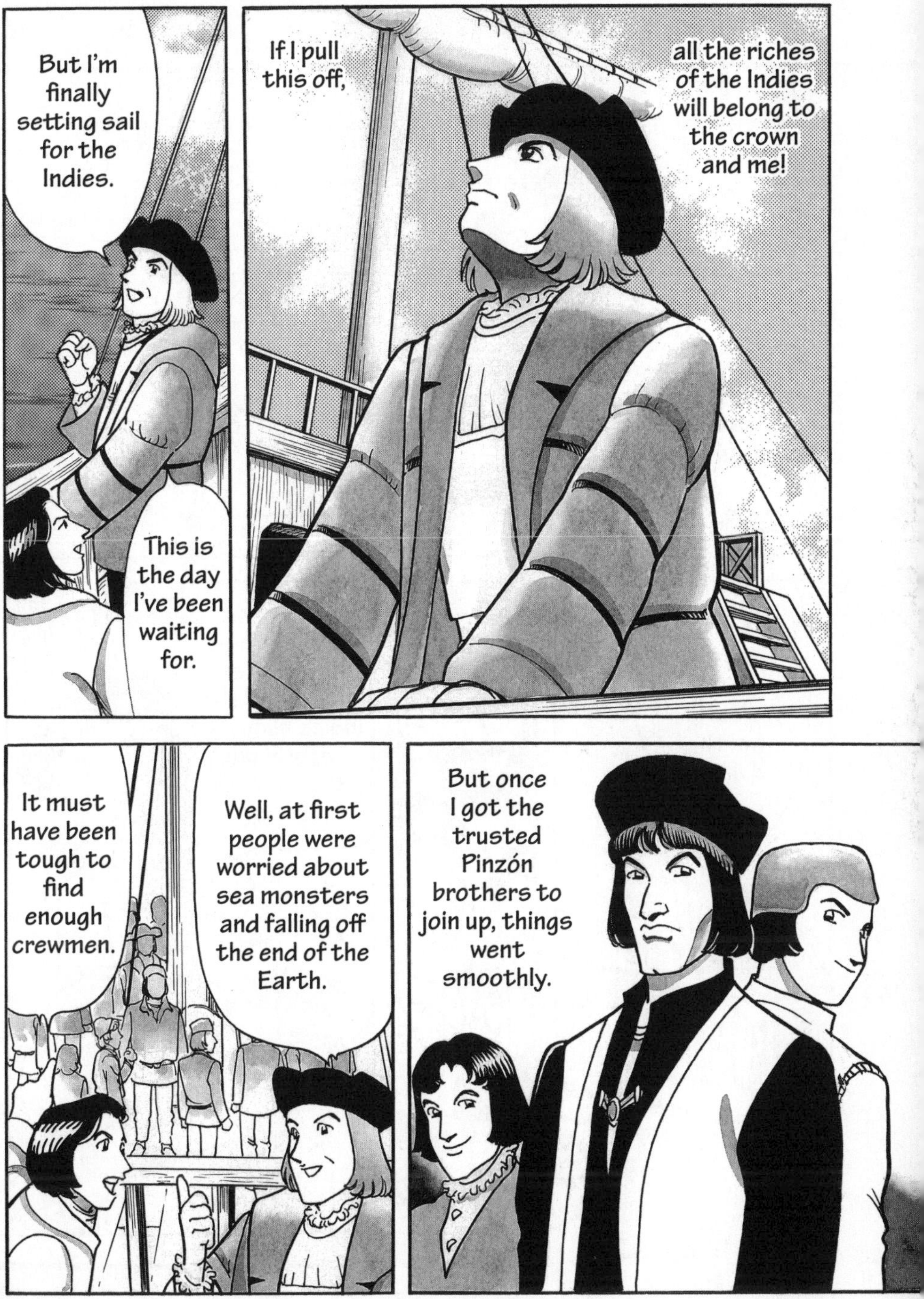
But I'm finally setting sail for the Indies.
This is the day I've been waiting for.
If I pull this off,
all the riches of the Indies will belong to the crown and me!
It must have been tough to find enough crewmen.
Well, at first people were worried about sea monsters and falling off the end of the Earth.
But once I got the trusted Pinzón brothers to join up, things went smoothly.

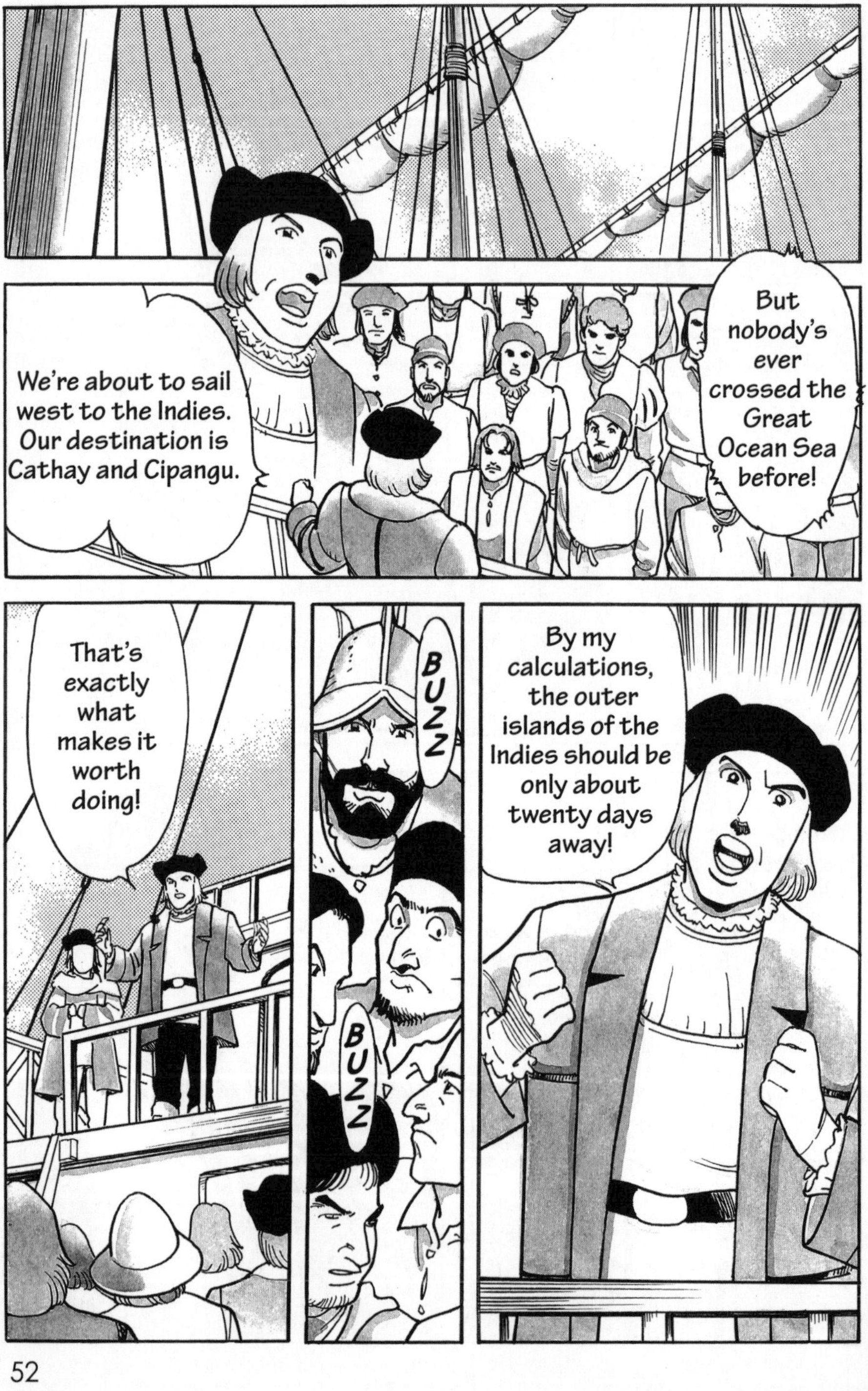
We're about to sail west to the Indies. Our destination is Cathay and Cipangu.
But nobody's ever crossed the Great Ocean Sea before!
That's exactly what makes it worth doing!
BUZZ
BUZZ
By my calculations, the outer islands of the Indies should be only about twenty days away!

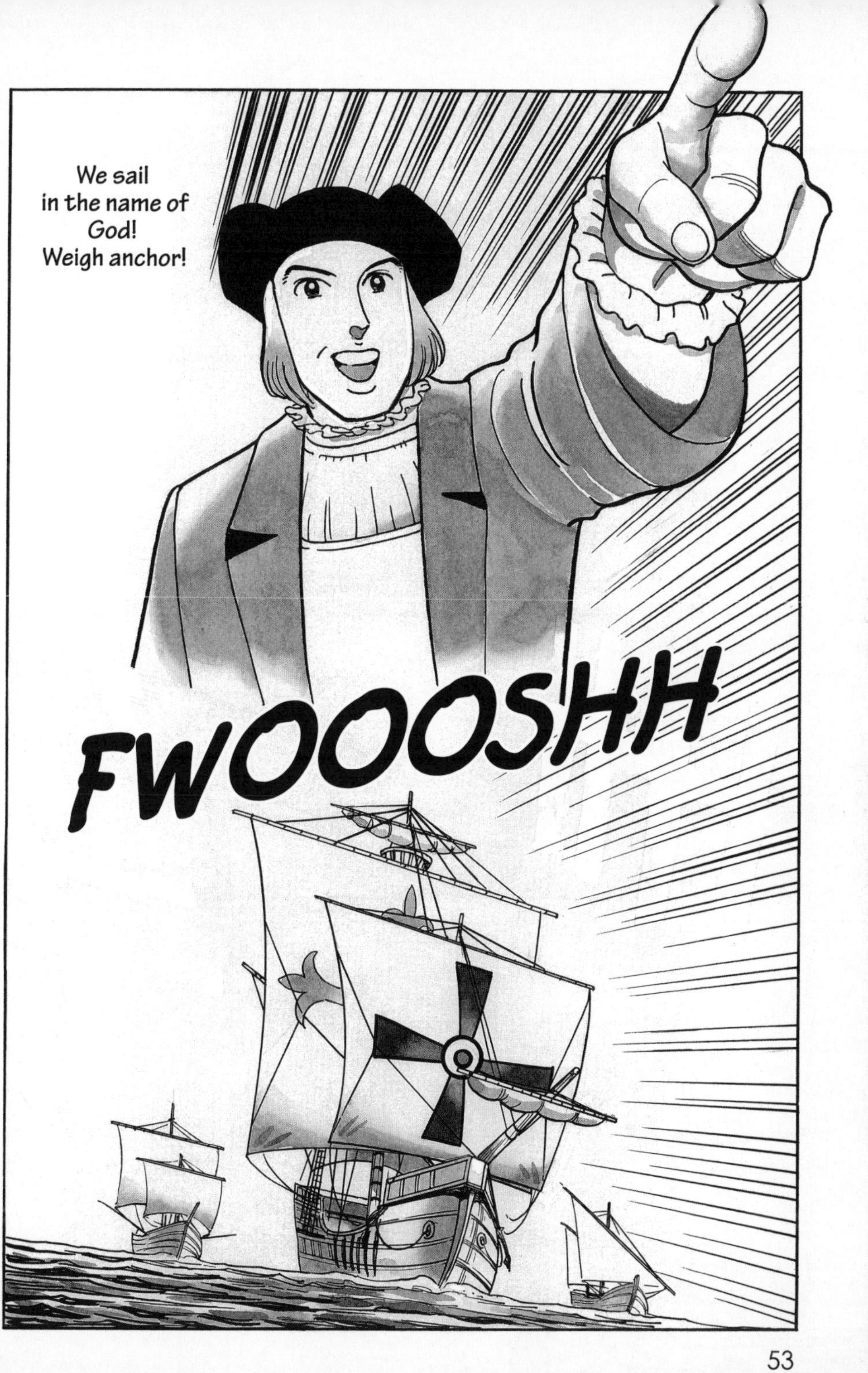
We sail in the name of God! Weigh anchor!
FWOOOSHH

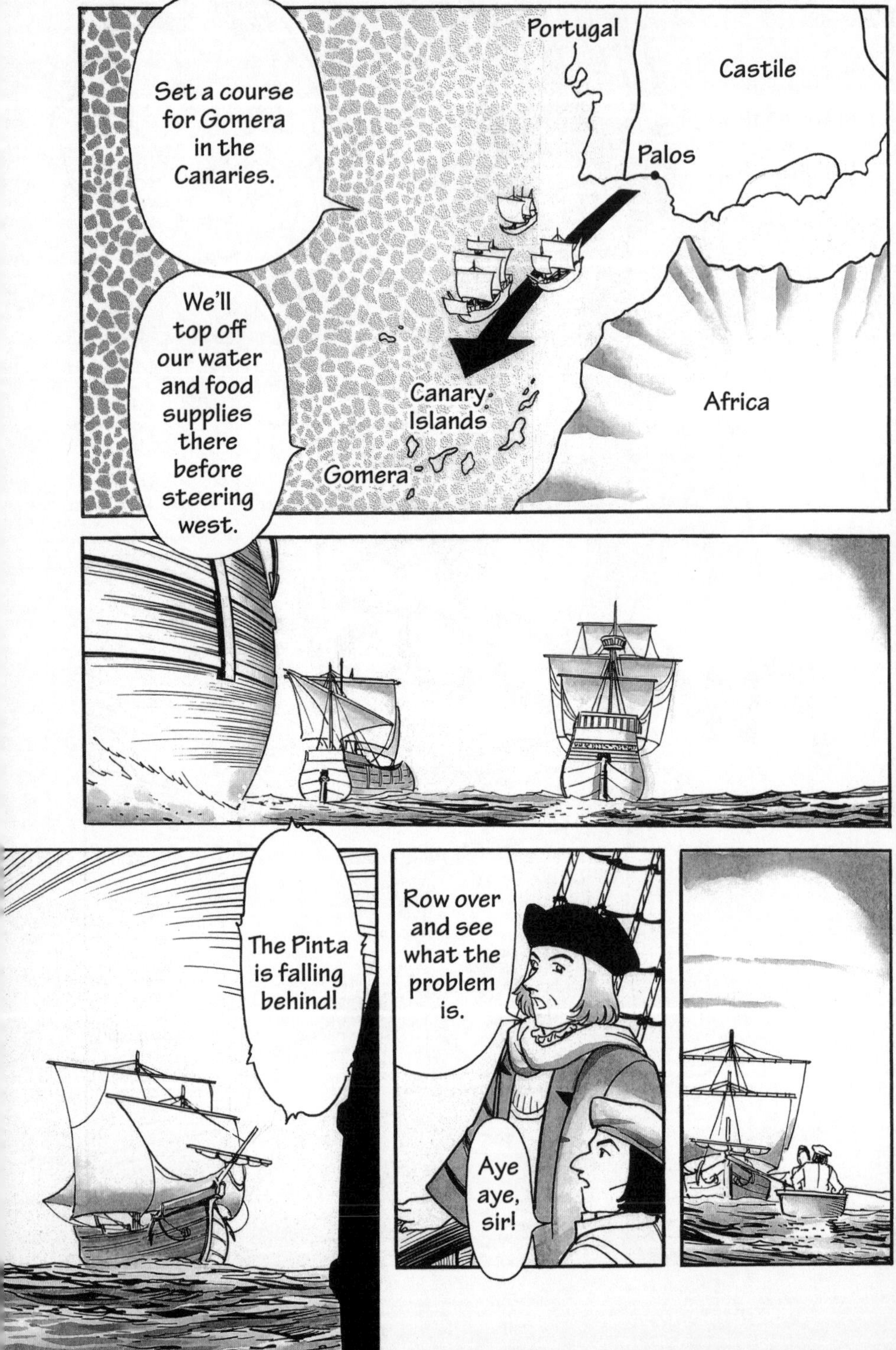
Set a course for Gomera in the Canaries.
Portugal
Castile
Palos
We'll top off our water and food supplies there before steering west.
Canary Islands
Gomera
Africa
The Pinta is falling behind!
Row over and see what the problem is.
Aye aye, sir!

Captain Pinzón, the admiral wishes to know why you're falling behind.

Send him my apologies.

We're having a bit of trouble with our rudder. Repairs will take some time.

We'll catch up at Gomera.

Very well, sir.

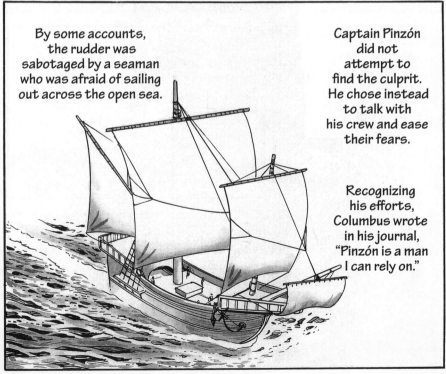

By some accounts, the rudder was sabotaged by a seaman who was afraid of sailing out across the open sea.

Captain Pinzón did not attempt to find the culprit. He chose instead to talk with his crew and ease their fears.

Recognizing his efforts, Columbus wrote in his journal, "Pinzón is a man I can rely on."

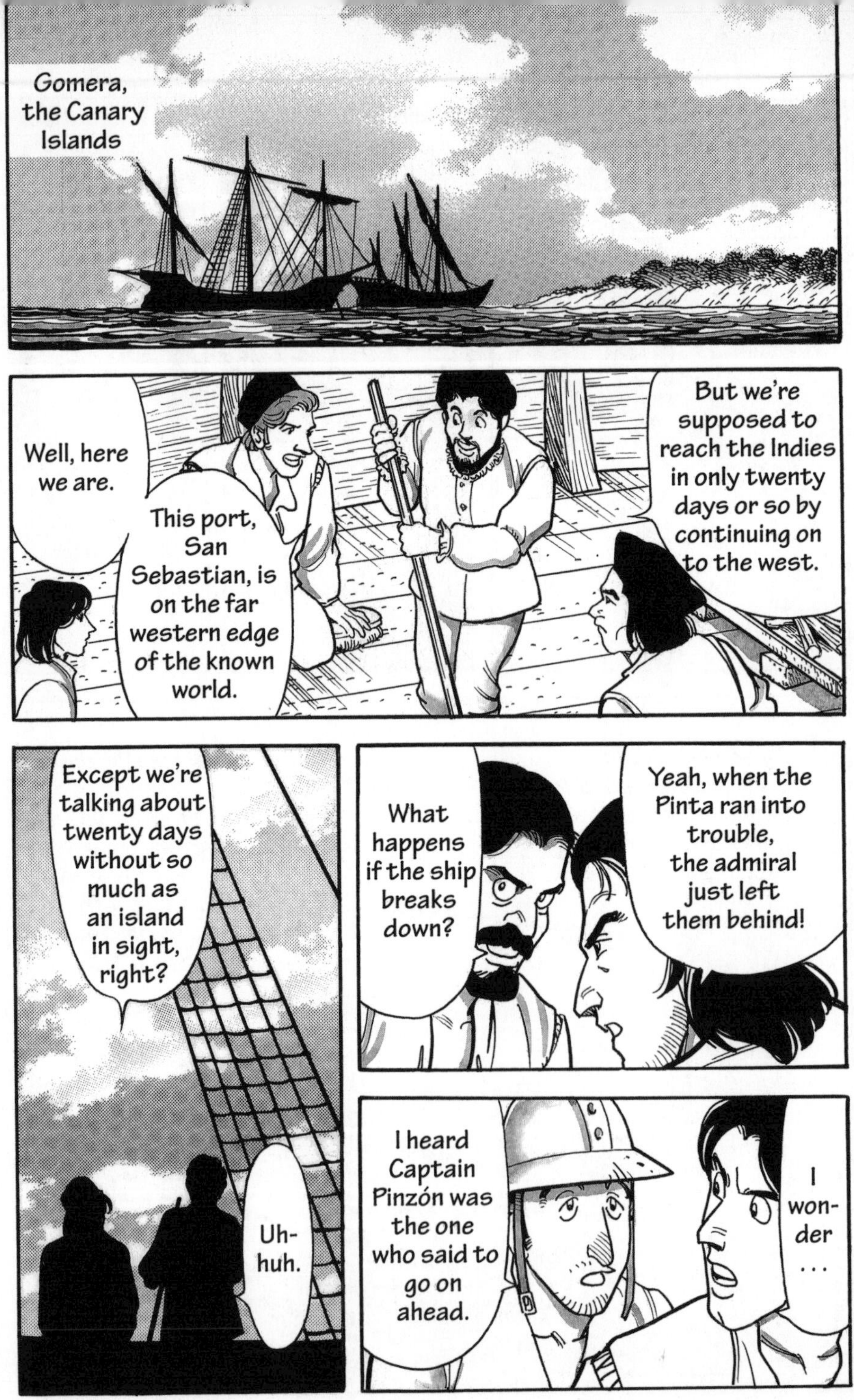
Gomera, the Canary Islands
Well, here we are.
This port, San Sebastian, is on the far western edge of the known world.
But we're supposed to reach the Indies in only twenty days or so by continuing on to the west.
Except we're talking about twenty days without so much as an island in sight, right?
Uh-huh.
What happens if the ship breaks down?
Yeah, when the Pinta ran into trouble, the admiral just left them behind!
I heard Captain Pinzón was the one who said to go on ahead.
I won-der . . .

Well, now that we've come this far, I guess there's no turning back.

Too bad!

Hey!

Look at that!

It's the Pinta! The Pinta's coming!

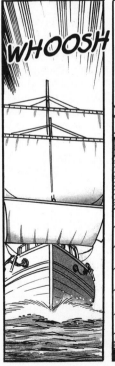

WHOOSH

Sorry for the delay.

I'm glad you made it!

We're finally ready to strike out into the unknown.

I know we'll find land again if we sail west from here!

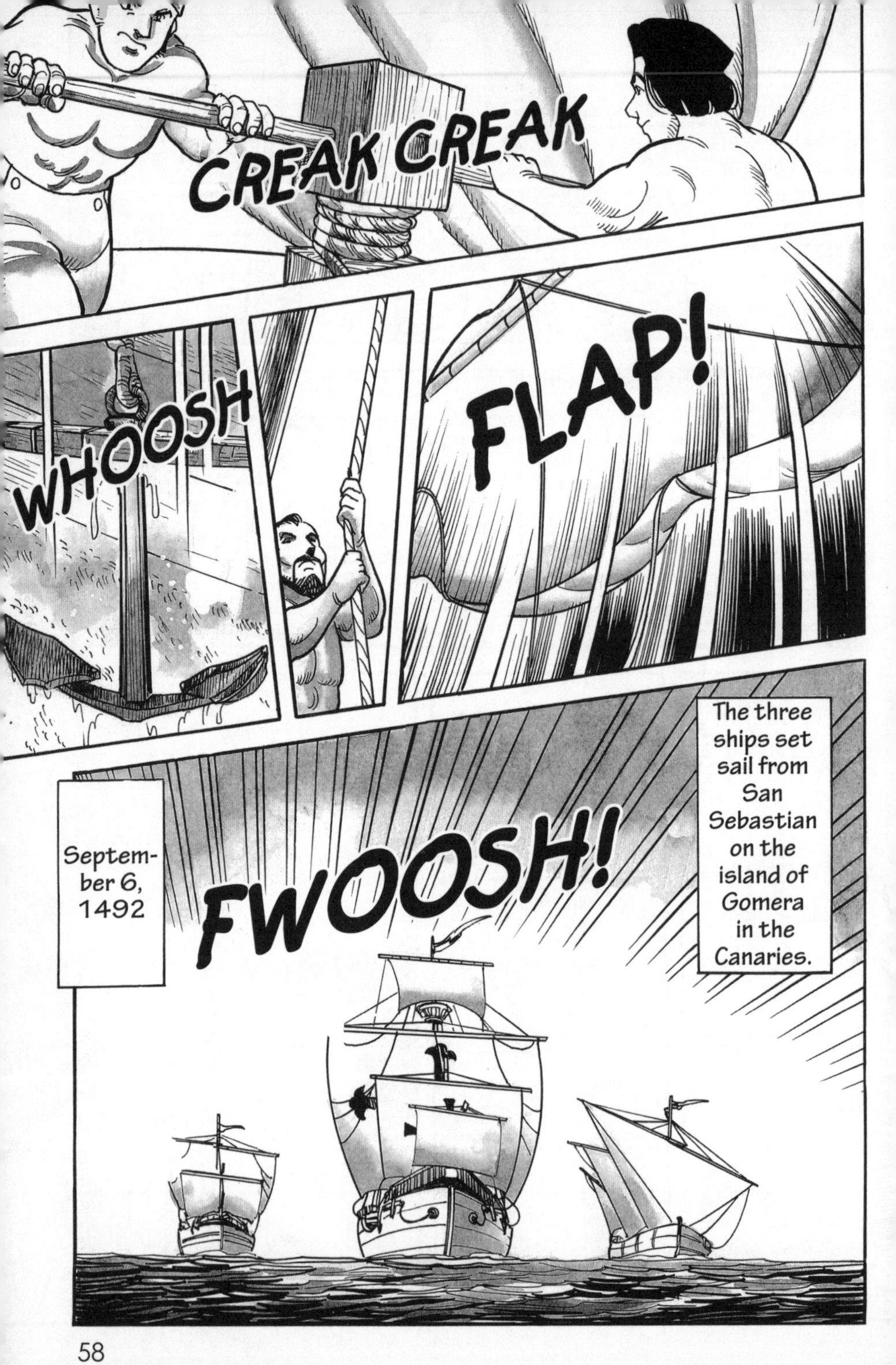
CREAK CREAK
WHOOSH
FLAP!
September 6, 1492
FWOOSH!
The three ships set sail from San Sebastian on the island of Gomera in the Canaries.

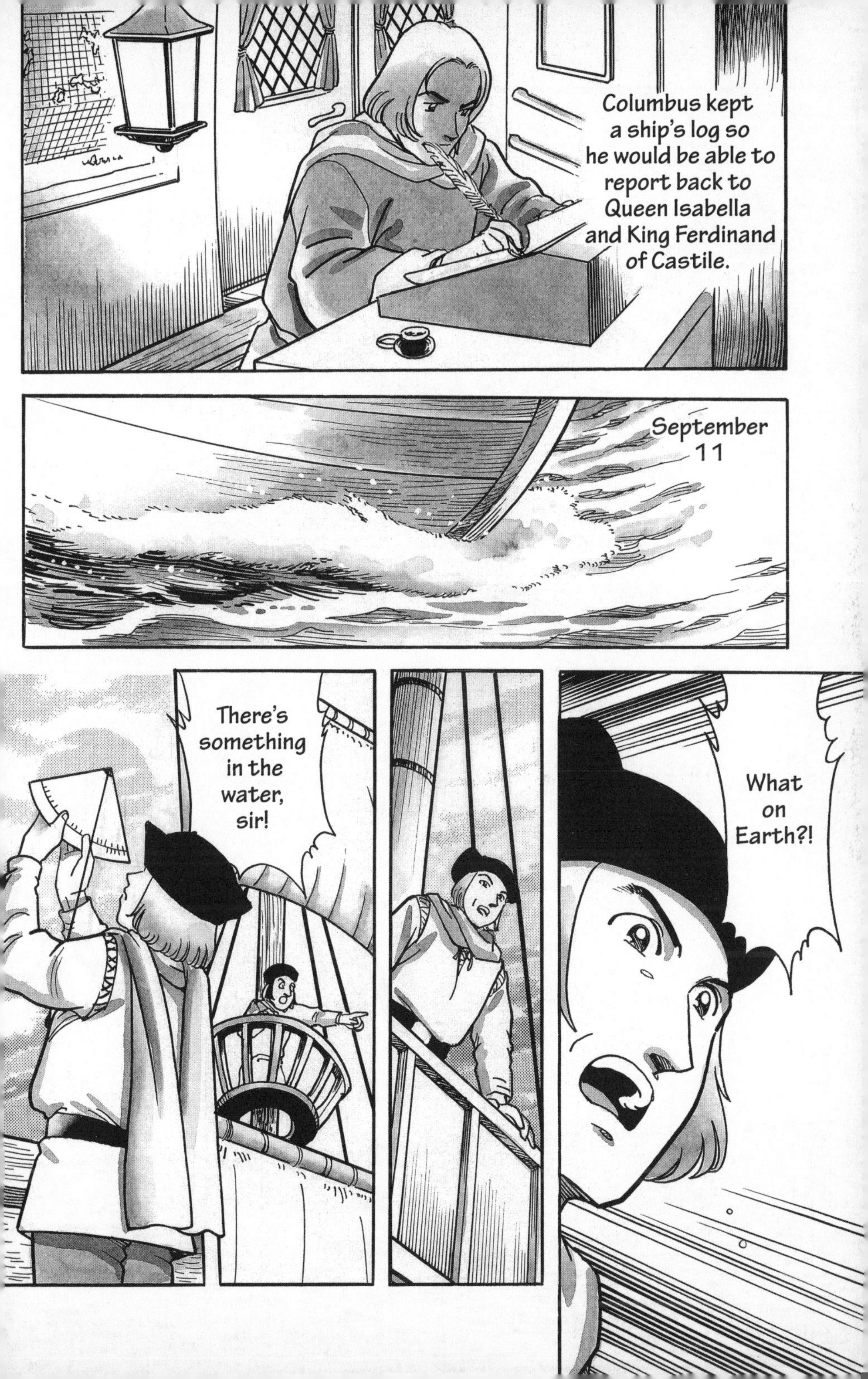
Columbus kept a ship's log so he would be able to report back to Queen Isabella and King Ferdinand of Castile.
September 11
There's something in the water, sir!
What on Earth?!

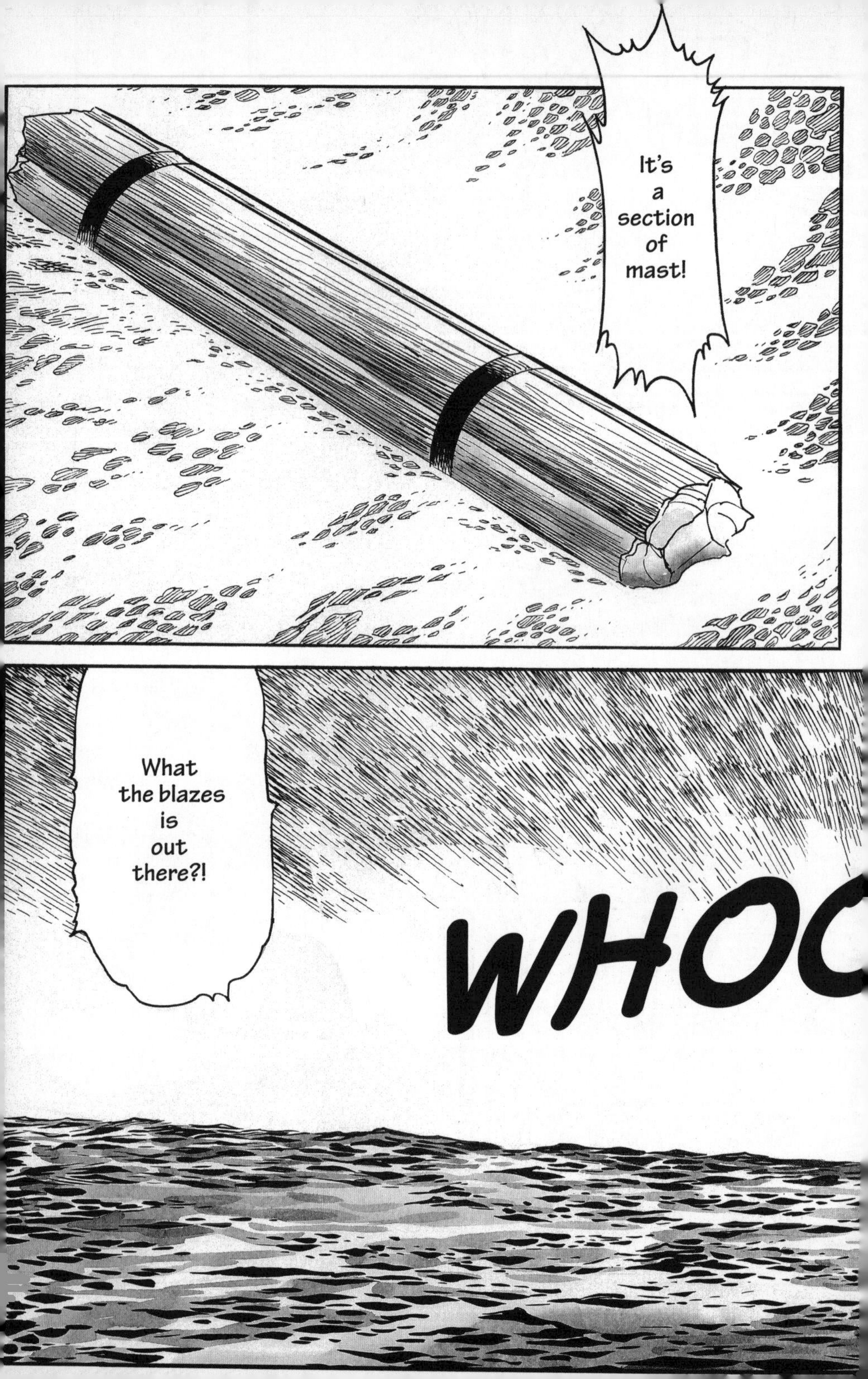
It's a section of mast!
What the blazes is out there?!
WHOO

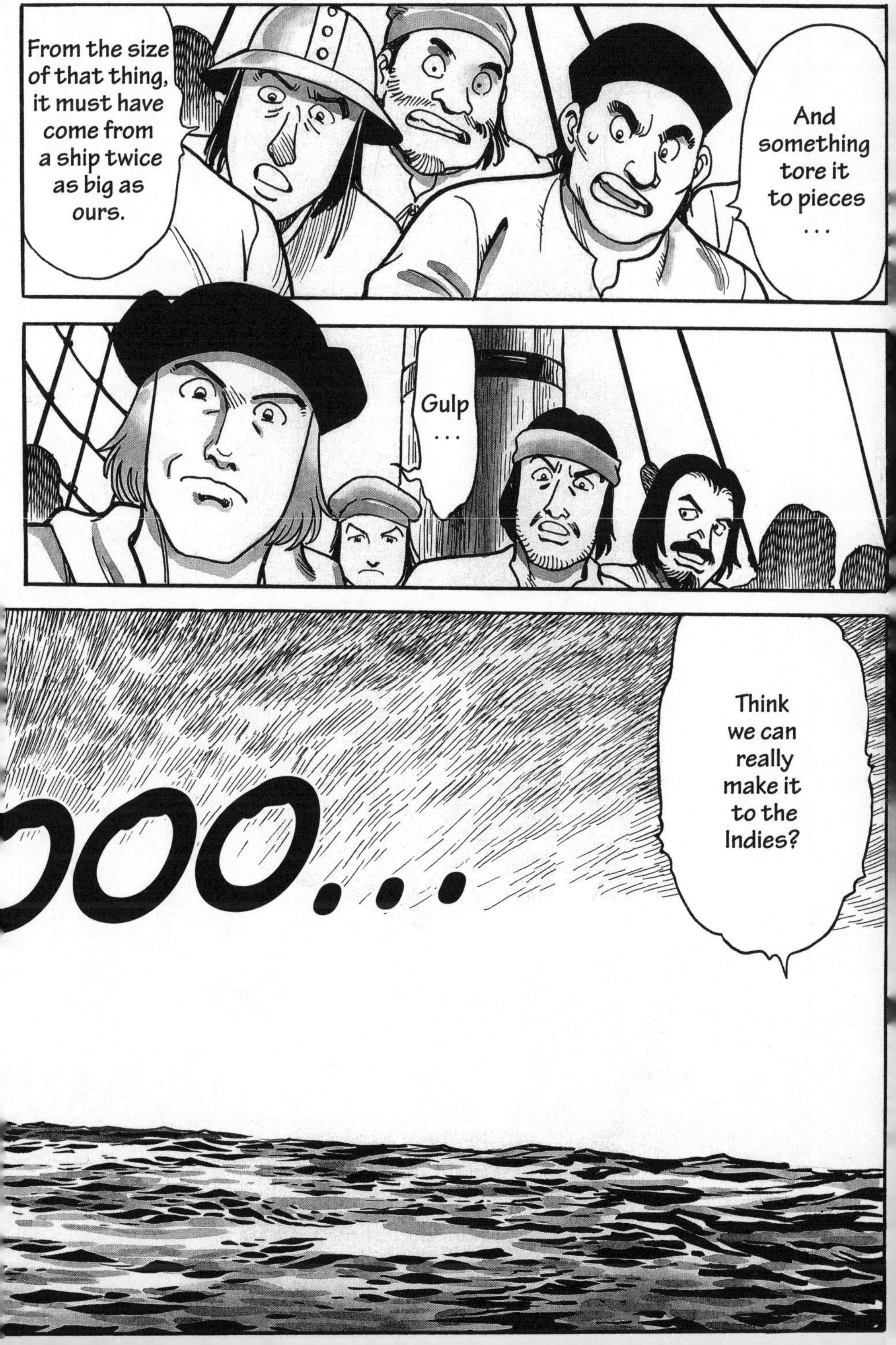
From the size of that thing, it must have come from a ship twice as big as ours.
And something tore it to pieces . . .
Gulp . . .
ooo...
Think we can really make it to the Indies?

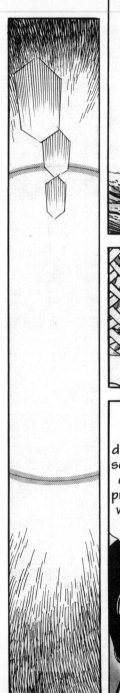

SIZZLE

Man, it's hot...

Stop drinking so much of our precious water!

Shut up! I'm hot.

The heat is getting to everyone.

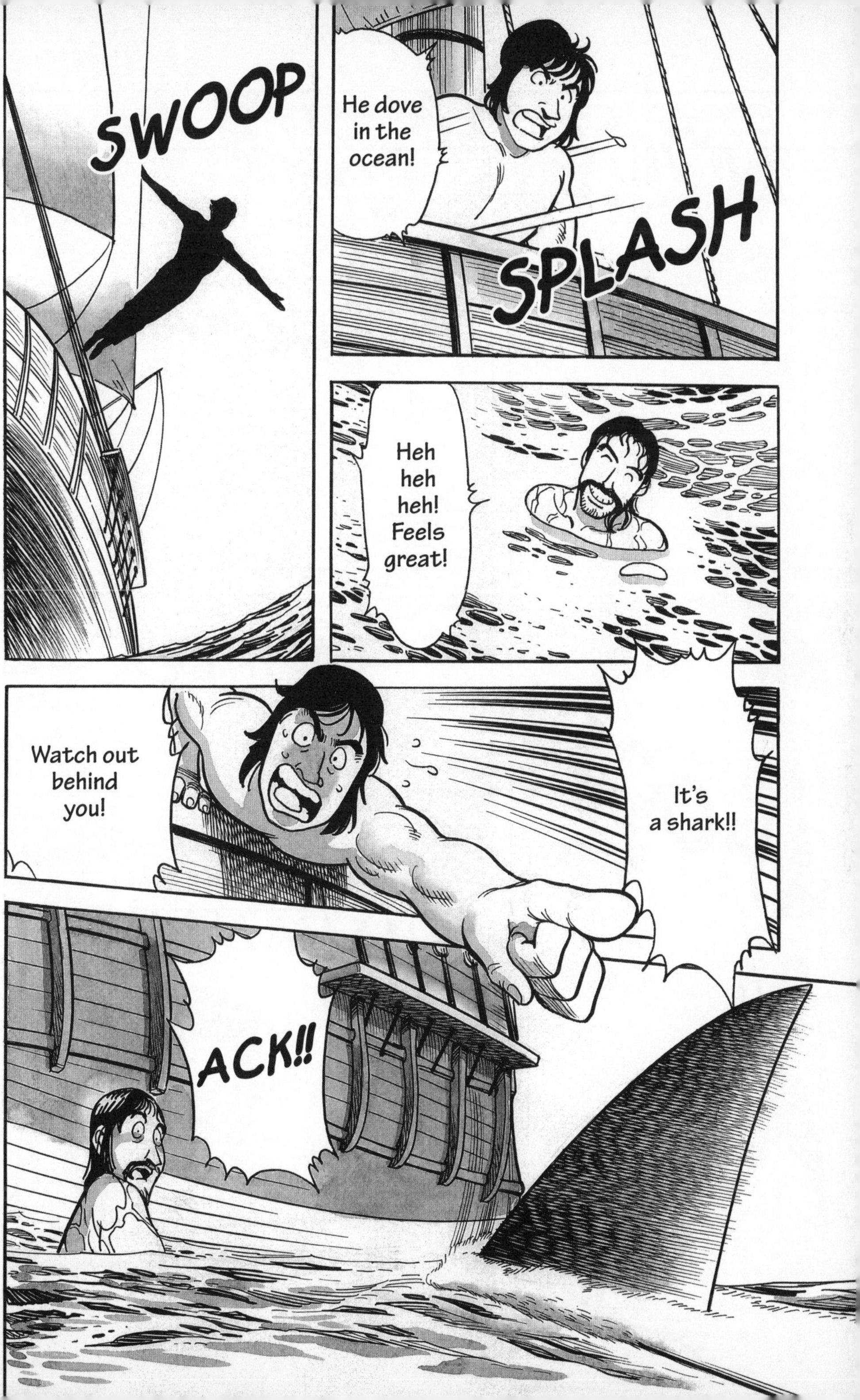
SWOOP
He dove in the ocean!
SPLASH
Heh heh heh! Feels great!
Watch out behind you!
It's a shark!!
ACK!!

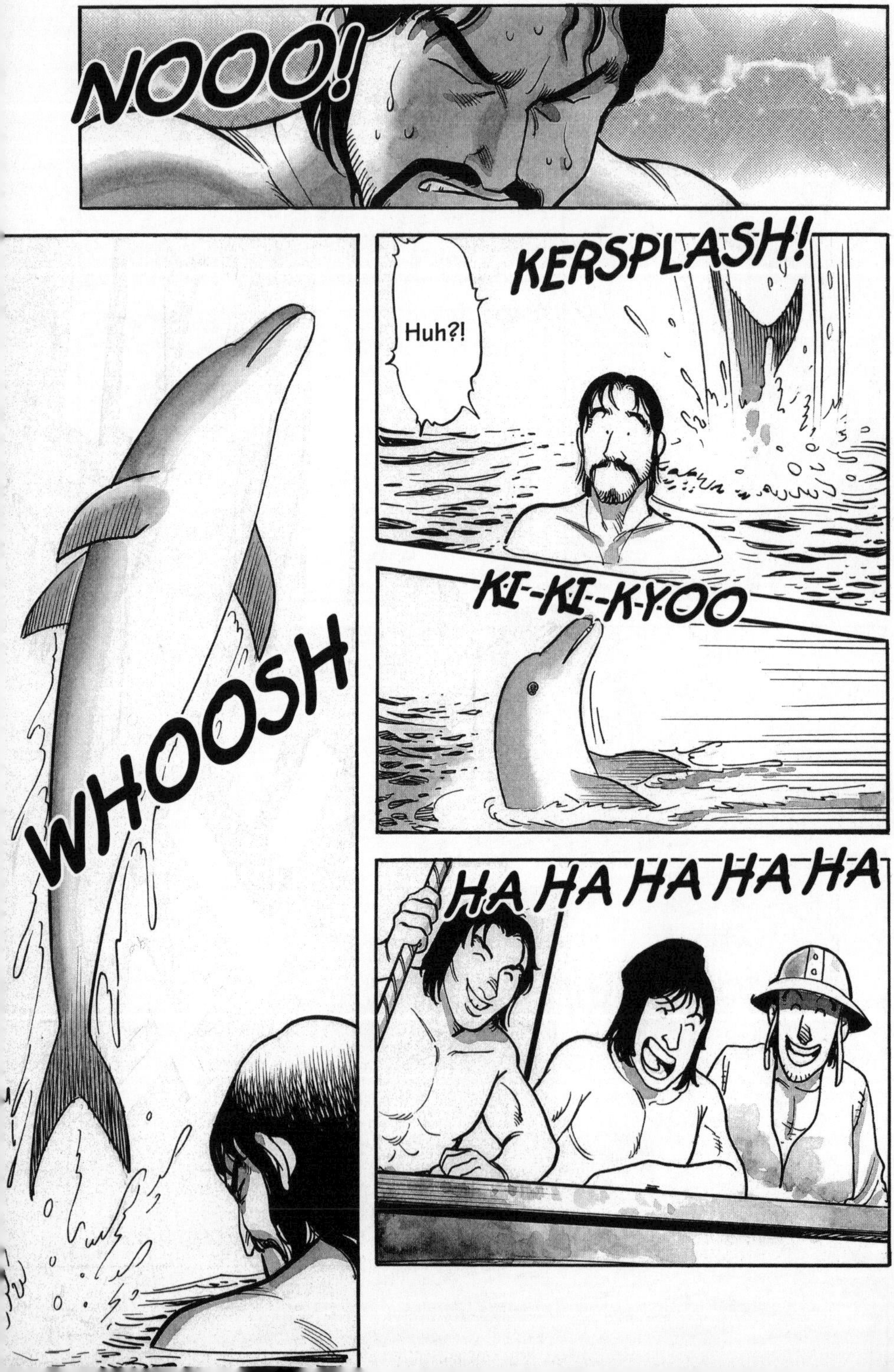
NOOO!
WHOOSH
KERSPLASH!
Huh?!
KI-KI-KYOO
HA HA HA HA HA HA

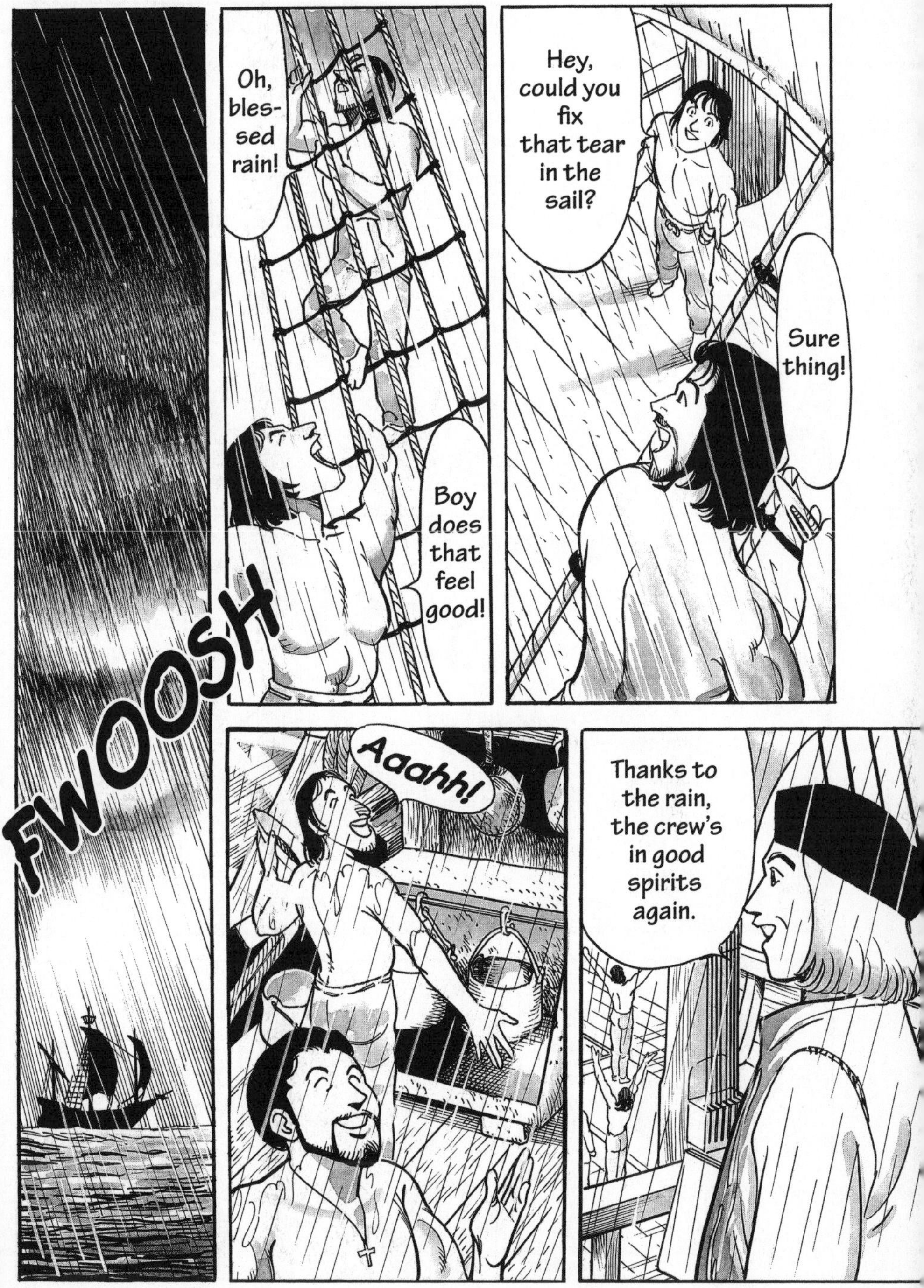
FWOOSH
Oh, bles-sed rain!
Boy does that feel good!
Hey, could you fix that tear in the sail?
Sure thing!
Aaahh!
Thanks to the rain, the crew's in good spirits again.

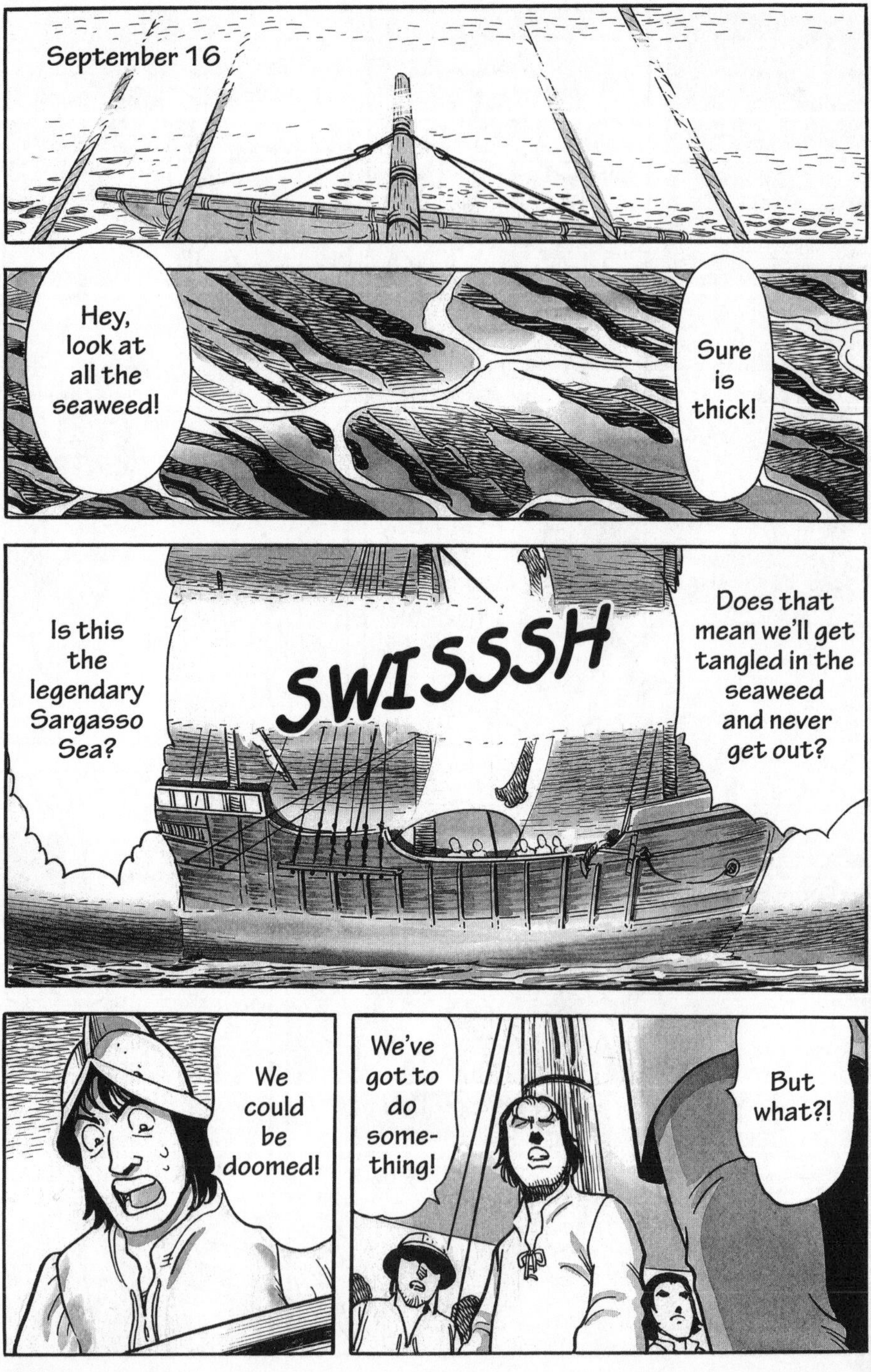
September 16
Hey, look at all the seaweed!
Sure is thick!
Is this the legendary Sargasso Sea?
SWISSSH
Does that mean we'll get tangled in the seaweed and never get out?
We could be doomed!
We've got to do some-thing!
But what?!

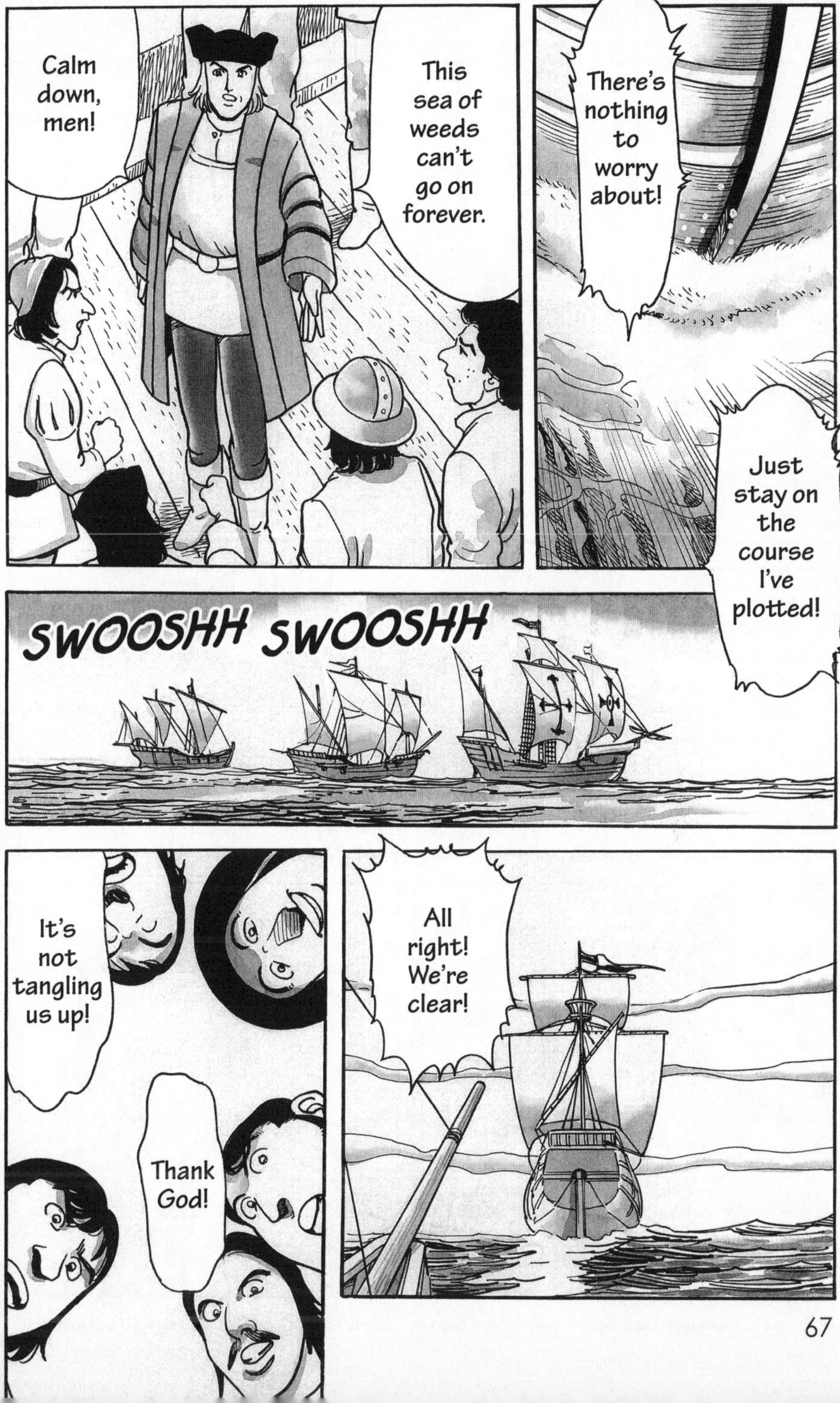
Calm down, men!
This sea of weeds can't go on forever.
There's nothing to worry about!
Just stay on the course I've plotted!
SWOOSHH SWOOSHH
It's not tangling us up!
Thank God!
All right! We're clear!

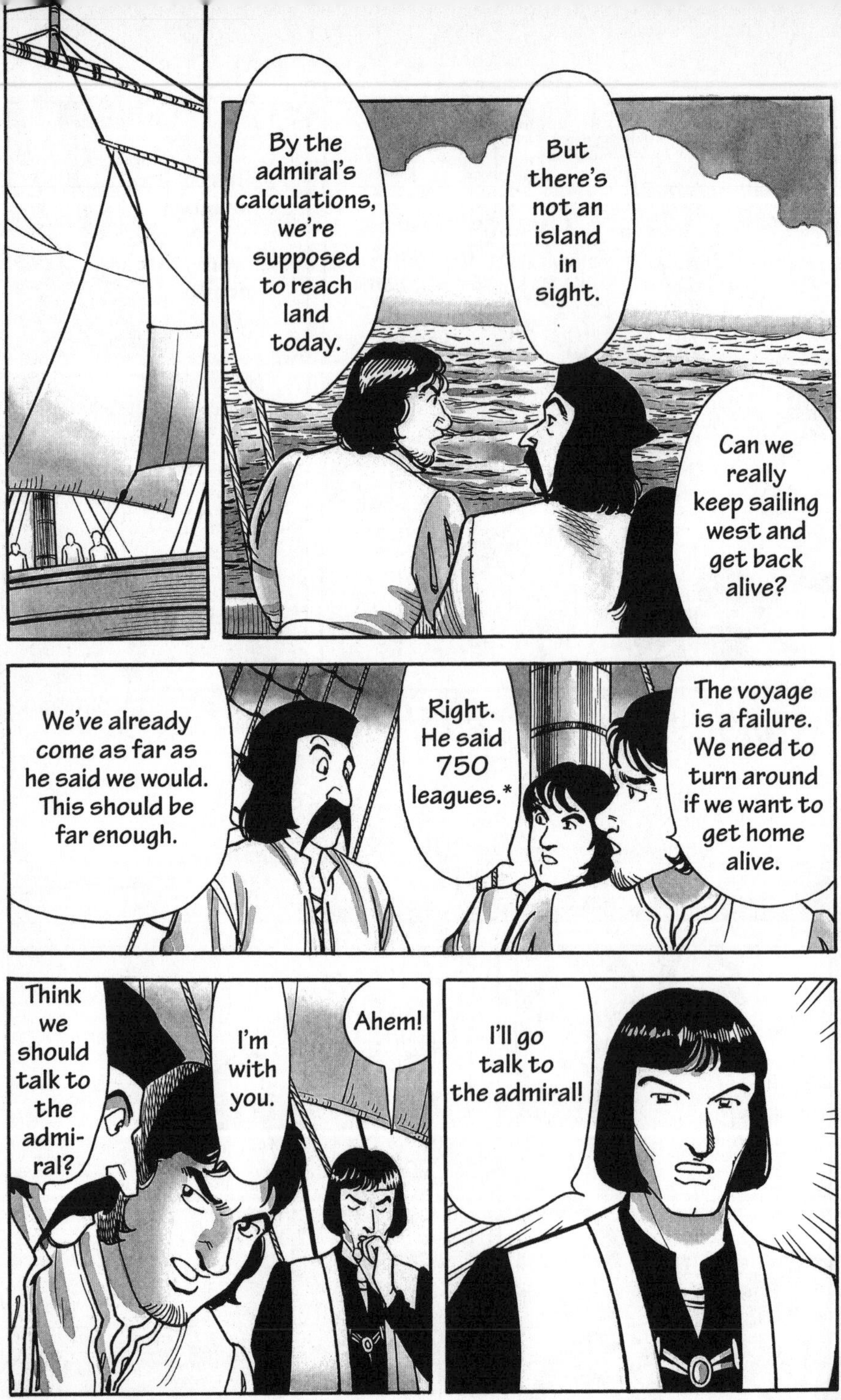
By the admiral's calculations, we're supposed to reach land today.
But there's not an island in sight.
Can we really keep sailing west and get back alive?
We've already come as far as he said we would. This should be far enough.
Right. He said 750 leagues.*
The voyage is a failure. We need to turn around if we want to get home alive.
Think we should talk to the admi-ral?
I'm with you.
Ahem!
I'll go talk to the admiral!

*League: One league is a little less than 3.7 miles, so 750 leagues is about 2,750 miles.

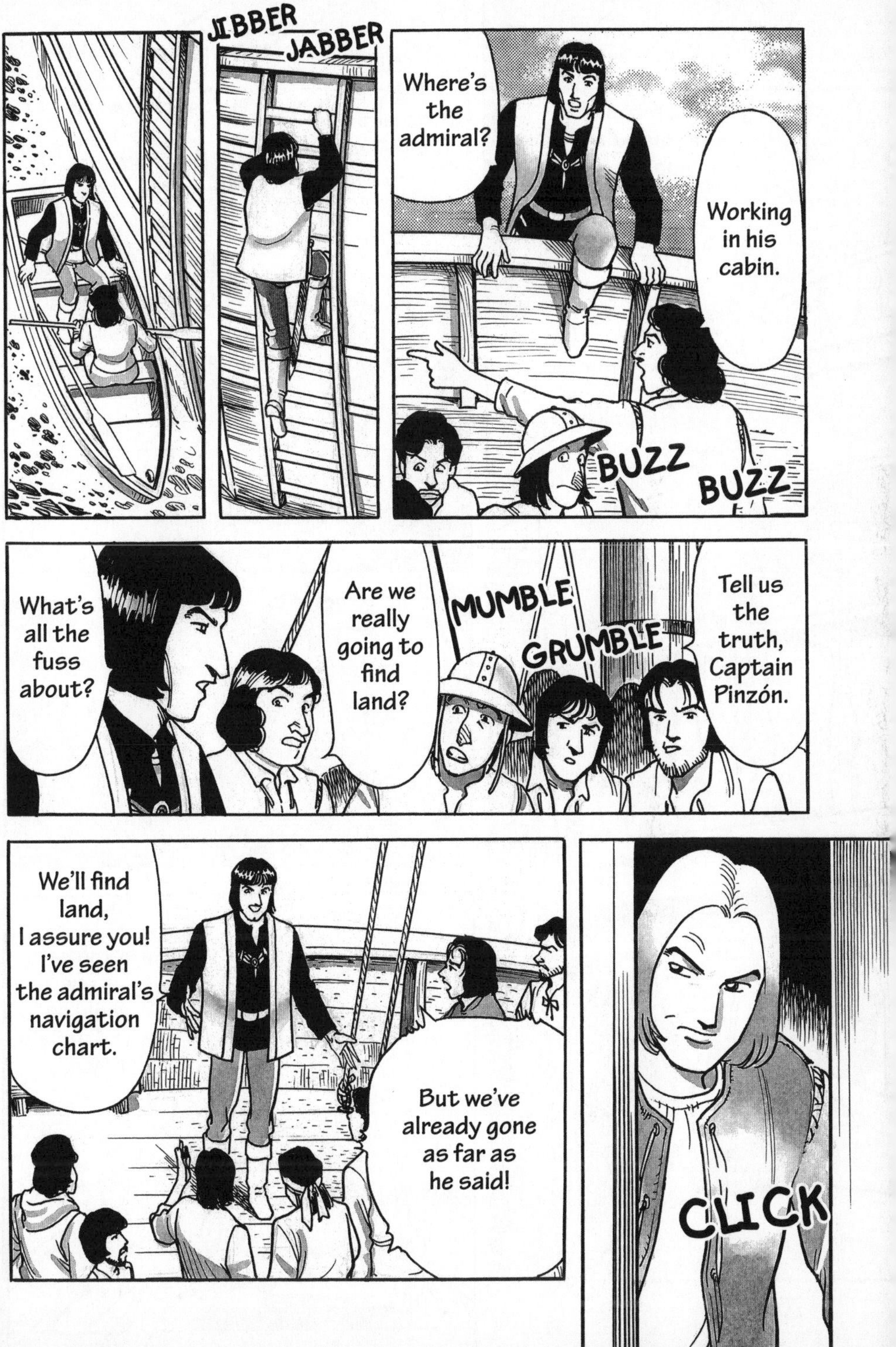
JIBBER
JABBER
Where's the admiral?
Working in his cabin.
BUZZ
BUZZ
What's all the fuss about?
Are we really going to find land?
MUMBLE
GRUMBLE
Tell us the truth, Captain Pinzón.
We'll find land, I assure you! I've seen the admiral's navigation chart.
But we've already gone as far as he said!
CLICK

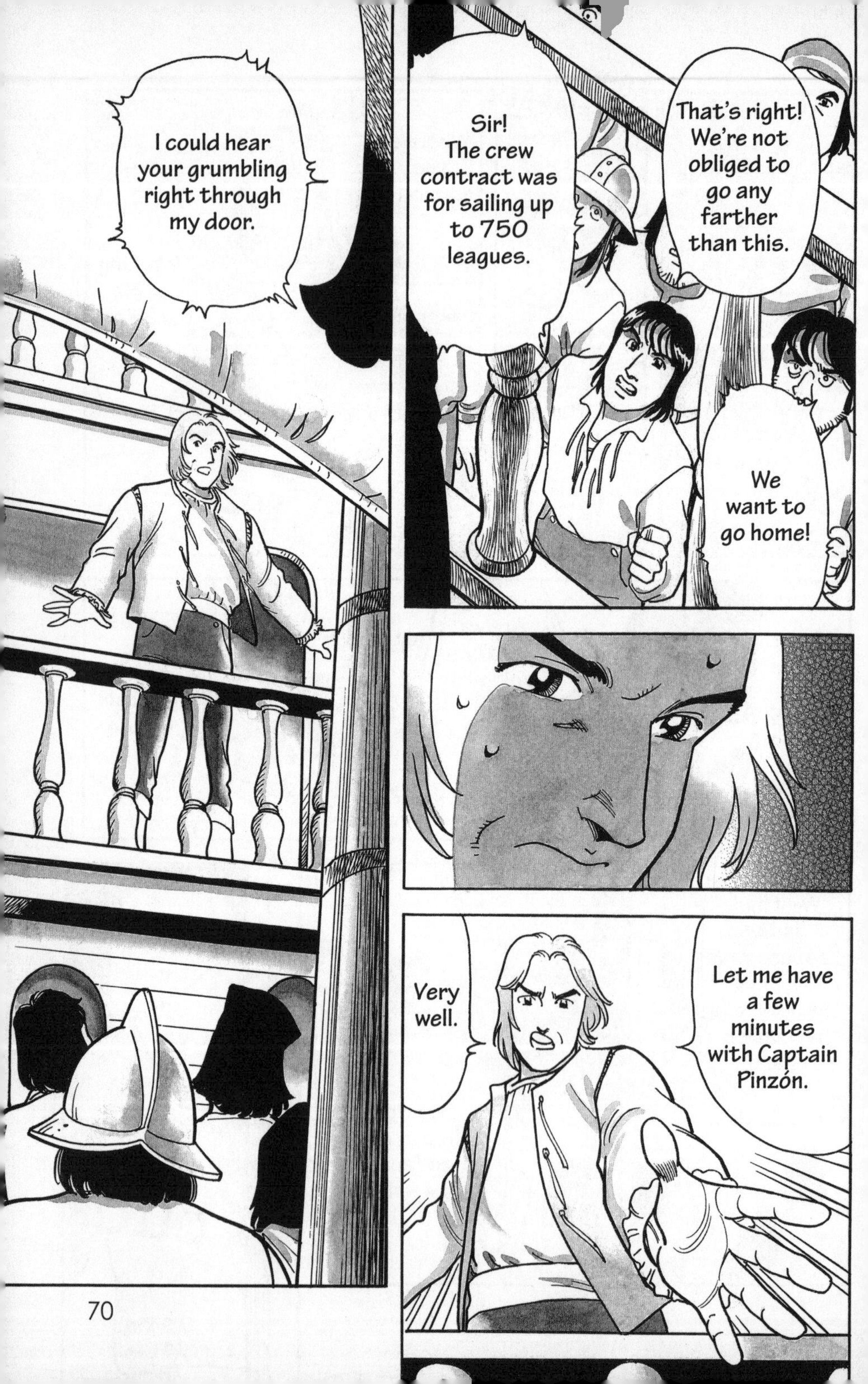
I could hear your grumbling right through my door.
Sir! The crew contract was for sailing up to 750 leagues.
That's right! We're not obliged to go any farther than this.
We want to go home!
Very well.
Let me have a few minutes with Captain Pinzón.

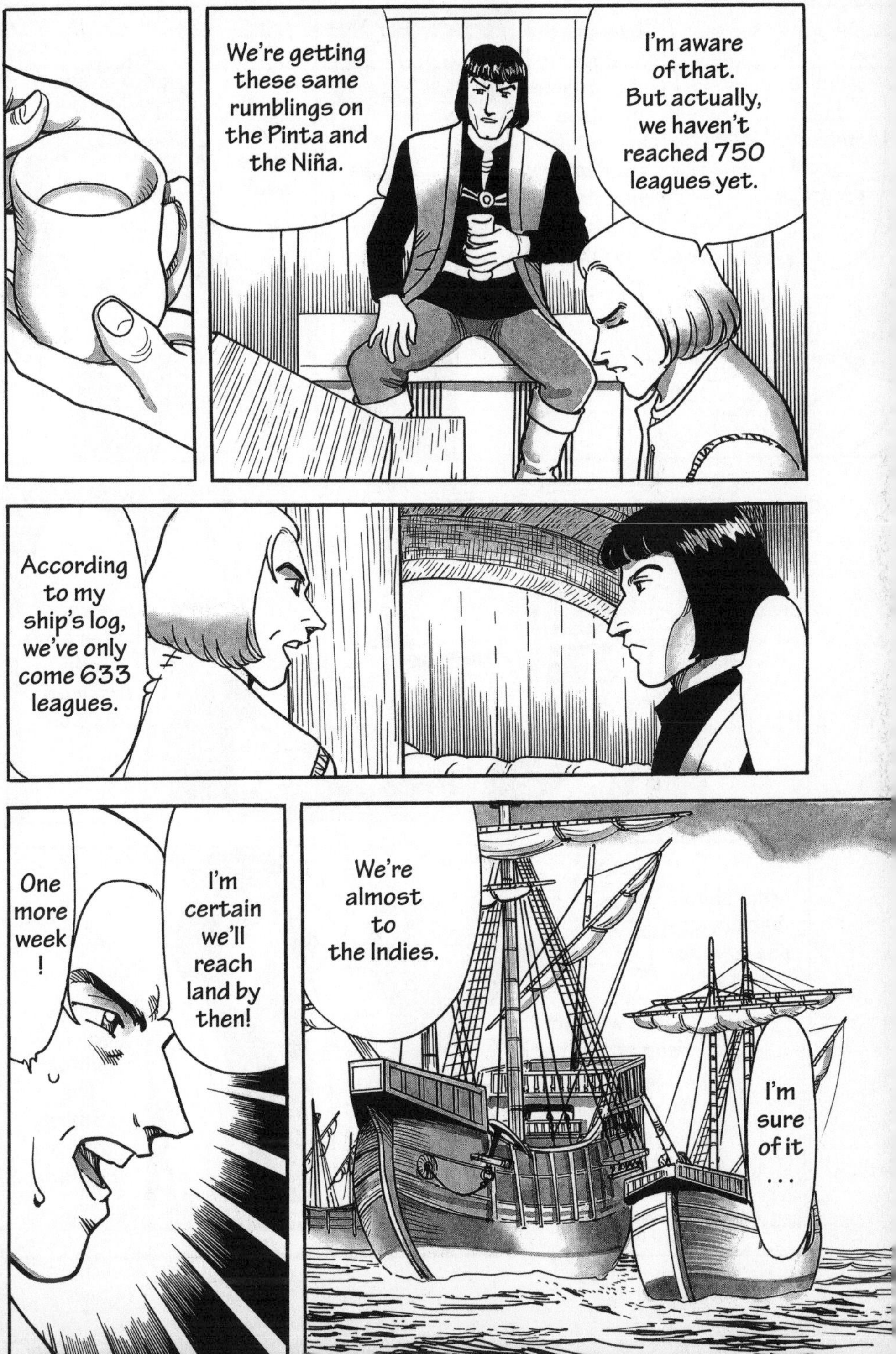

We're getting these same rumblings on the Pinta and the Niña.
I'm aware of that. But actually, we haven't reached 750 leagues yet.
According to my ship's log, we've only come 633 leagues.
One more week!
I'm certain we'll reach land by then!
We're almost to the Indies.
I'm sure of it . . .

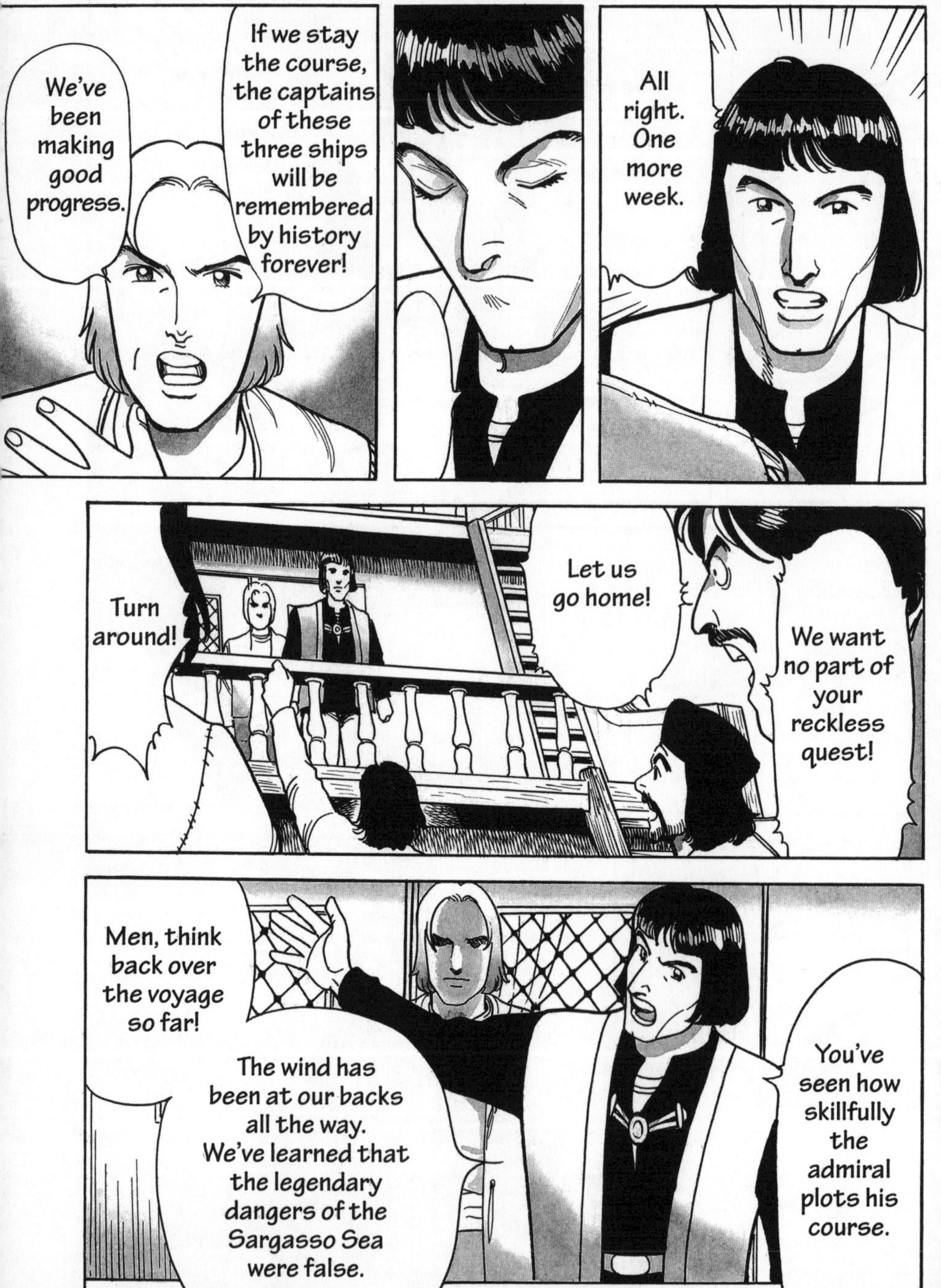
We've been making good progress.
If we stay the course, the captains of these three ships will be remembered by history forever!
All right. One more week.
Turn around!
Let us go home!
We want no part of your reckless quest!
Men, think back over the voyage so far!
The wind has been at our backs all the way. We've learned that the legendary dangers of the Sargasso Sea were false.
You've seen how skillfully the admiral plots his course.

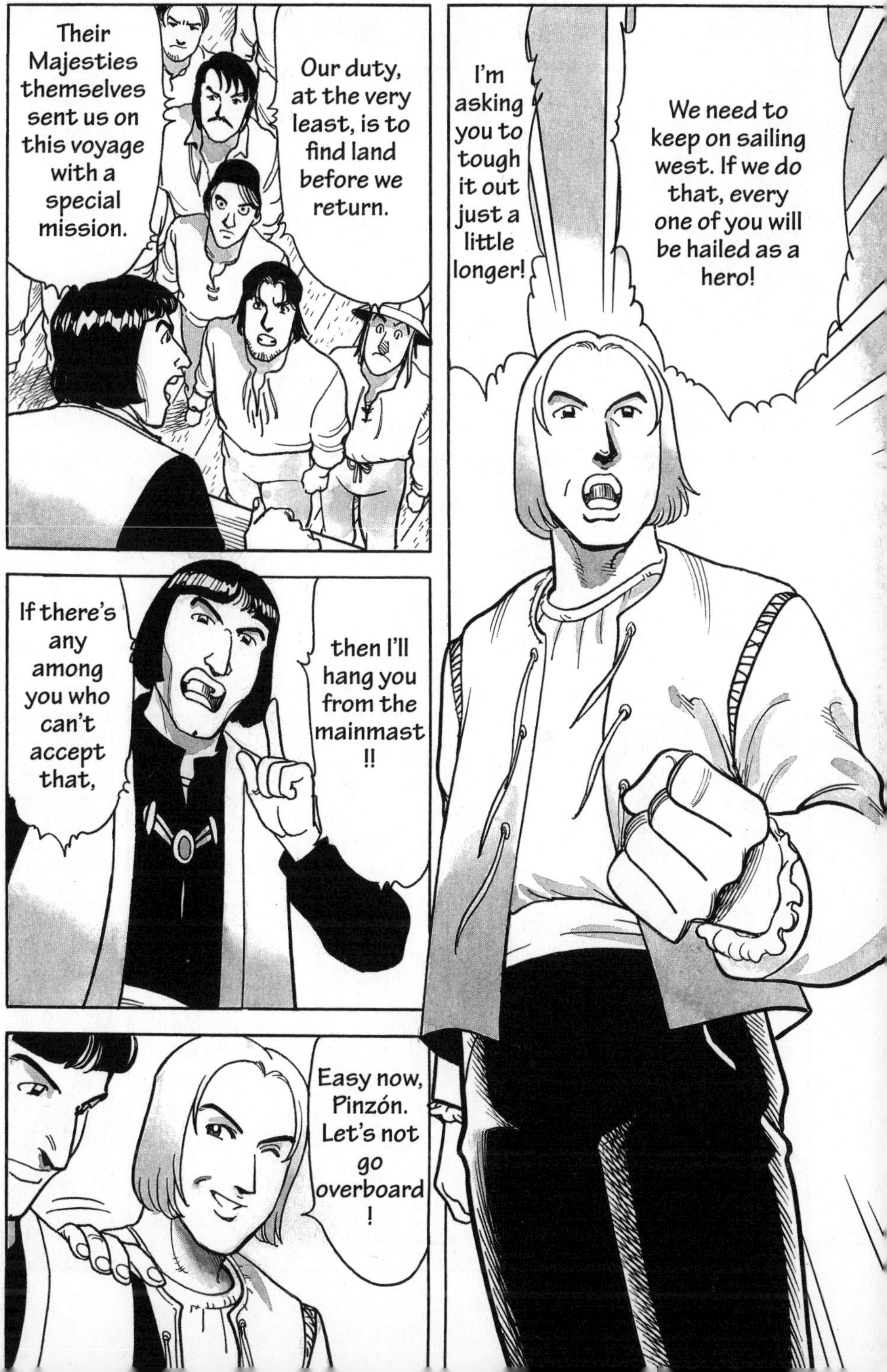
Their Majesties themselves sent us on this voyage with a special mission.
Our duty, at the very least, is to find land before we return.
If there's any among you who can't accept that,
then I'll hang you from the mainmast !!
Easy now, Pinzón. Let's not go overboard !
I'm asking you to tough it out just a little longer!
We need to keep on sailing west. If we do that, every one of you will be hailed as a hero!

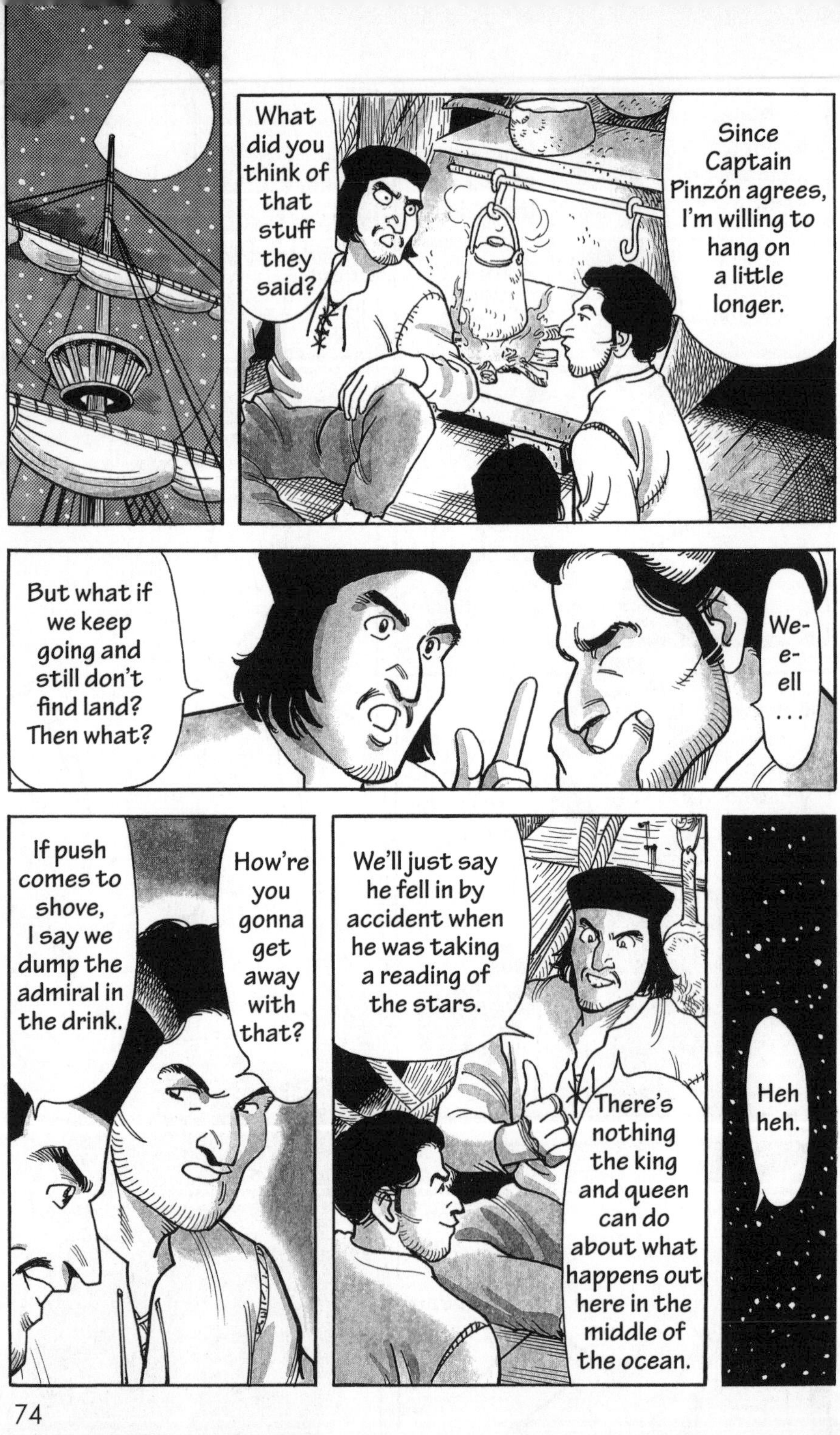
What did you think of that stuff they said?
Since Captain Pinzón agrees, I'm willing to hang on a little longer.
But what if we keep going and still don't find land? Then what?
We-e-ell . . .
If push comes to shove, I say we dump the admiral in the drink.
How're you gonna get away with that?
We'll just say he fell in by accident when he was taking a reading of the stars.
There's nothing the king and queen can do about what happens out here in the middle of the ocean.
Heh heh.

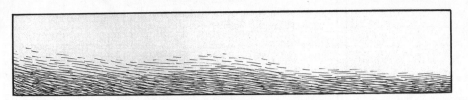

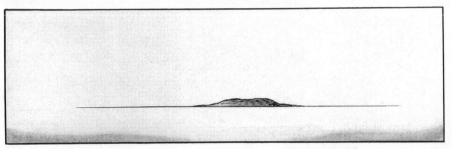

LAND
HO!!

What?!

Land?
At what
bearing?

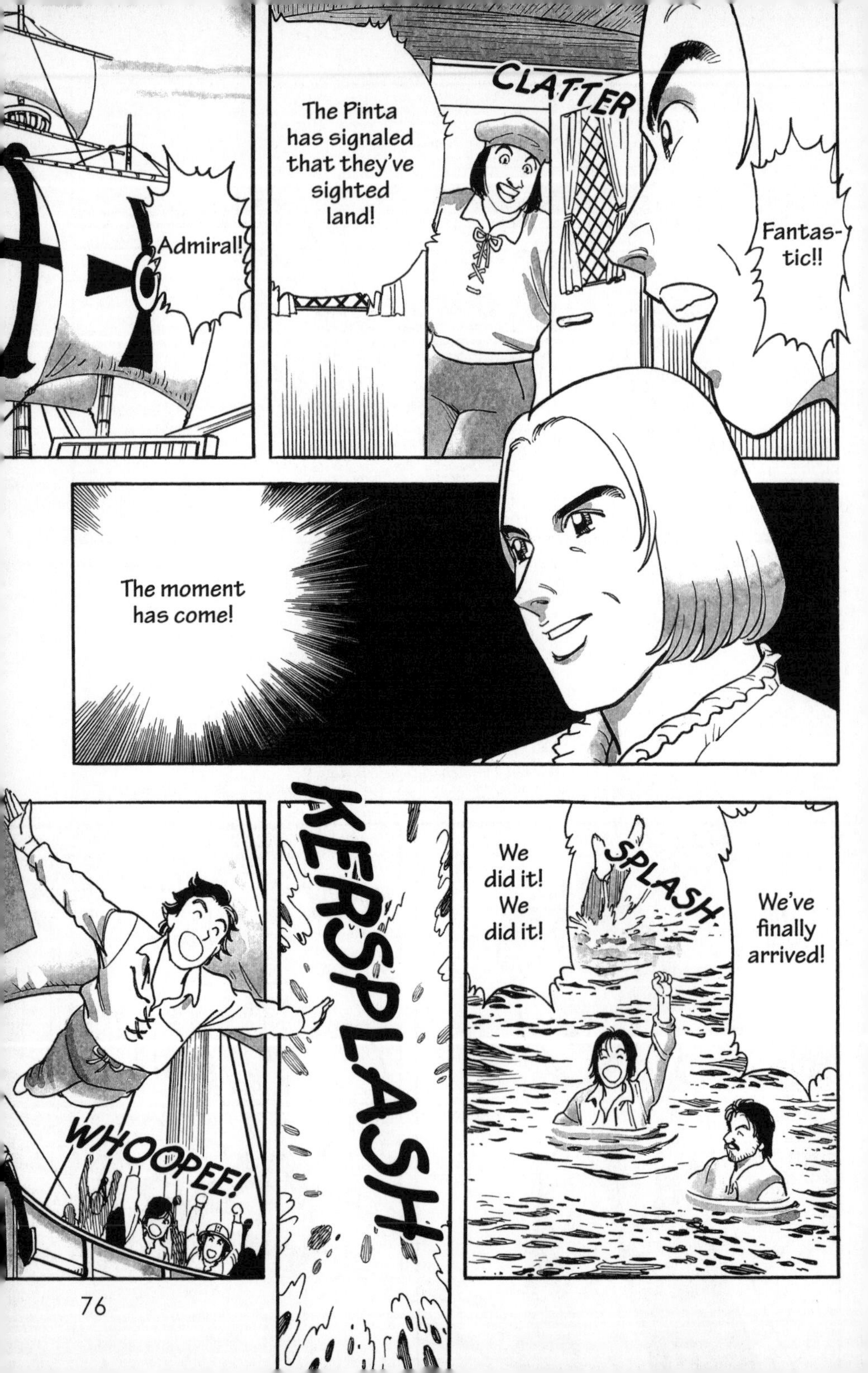
Admiral!
The Pinta has signaled that they've sighted land!
CLATTER
Fantas-tic!!
The moment has come!
WHOOPEE!
KERSPLASH
We did it! We did it!
SPLASH
We've finally arrived!

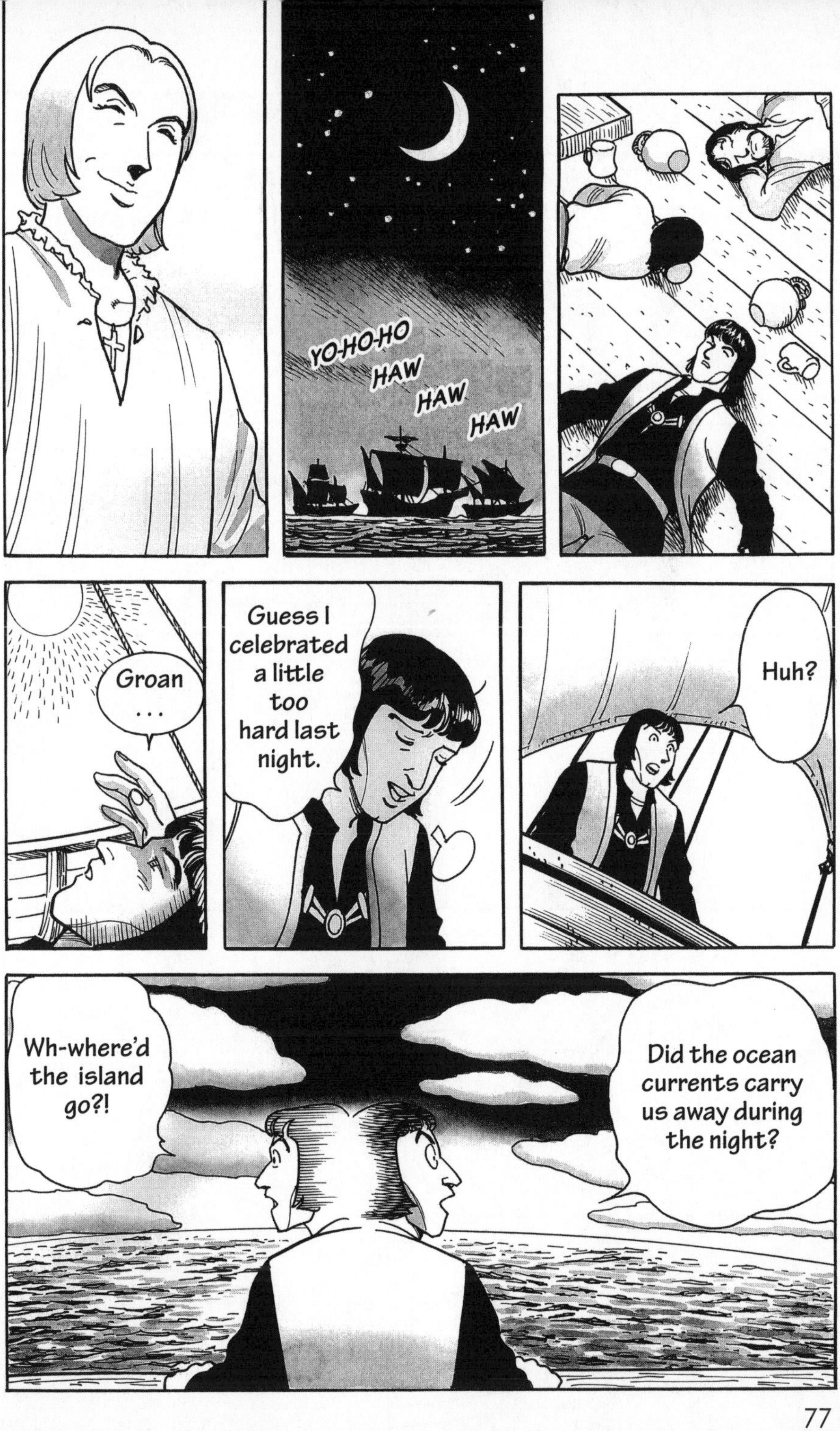
YO-HO-HO
HAW
HAW
HAW
Groan ...
Guess I celebrated a little too hard last night.
Huh?
Wh-where'd the island go?!
Did the ocean currents carry us away during the night?

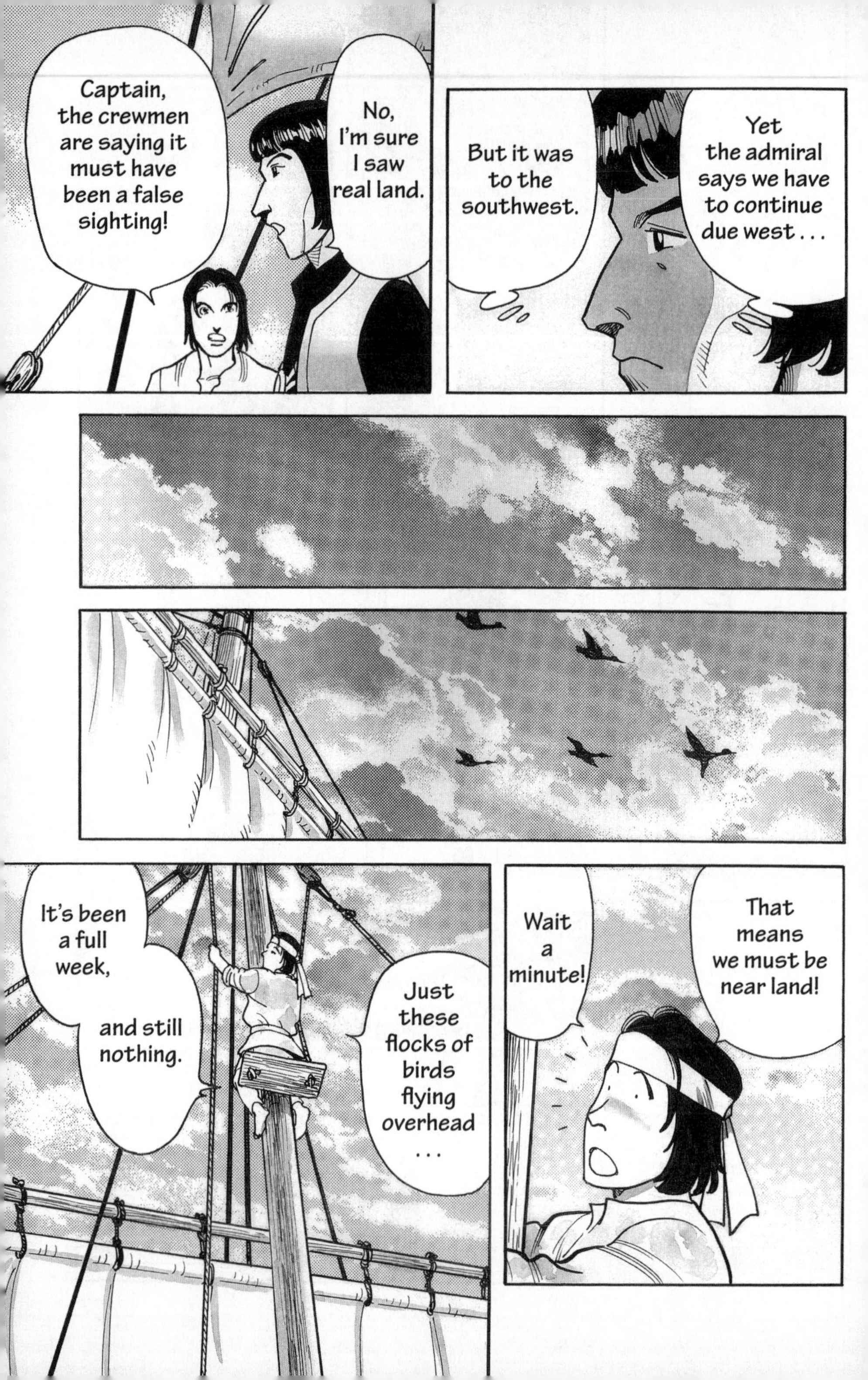
Captain, the crewmen are saying it must have been a false sighting!
No, I'm sure I saw real land.
But it was to the southwest.
Yet the admiral says we have to continue due west . . .
It's been a full week,
and still nothing.
Just these flocks of birds flying overhead . . .
Wait a minute!
That means we must be near land!

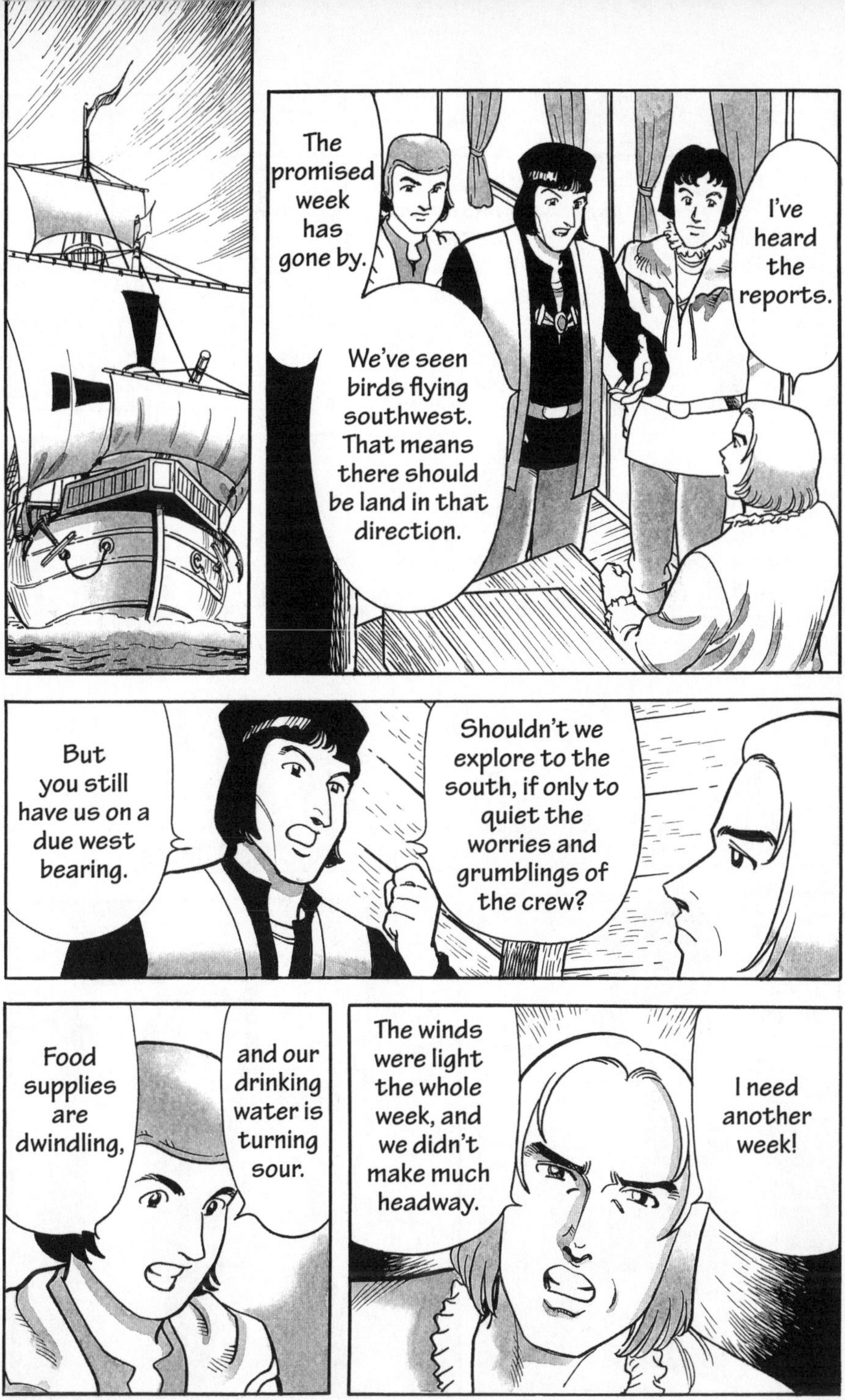

The promised week has gone by.
We've seen birds flying southwest. That means there should be land in that direction.
I've heard the reports.
But you still have us on a due west bearing.
Shouldn't we explore to the south, if only to quiet the worries and grumblings of the crew?
Food supplies are dwindling,
and our drinking water is turning sour.
The winds were light the whole week, and we didn't make much headway.
I need another week!

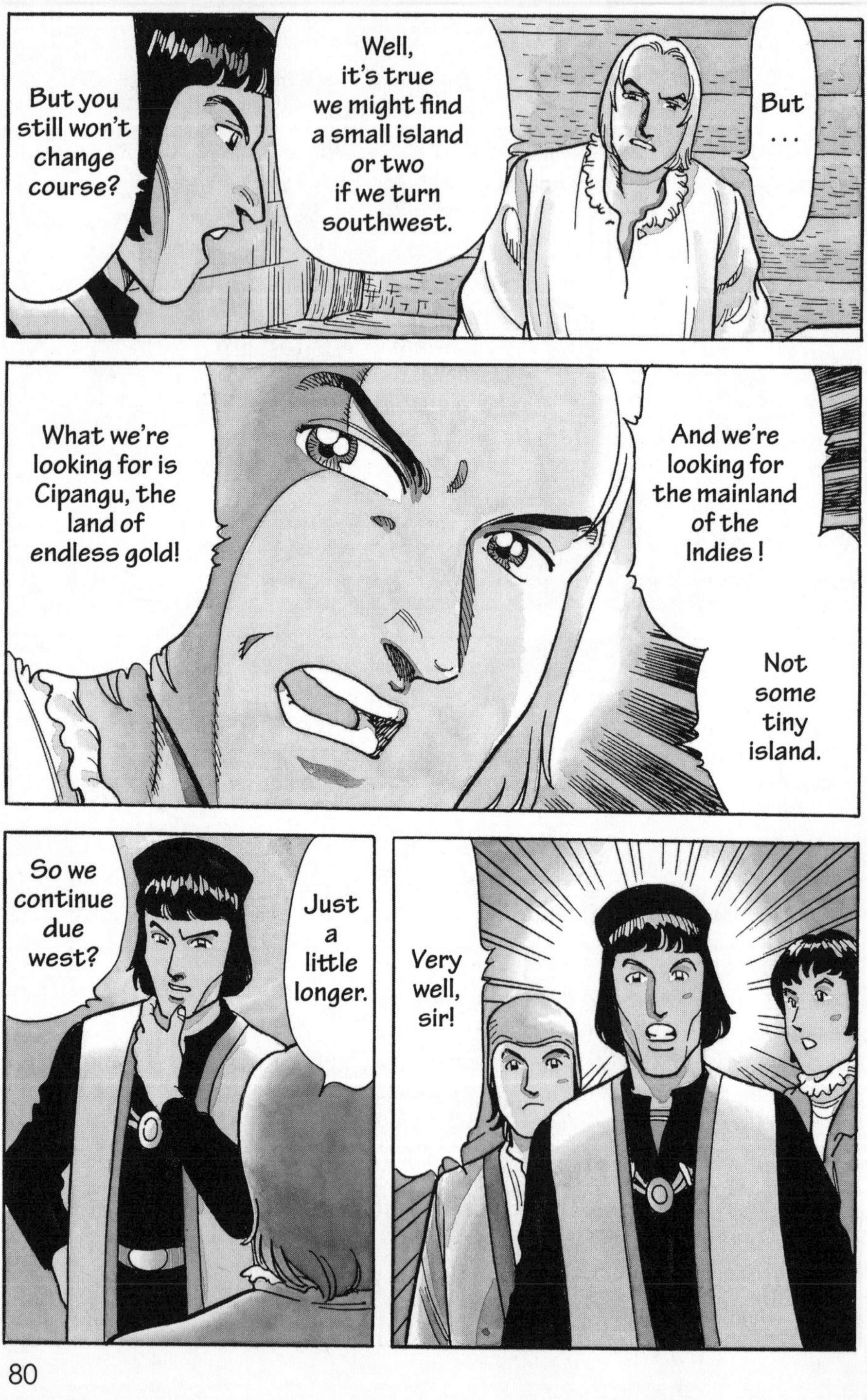
But you still won't change course?
Well, it's true we might find a small island or two if we turn southwest.
But . . .
What we're looking for is Cipangu, the land of endless gold!
And we're looking for the mainland of the Indies !
Not some tiny island.
So we continue due west?
Just a little longer.
Very well, sir!

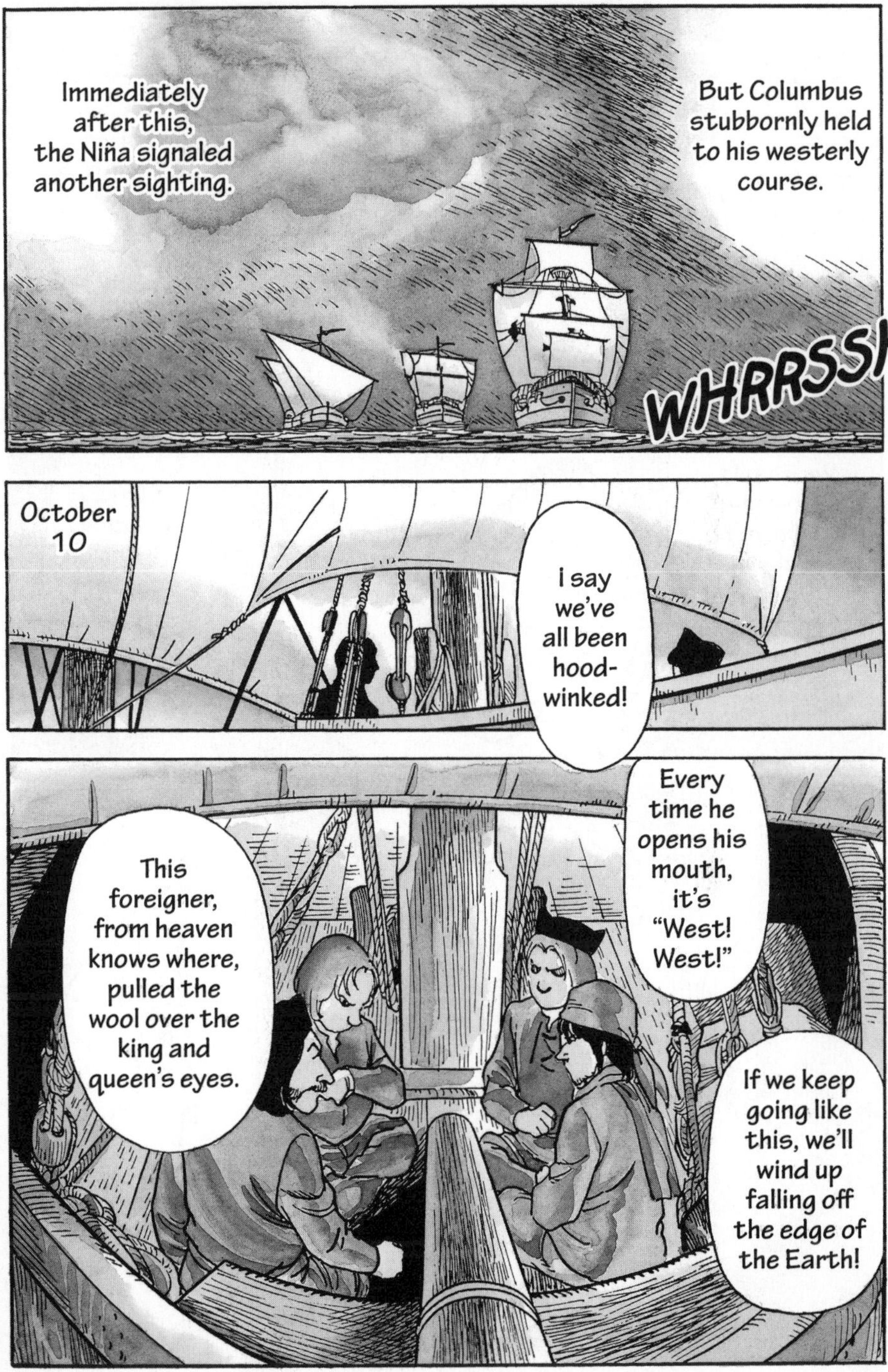
Immediately after this, the Niña signaled another sighting.
But Columbus stubbornly held to his westerly course.
WHRRSSH
October 10
I say we've all been hood-winked!
This foreigner, from heaven knows where, pulled the wool over the king and queen's eyes.
Every time he opens his mouth, it's "West! West!"
If we keep going like this, we'll wind up falling off the edge of the Earth!

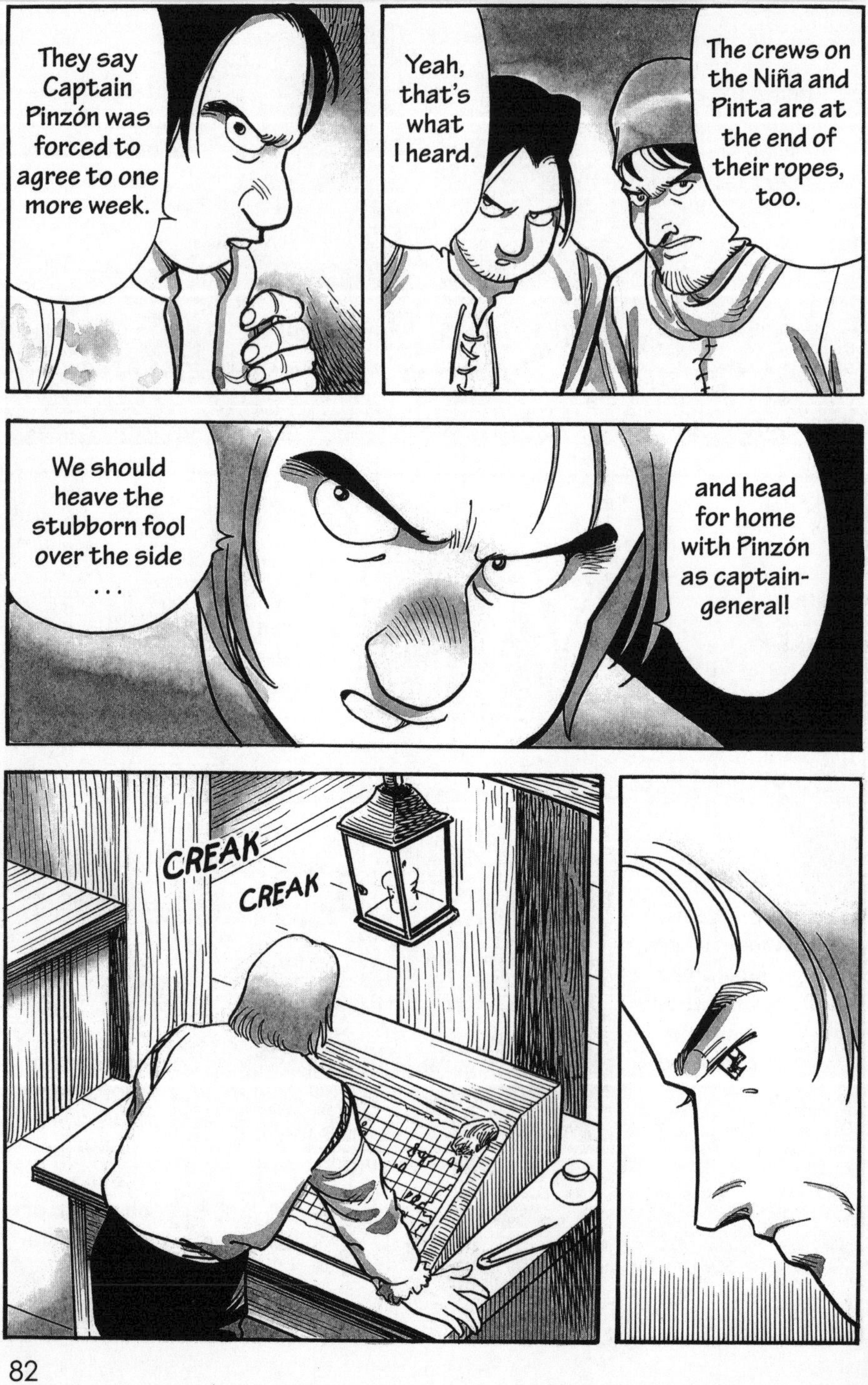
They say Captain Pinzón was forced to agree to one more week.
Yeah, that's what I heard.
The crews on the Niña and Pinta are at the end of their ropes, too.
We should heave the stubborn fool over the side . . .
and head for home with Pinzón as captain-general!
CREAK
CREAK

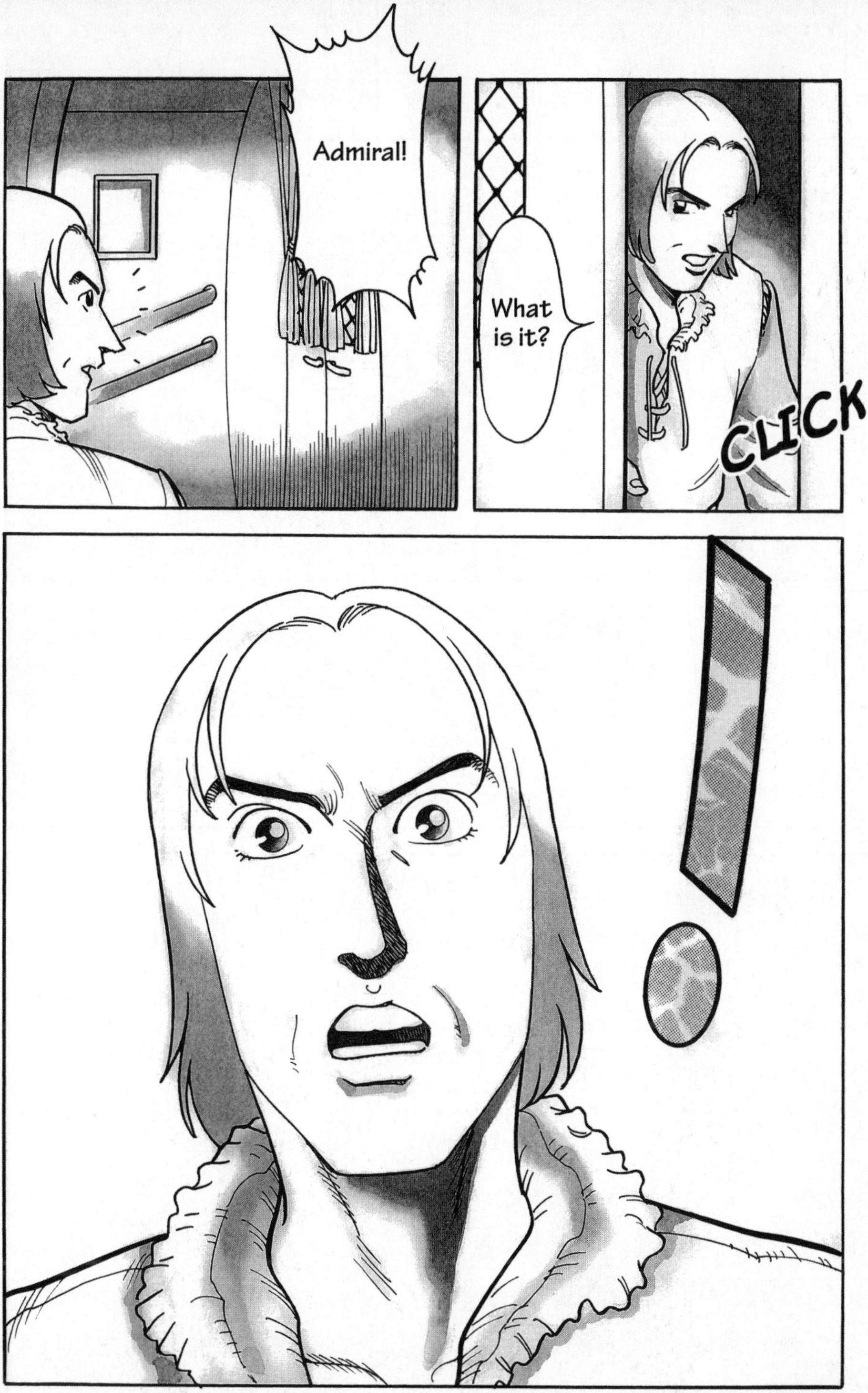
Admiral!
What is it?
CLICK

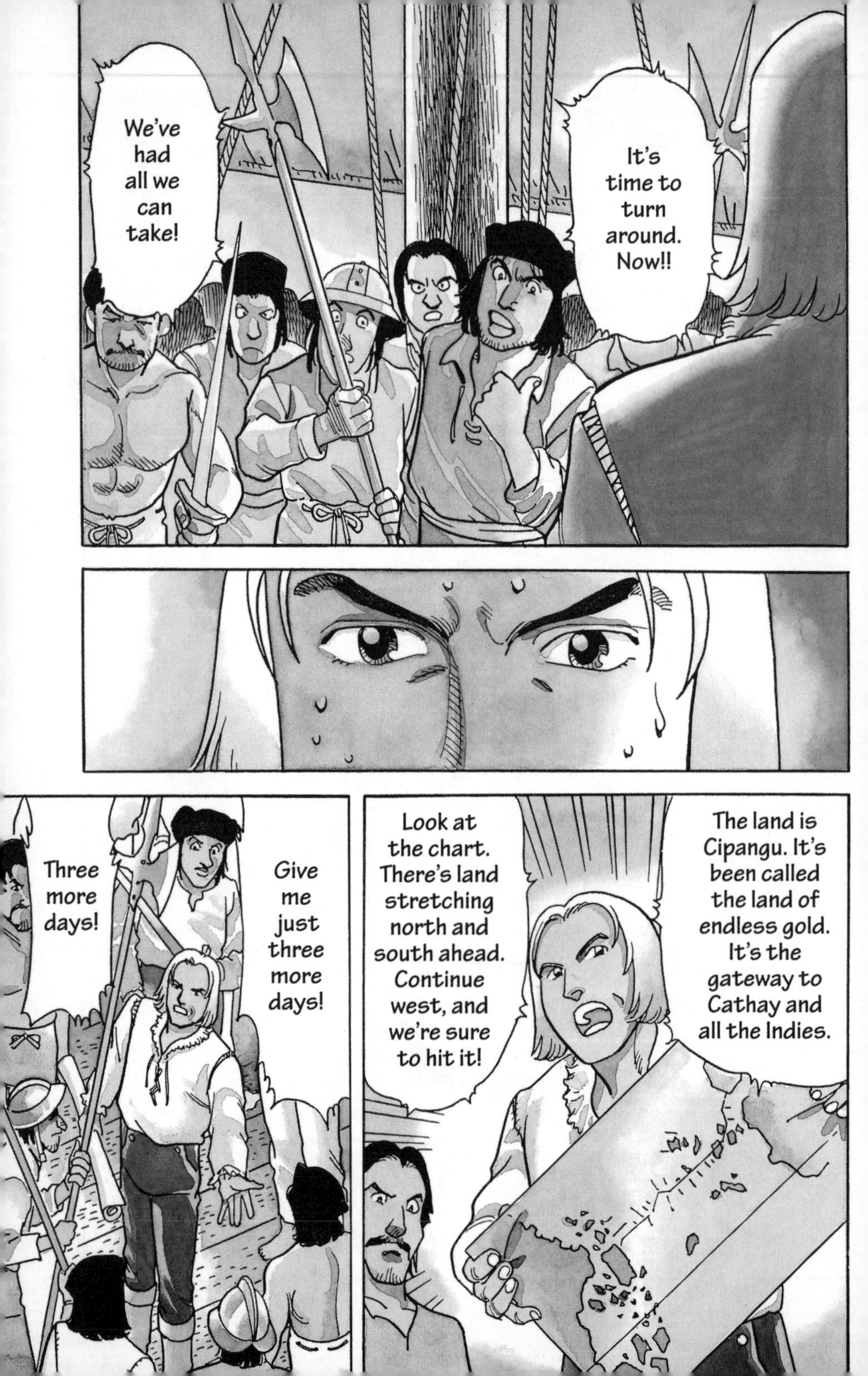
We've had all we can take!
It's time to turn around. Now!!
Three more days!
Give me just three more days!
Look at the chart. There's land stretching north and south ahead. Continue west, and we're sure to hit it!
The land is Cipangu. It's been called the land of endless gold. It's the gateway to Cathay and all the Indies.

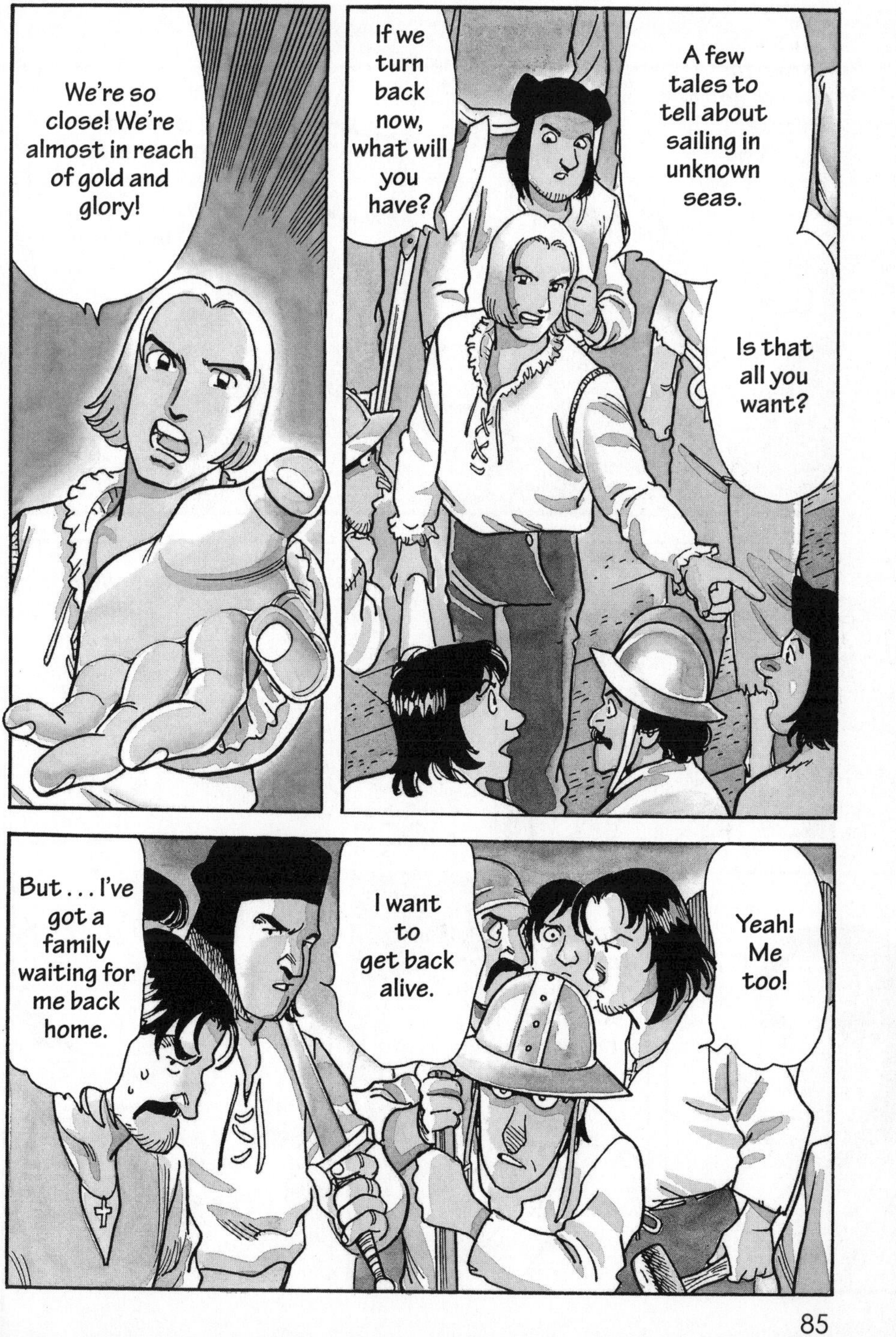
We're so close! We're almost in reach of gold and glory!
If we turn back now, what will you have?
A few tales to tell about sailing in unknown seas.
Is that all you want?
But . . . I've got a family waiting for me back home.
I want to get back alive.
Yeah! Me too!

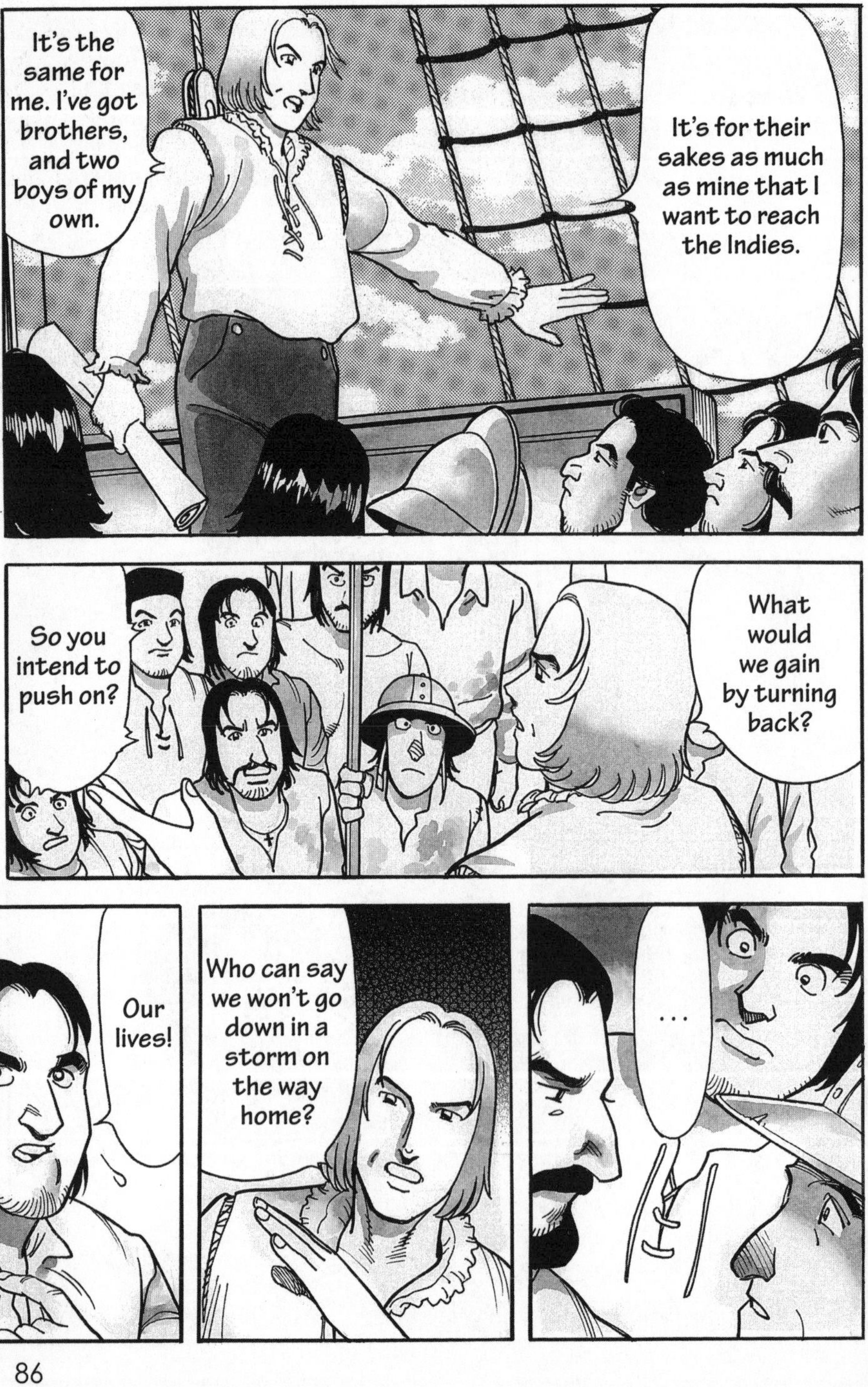
It's the same for me. I've got brothers, and two boys of my own.
It's for their sakes as much as mine that I want to reach the Indies.
So you intend to push on?
What would we gain by turning back?
Our lives!
Who can say we won't go down in a storm on the way home?
. . .

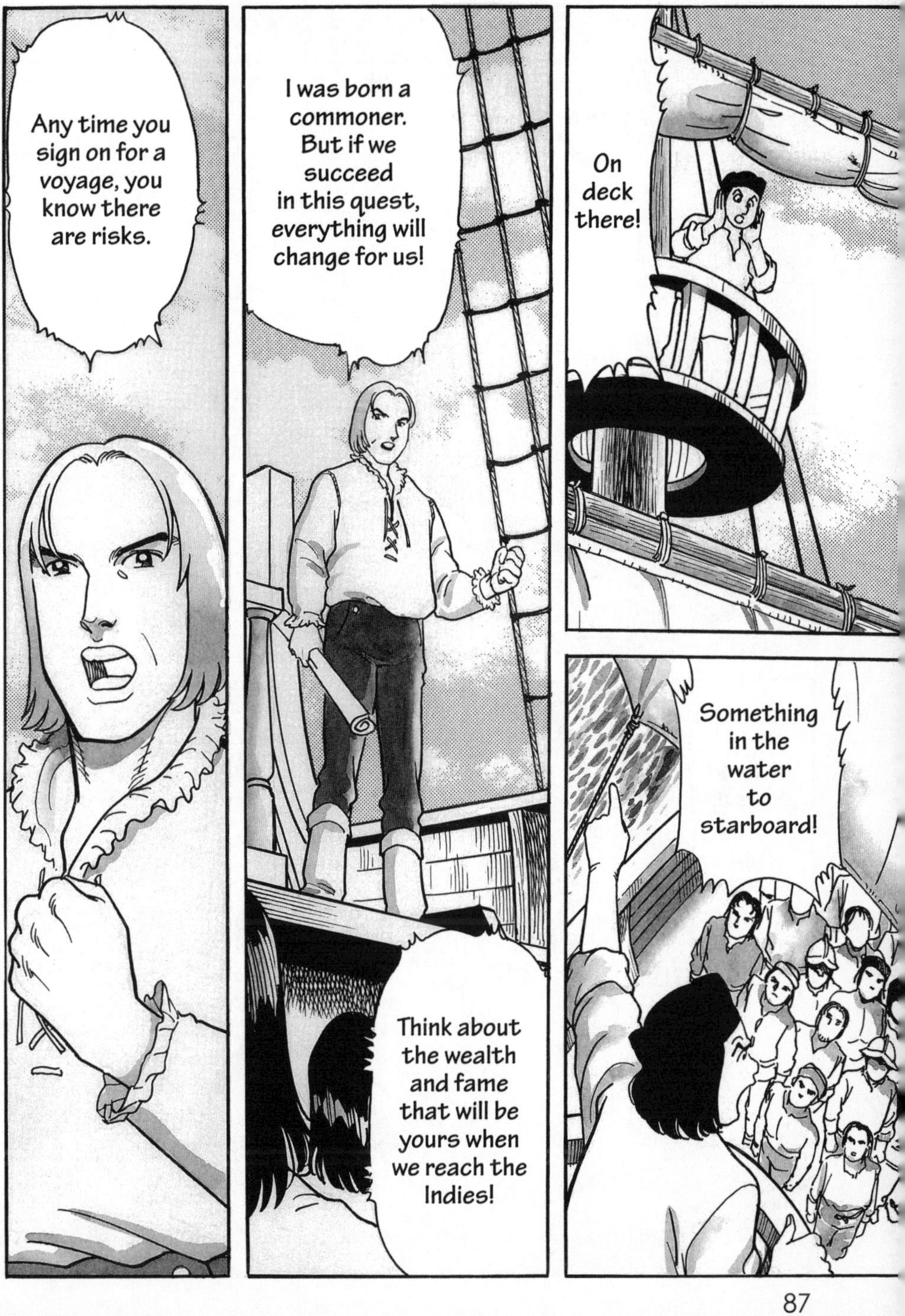

Any time you sign on for a voyage, you know there are risks.
I was born a commoner. But if we succeed in this quest, everything will change for us!
Think about the wealth and fame that will be yours when we reach the Indies!
On deck there!
Something in the water to starboard!

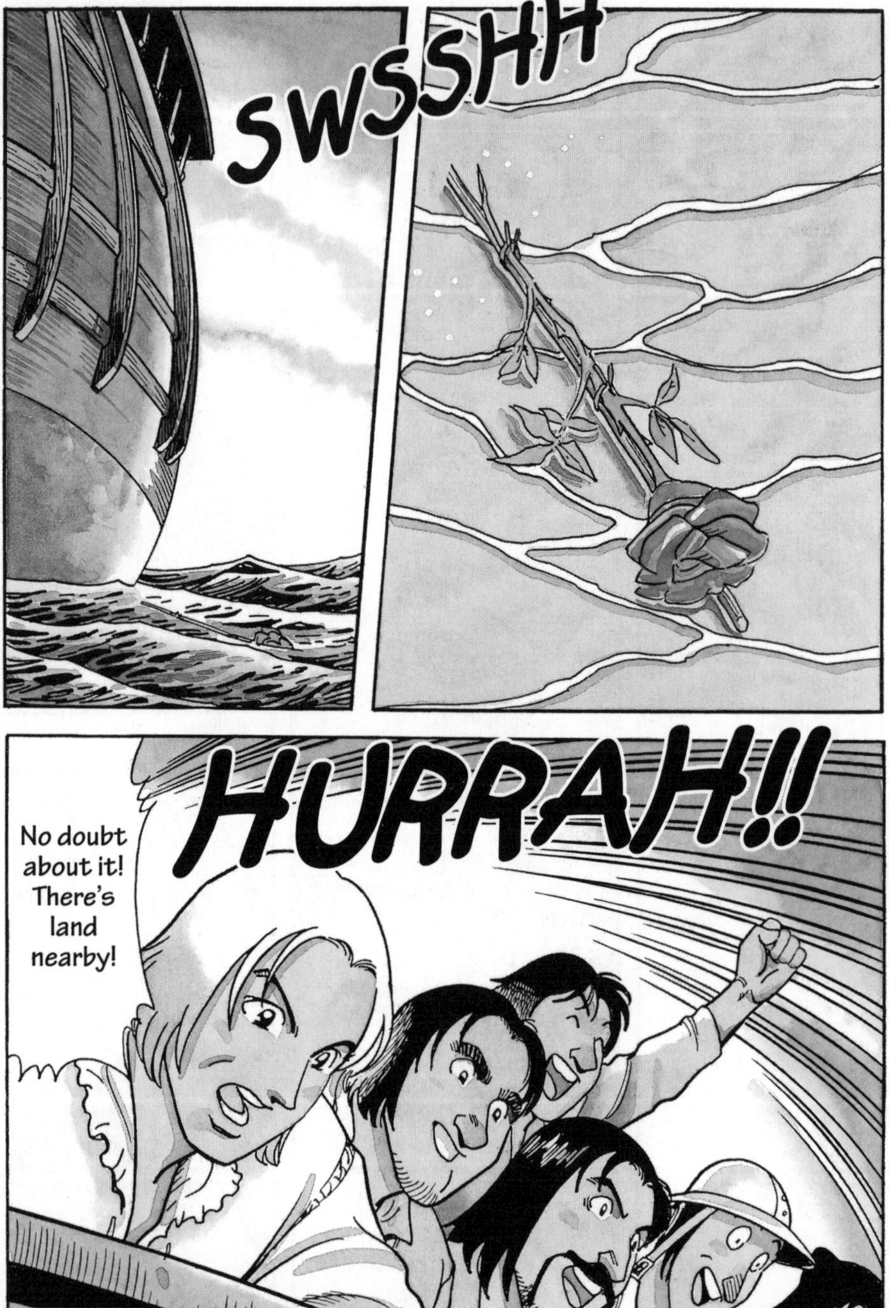
SWSSHH
HURRAH!!
No doubt about it! There's land nearby!

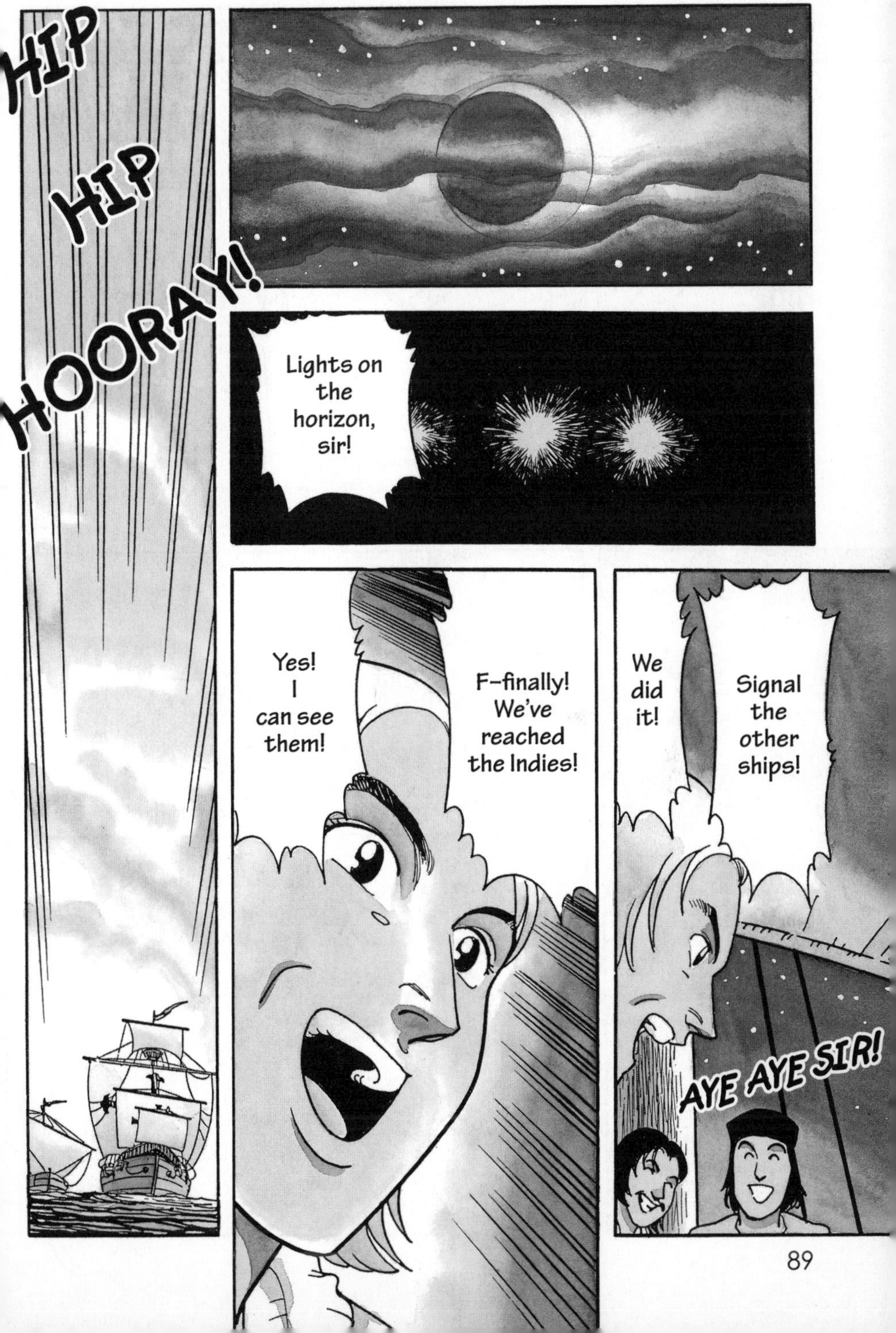
HIP
HIP
HOORAY!
Lights on the horizon, sir!
Yes! I can see them!
F-finally! We've reached the Indies!
We did it!
Signal the other ships!
AYE AYE SIR!

Chapter 5: Days of Discovery

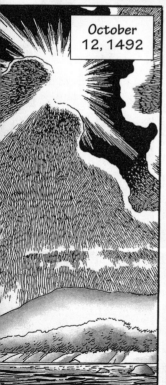

October 12, 1492

This time it really *is* real!

If this is a dream, don't let me wake up!

PINCH

How many days since we've been on dry land?

Thirty ...and six.

Wow! That long?!

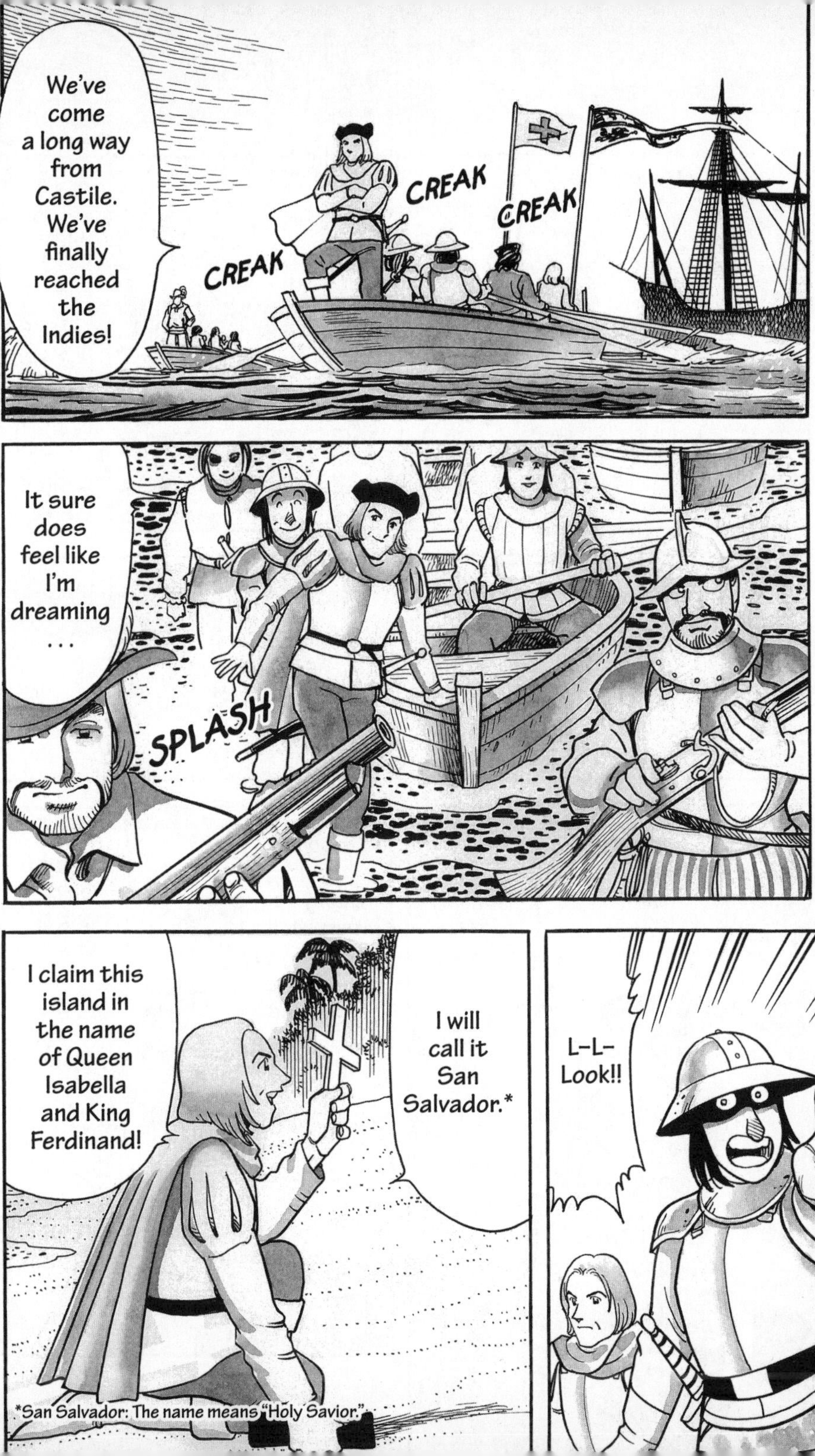
We've come a long way from Castile. We've finally reached the Indies!
CREAK
CREAK
CREAK
It sure does feel like I'm dreaming . . .
SPLASH
I claim this island in the name of Queen Isabella and King Ferdinand!
I will call it San Salvador.*
*San Salvador: The name means "Holy Savior."
L-L-Look!!

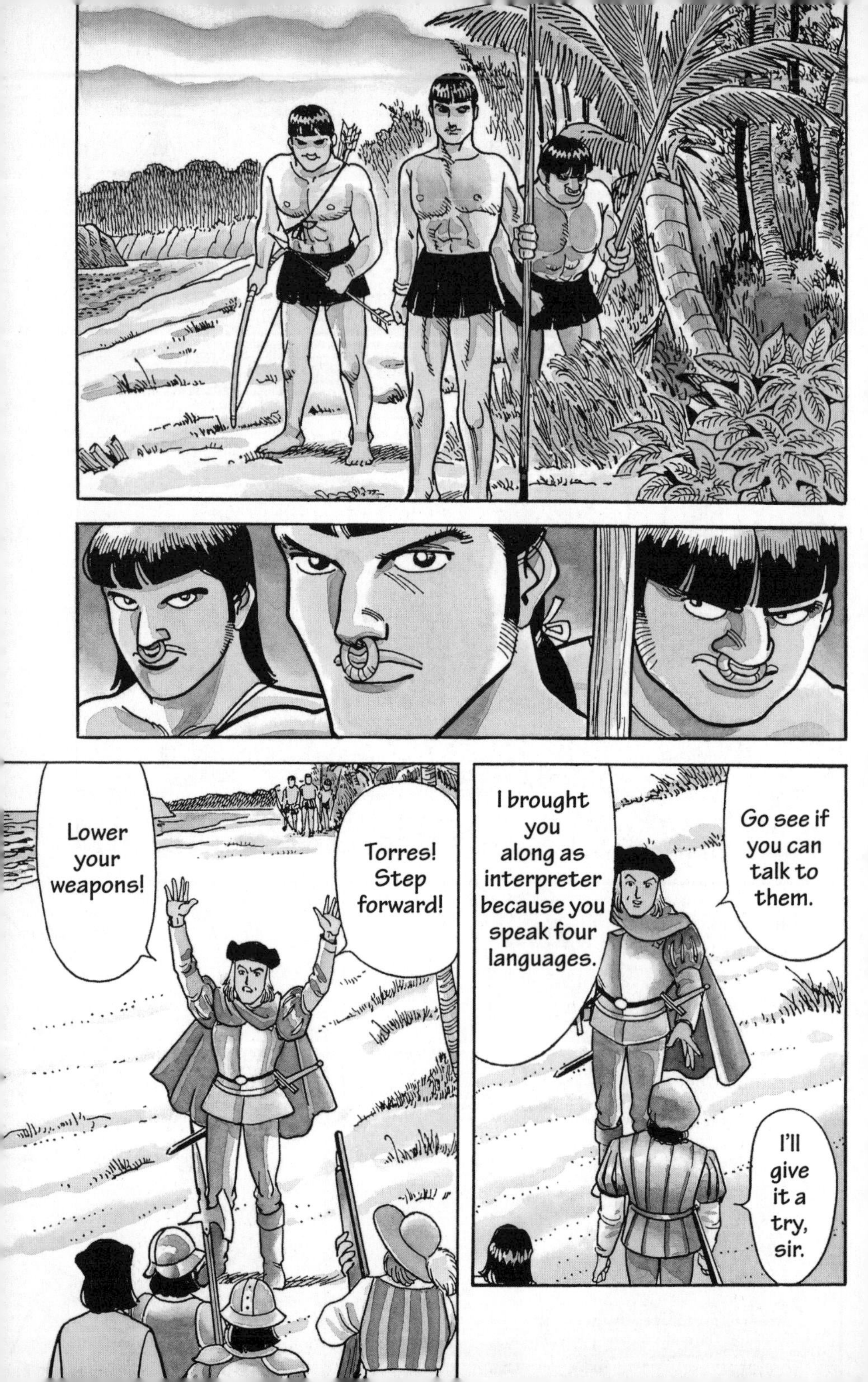
Lower your weapons!
Torres! Step forward!
I brought you along as interpreter because you speak four languages.
Go see if you can talk to them.
I'll give it a try, sir.

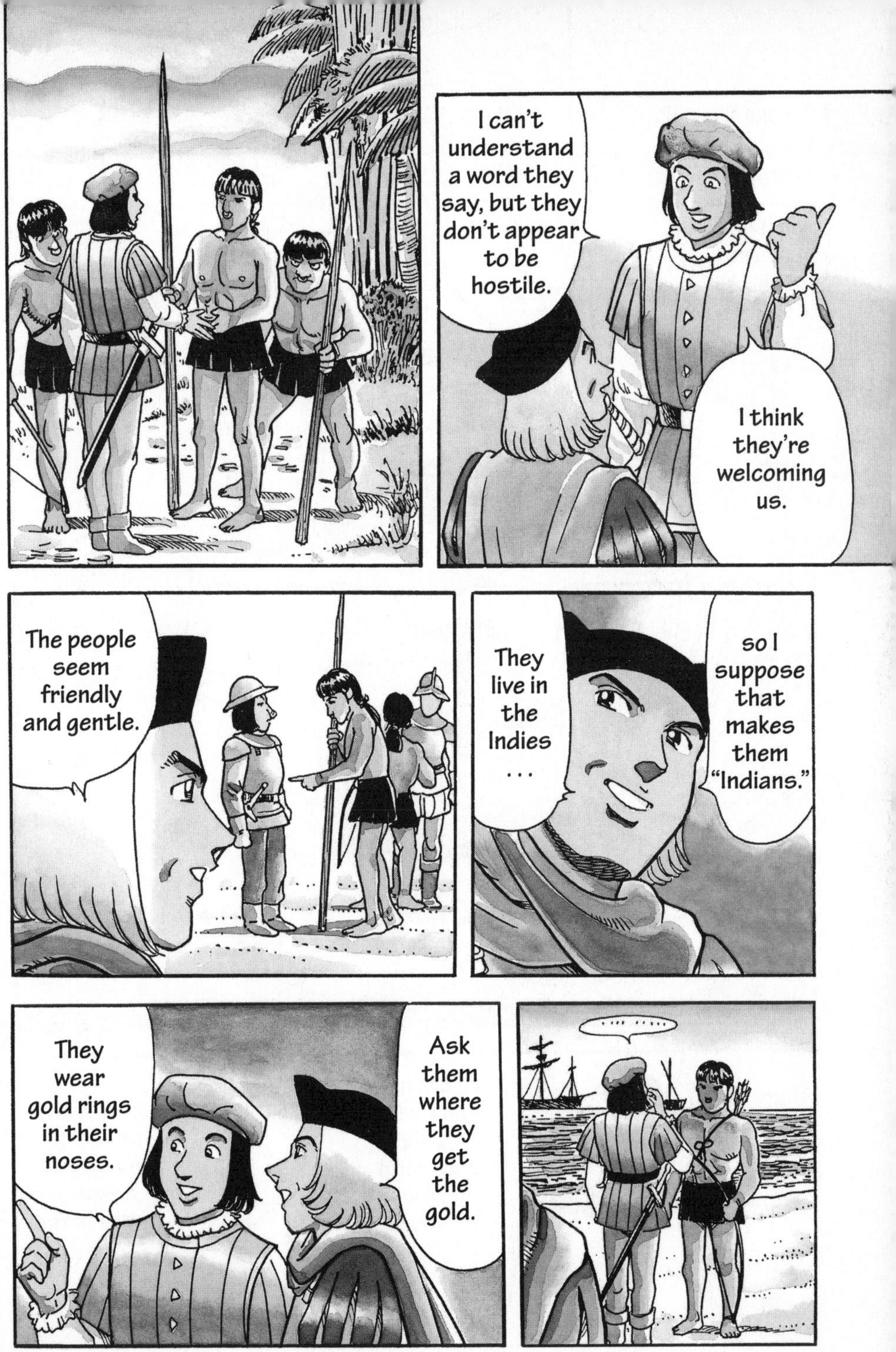
I can't understand a word they say, but they don't appear to be hostile.
I think they're welcoming us.
The people seem friendly and gentle.
They live in the Indies . . .
so I suppose that makes them "Indians."
They wear gold rings in their noses.
Ask them where they get the gold.
. . . .

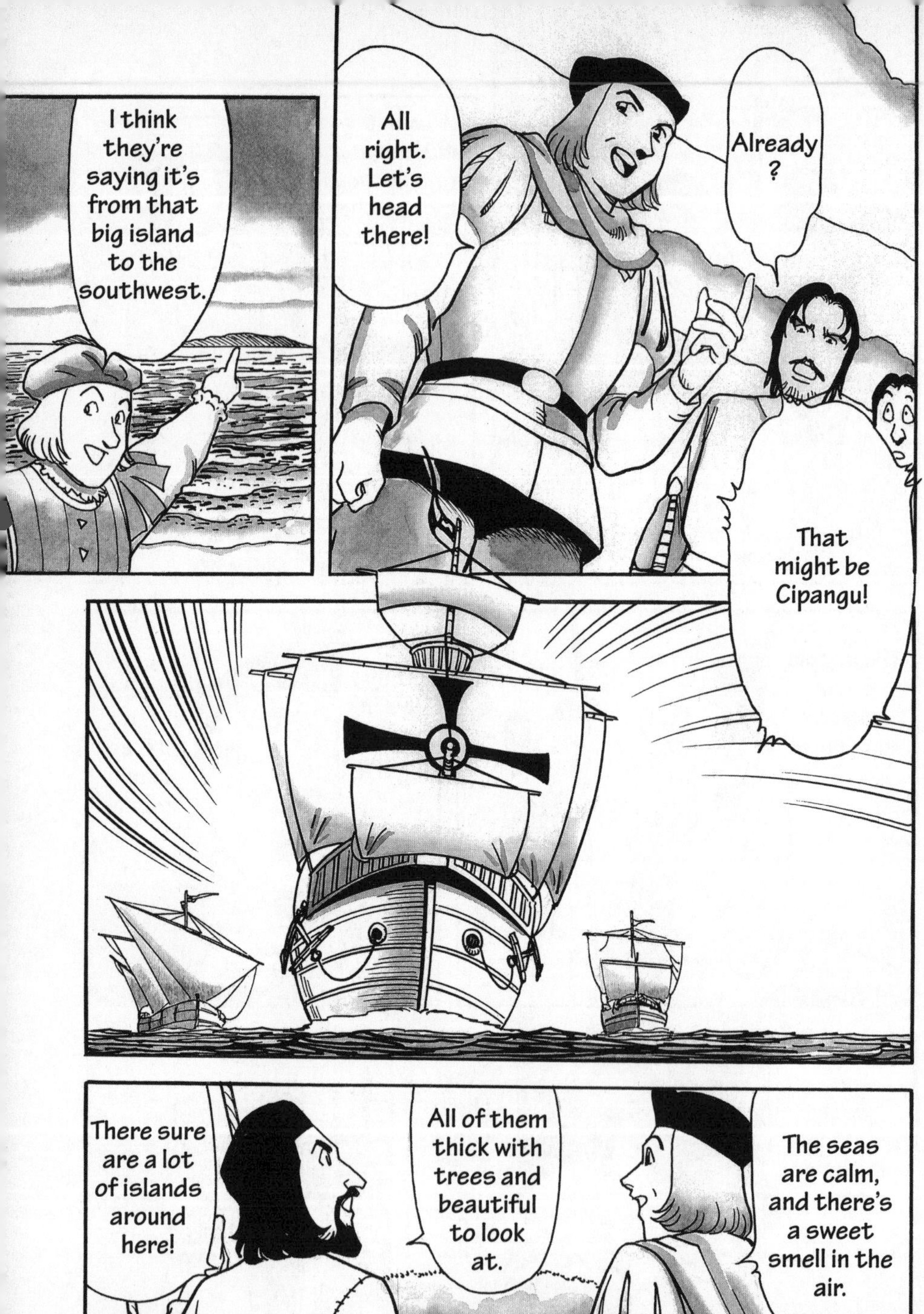
I think they're saying it's from that big island to the southwest.
All right. Let's head there!
Already?
That might be Cipangu!
There sure are a lot of islands around here!
All of them thick with trees and beautiful to look at.
The seas are calm, and there's a sweet smell in the air.

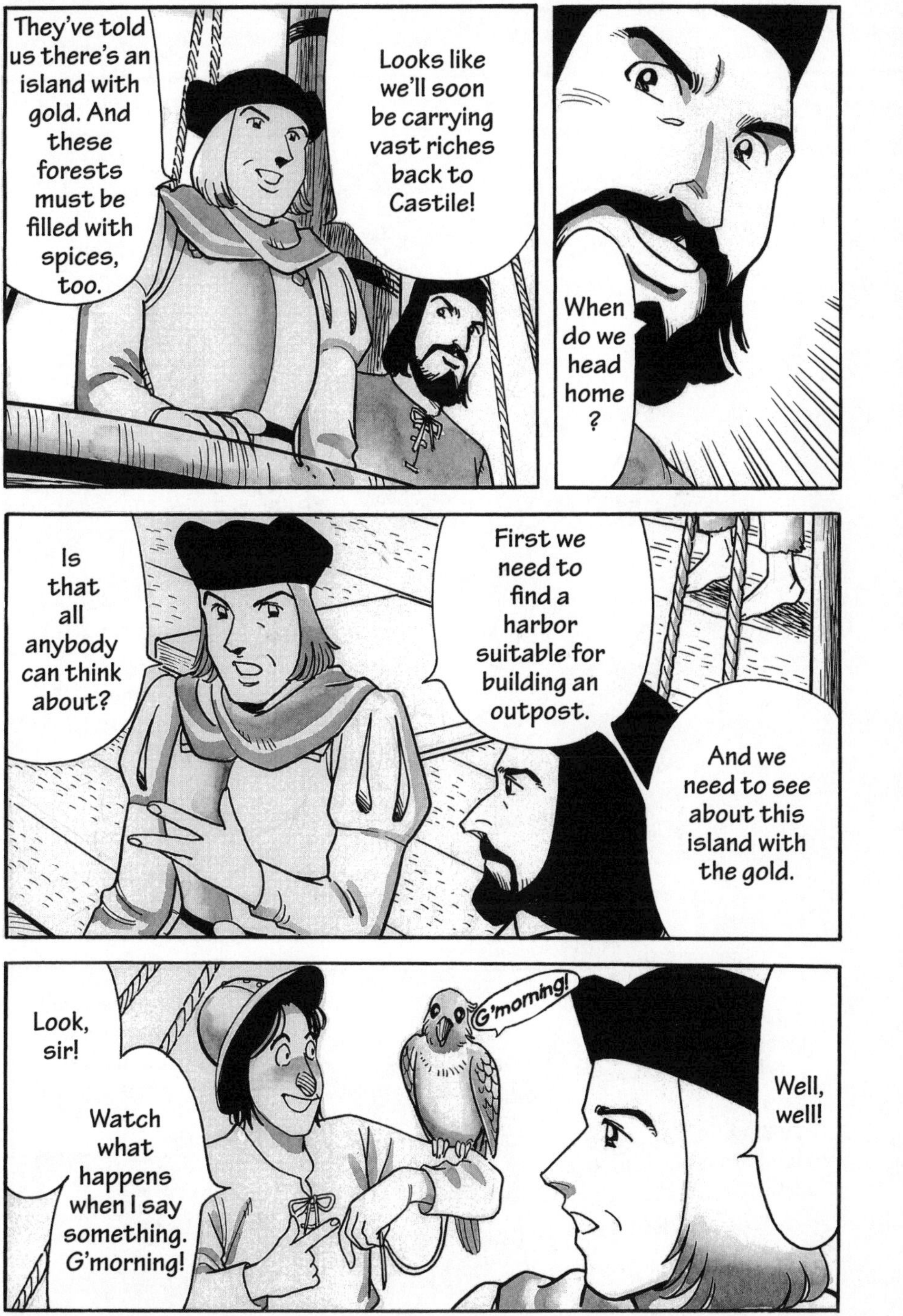
They've told us there's an island with gold. And these forests must be filled with spices, too.
Looks like we'll soon be carrying vast riches back to Castile!
When do we head home?
Is that all anybody can think about?
First we need to find a harbor suitable for building an outpost.
And we need to see about this island with the gold.
Look, sir!
G'morning!
Watch what happens when I say something. G'morning!
Well, well!

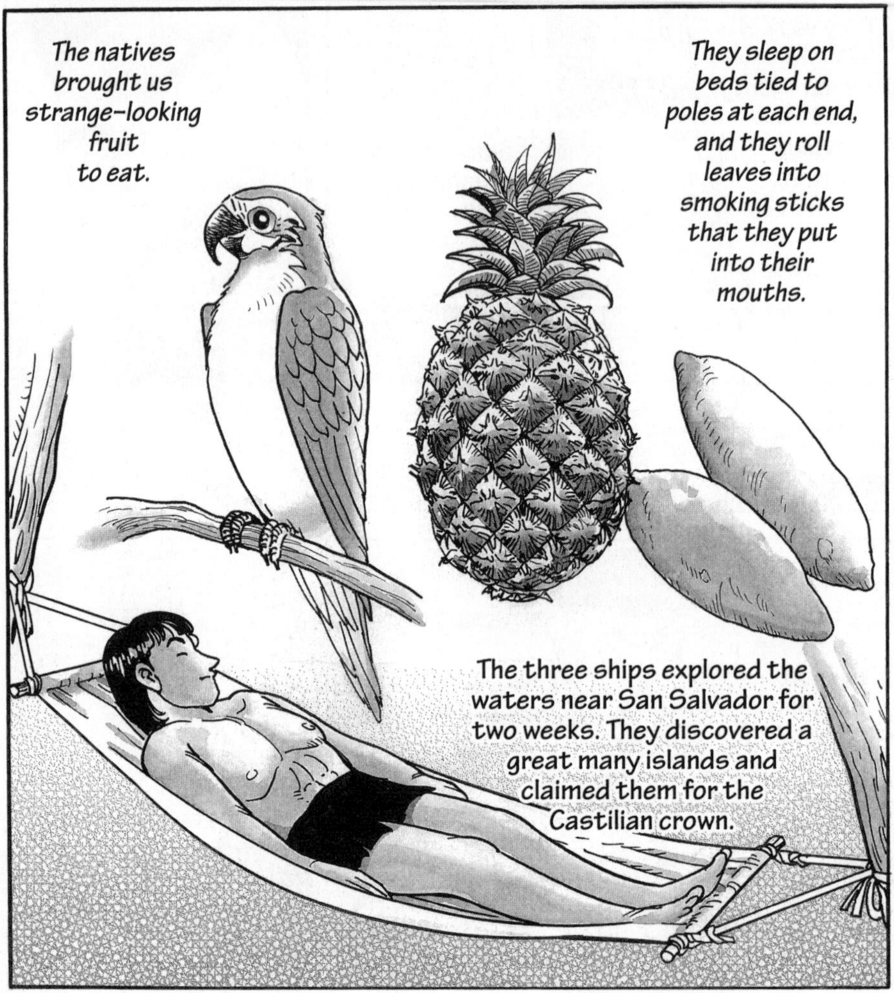
The natives brought us strange-looking fruit to eat.
They sleep on beds tied to poles at each end, and they roll leaves into smoking sticks that they put into their mouths.
The three ships explored the waters near San Salvador for two weeks. They discovered a great many islands and claimed them for the Castilian crown.

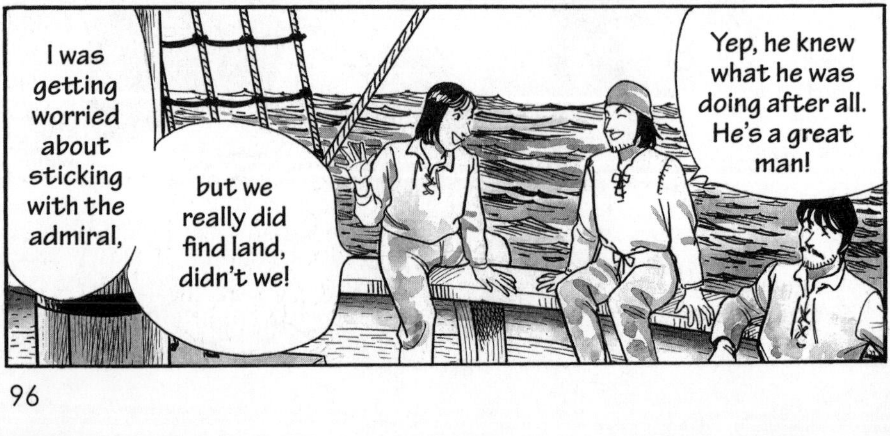
I was getting worried about sticking with the admiral,
but we really did find land, didn't we!
Yep, he knew what he was doing after all. He's a great man!

And a great navigator, that's for sure!

We've seen plenty of shallows and changing currents, but he always knows where to steer.

He wasn't just talking big to get us to come along, was he!

October 28

This island seems to stretch a long way east and west.

And it has natural harbors with waters deep enough for anchoring ships.

I'll name it in honor of Crown Prince Juan,

and call it Isla Juana.*

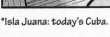

*Isla Juana: today's Cuba.

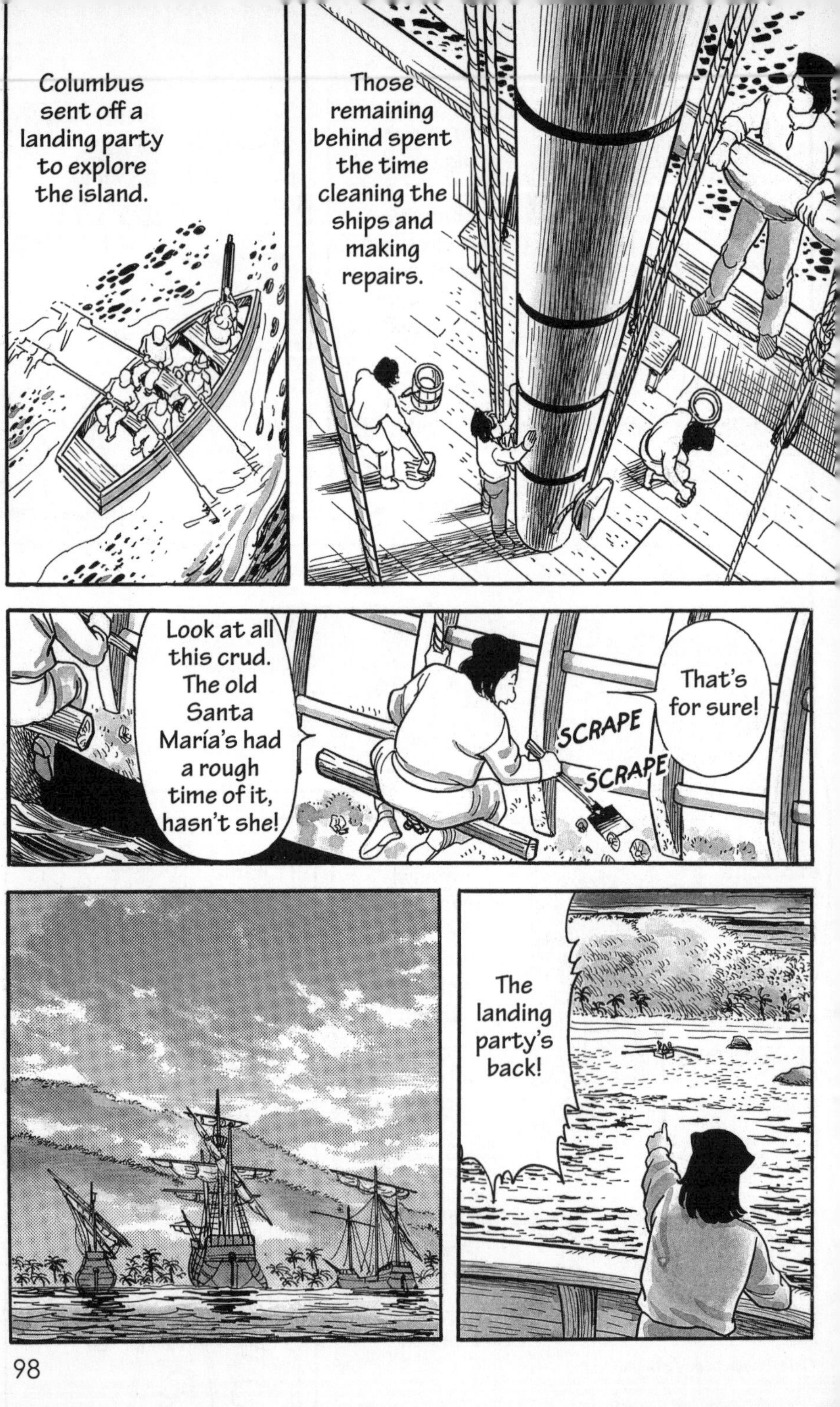
Columbus sent off a landing party to explore the island.
Those remaining behind spent the time cleaning the ships and making repairs.
Look at all this crud. The old Santa María's had a rough time of it, hasn't she!
SCRAPE
SCRAPE
That's for sure!
The landing party's back!

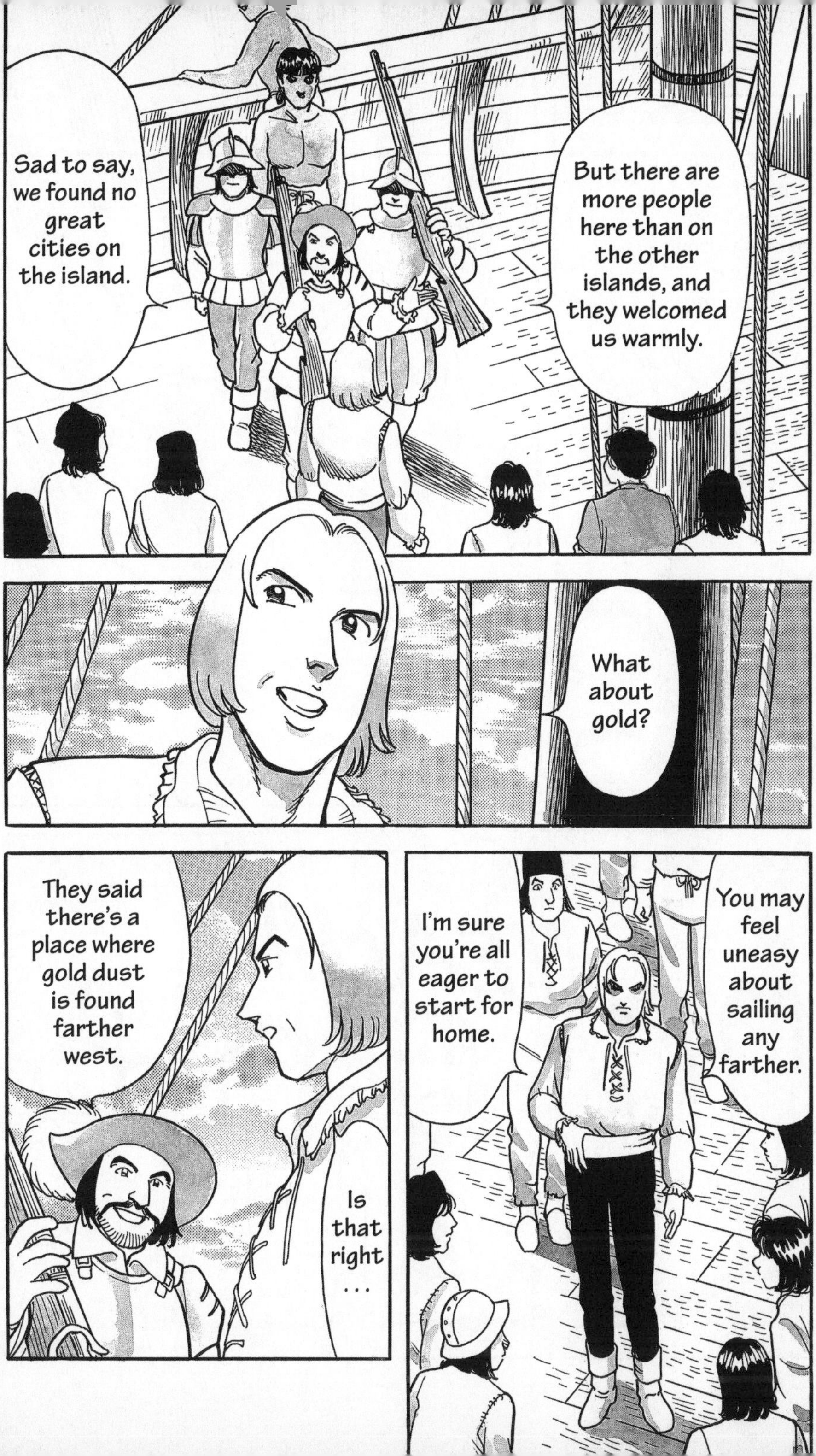
Sad to say, we found no great cities on the island.
But there are more people here than on the other islands, and they welcomed us warmly.
What about gold?
They said there's a place where gold dust is found farther west.
Is that right . . .
I'm sure you're all eager to start for home.
You may feel uneasy about sailing any farther.

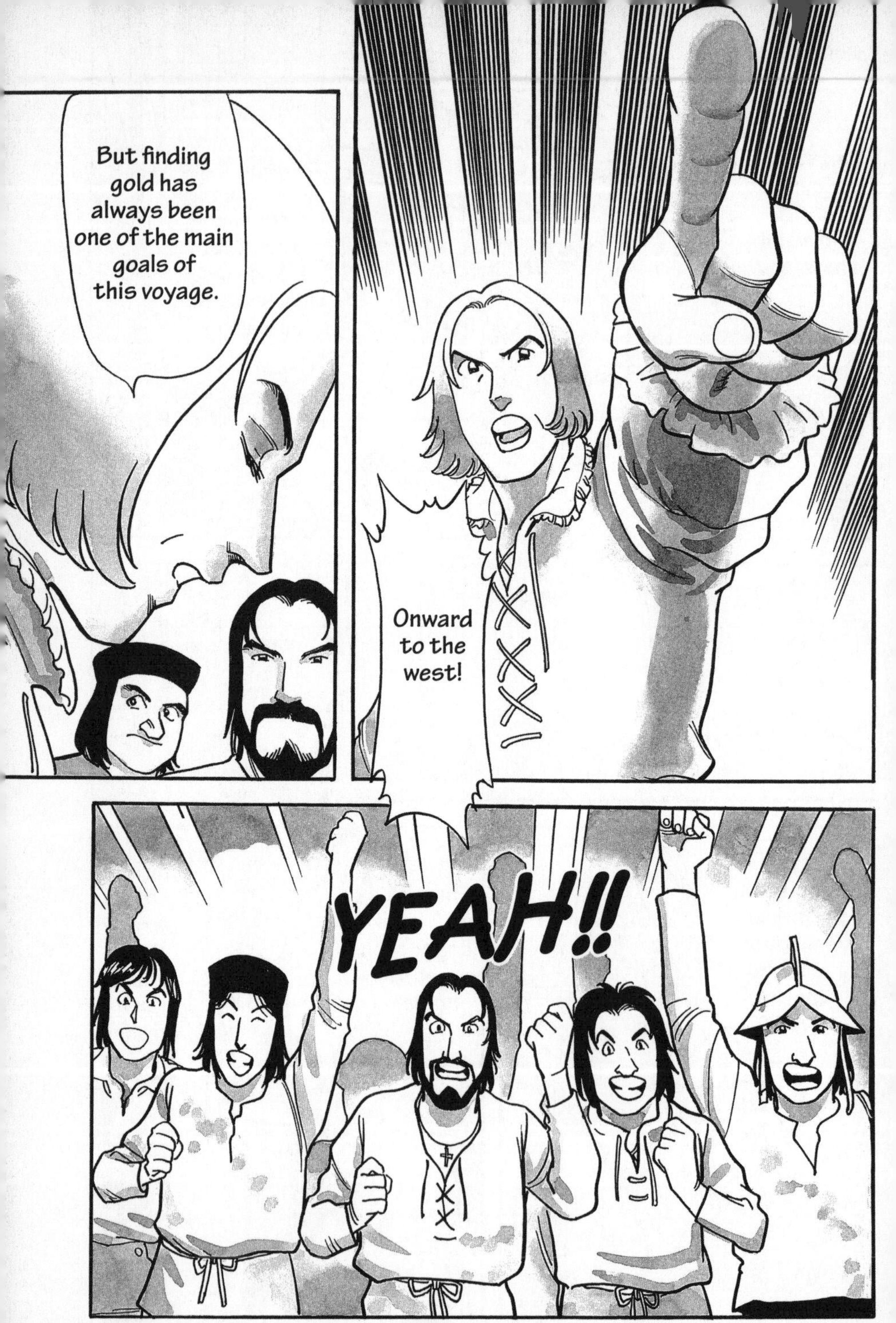
But finding gold has always been one of the main goals of this voyage.
Onward to the west!
YEAH!!

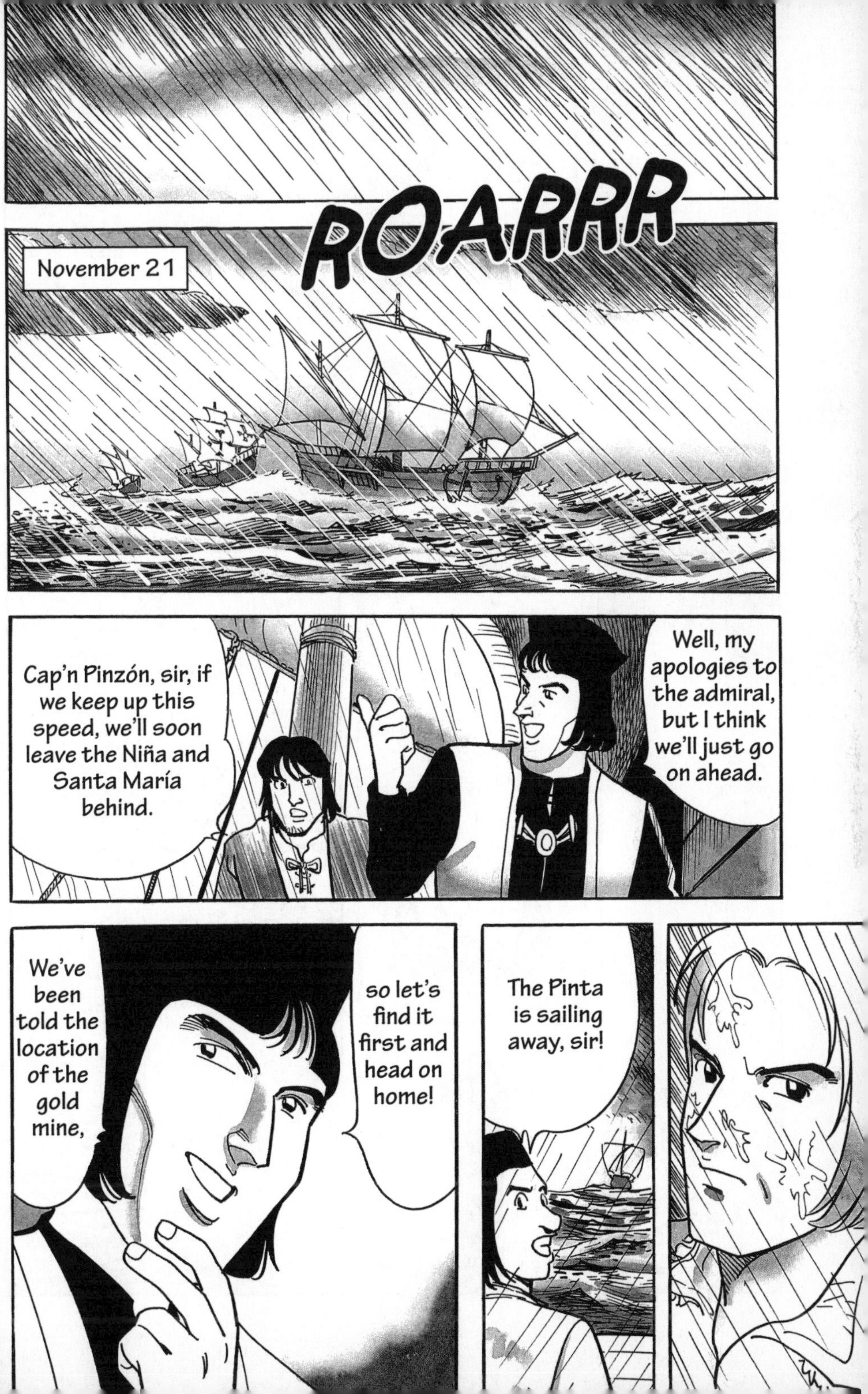
ROARRR
November 21
Cap'n Pinzón, sir, if we keep up this speed, we'll soon leave the Niña and Santa María behind.
Well, my apologies to the admiral, but I think we'll just go on ahead.
We've been told the location of the gold mine,
so let's find it first and head on home!
The Pinta is sailing away, sir!

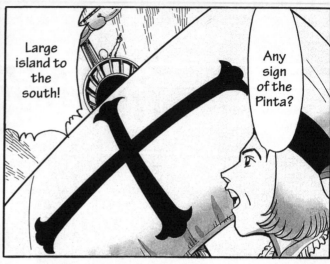

Large island to the south!

Any sign of the Pinta?

She's still missing, sir!

We'll anchor here to repair the damage from the storm.

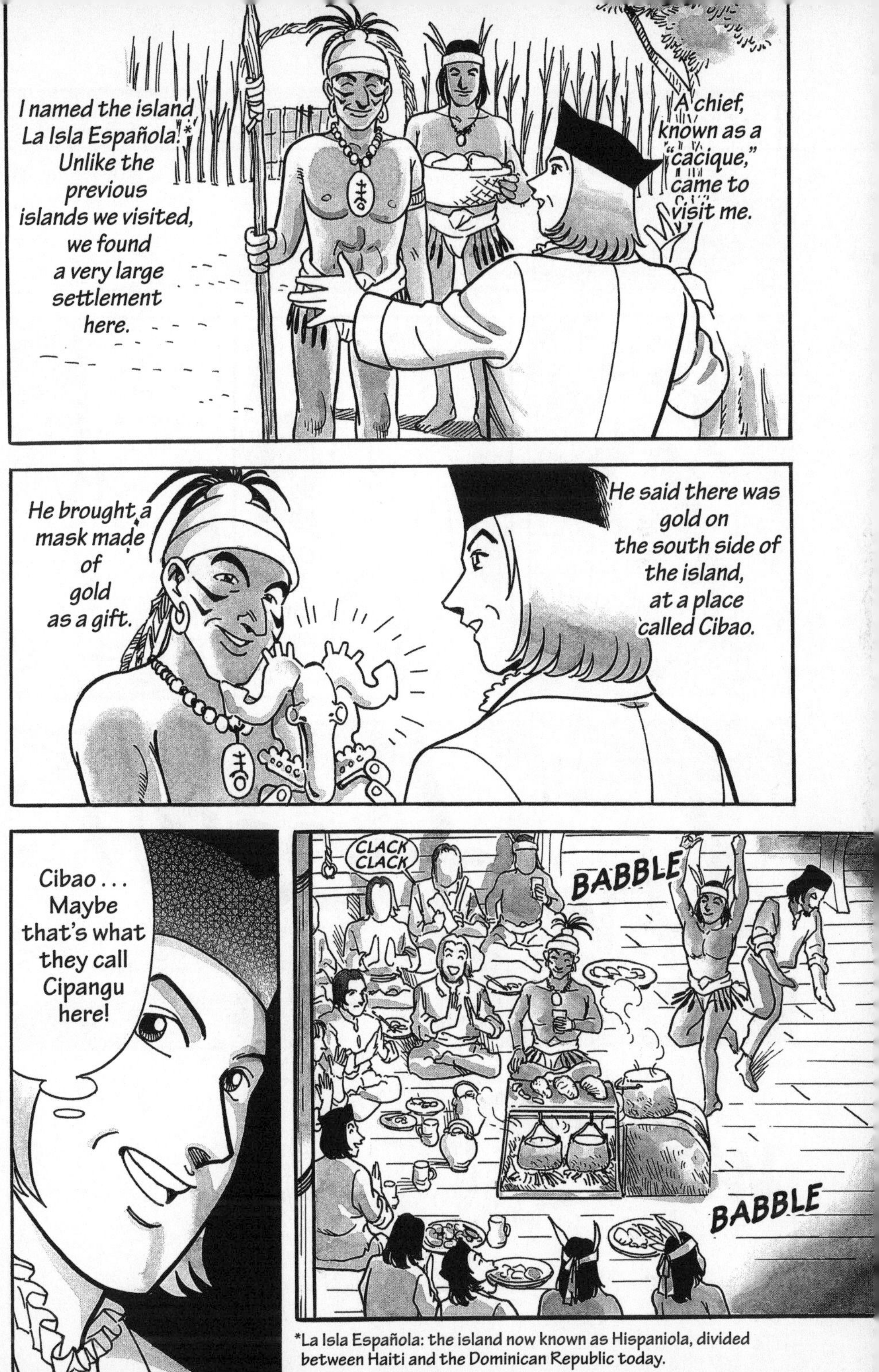
I named the island La Isla Española!* Unlike the previous islands we visited, we found a very large settlement here.
A chief, known as a "cacique," came to visit me.
He brought a mask made of gold as a gift.
He said there was gold on the south side of the island, at a place called Cibao.
Cibao . . . Maybe that's what they call Cipangu here!
CLACK CLACK
BABBLE
BABBLE

*La Isla Española: the island now known as Hispaniola, divided between Haiti and the Dominican Republic today.

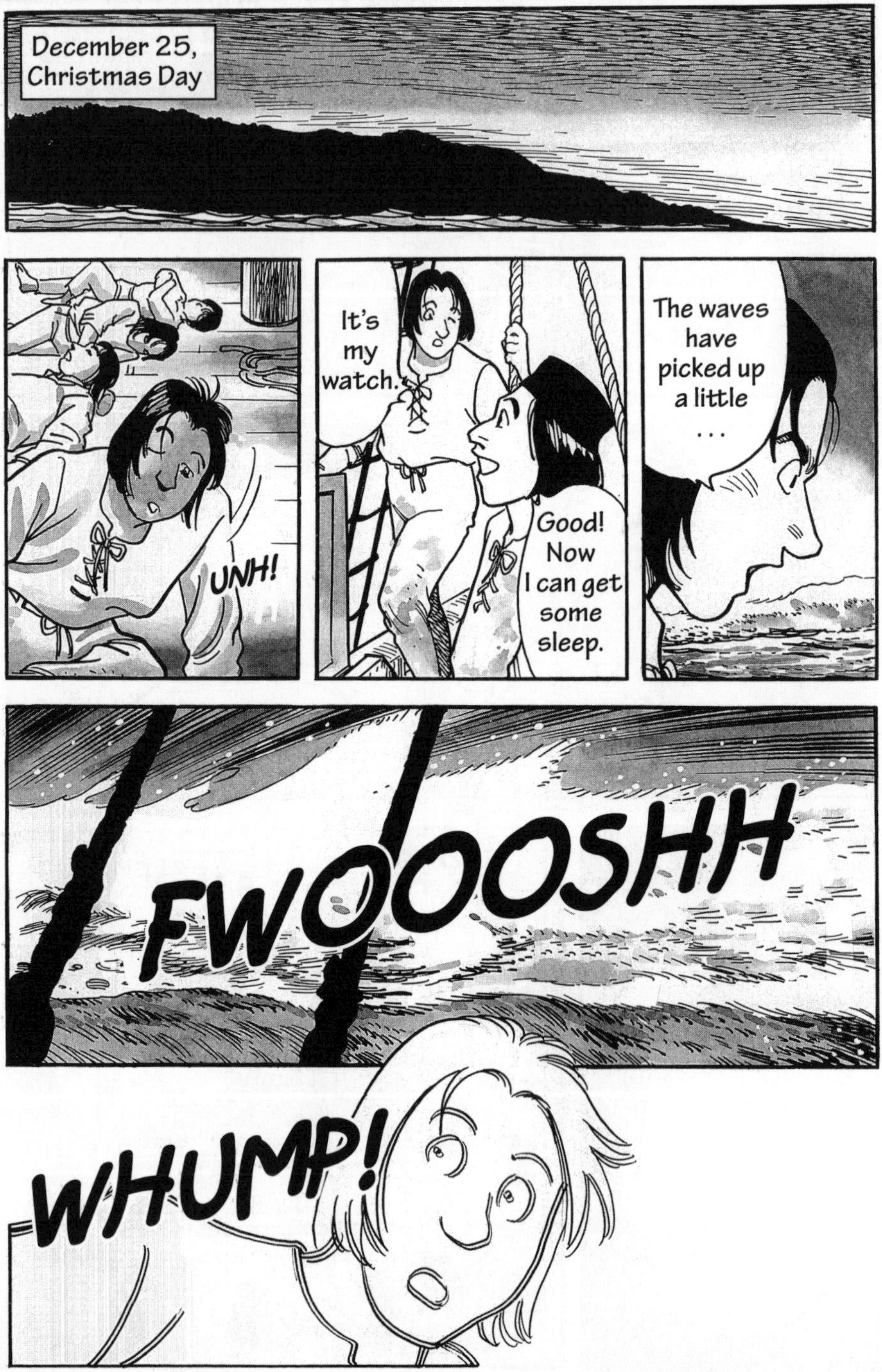
December 25, Christmas Day
UNH!
It's my watch.
Good! Now I can get some sleep.
The waves have picked up a little . . .
FWOOOSHH
WHUMP!

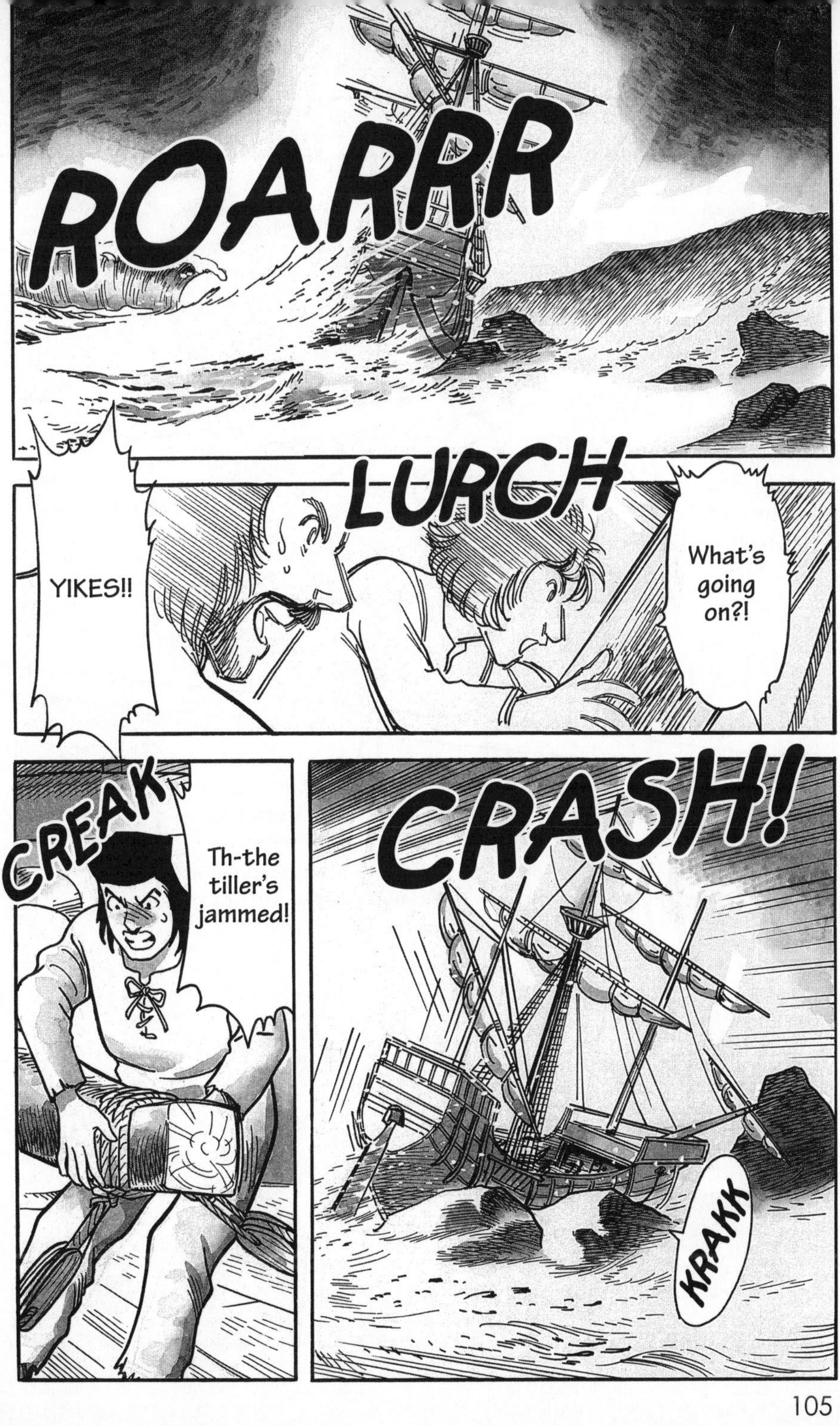
ROARRR
YIKES!!
LURCH
What's going on?!
CREAK
Th-the tiller's jammed!
CRASH!
KRAKK

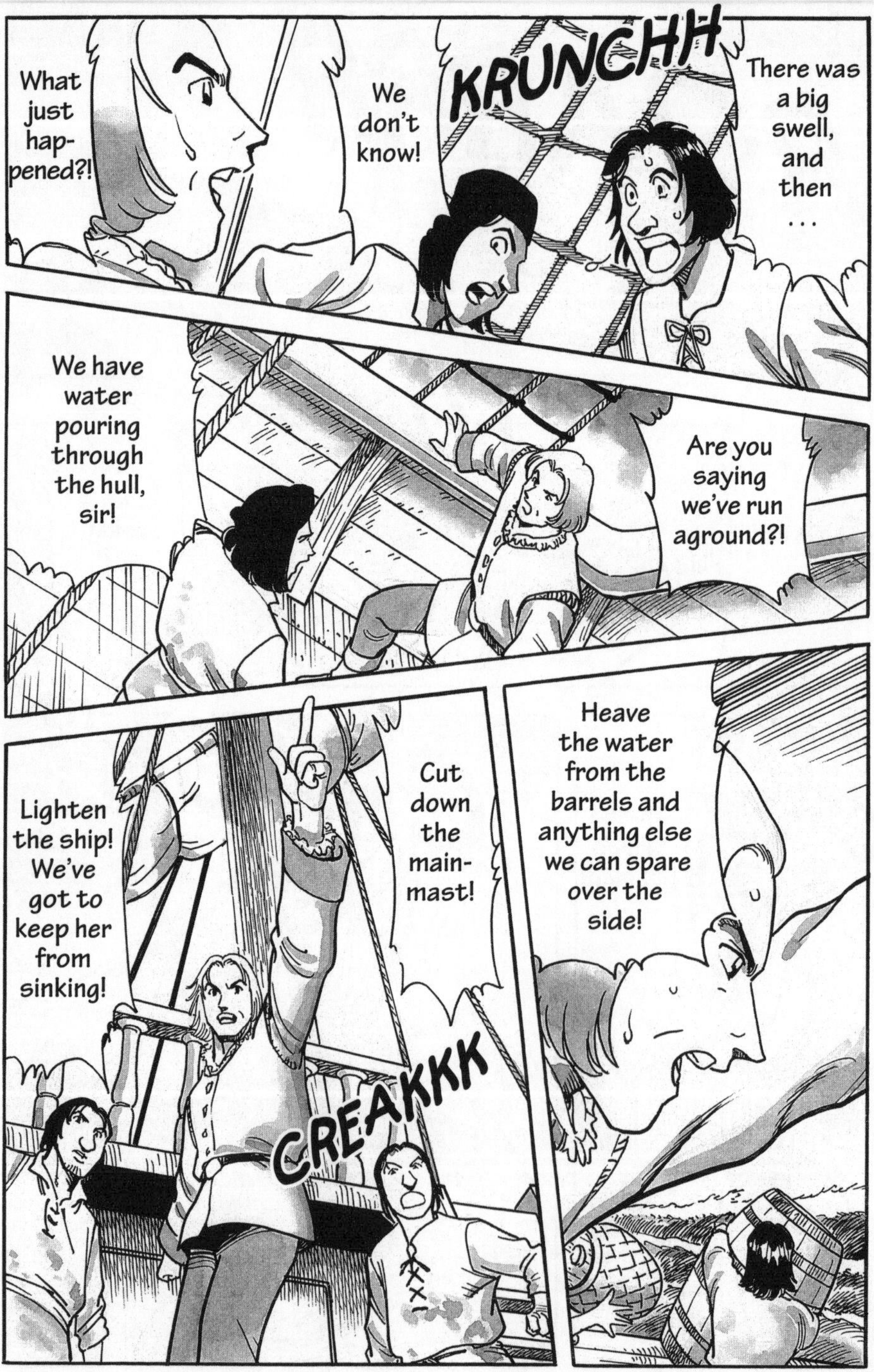
What just hap-pened?!
We don't know!
KRUNCHH
There was a big swell, and then . . .
We have water pouring through the hull, sir!
Are you saying we've run aground?!
Lighten the ship! We've got to keep her from sinking!
Cut down the main-mast!
CREAKKK
Heave the water from the barrels and anything else we can spare over the side!

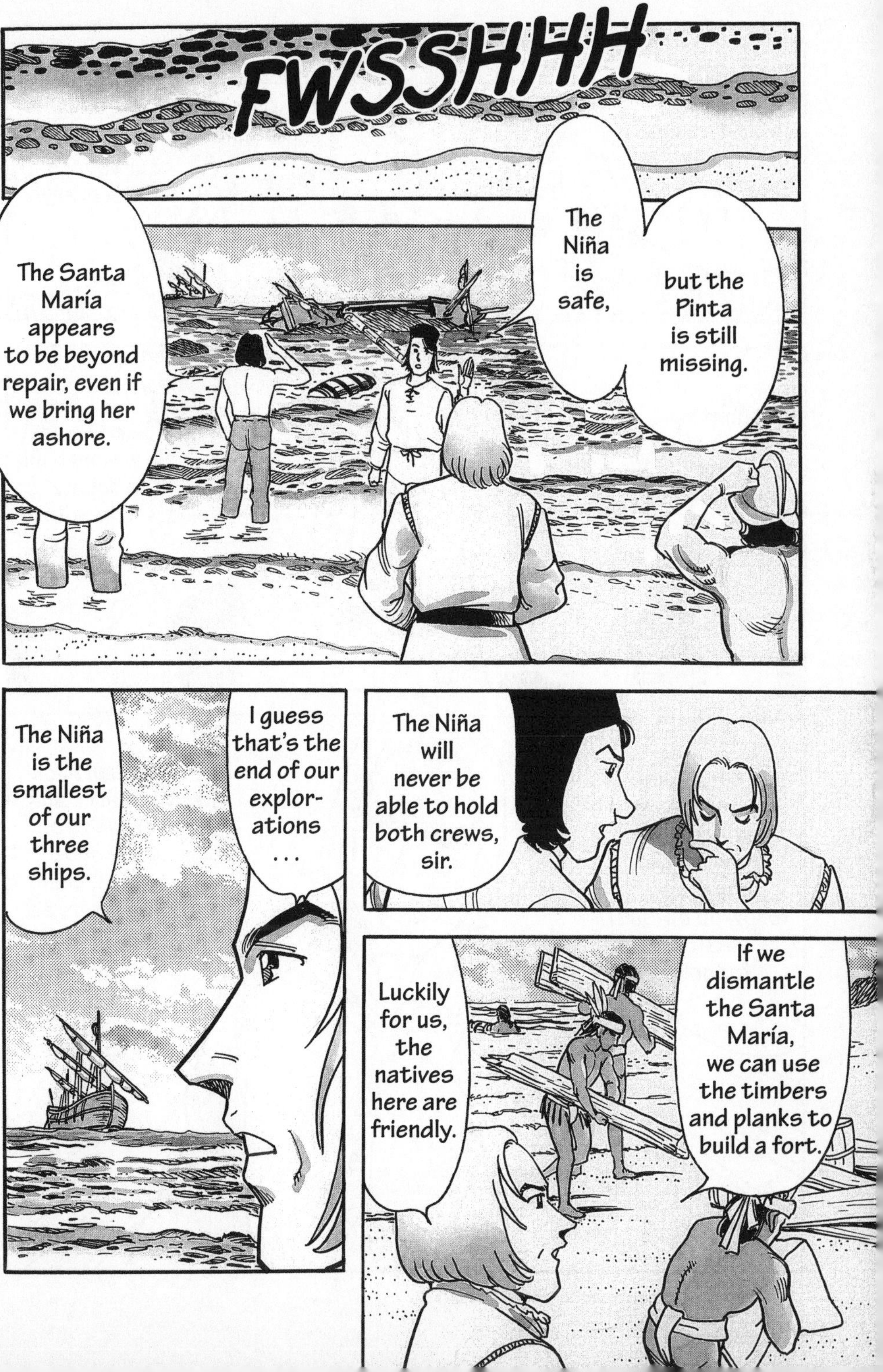
FWSSHHH
The Santa María appears to be beyond repair, even if we bring her ashore.
The Niña is safe,
but the Pinta is still missing.
The Niña is the smallest of our three ships.
I guess that's the end of our explorations . . .
The Niña will never be able to hold both crews, sir.
Luckily for us, the natives here are friendly.
If we dismantle the Santa María, we can use the timbers and planks to build a fort.

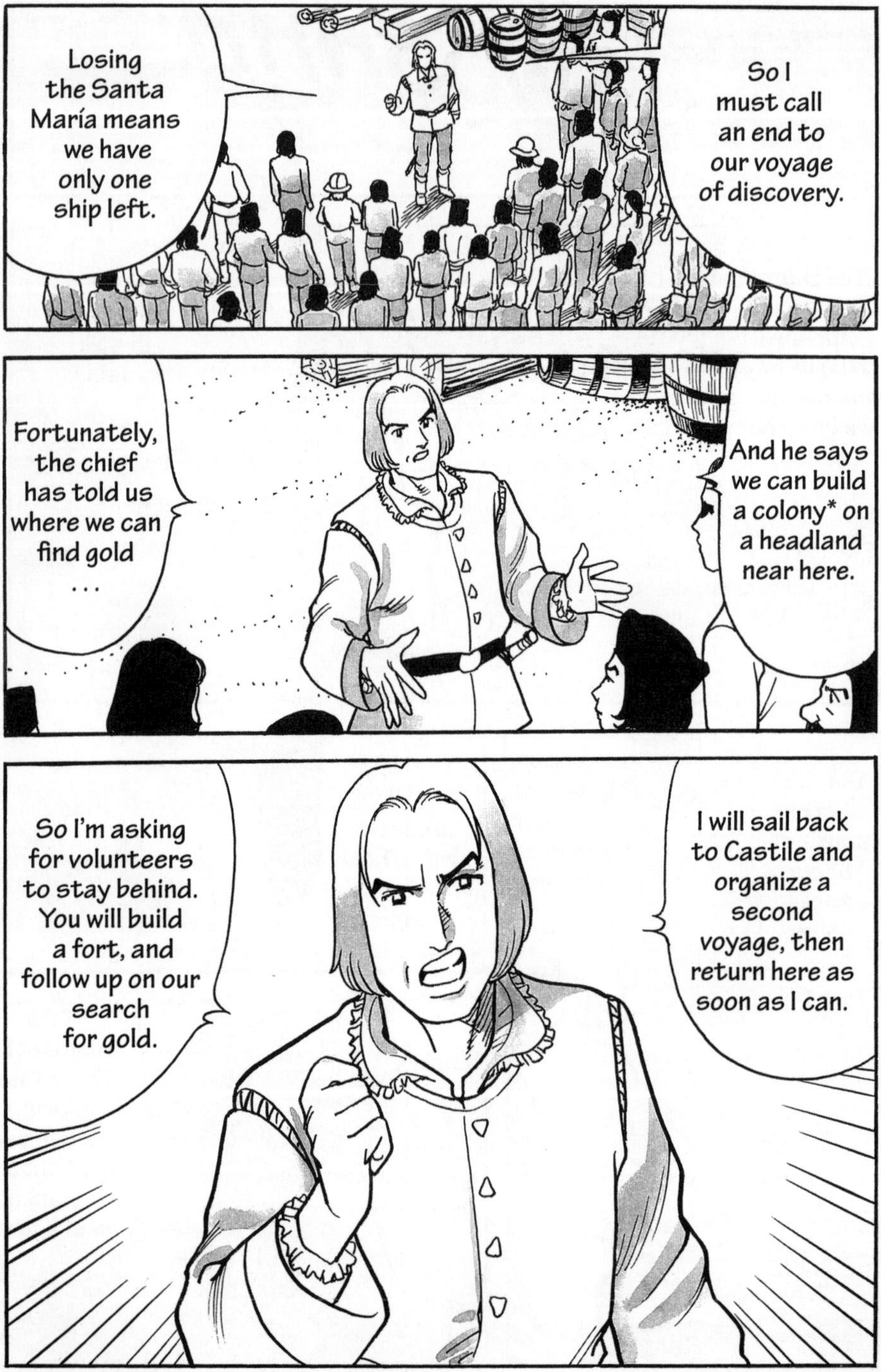

Losing the Santa María means we have only one ship left.
So I must call an end to our voyage of discovery.
Fortunately, the chief has told us where we can find gold . . .
And he says we can build a colony* on a headland near here.
So I'm asking for volunteers to stay behind. You will build a fort, and follow up on our search for gold.
I will sail back to Castile and organize a second voyage, then return here as soon as I can.

*Colony: a settlement on foreign soil.

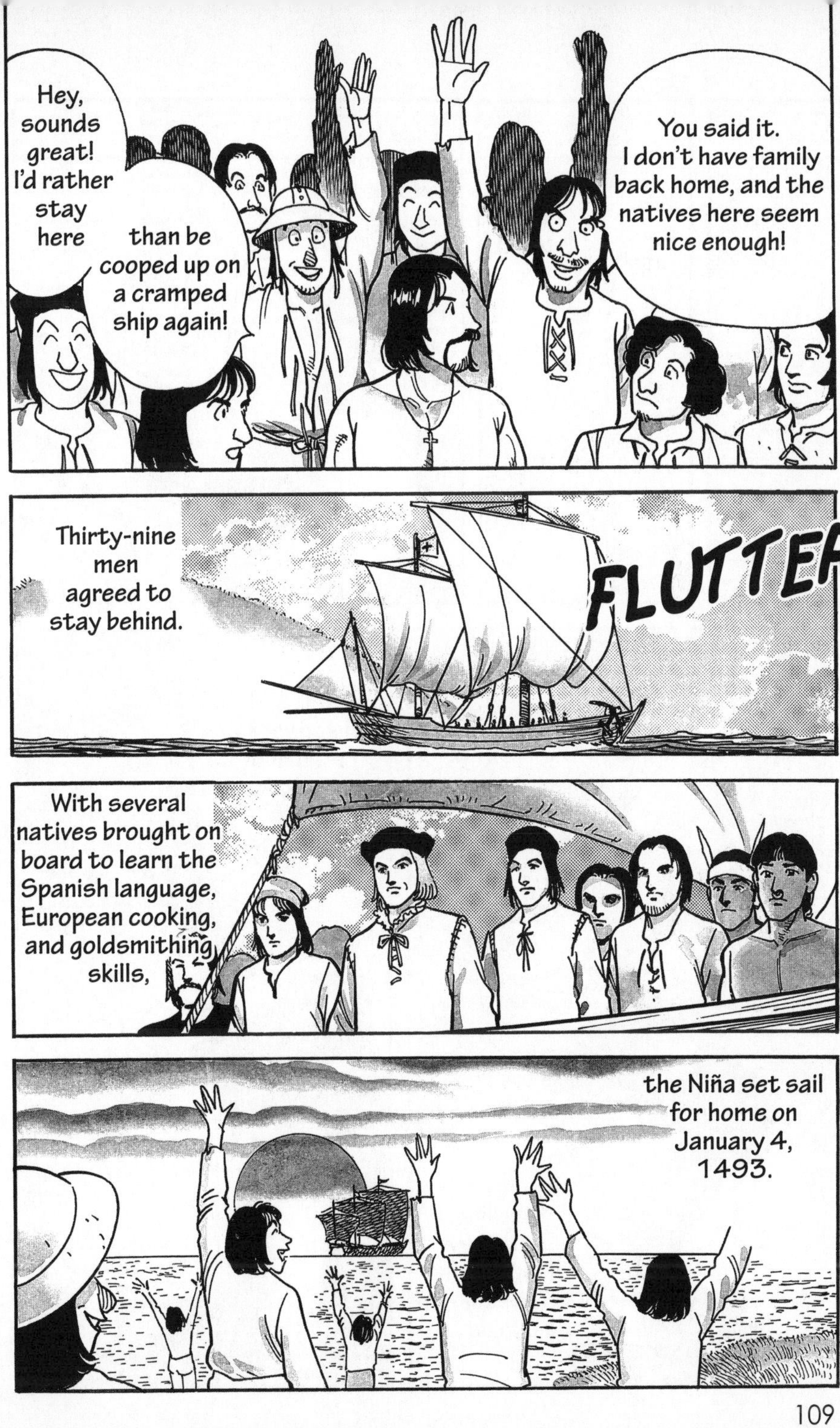
Hey, sounds great! I'd rather stay here
than be cooped up on a cramped ship again!
You said it. I don't have family back home, and the natives here seem nice enough!
Thirty-nine men agreed to stay behind.
FLUTTER
With several natives brought on board to learn the Spanish language, European cooking, and goldsmithing skills,
the Niña set sail for home on January 4, 1493.

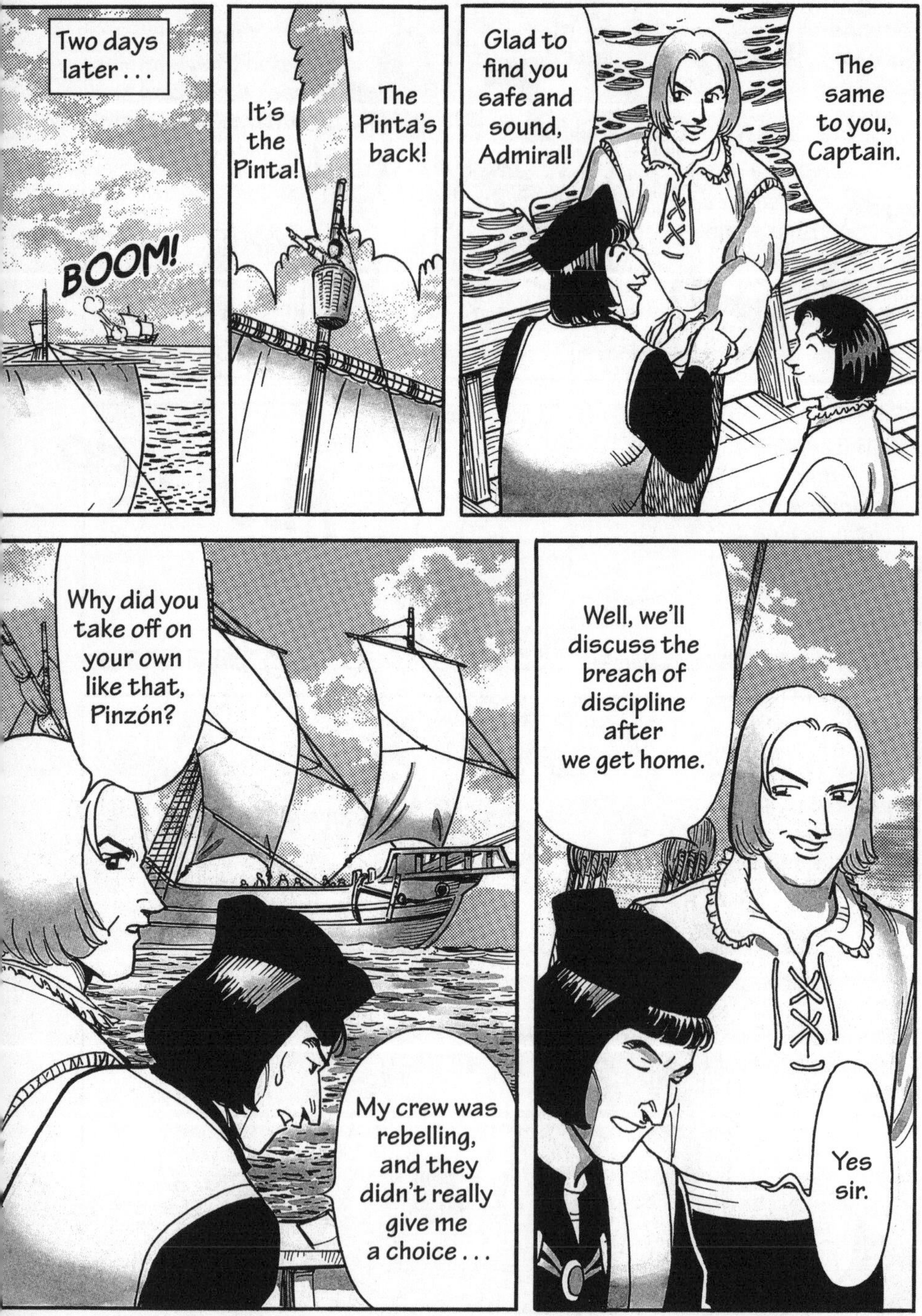
Two days later . . .
BOOM!
It's the Pinta!
The Pinta's back!
Glad to find you safe and sound, Admiral!
The same to you, Captain.
Why did you take off on your own like that, Pinzón?
My crew was rebelling, and they didn't really give me a choice . . .
Well, we'll discuss the breach of discipline after we get home.
Yes sir.

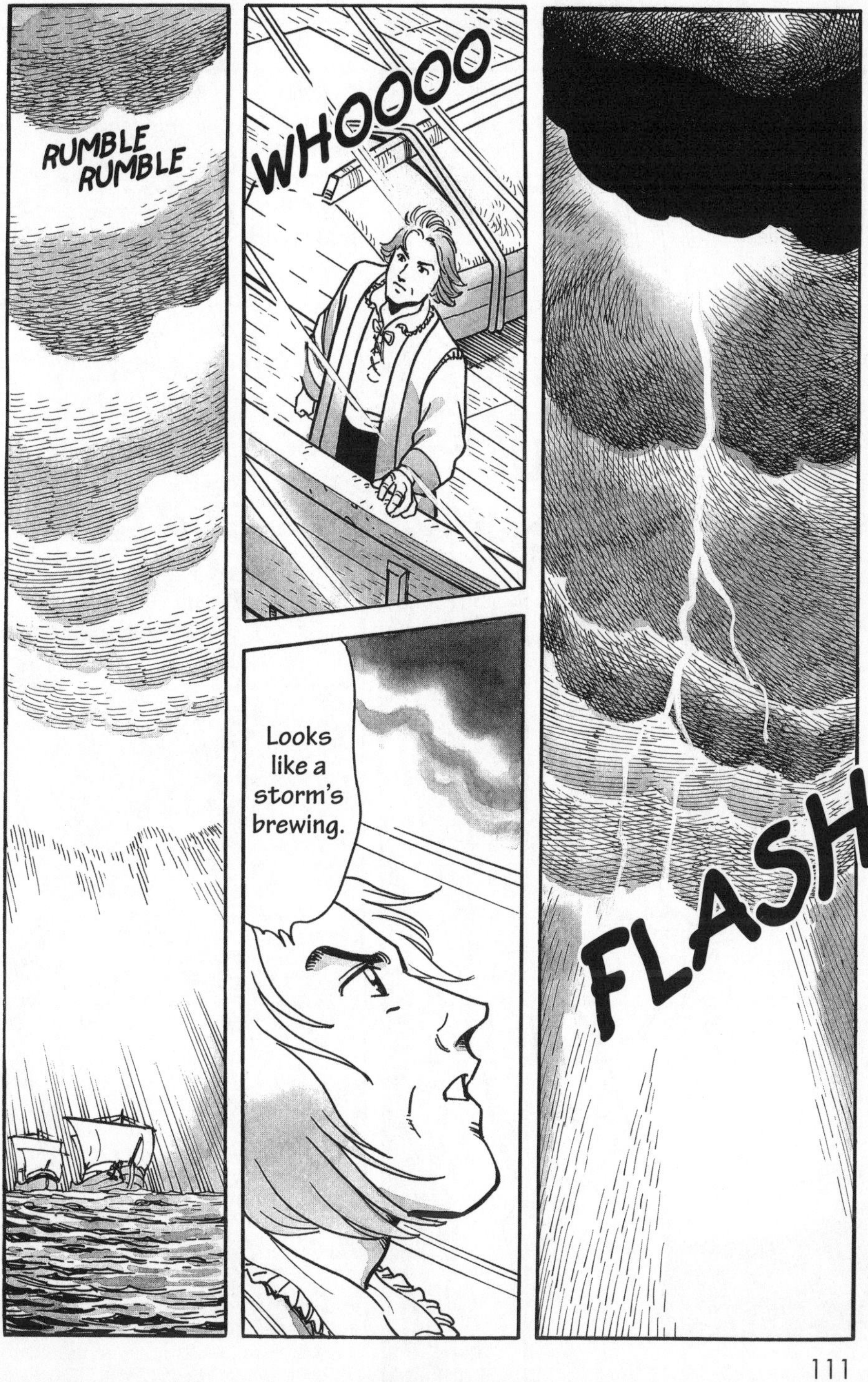
RUMBLE RUMBLE
WHOOOO
Looks like a storm's brewing.
FLASH

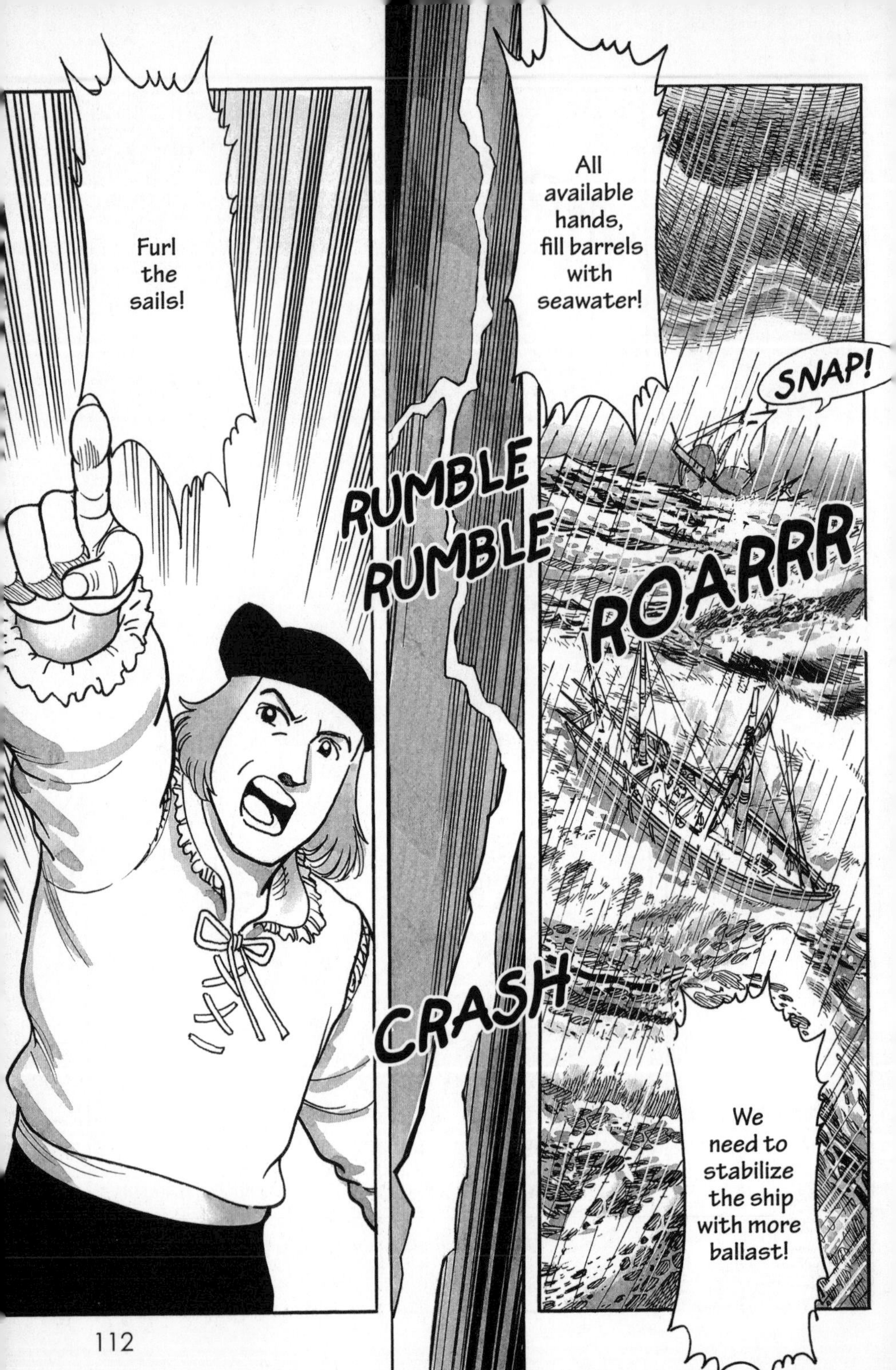

Furl the sails!
RUMBLE RUMBLE
CRASH
All available hands, fill barrels with seawater!
SNAP!
ROARRR
We need to stabilize the ship with more ballast!

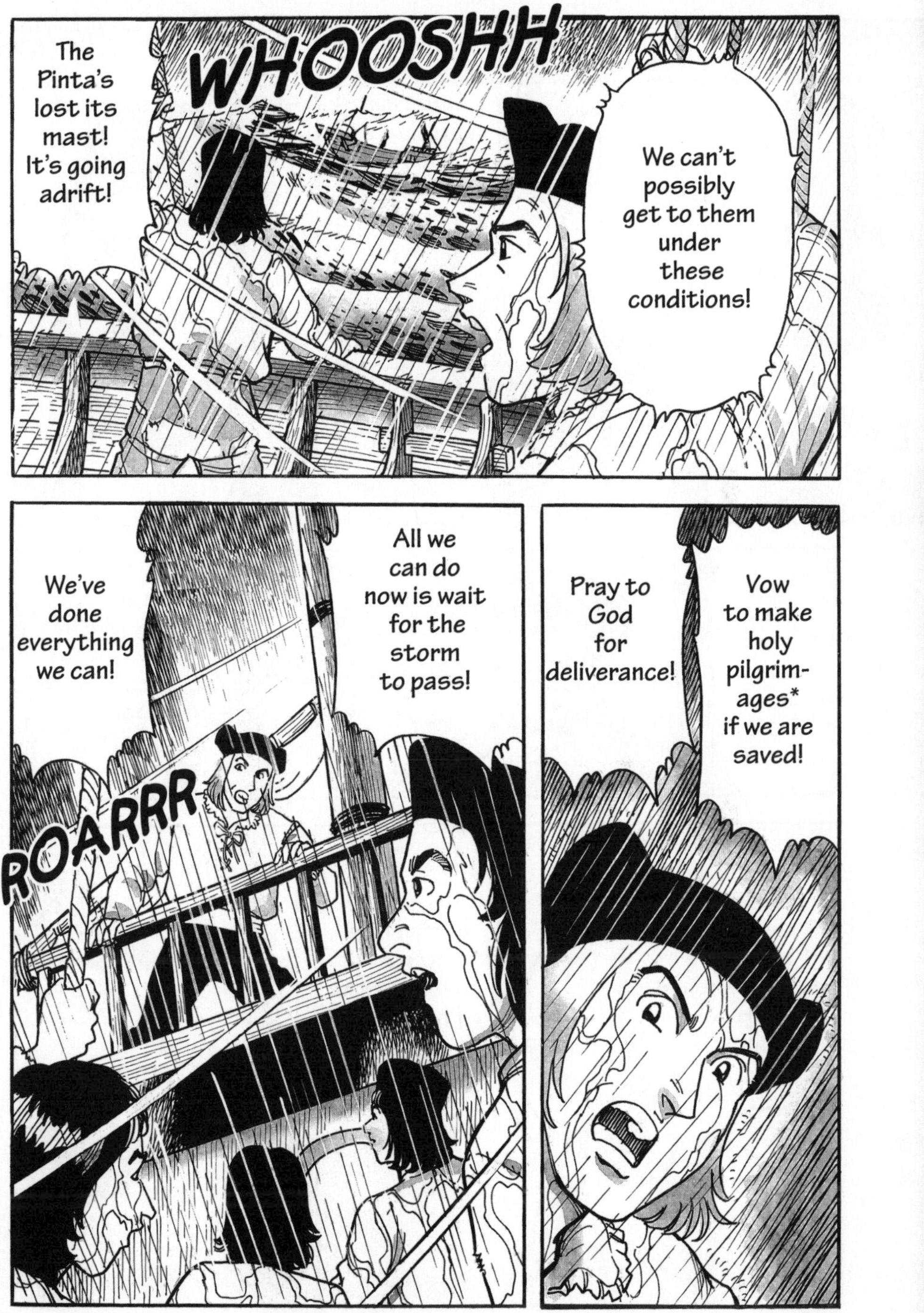
The Pinta's lost its mast! It's going adrift!
WHOOSHH
We can't possibly get to them under these conditions!
We've done everything we can!
All we can do now is wait for the storm to pass!
ROARRR
Pray to God for deliverance!
Vow to make holy pilgrimages* if we are saved!

*Holy pilgrimage: a journey to a church or holy place to show devotion and gratitude to God.

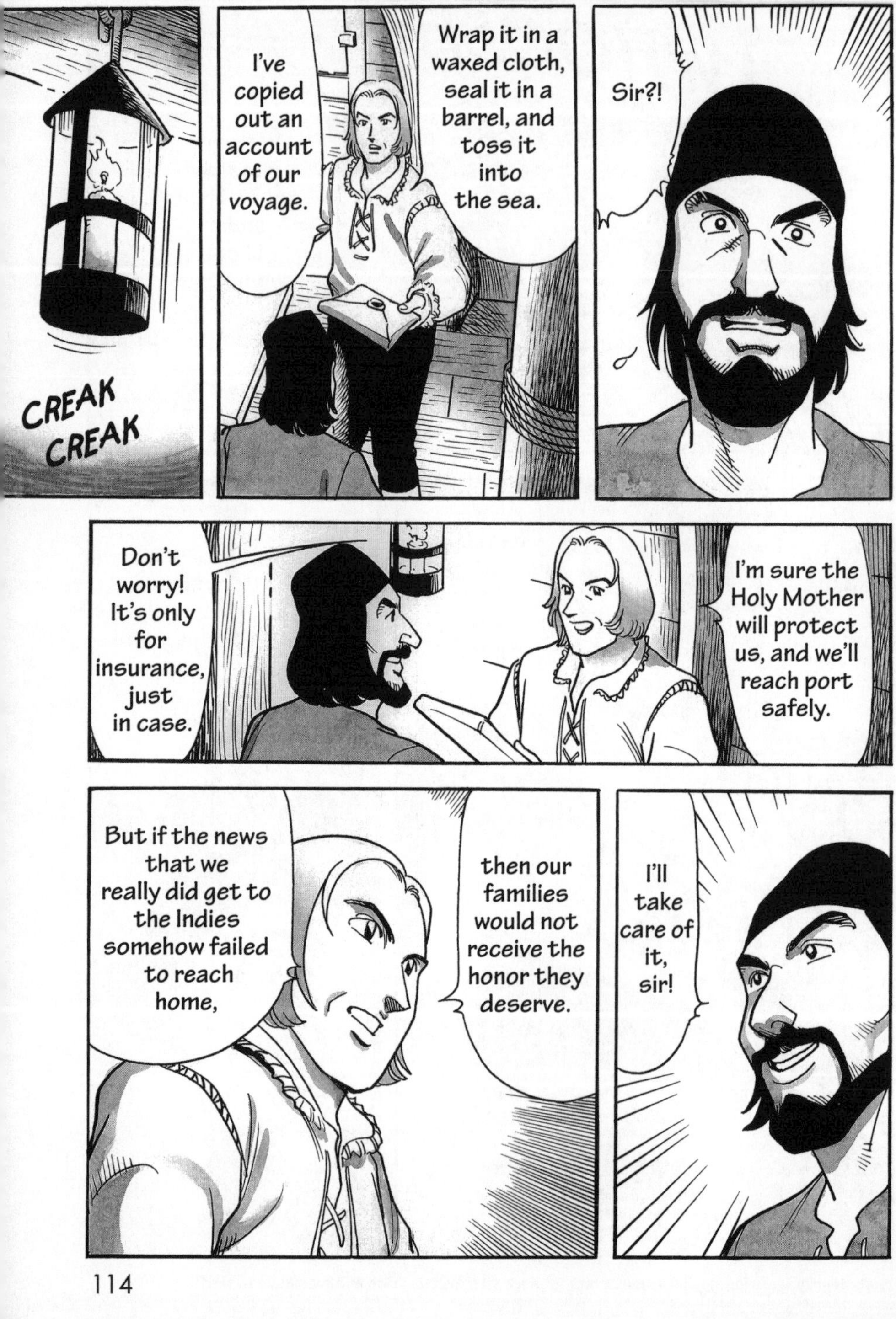
CREAK
CREAK
I've copied out an account of our voyage.
Wrap it in a waxed cloth, seal it in a barrel, and toss it into the sea.
Sir?!
Don't worry! It's only for insurance, just in case.
I'm sure the Holy Mother will protect us, and we'll reach port safely.
But if the news that we really did get to the Indies somehow failed to reach home,
then our families would not receive the honor they deserve.
I'll take care of it, sir!

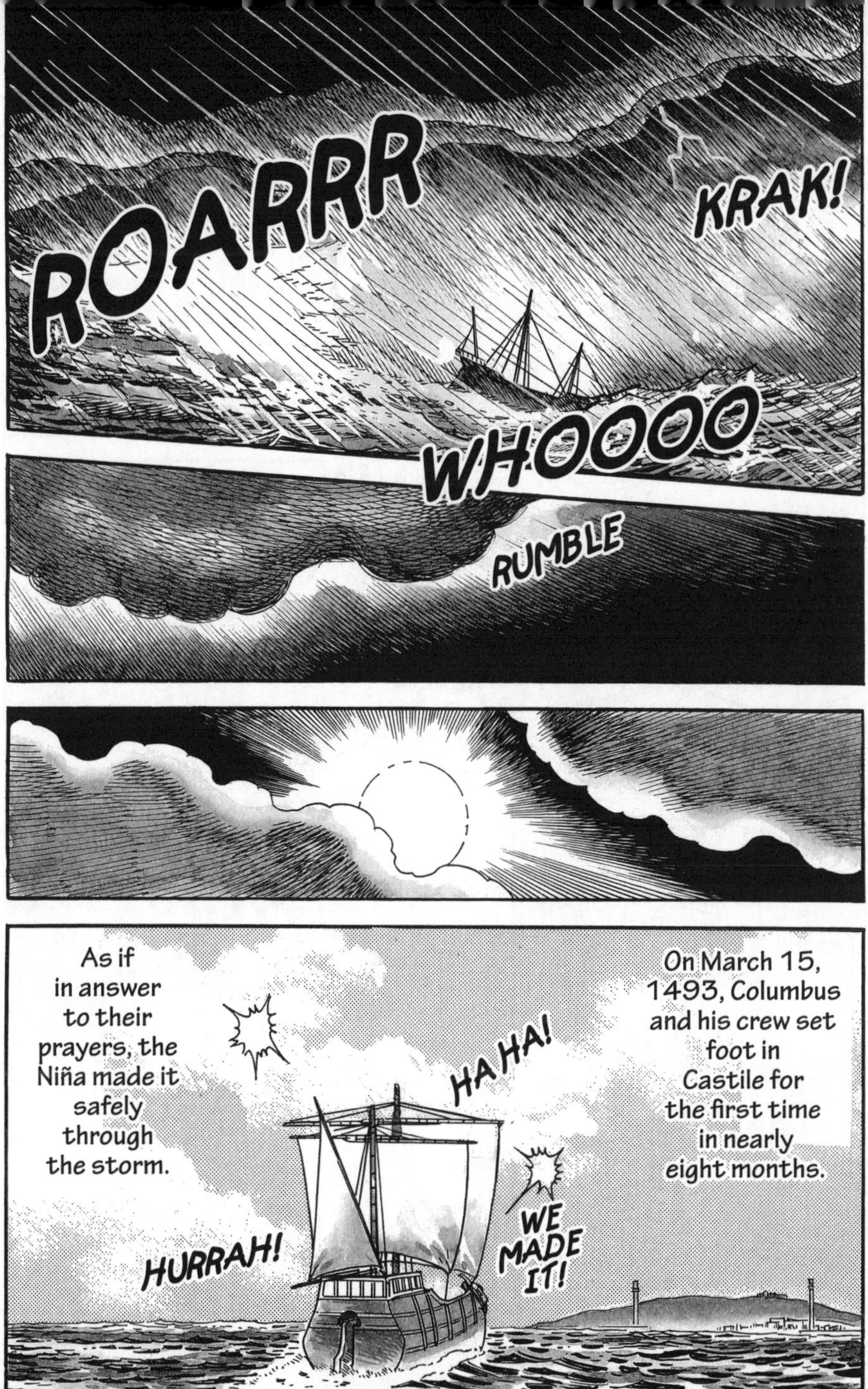
ROARRR
KRAK!
WHOOOO
RUMBLE
As if in answer to their prayers, the Niña made it safely through the storm.
HA HA!
HURRAH!
WE MADE IT!
On March 15, 1493, Columbus and his crew set foot in Castile for the first time in nearly eight months.

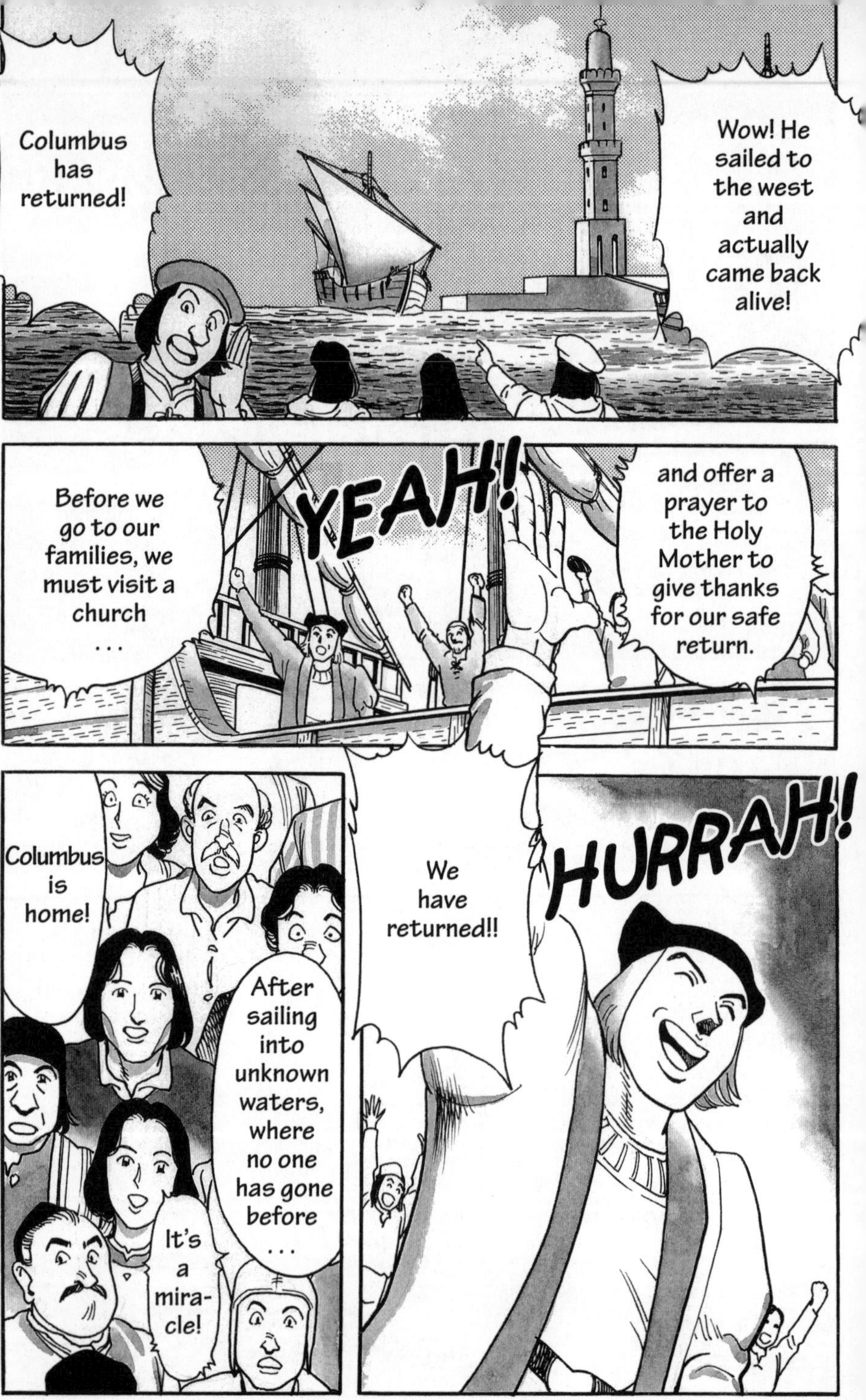
Columbus has returned!
Wow! He sailed to the west and actually came back alive!
Before we go to our families, we must visit a church . . .
YEAH!
and offer a prayer to the Holy Mother to give thanks for our safe return.
Columbus is home!
After sailing into unknown waters, where no one has gone before . . .
It's a mira-cle!
We have returned!!
HURRAH!

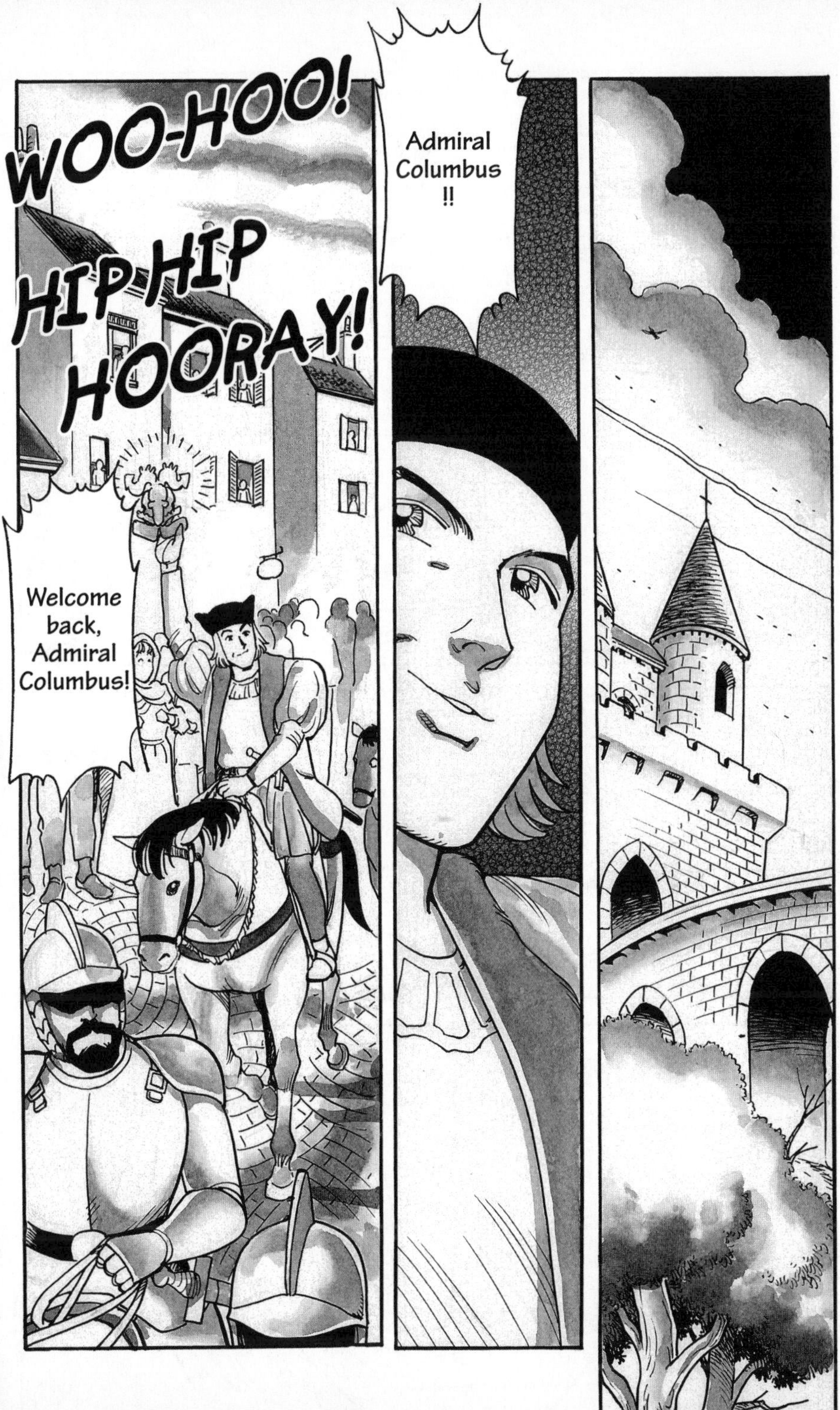
WOO-HOO!
HIP HIP HOORAY!
Welcome back, Admiral Columbus!
Admiral Columbus !!

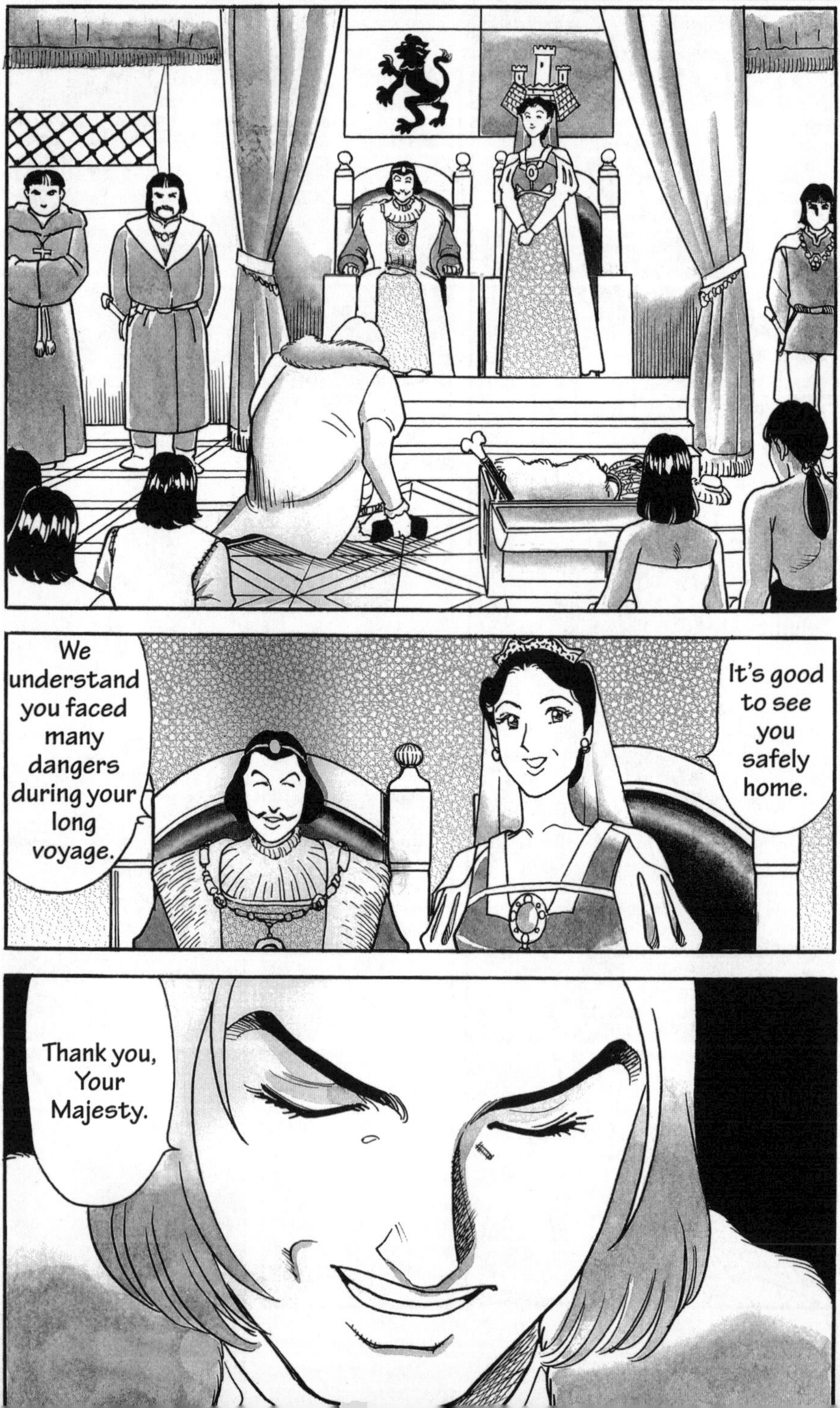
We understand you faced many dangers during your long voyage.
It's good to see you safely home.
Thank you, Your Majesty.

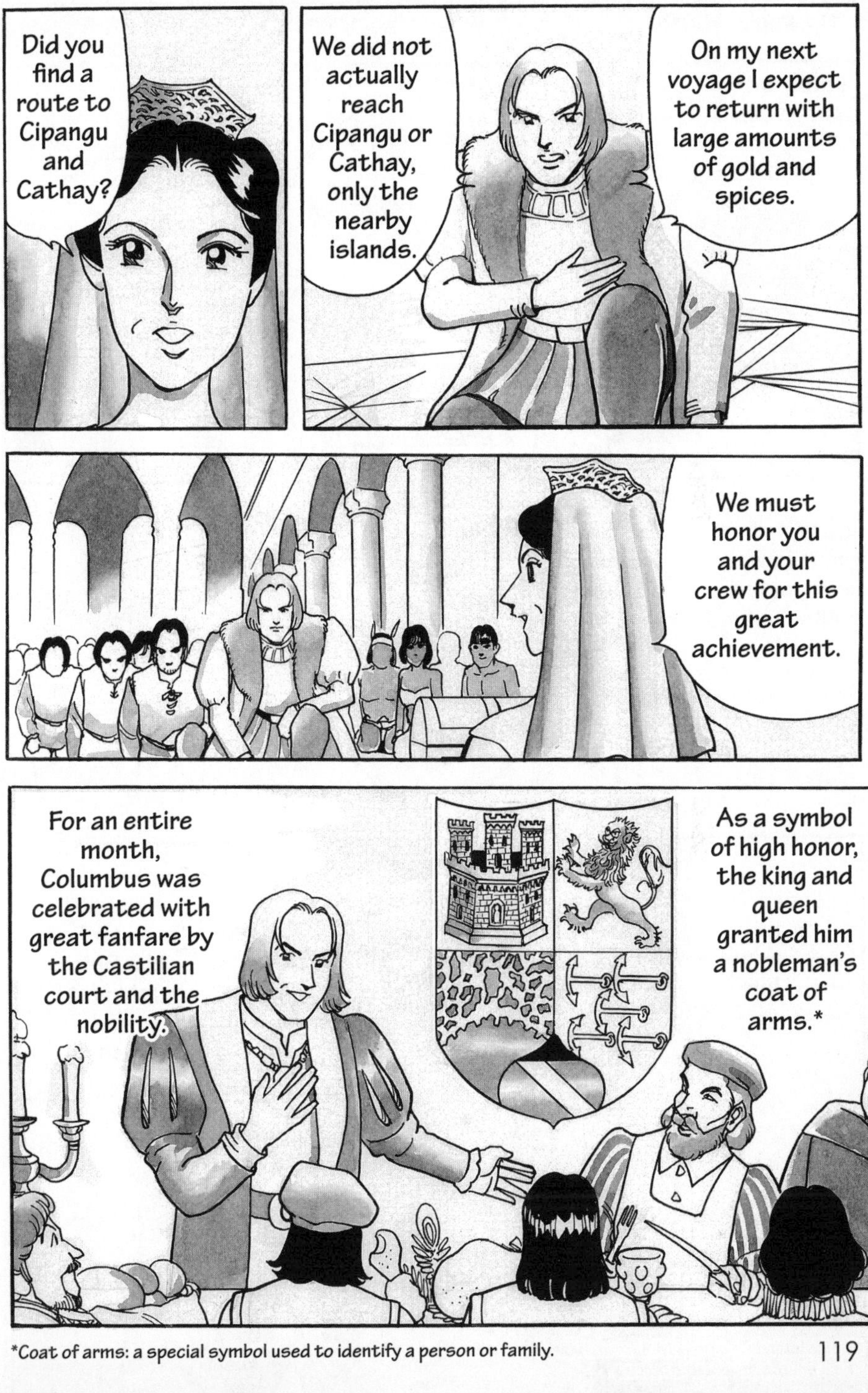
Did you find a route to Cipangu and Cathay?
We did not actually reach Cipangu or Cathay, only the nearby islands.
On my next voyage I expect to return with large amounts of gold and spices.
We must honor you and your crew for this great achievement.
For an entire month, Columbus was celebrated with great fanfare by the Castilian court and the nobility.
As a symbol of high honor, the king and queen granted him a nobleman's coat of arms.*

*Coat of arms: a special symbol used to identify a person or family.

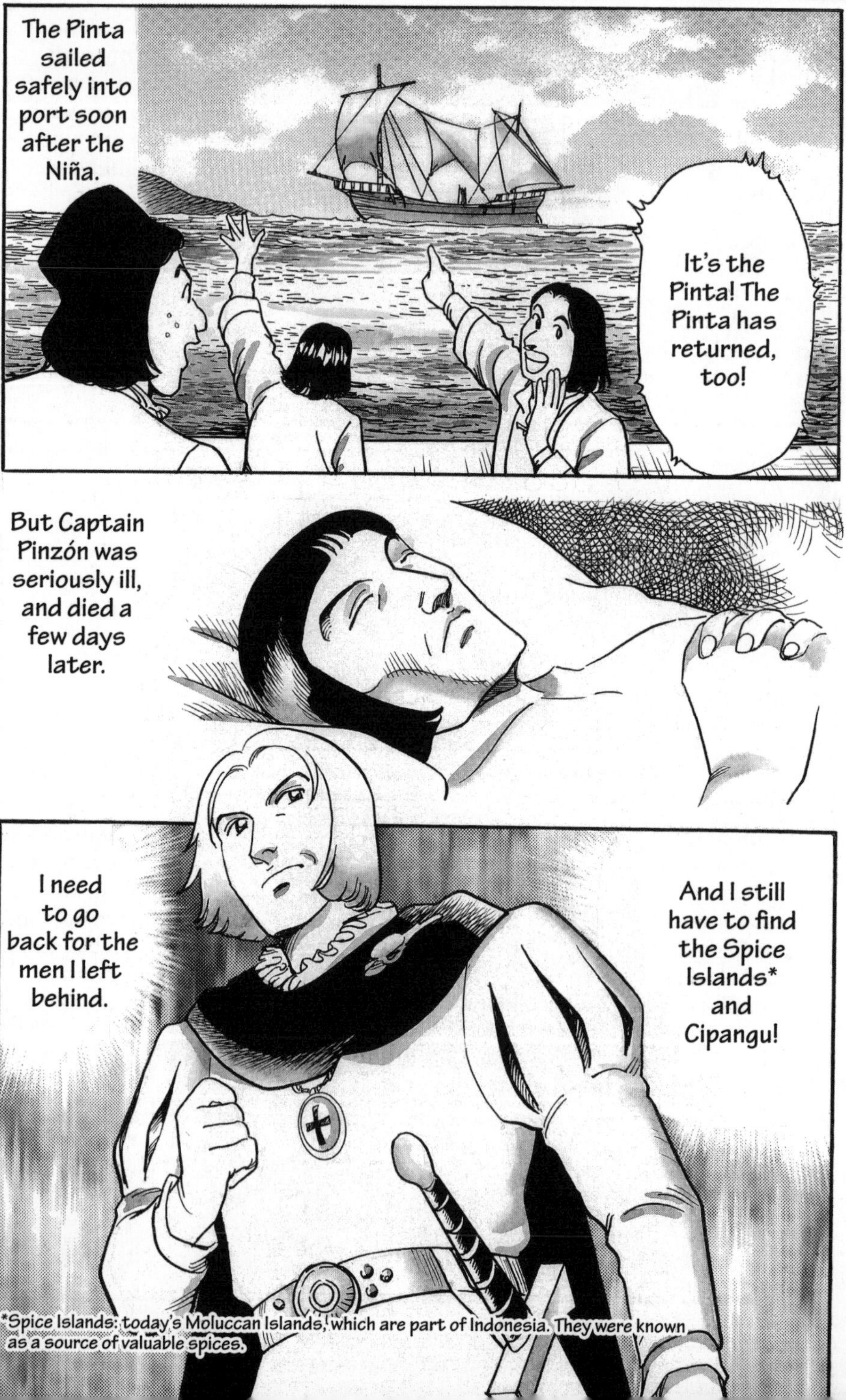
The Pinta sailed safely into port soon after the Niña.
It's the Pinta! The Pinta has returned, too!
But Captain Pinzón was seriously ill, and died a few days later.
I need to go back for the men I left behind.
And I still have to find the Spice Islands* and Cipangu!
*Spice Islands: today's Moluccan Islands, which are part of Indonesia. They were known as a source of valuable spices.

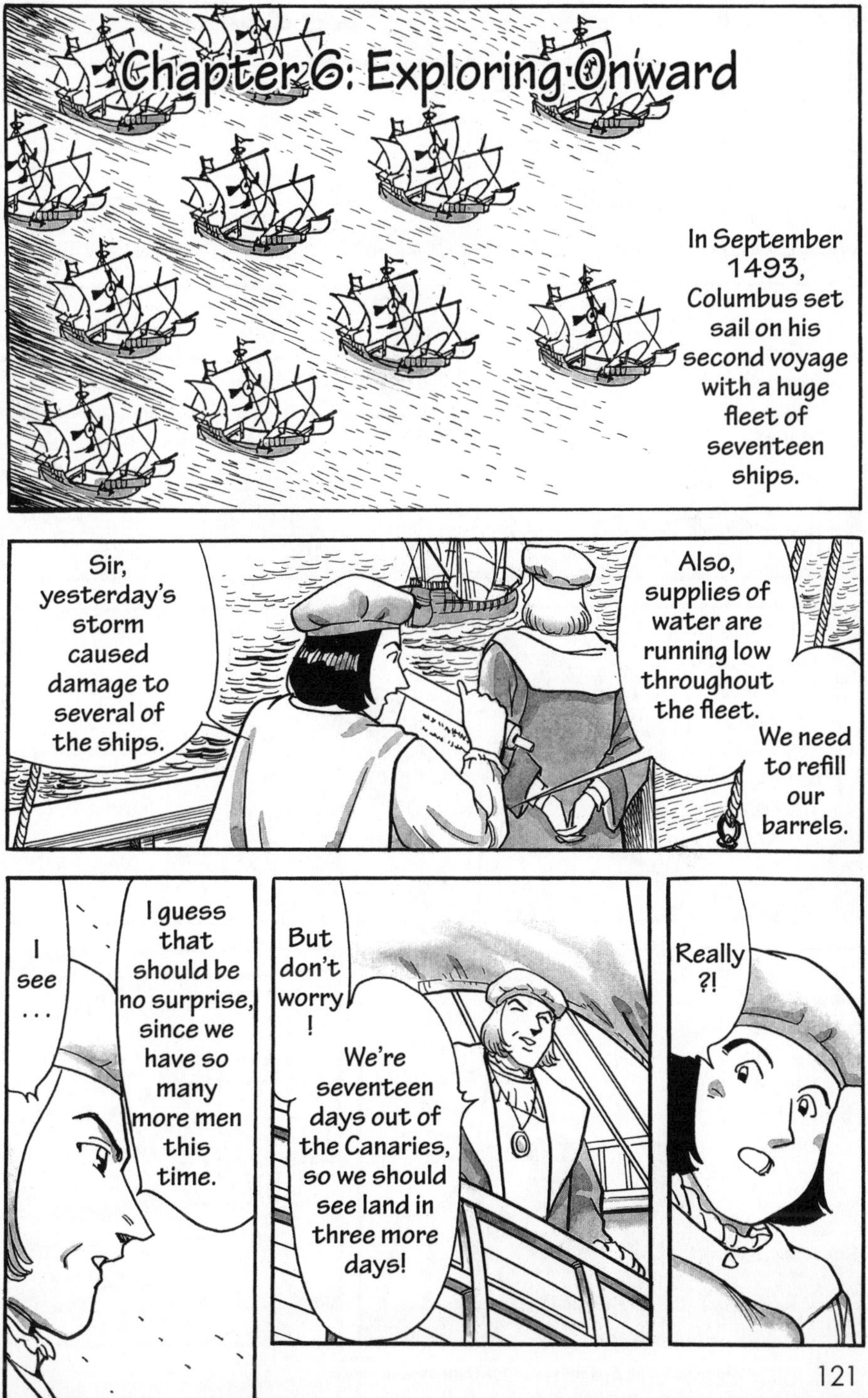
Chapter 6: Exploring Onward
In September 1493, Columbus set sail on his second voyage with a huge fleet of seventeen ships.
Sir, yesterday's storm caused damage to several of the ships.
Also, supplies of water are running low throughout the fleet.
We need to refill our barrels.
I see . . .
I guess that should be no surprise, since we have so many more men this time.
But don't worry!
We're seventeen days out of the Canaries, so we should see land in three more days!
Really?!

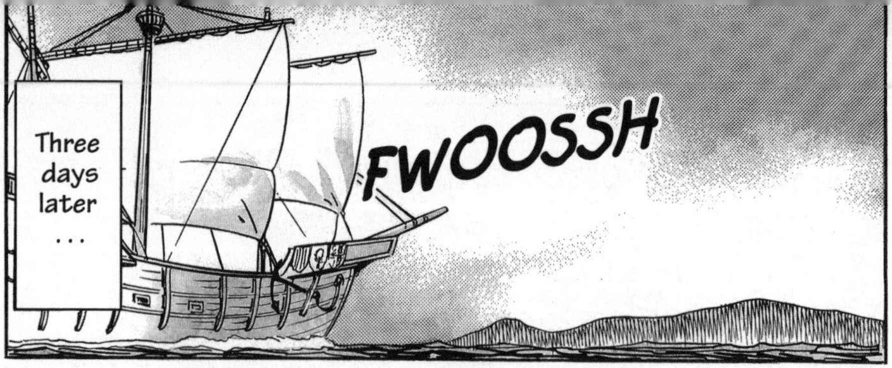
Three days later . . .
FWOOSSH

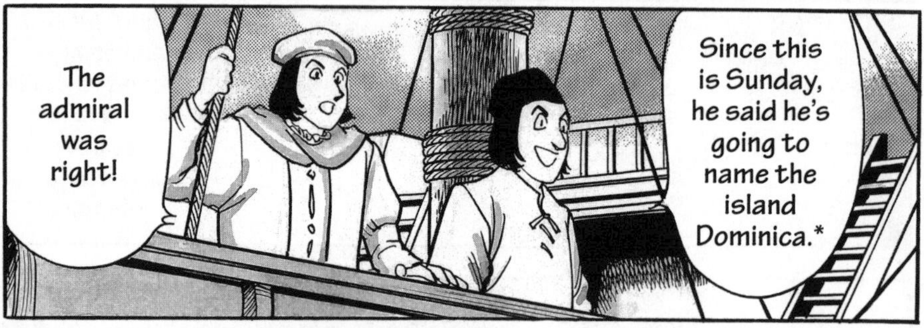
The admiral was right!
Since this is Sunday, he said he's going to name the island Dominica.*

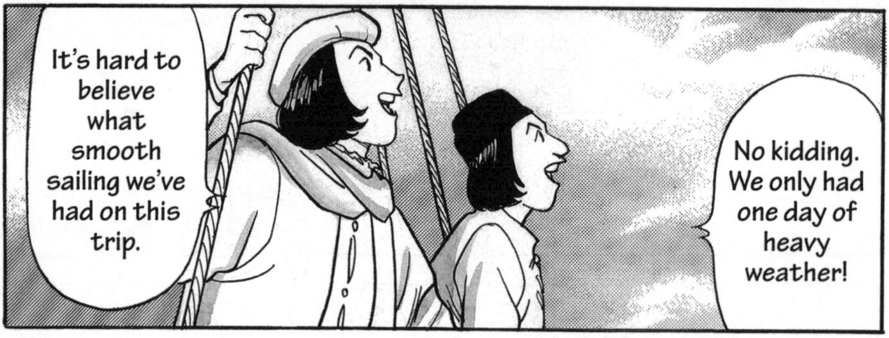
It's hard to believe what smooth sailing we've had on this trip.
No kidding. We only had one day of heavy weather!

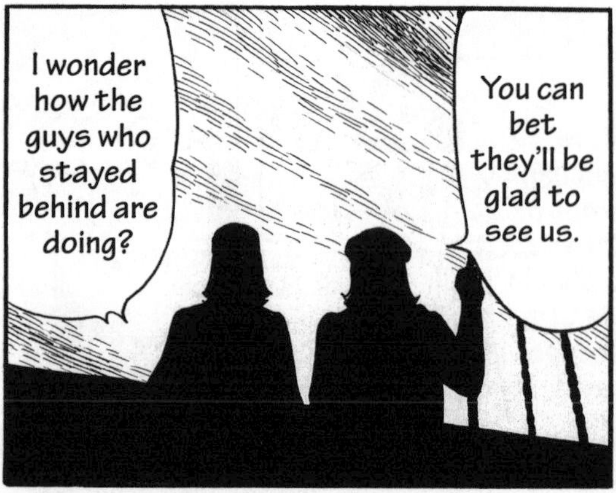
I wonder how the guys who stayed behind are doing?
You can bet they'll be glad to see us.

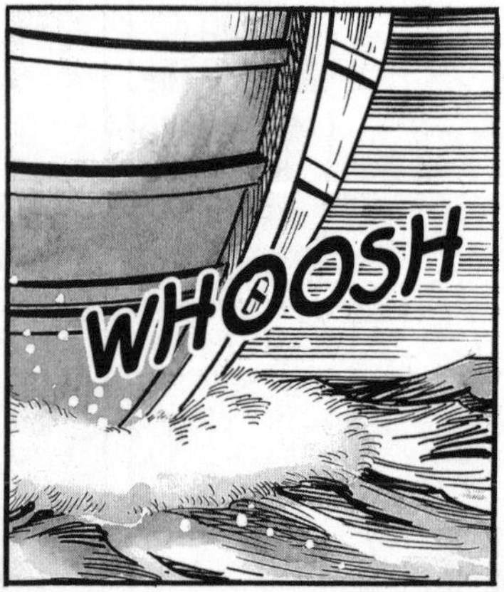
WHOOSH

*Dominica: The Spanish word for Sunday is *domingo*.

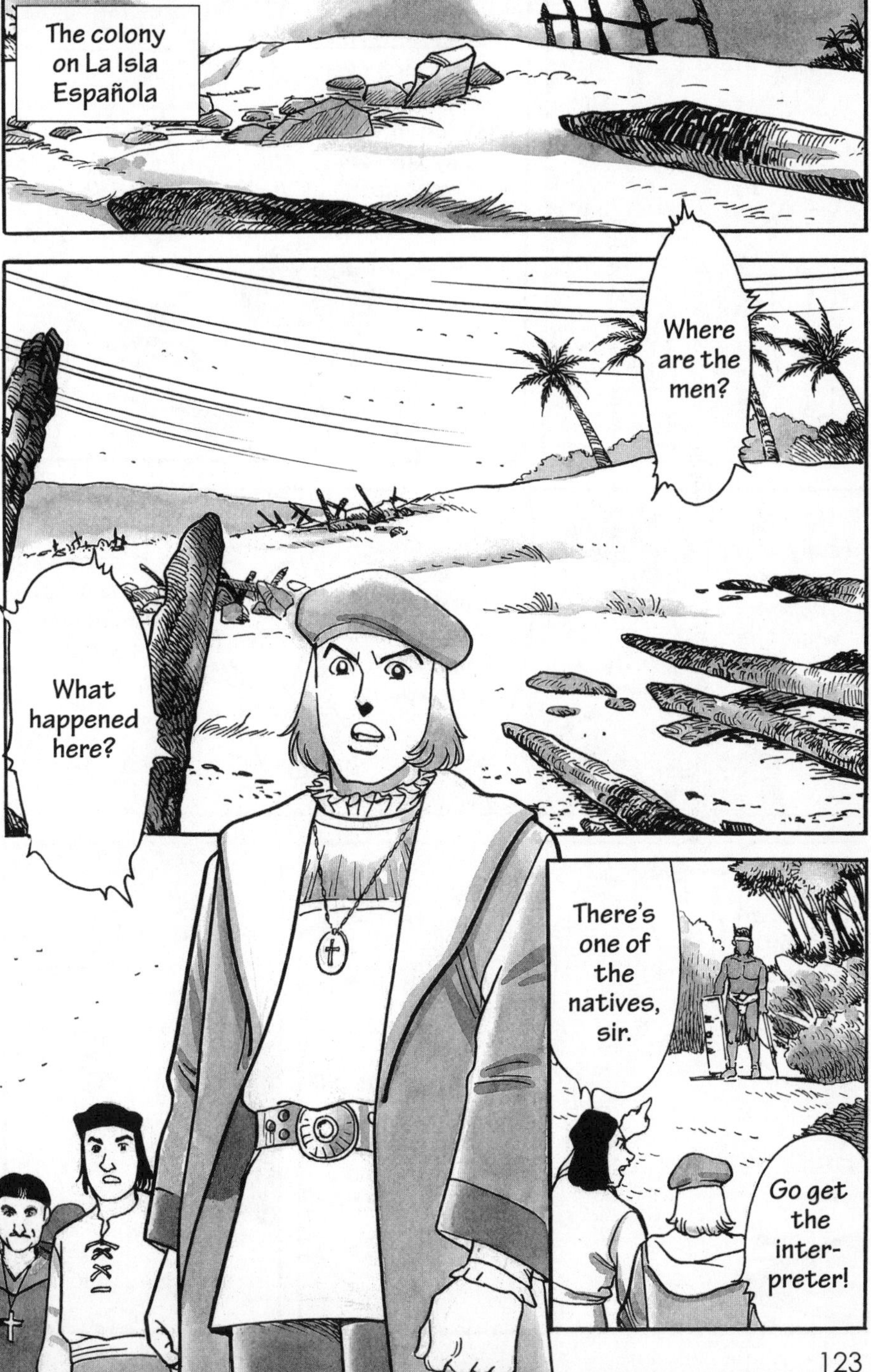
The colony on La Isla Española
Where are the men?
What happened here?
There's one of the natives, sir.
Go get the inter-preter!

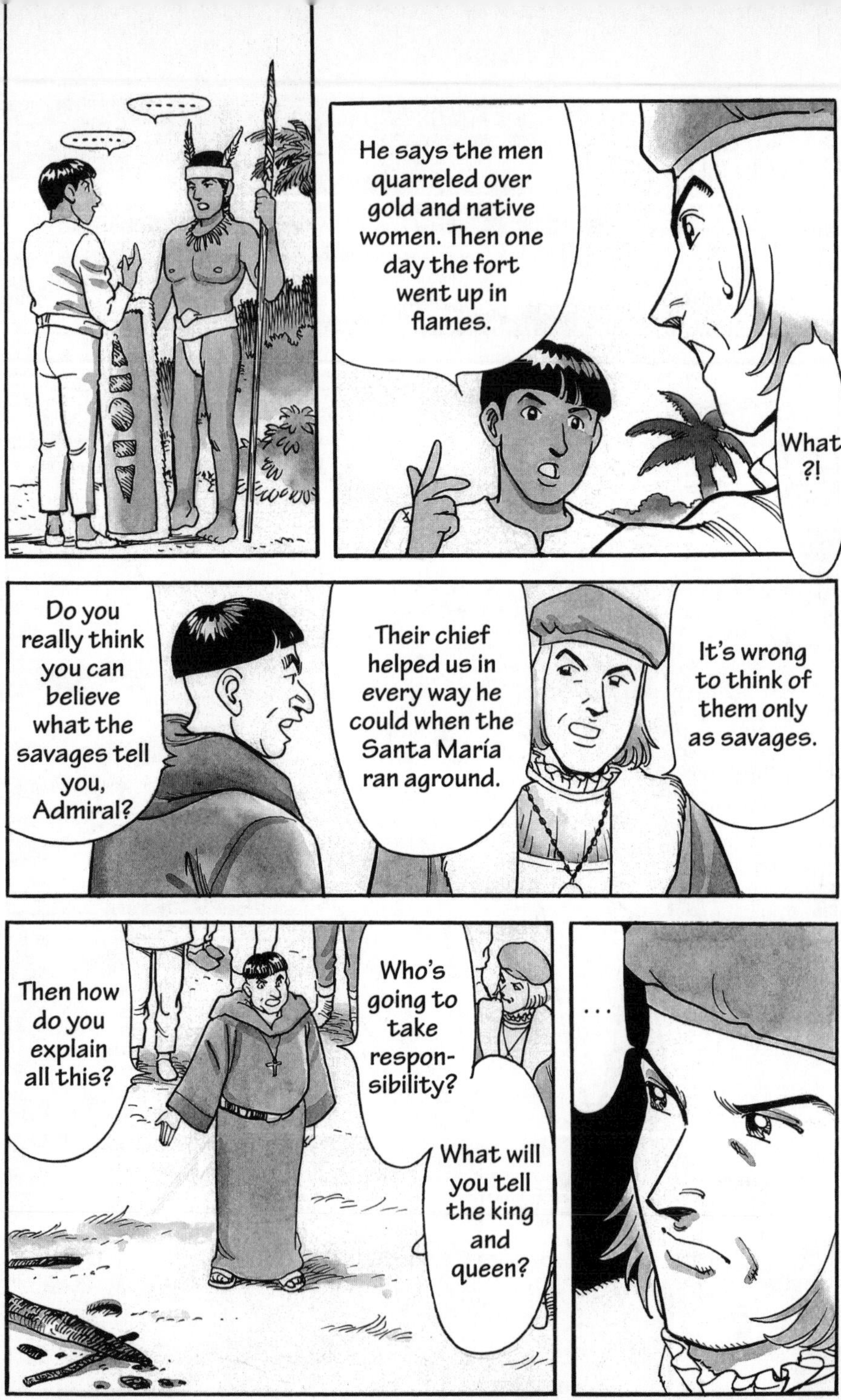

.....
......
He says the men quarreled over gold and native women. Then one day the fort went up in flames.
What?!
Do you really think you can believe what the savages tell you, Admiral?
Their chief helped us in every way he could when the Santa María ran aground.
It's wrong to think of them only as savages.
Then how do you explain all this?
Who's going to take respon-sibility?
What will you tell the king and queen?
...

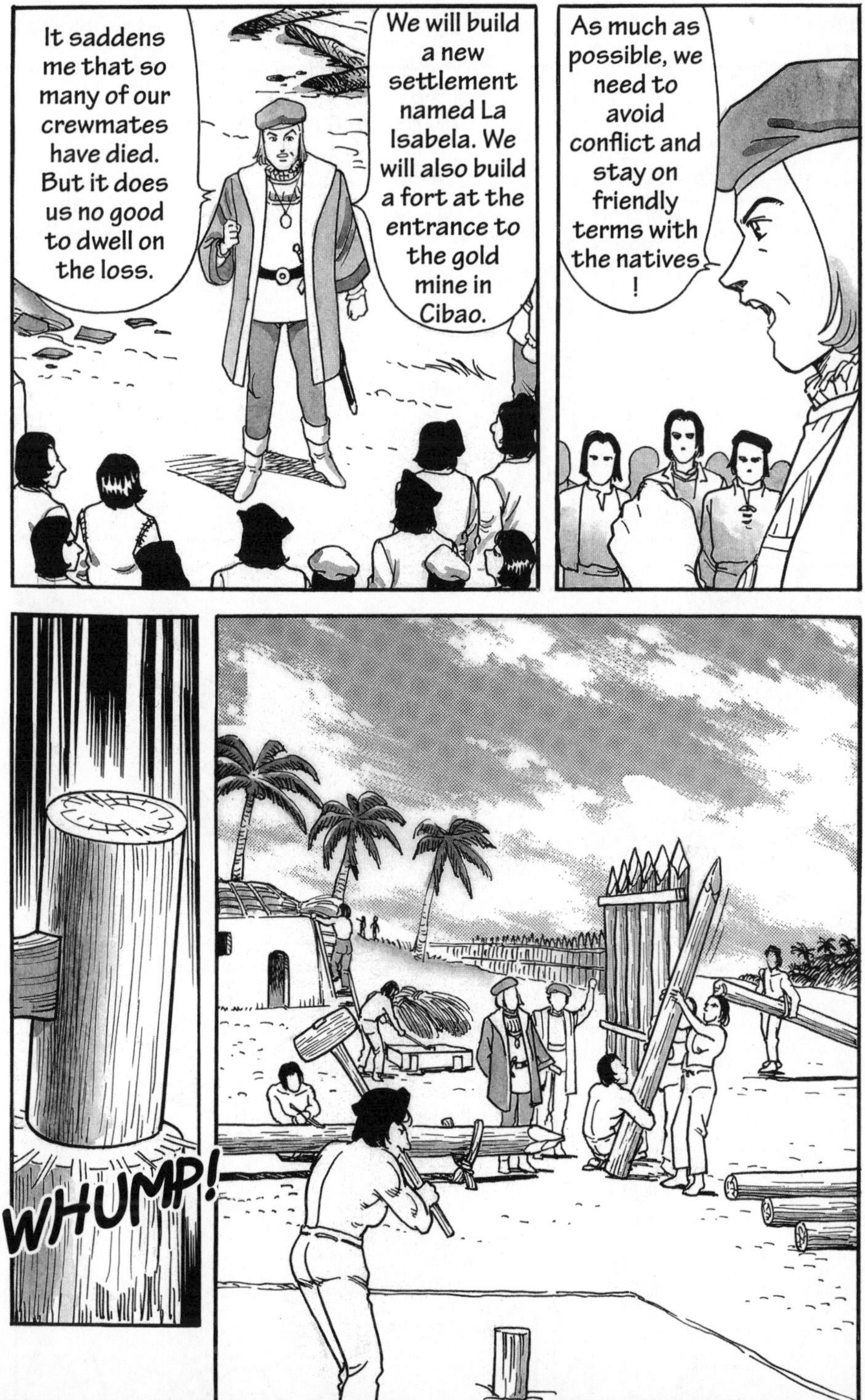
It saddens me that so many of our crewmates have died. But it does us no good to dwell on the loss.
We will build a new settlement named La Isabela. We will also build a fort at the entrance to the gold mine in Cibao.
As much as possible, we need to avoid conflict and stay on friendly terms with the natives!
WHUMP!

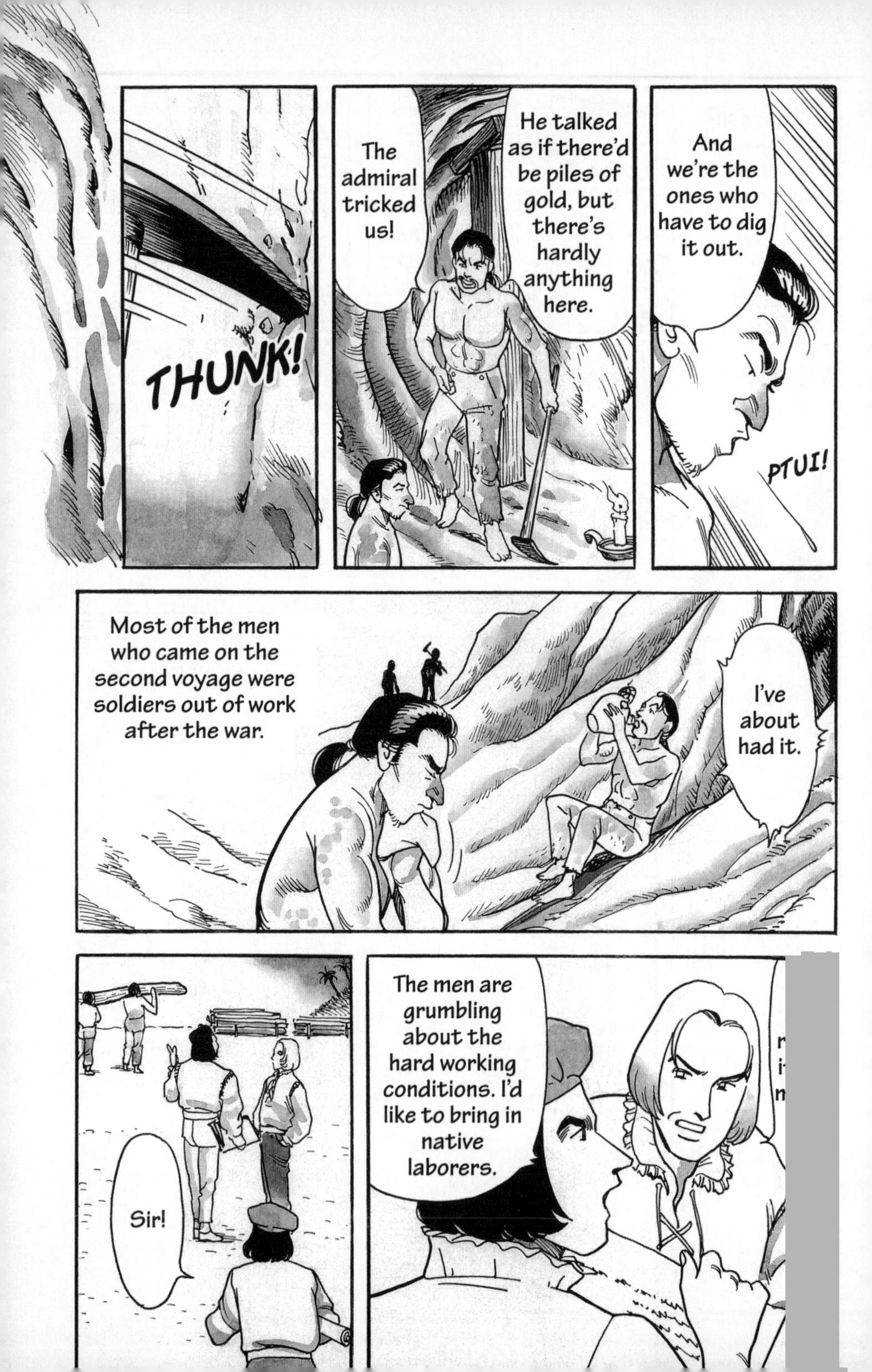
THUNK!
The admiral tricked us!
He talked as if there'd be piles of gold, but there's hardly anything here.
And we're the ones who have to dig it out.
PTUI!
Most of the men who came on the second voyage were soldiers out of work after the war.
I've about had it.
Sir!
The men are grumbling about the hard working conditions. I'd like to bring in native laborers.

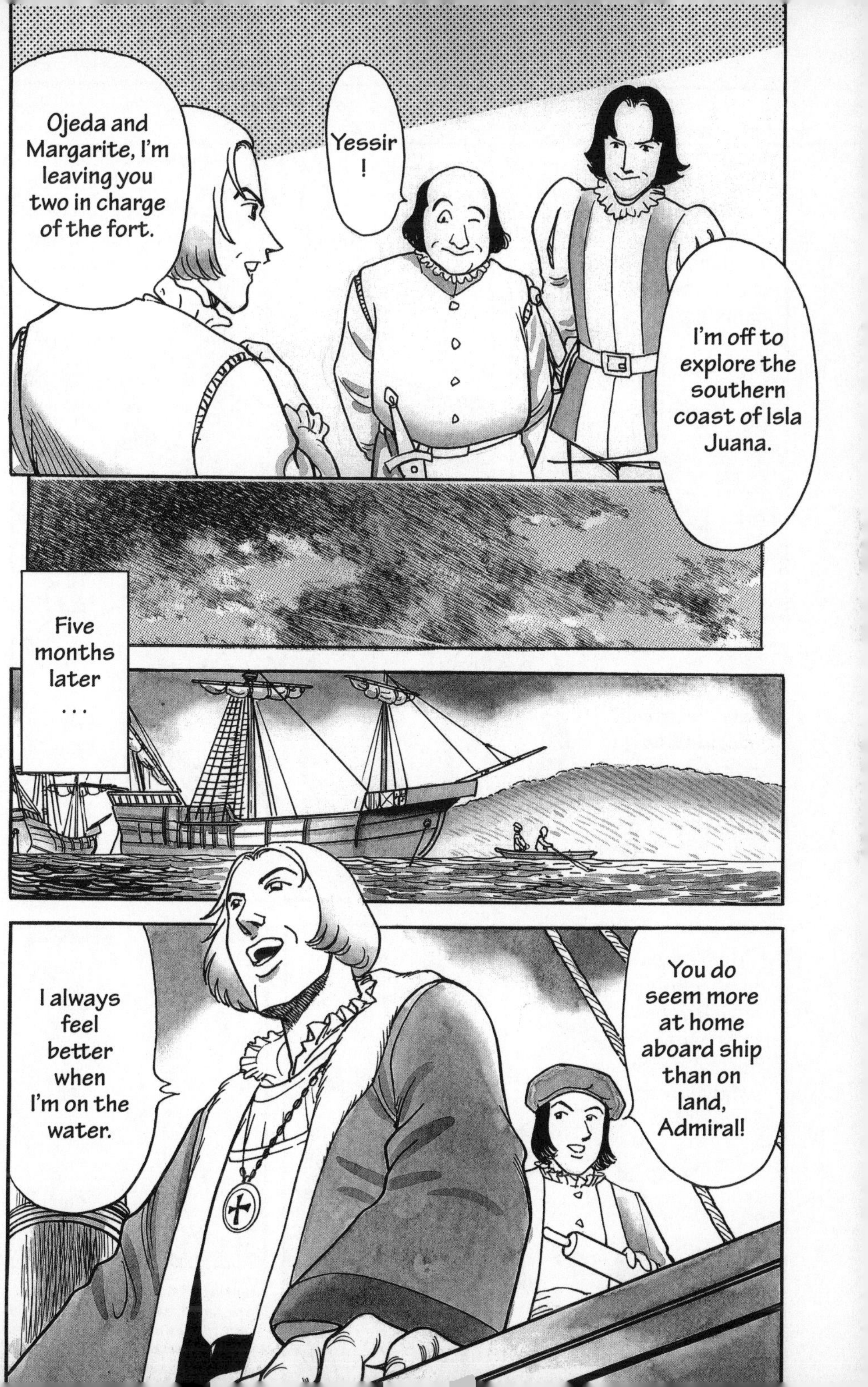
Ojeda and Margarite, I'm leaving you two in charge of the fort.
Yessir!
I'm off to explore the southern coast of Isla Juana.
Five months later . . .
I always feel better when I'm on the water.
You do seem more at home aboard ship than on land, Admiral!

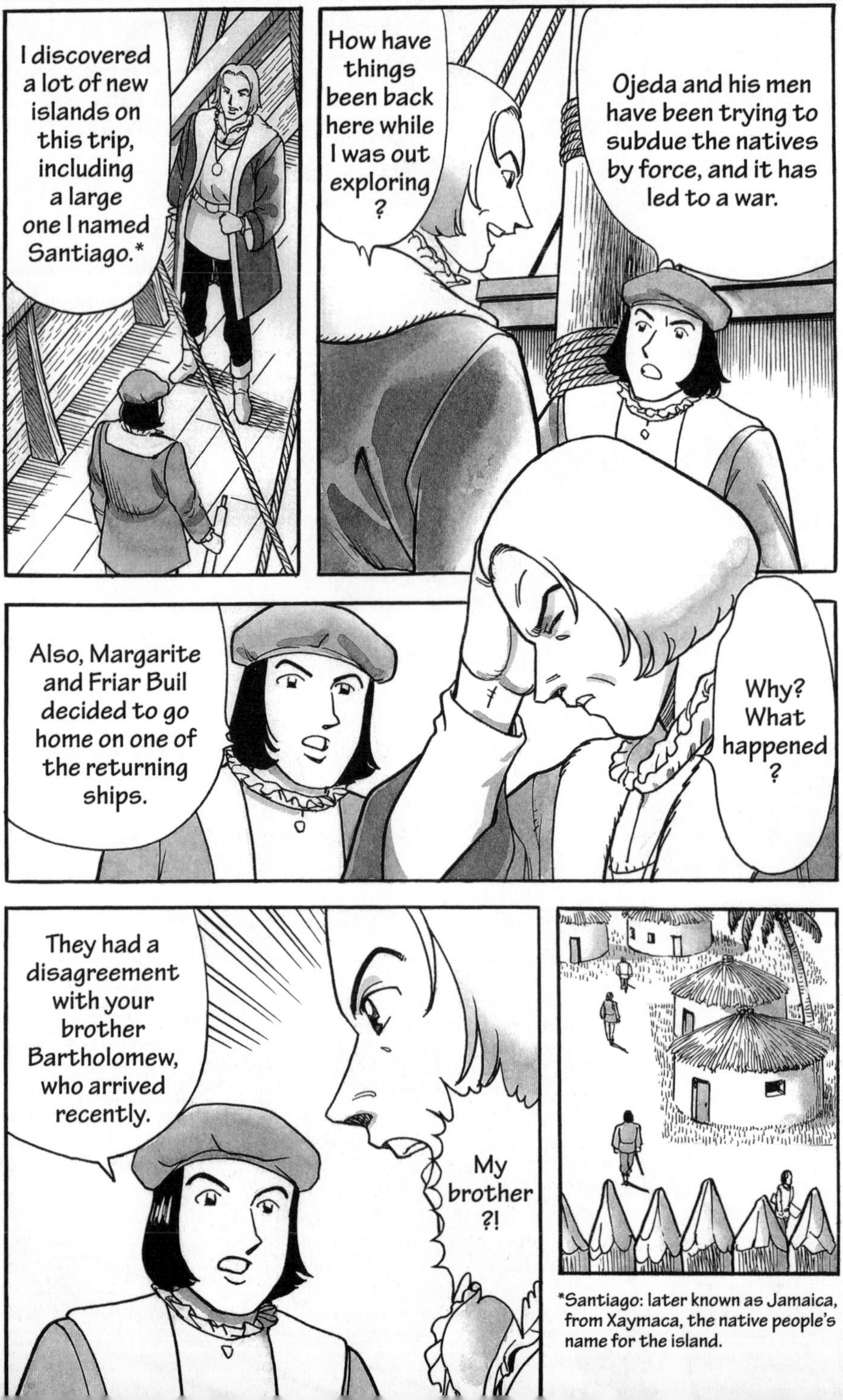
I discovered a lot of new islands on this trip, including a large one I named Santiago.*
How have things been back here while I was out exploring?
Ojeda and his men have been trying to subdue the natives by force, and it has led to a war.
Also, Margarite and Friar Buil decided to go home on one of the returning ships.
Why? What happened?
They had a disagreement with your brother Bartholomew, who arrived recently.
My brother?!

*Santiago: later known as Jamaica, from Xaymaca, the native people's name for the island.

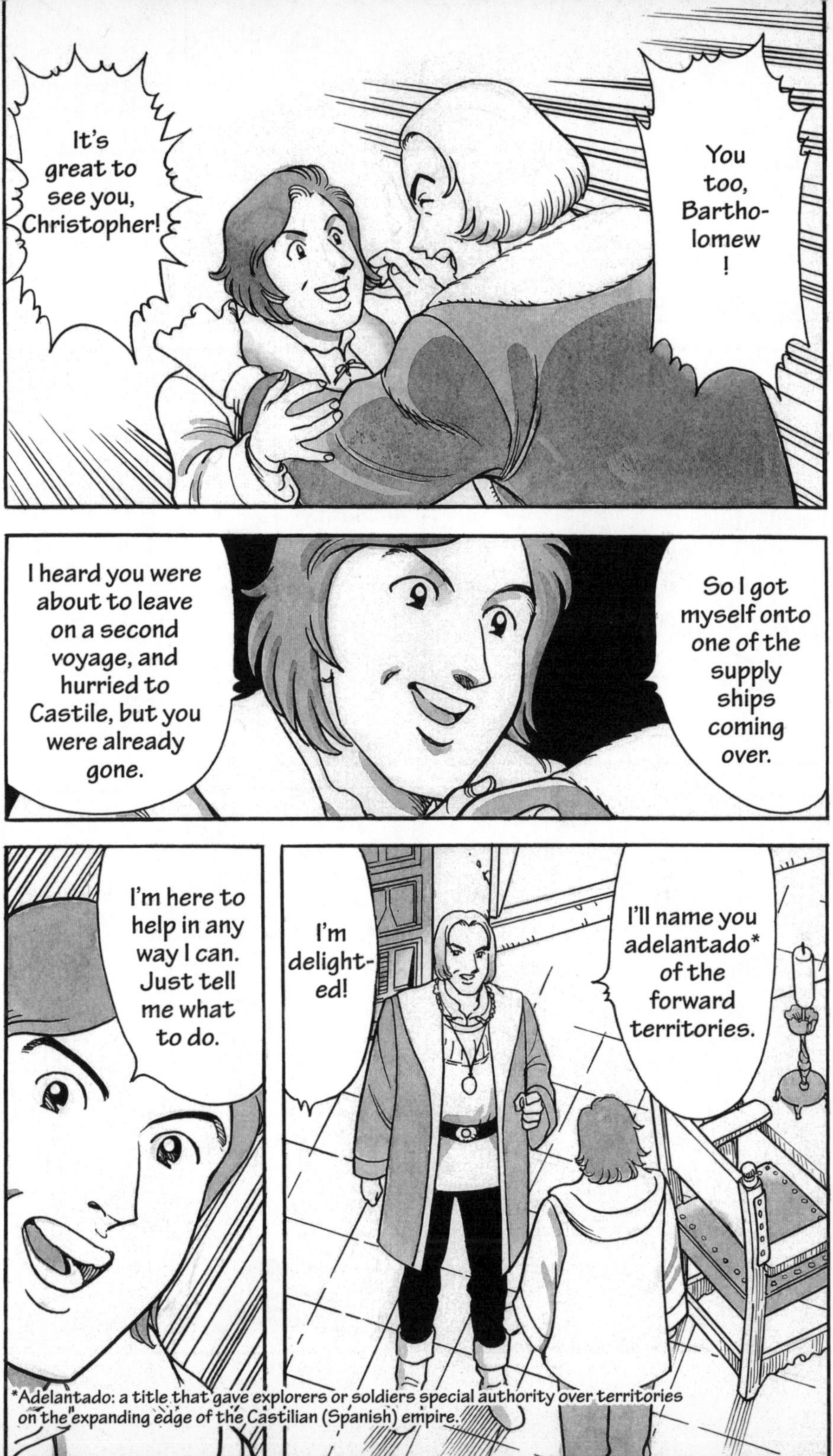
It's great to see you, Christopher!
You too, Bartho-lomew!
I heard you were about to leave on a second voyage, and hurried to Castile, but you were already gone.
So I got myself onto one of the supply ships coming over.
I'm here to help in any way I can. Just tell me what to do.
I'm delight-ed!
I'll name you adelantado* of the forward territories.

*Adelantado: a title that gave explorers or soldiers special authority over territories on the expanding edge of the Castilian (Spanish) empire.

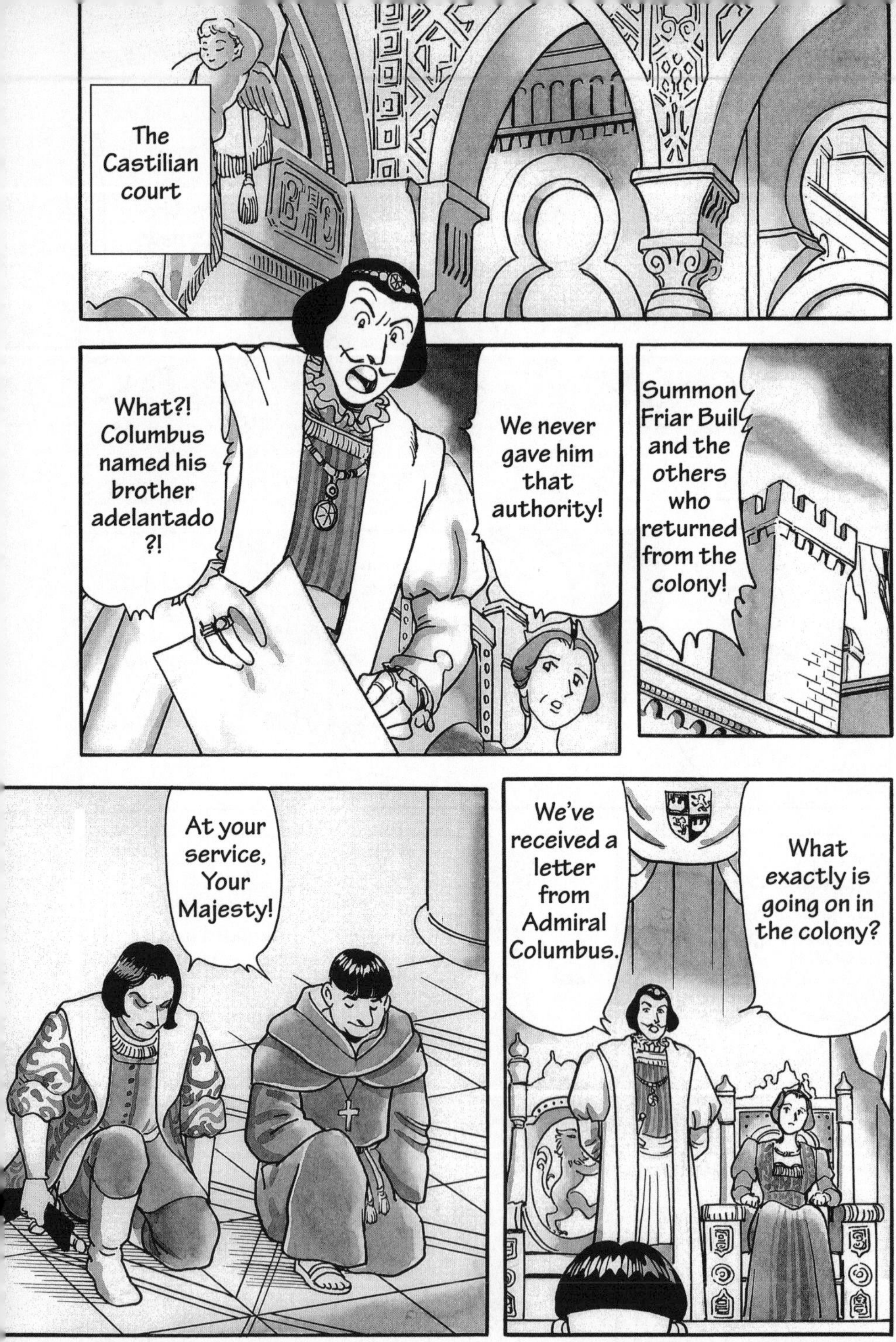

The Castilian court
What?! Columbus named his brother adelantado ?!
We never gave him that authority!
Summon Friar Buil and the others who returned from the colony!
At your service, Your Majesty!
We've received a letter from Admiral Columbus.
What exactly is going on in the colony?

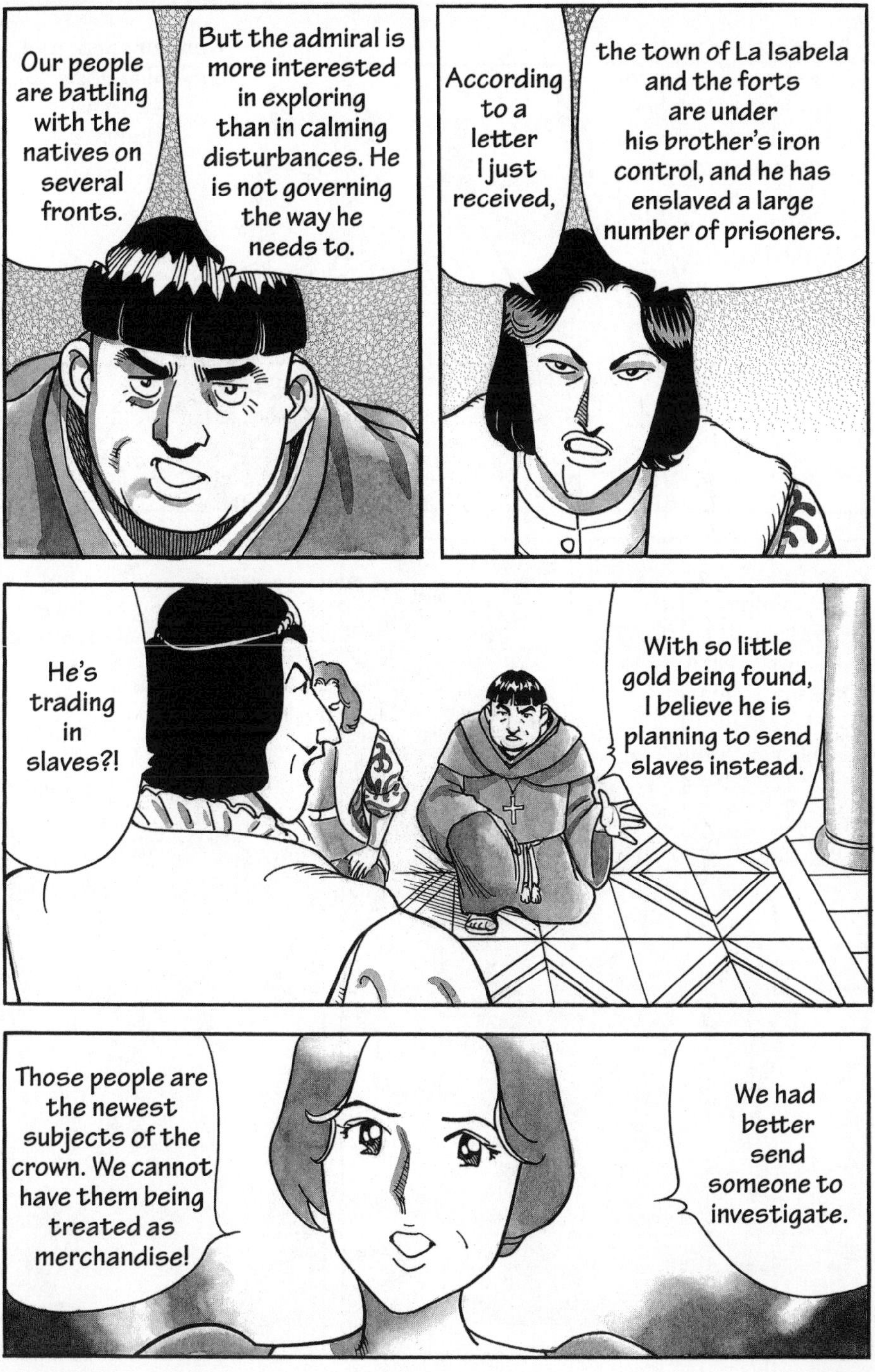
Our people are battling with the natives on several fronts.
But the admiral is more interested in exploring than in calming disturbances. He is not governing the way he needs to.
According to a letter I just received,
the town of La Isabela and the forts are under his brother's iron control, and he has enslaved a large number of prisoners.
He's trading in slaves?!
With so little gold being found, I believe he is planning to send slaves instead.
Those people are the newest subjects of the crown. We cannot have them being treated as merchandise!
We had better send someone to investigate.

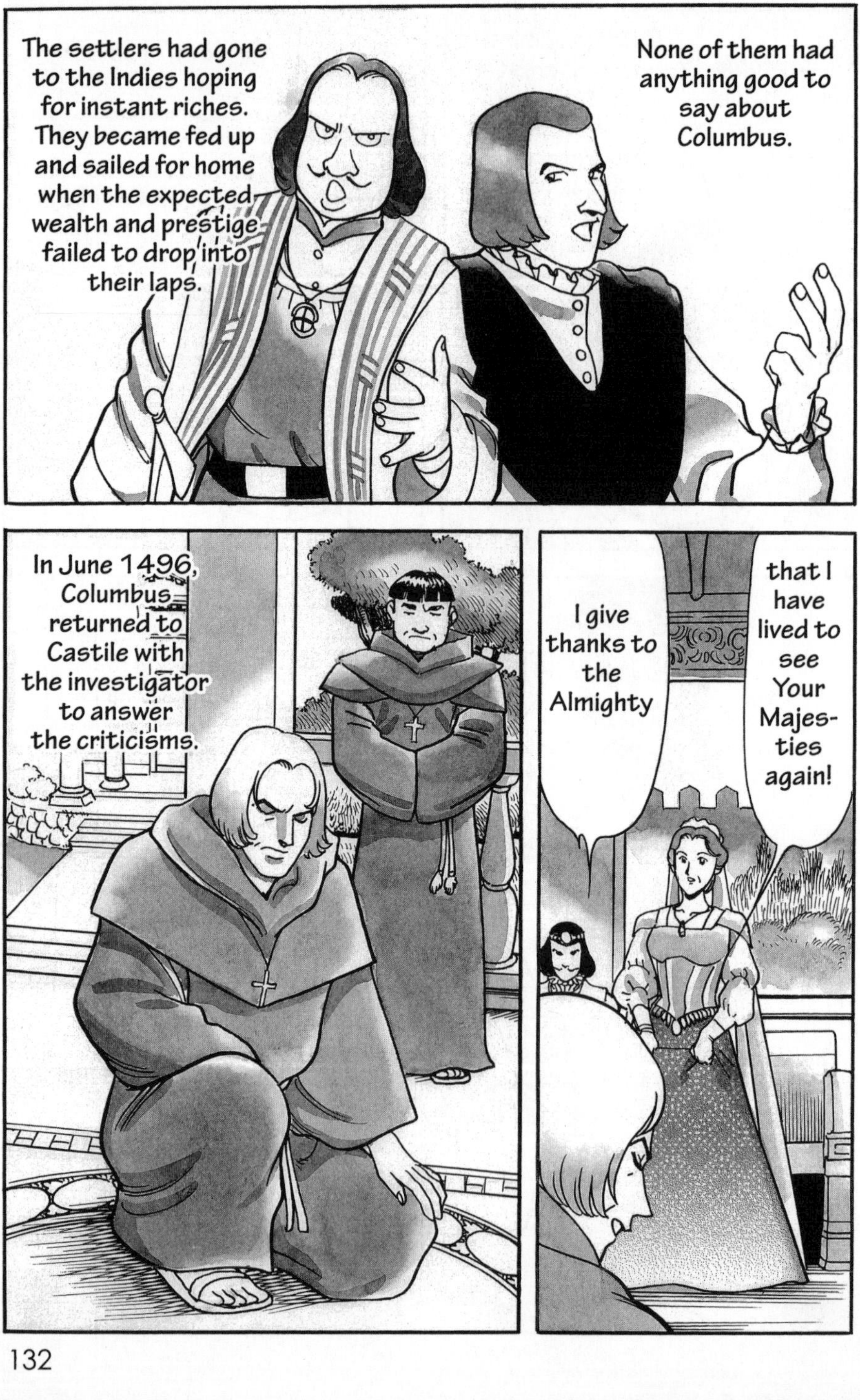
The settlers had gone to the Indies hoping for instant riches. They became fed up and sailed for home when the expected wealth and prestige failed to drop into their laps.
None of them had anything good to say about Columbus.
In June 1496, Columbus returned to Castile with the investigator to answer the criticisms.
I give thanks to the Almighty
that I have lived to see Your Majesties again!

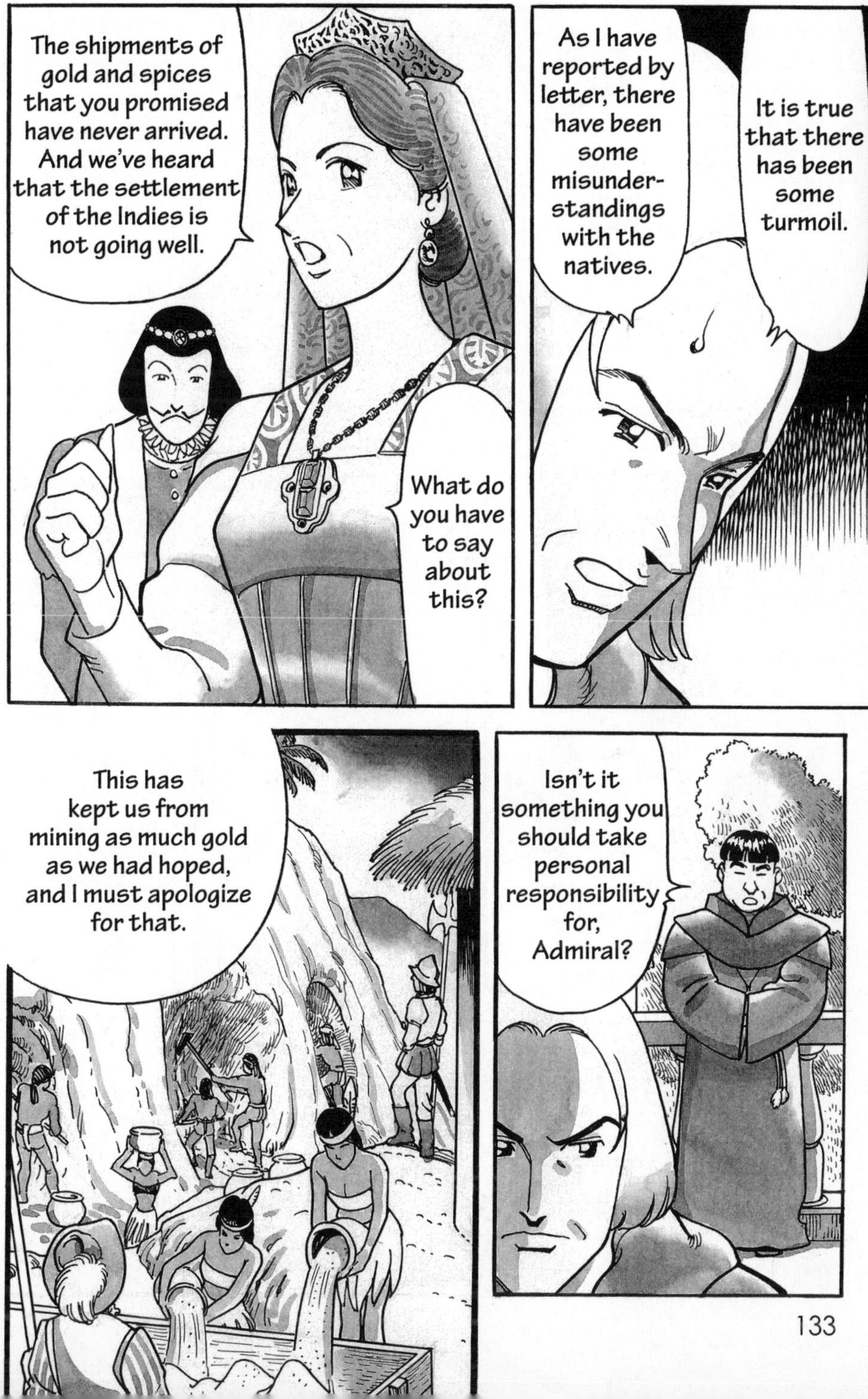
The shipments of gold and spices that you promised have never arrived. And we've heard that the settlement of the Indies is not going well.
What do you have to say about this?
As I have reported by letter, there have been some misunder-standings with the natives.
It is true that there has been some turmoil.
This has kept us from mining as much gold as we had hoped, and I must apologize for that.
Isn't it something you should take personal responsibility for, Admiral?

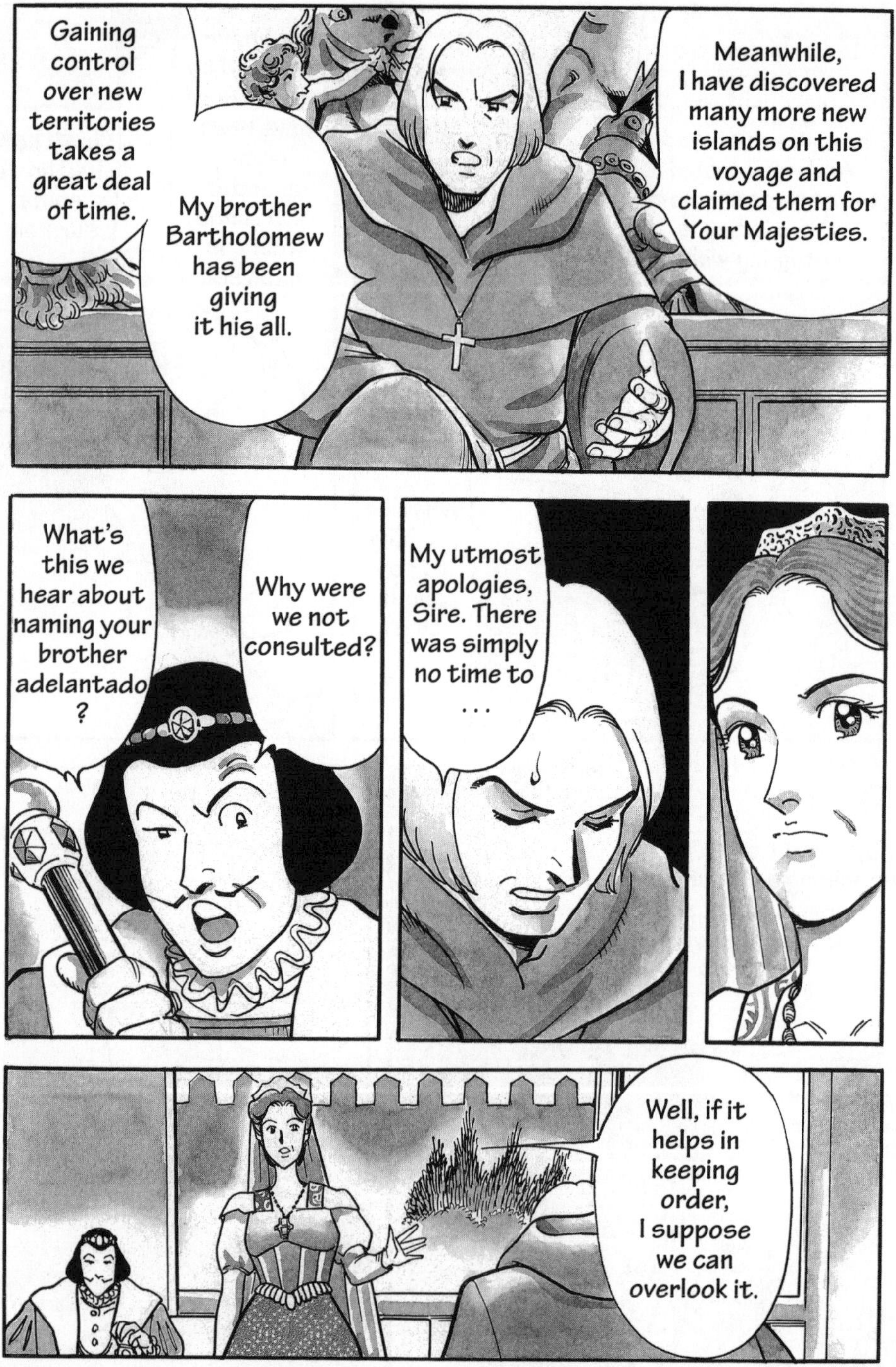
Gaining control over new territories takes a great deal of time.
My brother Bartholomew has been giving it his all.
Meanwhile, I have discovered many more new islands on this voyage and claimed them for Your Majesties.
What's this we hear about naming your brother adelantado?
Why were we not consulted?
My utmost apologies, Sire. There was simply no time to . . .
Well, if it helps in keeping order, I suppose we can overlook it.

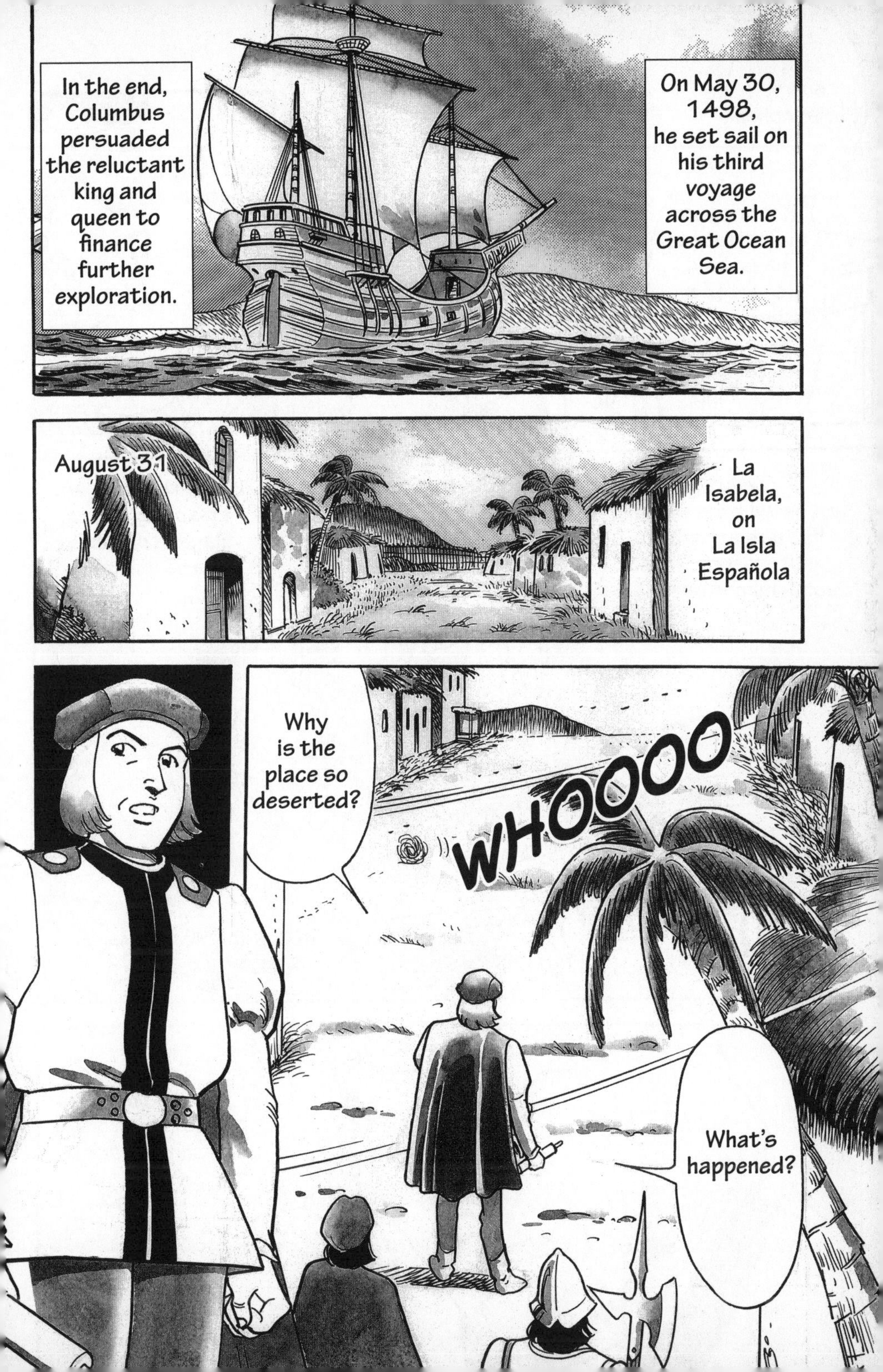
In the end, Columbus persuaded the reluctant king and queen to finance further exploration.
On May 30, 1498, he set sail on his third voyage across the Great Ocean Sea.
August 31
La Isabela, on La Isla Española
Why is the place so deserted?
WHOOOO
What's happened?

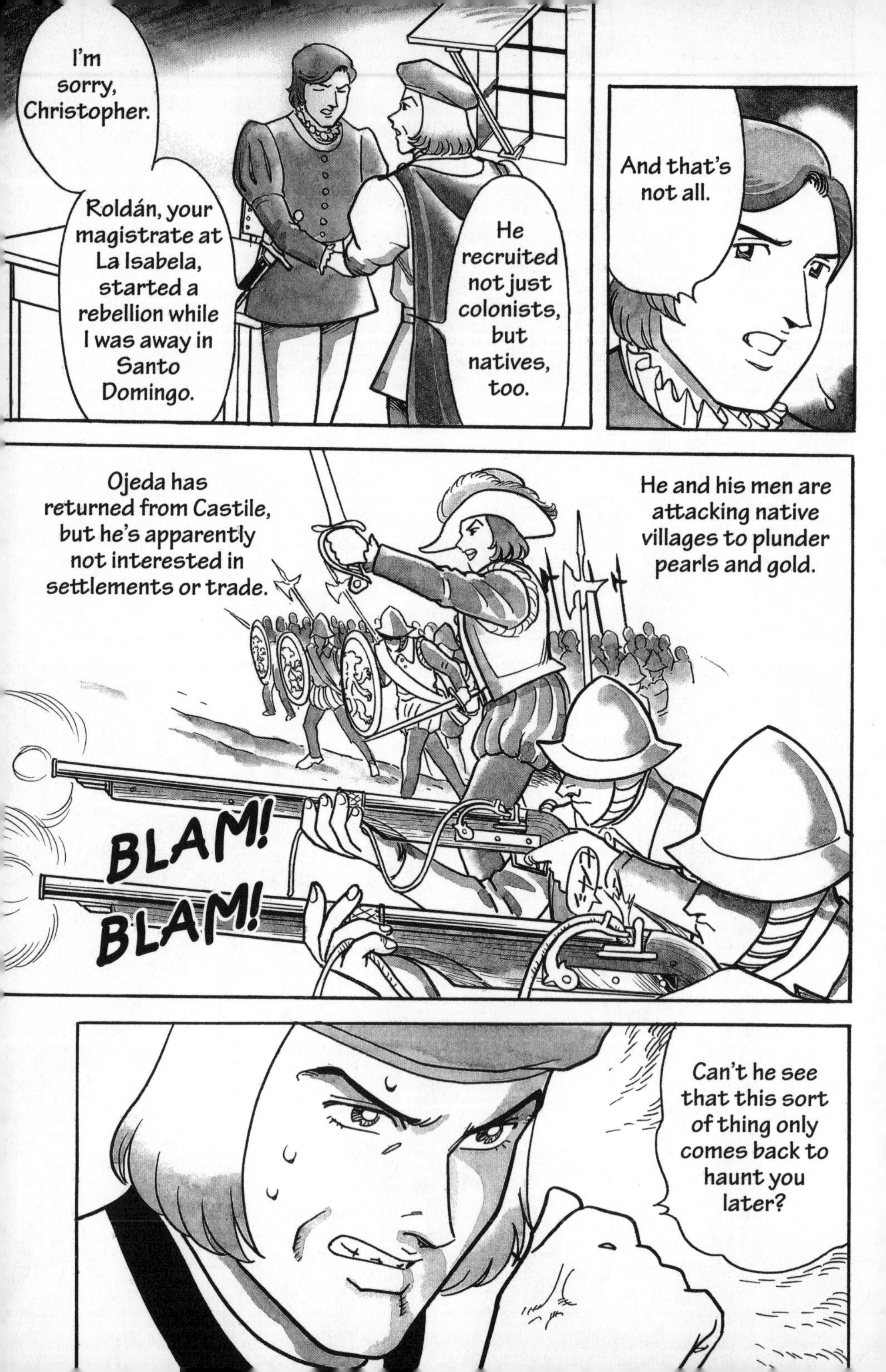
I'm sorry, Christopher.
Roldán, your magistrate at La Isabela, started a rebellion while I was away in Santo Domingo.
He recruited not just colonists, but natives, too.
And that's not all.
Ojeda has returned from Castile, but he's apparently not interested in settlements or trade.
He and his men are attacking native villages to plunder pearls and gold.
BLAM!
BLAM!
Can't he see that this sort of thing only comes back to haunt you later?

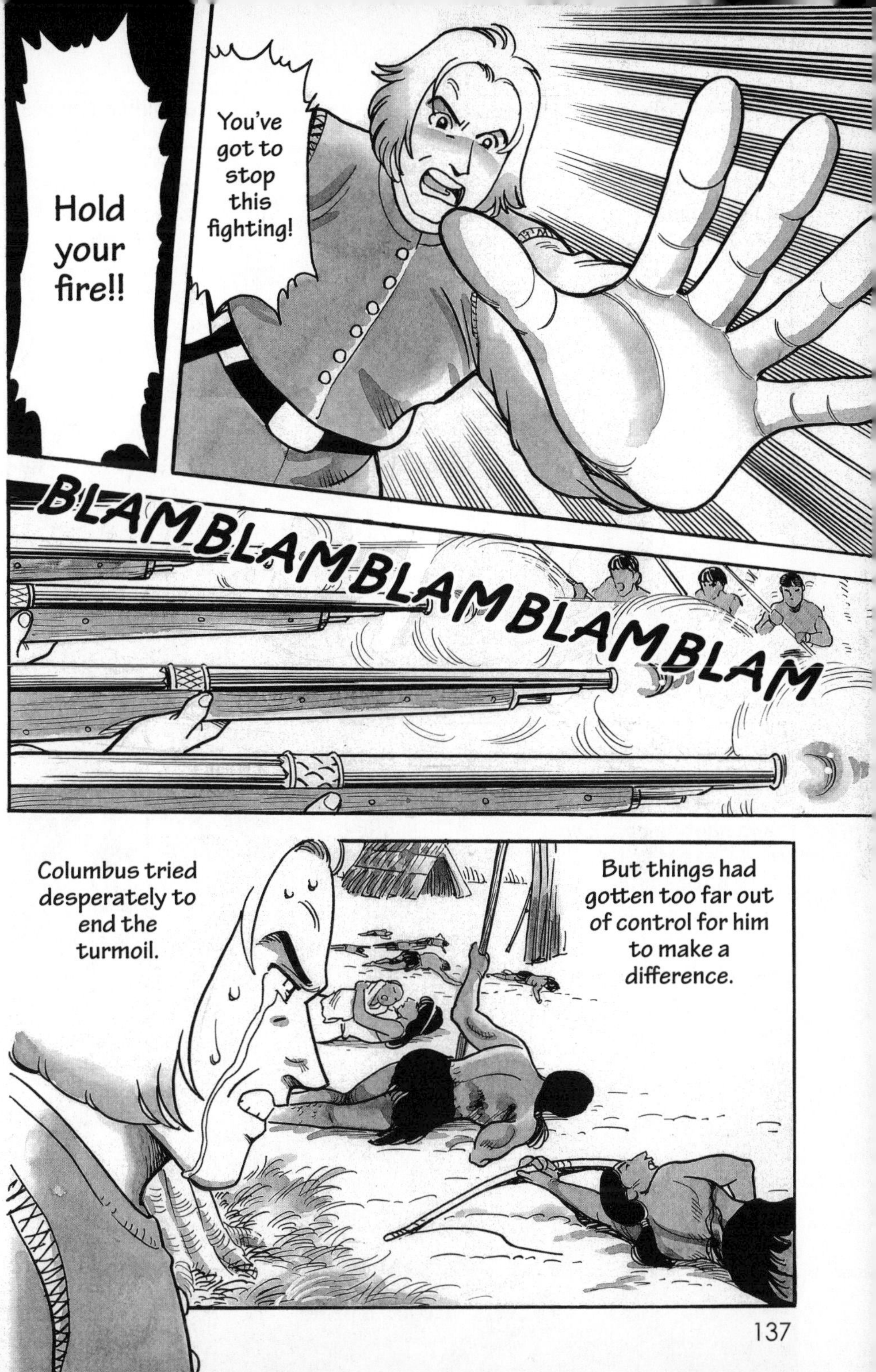

Hold your fire!!
You've got to stop this fighting!
BLAMBLAMBLAMBLAMBLAMBLAMBLAM
Columbus tried desperately to end the turmoil.
But things had gotten too far out of control for him to make a difference.

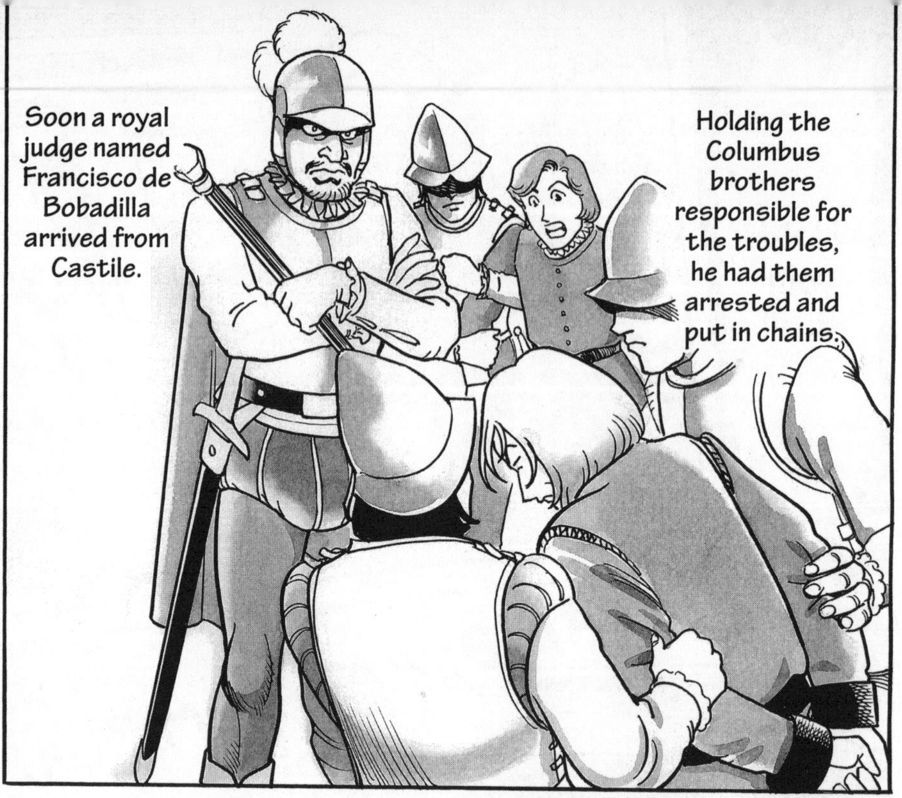
Soon a royal judge named Francisco de Bobadilla arrived from Castile.
Holding the Columbus brothers responsible for the troubles, he had them arrested and put in chains.
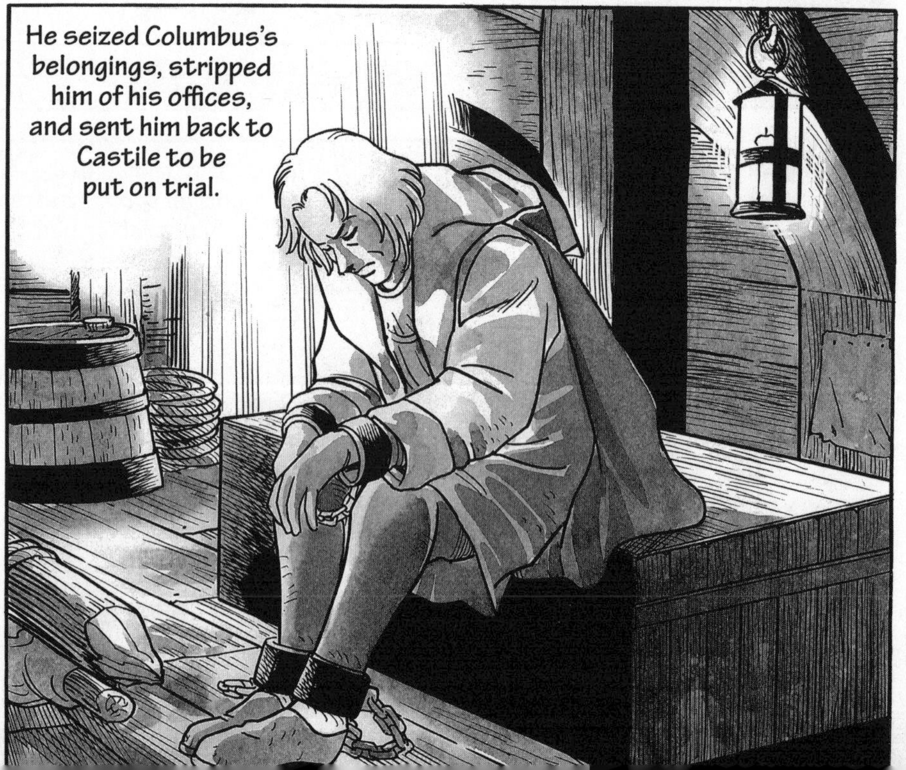
He seized Columbus's belongings, stripped him of his offices, and sent him back to Castile to be put on trial.

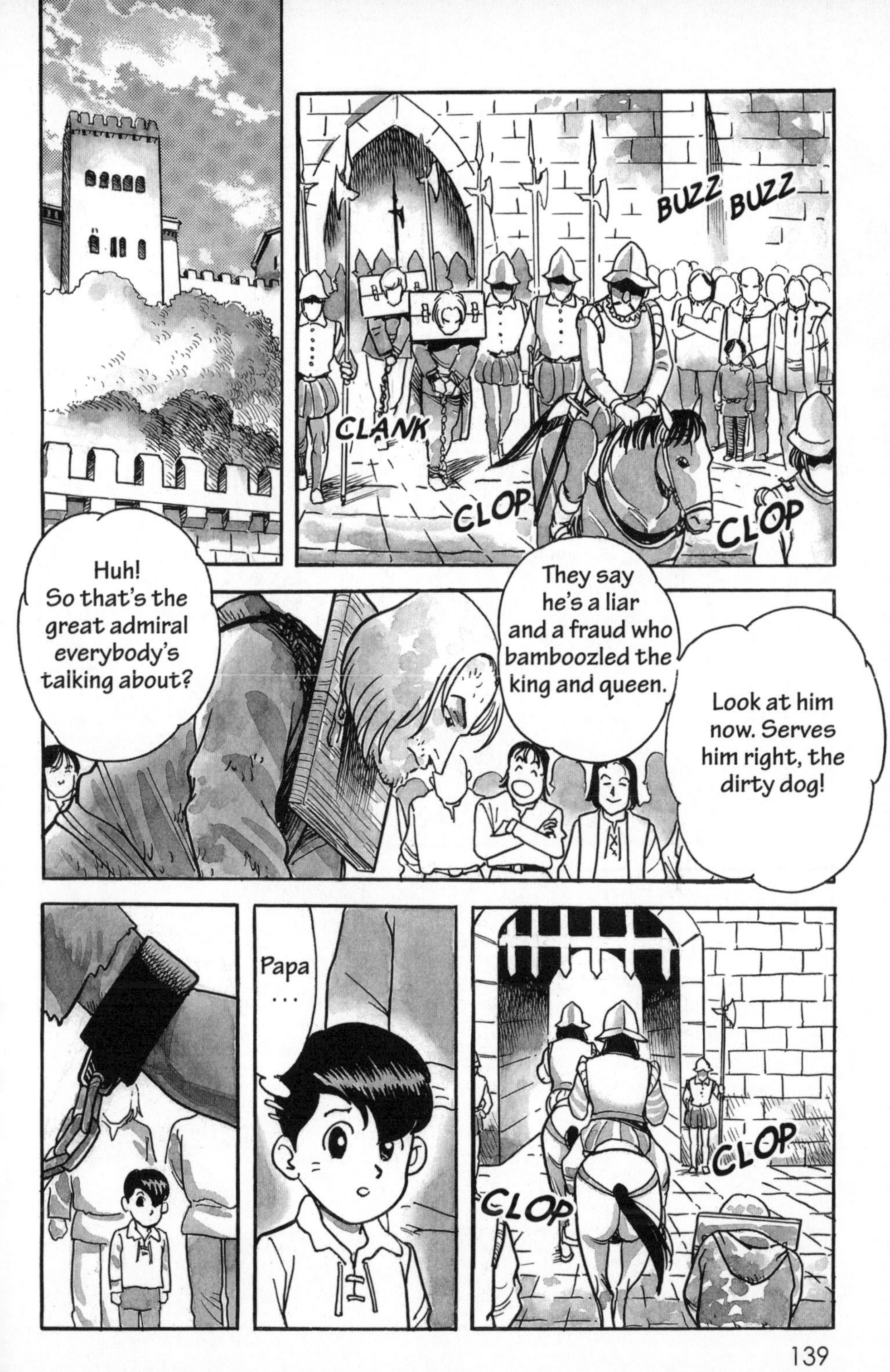
BUZZ BUZZ
CLANK
CLOP
CLOP
Huh! So that's the great admiral everybody's talking about?
They say he's a liar and a fraud who bamboozled the king and queen.
Look at him now. Serves him right, the dirty dog!
Papa . . .
CLOP
CLOP

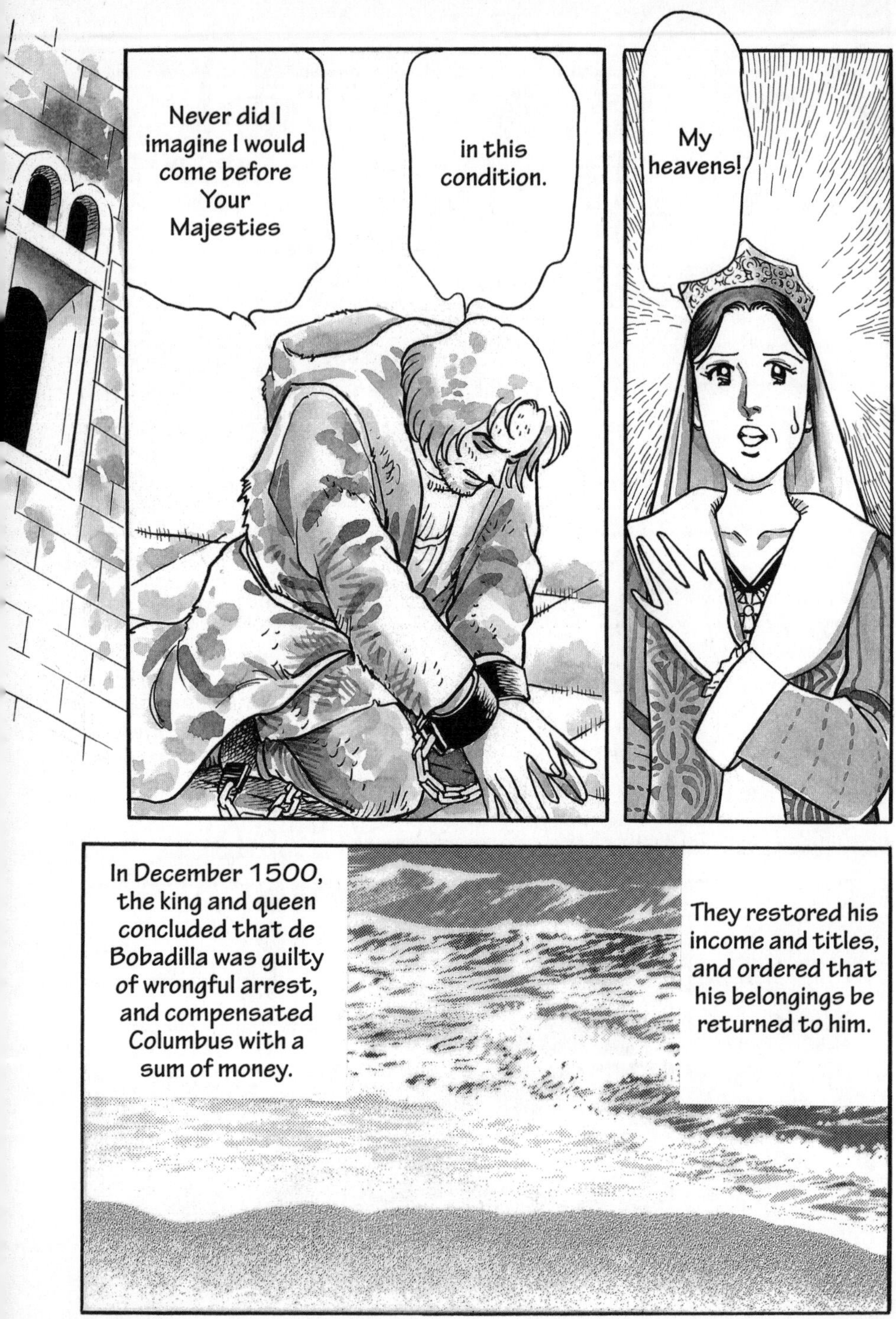
Never did I imagine I would come before Your Majesties
in this condition.
My heavens!
In December 1500, the king and queen concluded that de Bobadilla was guilty of wrongful arrest, and compensated Columbus with a sum of money.
They restored his income and titles, and ordered that his belongings be returned to him.

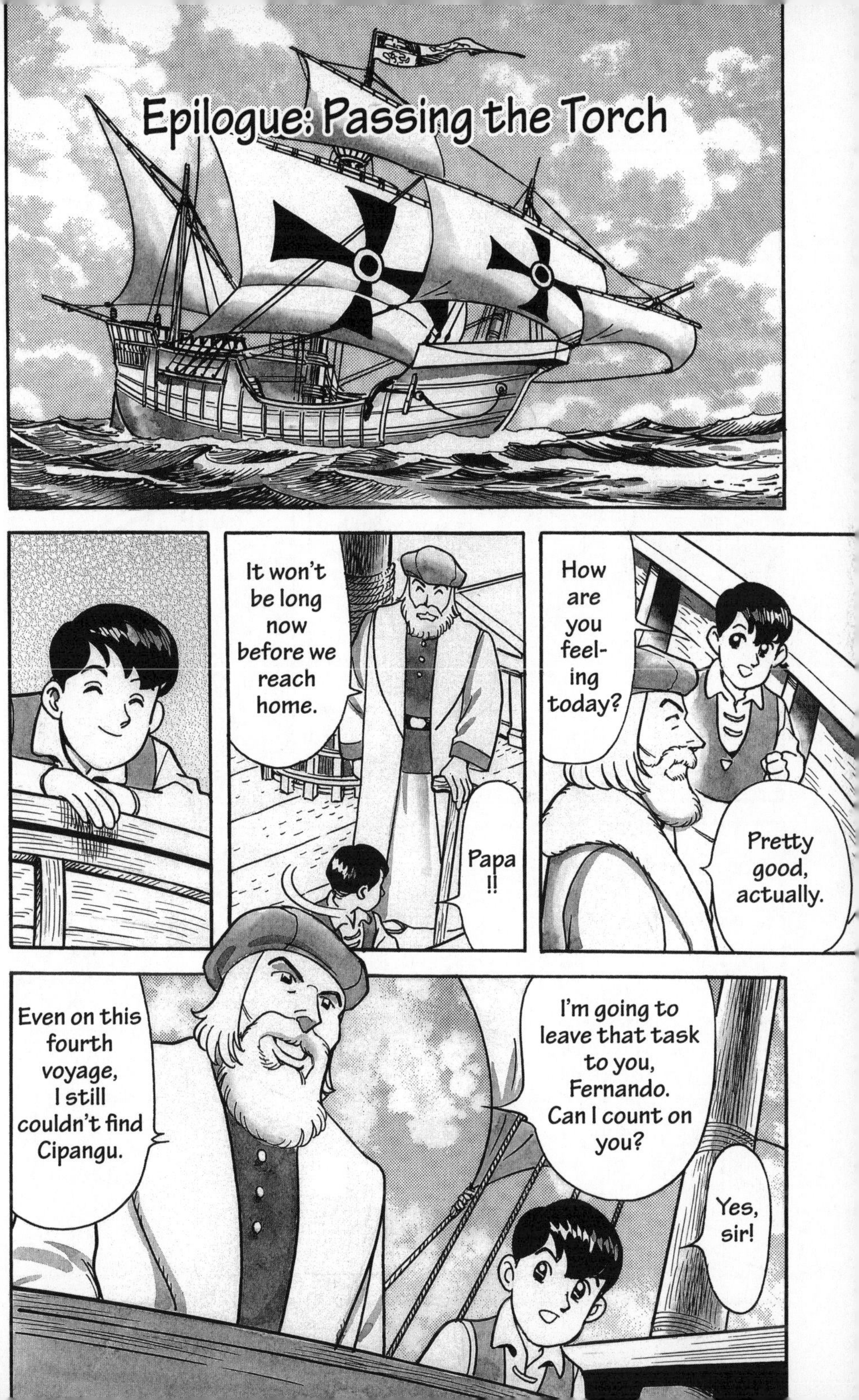
Epilogue: Passing the Torch
It won't be long now before we reach home.
Papa!!
How are you feeling today?
Pretty good, actually.
Even on this fourth voyage, I still couldn't find Cipangu.
I'm going to leave that task to you, Fernando. Can I count on you?
Yes, sir!

On his fourth voyage, Columbus sailed up and down the Central American coast, searching for a way through to the Spice Islands.

It was a voyage dogged by bad weather and trouble with both natives and colonists. Columbus finally returned to Castile in November 1504 without finding the passage he was looking for.

Within that same month, Queen Isabella died. She had been his greatest supporter over the years.

You never did have a chance to sail with me, did you, Diego.

Sorry I always left you holding down the fort here at home . . .

Fernando, I'm counting on you to help your brother defend the family's rights.

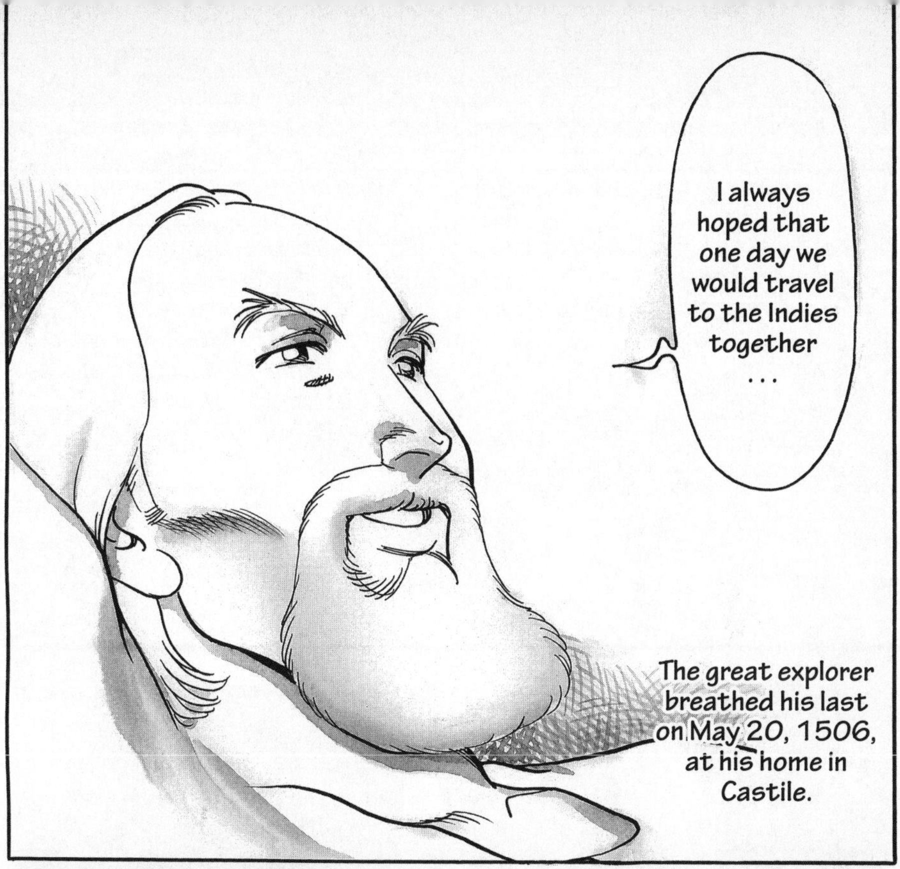
I always hoped that one day we would travel to the Indies together . . .
The great explorer breathed his last on May 20, 1506, at his home in Castile.

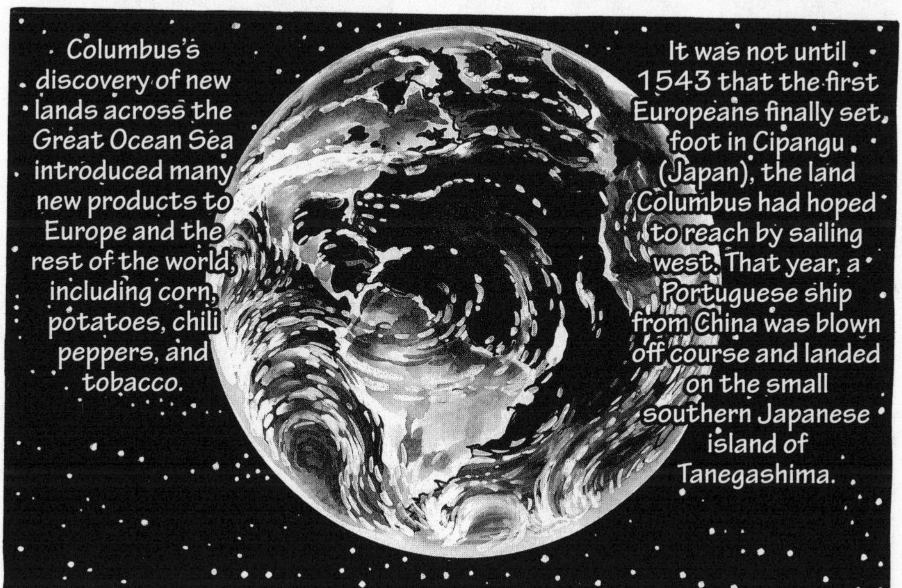
Columbus's discovery of new lands across the Great Ocean Sea introduced many new products to Europe and the rest of the world, including corn, potatoes, chili peppers, and tobacco.
It was not until 1543 that the first Europeans finally set foot in Cipangu (Japan), the land Columbus had hoped to reach by sailing west. That year, a Portuguese ship from China was blown off course and landed on the small southern Japanese island of Tanegashima.

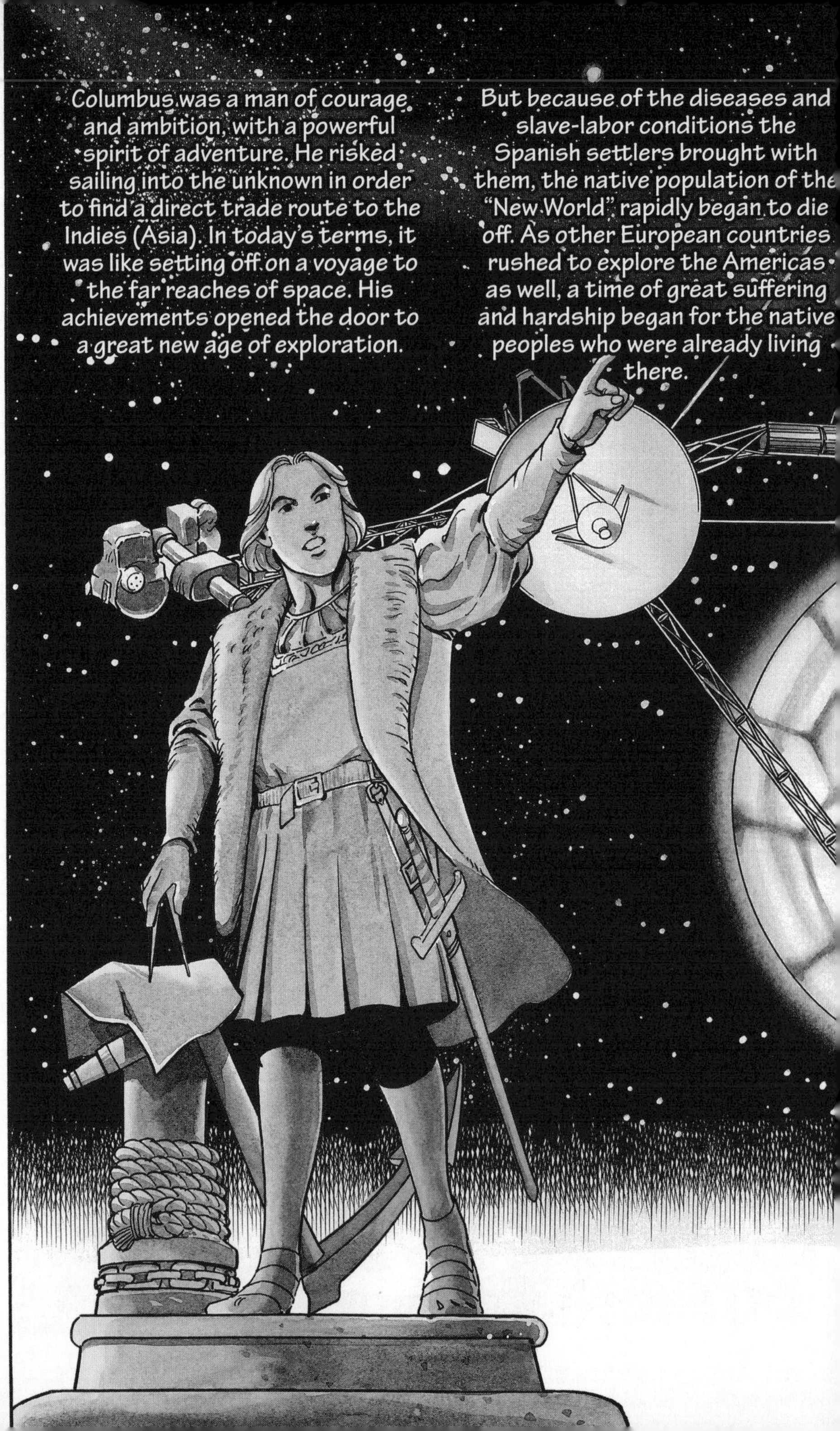
Columbus was a man of courage and ambition, with a powerful spirit of adventure. He risked sailing into the unknown in order to find a direct trade route to the Indies (Asia). In today's terms, it was like setting off on a voyage to the far reaches of space. His achievements opened the door to a great new age of exploration.
But because of the diseases and slave-labor conditions the Spanish settlers brought with them, the native population of the "New World" rapidly began to die off. As other European countries rushed to explore the Americas as well, a time of great suffering and hardship began for the native peoples who were already living there.

Timeline: The Life of Christopher Columbus

Timeline: The Life of Christopher Columbus

Year	Age	Event
1451	0	Born in Genoa, Italy.
1476	25	Signs on with a Genoese merchant fleet headed for England. Leaps from a burning ship and swims to shore when the fleet is attacked by a joint French-Portuguese force off Cape St. Vincent in southwest Portugal. Goes on to Lisbon.
1477	26	Sails to England from Lisbon on a Genoese merchant ship. From there, sails north toward Iceland.
1479	28	Meets and marries Filipa Moniz Perestrelo in Lisbon around this time.
1480	29	First son, Diego, is born.
1484	33	Presents King John II of Portugal with his plan for sailing to the Indies, but fails to gain the king's backing.
1485	34	Moves to Castile (today's Spain) after the death of his wife Filipa.
1486	35	Gains an audience with Queen Isabella of Castile and presents his plan to her. She appoints a committee of experts to study it. They fail to support the plan, and Columbus is left waiting.
1488	37	Second son, Fernando, is born.
1491	40	Giving up on support from Isabella, Columbus sets out for France to appeal to King Charles VIII, but is called back.
1492	41	January 2: The surrender of Granada finally makes support from Castile possible.
		April 17: King Ferdinand and Queen Isabella sign the "Capitulations of Santa Fé," their contract with Columbus.
		August 3: Sails out of Palos on three ships, the Santa María, the Pinta, and the Niña.
		October 12: Land is sighted and a landing party goes ashore; Columbus names the island San Salvador. Claims many islands for the crown in the following weeks, including Cuba (Isla Juana) and Hispaniola (La Isla Española).

146

Year	Age	Event
1492	41	December 25: The Santa María runs aground and is destroyed. Columbus asks 39 men to remain behind and start a colony.
1493	42	January 4: Sets sail on the Niña for Castile.
		March 4: Reaches Lisbon after being badly battered by storms.
		March 9: Has an audience with King John II.
		March 15: Makes his triumphal return to Palos.
		April: Reports on his voyage to King Ferdinand and Queen Isabella.
		September 25: Sets out from the port of Cadiz on his second voyage, with a fleet of 17 ships carrying some 1,500 men. Arrives at Hispaniola in November.
1496	45	June: Returns to Castile.
1498	47	May 30: Sets sail on his third voyage with a fleet of six ships. Two months later discovers the southernmost of the Lesser Antilles islands, which he names Trinidad. Next explores the coast of Venezuela before arriving in Santo Domingo on Hispaniola at the end of August. Finds a rebellion in progress.
1500	49	March: Royal Judge Francisco de Bobadilla holds Columbus responsible for the disturbances on Hispaniola, puts him in chains and sends him home.
1502	51	May 9: Sails on his fourth and final voyage. Second son Fernando accompanies him. Explores the shores of today's Honduras, Nicaragua, and Panama.
1504	53	September: Sails for home, arriving in November.
1506	54	May 20: Dies at Valladolid, Castile (Spain).

REFERENCES

Aoki, Yasuyuki. *Columbus*. Chuo Koronsha, 1989
Columbus, Christopher. *The Four Voyages* (translation by Yasuyuki Aoki). Heibonsha, 1993

Shogakukan Biographical Comics is a series of biographies of inspiring historical figures in an easy-to-read manga format. These books are as fun to read as any comic, but the stories they tell are based entirely on fact. Every volume includes maps and a historical timeline, rounding out a package that teaches even as it entertains.

- -

"The desire to fly is an idea handed down to us by our ancestors who, in their grueling travels across trackless lands in prehistoric times, looked enviously on the birds soaring freely through space, at full speed, above all obstacles, on the infinite highway of the air."
—Orville Wright

The Wright Brothers
Challengers of the Air
Illustrator: Kaoru Oobayashi Writer: Keiko Imamura

THE STORY

Wilbur and Orville Wright started out repairing bicycles in a shop in a small midwestern American city and went on to complete the first piloted, self-propelled flight in history. Since that fateful day in 1903, aviation and aerospace technology has developed by leaps and bounds. Now, in the 21st century, we are close to the day when people will travel freely between the earth and outer space. But we should never forget that the invention of the airplane began with two brothers tinkering in their bicycle shop. The Wright brothers achieved their vision of human flight through hard work, patience, and an unwavering belief in themselves and their dreams.

Hardcover ISBN: 978-1-4215-4320-8
Paperback ISBN: 978-1-4215-4321-5
Shogakukan
VIZ Media, LLC www.viz.com store.viz.com